Cry of the
Justice Bird

Cry of the Justice Bird

JON HAYLETT

PaperBooks

First published 2007 by PaperBooks
PaperBooks Ltd, Neville House, Station Approach
Wendens Ambo, Essex CB11 4LB
www.paperbooks.co.uk

ISBN 0 9551094 8 5
ISBN 978 0 9551094 8 5

1 3 5 7 9 8 6 4 2

A CIP catalogue record for this book is available from
the British Library.

Cover design by Chris Gooch – Bene Imprimatur Ltd

Typeset by SetSystems Ltd, Saffron Walden, Essex
Printed and bound in Great Britain by
Cox & Wyman, Reading

For Gill

1   Boromundi

I first met Chloris at the funeral of Smallboy Mushewa. Temba and I had arrived with the intention of arranging it, but we were too late – Aids had beaten us to it. So, all we could do was watch while Chloris and a straggly group from the rehab centre stood around the grave as Father Kaze mouthed the Christian burial the little bastard didn't deserve. To make up for our missed opportunity, we came back that night and dug him up. We'd wanted him alive very, very badly, but dead had to do: we weren't going to let it ruin our carefully arranged plan. So, we drove him a couple of miles out into the bush and, by the light of the two Maglite torches I'd bought, dumped him and our kit on to a groundsheet.

It took us a couple of hours to take him apart. We didn't want to prolong the process but we both teetered on the edge of a screaming, murderous breakdown, so remained tightly controlled. Had we not, we might have lost it completely and smashed his remains to a bloody pulp – which would have made the whole exercise pointless.

We didn't know all the horrors he had been party to, because, in the years he and his gang had rampaged across Boromundi, there had been so many, and so much misery, but the girls had collected a remarkable amount of detail and we knew what he had done to Rebecca and Annabel. That, alone, was enough.

When we'd finished, we loaded him into a couple of plastic bin-bags and chucked them into the back of the school truck. Being Boromundi, by that time it was raining, but this didn't prevent Temba from driving us through the village while I sat in the back and threw Smallboy's remains out behind us into the main street. The whole village must have heard us coming because it was deserted and in darkness as we passed, but the pye dogs welcomed us and seemed quite pleased with what we had to offer. We stopped twice, once at the village shop, where I climbed onto Temba's shoulders to hook Smallboy's testicles over the front door, then again on our way out to leave his head on the top step of the rehab centre, his eyes blankly staring out across that same countryside which had been the backdrop to the horrors he had helped create.

Smallboy was only fourteen. There are people who will say that it wasn't his fault he'd turned out so rotten, that, as a kid, he'd been deprived, traumatised, brutalised, bestialised and brainwashed. Personally I don't care what had happened to him or whose fault it was. Smallboy wasn't stupid. He had plenty of chances to behave himself, just like the rest of us but he thought that he could get away with it, and, because we failed to catch him alive, he did.

After Smallboy's funeral, as the others trailed back towards the rehab centre, Chloris headed towards us. Dressed as we were, with our faces painted black and white, and with Temba carrying that evil American M16 carbine of his, we might have done better to make ourselves scarce, but neither of us were going to be seen running from a nun.

What confronted us, however, was no ordinary nun. She was young, my age, medium height and as best I could tell, slim. The coarse black cloth of her habit suited her because it contrasted with her pale, flawless, almost doll-like skin, and with deep, sapphire blue eyes set in the softest and gentlest of faces. As she talked to us, as she described how she had nursed Smallboy through hours of screaming agony, her innocence, her transparent virtue, her cloud-cuckooland otherworldliness suddenly infuriated me. Beautiful she might have been, but she was so utterly naïve, such a suicidal innocent in a land ravaged by monsters, that I stood, staring at her, struggling with an insane urge to grab her by the throat, drag her to the truck, and sit on her head until darkness fell, when I would force her to witness the justice which, given the chance, Temba and I would have meted out to a living Hezikiah 'Smallboy' Mushewa.

I don't want you to have any illusions about how nasty this story is. The way I was when it all started, I wouldn't have wished any of these experiences upon my worst enemy. But that was in the days when I didn't understand what an enemy was. To me an enemy was someone, often faceless and remote, who provided the opposition in films and books about war. Someone someone else hated. I had met a bloke in a pub once who had been in the paras in the Falklands who spoke of the Argies as enemies. He had every justification since they'd done their damnedest to kill him – though he had a quiet respect for some of them, particularly their pilots. But I really didn't know what an enemy was because I'd never had one.

My name is Armstrong McKay and at the time this started I was twenty-four and a much more ordinary man than my first name might suggest. Anyone rummaging through my life history hoping to unearth something of interest would have fallen asleep on the job. I was a teacher in a big comprehensive school in a small English town. The kids I taught seemed to like me, we'd have a laugh together and running trips and the second eleven football team meant I got to know them. I felt reasonably happy with my life but I did catch myself wondering whether this was all there was. I had this nagging worry that, when I lay on my death bed, thinking back, I might feel I'd wasted my time. That was until Rebecca joined the staff.

I met Rebecca on the first day of the autumn term 1997. I'd spent the whole of the previous afternoon and evening in the pub, pretending so successfully that it wasn't the last day of the summer holidays that, when I staggered into the staff room for the inservice day that Monday, the hangover was still hours ahead. The first thing I saw was Rebecca. She was so strikingly beautiful that the words that sprang to mind just came straight out, 'God, who's this gorgeous . . . ?' When you say something like that and everyone falls silent and stares at you, you either have to apologise, or follow it up.

I knelt down on the worn carpet in front of the armchair where she was sitting, kissed her hand and said, 'I'm Armstrong and I think you're beautiful.'

Rebeccca always remembered it. We often laughed about it, and she would tell me how secretly thrilled she'd been by the attention.

Rebecca was a dark beauty. She had eyes the colour of newly shelled conkers set in a very strong, rectangular face framed by a tangle of curly black hair that fell below her shoulders. The first time she pinned her hair up, exposing the soft, caramel skin of her neck and shoulders, I had difficulty breathing. It's the nearest I've come to an asthma attack.

At first all I saw in Rebecca was her body – and I just wanted to persuade it into my bed. I made a point of seeing a lot of her: she hung around with our group, I persuaded her to come on one of my Geography field trips because we were short of a woman to look after the girls. She was always good fun, but she eased herself away from me the first time I made a move, and each time I declared my undying love for her she'd laugh it off. I couldn't understand why she was so stand-offish. One day I slipped. I got quite angry with her. Perhaps it was a good thing as it gave her the chance to be honest with me. She liked me, but she wasn't ready for commitment and, anyway, she was the sort of Christian who believed enough in her faith to want to go to her marriage bed a virgin.

A virgin! Christ, I wasn't having any of it. She, her virginity, and the ramparts of her ideals became a challenge, perhaps the greatest challenge of my life. Everyone knew what I was doing and watched our goings-on with anything from interest to growing amusement. It might have been fun, up to a point, but some of us saw it as very serious. My best mate, the bastard, began taking bets. When he told me how much had been wagered on my getting Rebecca laid I couldn't believe it, although admittedly the challenge made me work harder.

She'd been at the school less than a year when she announced she was leaving, that she was going to central Africa to teach Geography and Maths in a mission school deep in the equatorial forest. On first hearing the news I thought it was a joke. When I realised she meant it, sanity abandoned me. I ambushed her in her classroom at the end of a lesson – I couldn't wait for the kids to get out, and, after kicking the door closed and telling her how upset I was that she hadn't told me first, begged her not to go. I said the reason I didn't want her to go must be pretty obvious. I loved her. I wanted to marry her. When I said that, about marrying her, when I heard those words coming out of my mouth, somehow very far away but entirely real, I knew I meant it. I had never thought of it before now, but suddenly and at this moment, I really meant it. So I tried repeating the trick of kneeling to kiss her hand while I begged her.

What happened next destroyed me. She knelt, put her arms round me and pressed a wet cheek against mine. We must have looked ridiculous to the kids lining up for her next lesson. She whispered in my ear, things like, 'sorry' and 'perhaps' and 'a couple of years' time' and . . . how much, really, she did love me.

Rebecca flew to Boromundi in late August. She managed just six weeks of teaching before she was killed. She died on Saturday 10th October 1998, face down in the roadside mud. There was no accident. She was murdered. Had the motive been comprehensible, say, a robbery, it would have been bad enough. Had she been martyred for the faith she held so dear, I might have coped with it. But she wasn't. She was butchered for the very thing I had so painfully respected: her virginity. Smallboy Mushewa was one of the bastards who did it, and that's why Temba and I set out to kill him. There were four others involved and it took us seven months to track them down and arrange their deaths. But, in seeking justice for Rebecca and later, fighting for a country and a people we loved, we stirred up a snakes' nest of horror and hatred. And I learned what an enemy is.

The Thursday following Rebecca's death, Joan Wishart, the new deputy head with responsibility for inservice training and staff development, organised a memorial service for Rebecca in the parish church. The school very rarely went to the parish church so it was a pretty heavy event. I saw the Head and said I couldn't face it. He told me I had to go. So I went and I met Rebecca's parents.

The Head caught my sleeve on the way out and said he wanted me in his study as soon as we were back in school – he'd arrange to cover my class. When I arrived Mr and Mrs Wise, Rebecca's parents, were sitting waiting for me. They were old, not only from their grief. I put Mr Wise, a small man with the same tangled hair as Rebecca, except his was white, at seventy, and his wife a few years younger. Rebecca was their only child. They were in control of themselves but only just.

The Head left us together. Mr Wise didn't beat around the bush. He asked me if I would go out to Boromundi with them to bring back her body. No, they hadn't arranged this with the Head, they'd simply asked if they could have a few minutes privately with me. They couldn't face the ordeal alone and they had no-one else to turn to. They knew how much I'd loved her – it's the phrase they used and it made me stop and think a bit – and, please.

I said, yes. I said it without hesitation. I saw the Head later and explained. I didn't say as much, but I was going whether he gave permission or not. In the event, he was very decent about it: he would have a word with the Chairman of Governors and arrange a week's paid leave. I wasn't to worry about it.

We arrived in Mateka, the capital of Boromundi, in the early afternoon of Monday 19th October. We had rooms booked in the Palace Hotel, the best hotel in town. I don't remember much about the drive from the airport because by that time it was fairly obvious that George Wise was ill. We helped him up to their room and persuaded him to lie down. The air conditioning wasn't working. It was the rainy season in Boromundi and Mateka was stiflingly hot with the humidity knocking one hundred percent. The room was like a bread oven. I went down to reception and demanded to see the manager. I had their room changed to one which had air conditioning that worked and arranged for a doctor to see George. It was while I was in the lobby that Temba turned up.

Temba stood six foot six. He had the physique of one of those Afro-American professional boxers and skin the blackness and texture of tar. He shaved his head, which was remarkably small for such a massive man. It looked just like a cannon ball except his ears stuck out. His movements always seemed as lethargic as his mind was quick, but that slowness of movement was an illusion: it was simply that, whatever part of his body moved, there was a lot of it. It's like a sailing dinghy making five knots looks as if it's skipping along, when a bulk carrier doing the same is crawling. And, when he shook hands, he crushed bones.

Yet he had a restraint about him, a remoteness. He didn't string many words together. I didn't mind that – most people babble too much. Everything Temba said was worth listening to. There was an honesty about the guy, an open-ness; and a deep personal strength. I liked him. From the moment I met him I liked him.

The school Rebecca had taught at, St Faith's, hadn't been told by the British High Commission that we were coming. They'd found out by chance. Temba had been dispatched to collect us: the Head, the staff and the students were desperate to meet us, to tell us about Rebecca, to share our grief. I remember Temba saying all those things, his voice low and hard with emotion, until I stopped him. I explained about Mr Wise. I said I didn't think the Wises would be able to do anything, not until they'd recovered from the journey. But I'd like to come.

He'd driven me as far as the edge of the city when I told him to turn round and take me straight back to the hotel. What he had told me in those few minutes about how Rebecca had died, bore no relationship whatsoever to what we had heard back home. The Foreign Office had said that Rebecca had been killed in a traffic accident, a minibus skidding on a slippery road during a rainstorm. Temba told me she'd been murdered. And she hadn't died alone. Temba's wife, Annabel, had been with her and had died face down in the roadside mud beside her. Worse, the two women had been badly beaten. In defending herself, Annabel's arm had been severed. The rest of the passengers had escaped, abandoning the two girls to their fate. As they fled they had seen the beginning of what had been a prolonged and brutal rape. Temba had no idea how long this assault had continued but when, finally, they were dead they had been severely mutilated. Lastly, they had been chopped up into small pieces.

If what I heard sickened me, it was then that I understood Temba's suppressed emotion. He was restraining a murderous fury, the fury that found its first release when we finally caught up with Smallboy Mushewa.

We had a problem. We sat down to solve it in my room at the Palace Hotel with the help of a litre of duty-free Glenfiddich I'd bought at Heathrow.

Mr and Mrs Wise could not be told the truth and there was no way they could be allowed to see their daughter's remains. I was convinced it would kill them. It also meant that Rebecca's body couldn't travel back to England with us, as we'd planned, because that would mean a post-mortem and complications with the Coroner. When Temba began the task of phoning round to see what we could achieve, he found that others were miles ahead of us. Nobody wanted the truth known, not the Boromundi government, not the British High Commission, not the undertakers; even the local newspapers had been squared. For all of them, the murder, dismemberment and butchery of a twenty three year old British girl was bad news. It would affect tourism. It would damage the rapidly improving relations between the Boromundi and British governments. It might threaten a vital IMF loan. The country was still recovering from its second civil war and the last thing its people needed was a reminder of the atrocities they believed were behind them. And the undertakers couldn't do anything to make Rebecca's remains look decent.

So Temba and I connived in what the newspapers would call a cover-up. It was done for the very best reasons, but it was a mistake. That evening, with George much recovered, I explained to the Wises that Rebecca's body was already beginning to decompose and needed immediate burial. We broke the news to them that she had not died alone, that she had died with Temba's wife, her friend Annabel. We suggested that a quick burial, next to Annabel in the little churchyard at St Faith's School, would be the best solution. I think they were too tired and too distraught to do anything but agree.

A message to the school arranged the service for the next afternoon. Early the following morning Temba and I drove out with the hearse while the Wises followed in a taxi. At five in the afternoon we buried Rebecca under the shade trees in St Faith's churchyard.

You've heard Africans sing, Ladysmith Black Mambazo, the Bhundu Boys, those sorts of people. There's a richness in their voices, a vibrancy, and they have this miraculous ability to harmonise. The singing at Rebecca's service was glorious. The church was packed, not only with St Faith's staff and pupils but also with people from the surrounding villages. Most of them had never met Rebecca but they had heard that a stranger, a young white woman, had come many thousands of miles to teach their children – and that was enough. The congregation spilled into the yard in front of the building and out of the gate into the road. The priest, Father Chitembe, who was also the Deputy Head in the school and had come to know Rebecca well, spoke.

Temba, the Head, one of the other teachers and I, bore her coffin out of the church. The box was so light I remember wondering at the time whether all of her was there. They'd dug the grave in a corner of the churchyard, next to Annabel, shaded by a flame tree but with a view. And that's when I began to look around. Which is strange, because the act of burial is the worst moment in any funeral service. It's the final act, the farewell, the moment when a warm body – because that's the only way I could ever imagine Rebecca – is committed to darkness, dirt and decomposition; and, usually, I'm hopeless with tears. But as we turned with the coffin, as we steadied ourselves before lowering it, I looked up and saw the view that Rebecca would sleep with.

Boromundi is a mountainous country. Only on the western side, where the land falls precipitously to the Rift Valley and the shores of Lake Kenge, does it drop below two thousand metres. It's a land of sheer-sided valleys, of red lateritic soils contrasted against brash green vegetation, of bright flowers and jewelled birds, of torrential rain, cloying mists and sparkling sunshine. It had rained just before the service began so everything was sopping wet, but the setting sun peeped out from under ragged clouds and the place looked clean, the colours sharp in the clear light. The church stood on a spur which protruded into a deep valley dense with evening shadows. From where we stood, from where Rebecca would lie, we looked out across a pattern of farmsteads that seemed to hang from the valley walls, and across ridge after ridge of mountains, each paler and bluer and mistier than the one before. We looked west, towards where the sun was beginning to set; and north-west towards England, to the land where Rebecca had been born and grown so lovely, towards where her parents and I would shortly return.

At the reception Temba introduced me to the local, home made millet brew. Back in England, and given different circumstances, I'd probably have described what followed as the most massive piss-up I've ever encountered, although it had a very practical purpose. The alcohol freed the emotions. There was a lot of crying, but there was more laughter. It was a catharsis, a purging, a farewell, a closing of a very good book.

Later, there was dancing. At first, I suppose in deference to their older visitors, someone found a record of Victor Sylvester ballroom dancing. And they danced to it, very formally, waltzes and quicksteps, mostly pairs of women bumping rather awkwardly round the room in their brightly patterned cotton dresses and turban-like head-gear. Then the Head asked the Wises if they'd mind something a little more modern. I don't know what went on the record player next, but it was African and noisy and it brought everyone to their feet. Around eleven, when things were, for me, little more than a haze, men appeared with drums and rattles, with strangely shaped stringed instruments and what they called finger pianos, and Rebecca's wake really got cracking.

Some time later Temba found me and dragged me out of the hall. We walked down the front steps with the warm Boromundi rain running down our faces, keeping going until we stood on the edge of the great darkness that filled the valley. He held my arm very tightly.

I remember the brief conversation that followed. I remember every word of it, because it was the beginning of what was to come.

'Listen,' Temba said.

At first I thought the command was a preliminary to some important statement so I tried to look intelligent.

'You hear it?'

I rearranged my expectations and shook my head. I couldn't hear anything, not above the spatter of the rain and the gurgle of the water in the storm gullies.

'There!' His head was cocked on one side.

'What is it?' I whispered. It helps when you're listening for something if you have some idea what you're listening for.

'It is *Kisasi*, the Justice Bird.' He paused. 'I heard him . . . a moment ago.'

'Oh?' I croaked. I still couldn't hear anything.

'The villagers have heard him. The students on their way to school – they hear him. Now, now *I* have heard him.'

He didn't sound very sure. Yet I felt guilty, stupidly guilty, that I hadn't heard him too.

'What is this . . . Justice Bird?'

'It is a bird that is found only in the deep forests. People say that he only comes near to human habitation if a great injustice has been done, that he sings because those who have gone cannot rest. So he calls to those that loved them . . .'

The Wises left in their taxi just before one. I never left. At some point in the evening I found myself begging the Headmaster to allow me to stay at St Faith's and teach Rebecca's classes. And then I found Temba and told him I wasn't going until we made damn sure this *Kisasi* bird stopped singing.

I remember that conversation so exactly and it all seems so simple, so straightforward, so black and white. But thinking back, I wonder whether the perception I had of events was in fact wrong. For example, I wonder whether Temba deliberately didn't tell me about the attitude of the police until later; whether, if he had told me when we first met, I would have agreed to hush up the circumstances of Rebecca's death. Or whether Temba thought I was intelligent enough to have worked it out for myself before I made that decision – which I evidently wasn't.

Because it's quite logical that, if two girls are killed in what everyone agrees was an unfortunate accident, there's no need to carry out an intensive police investigation. The minibus skidded on a muddy road. It slid into a ditch and rolled. The two girls, who were not belted in – the minibus didn't have seatbelts – were thrown clear and died at the scene. The driver and the other passengers survived, though the latter conveniently disappeared before they could be questioned. No criminal offence had occurred. The file on the accident was closed.

The police were going to do nothing. I'd assumed that they would continue to investigate, if surreptitiously. So who do you turn to? The British High Commission? 'Look, old boy, I thought we'd agreed . . .' A Boromundi Government desperately anxious about tourism and IMF loans? The local newspapers? Your MP at home? The British press? And if I'd done any of these, what effect would it have had on the Wises?

All these pennies dropped long after Temba and I talked outside the school hall. 'Pennies dropped', it was more as if the ground opened up underneath me.

Still I had no hesitation in making the decision I made that night and, in retrospect, it was the right one. I was pissed. I was emotionally as charged as a thundercloud. I was overawed by the place, by its strangeness, by its excitement. Nevertheless, my decision to stay was made coldly, lucidly and with a very real awareness of what I was letting myself in for. Because, before I made it, Temba told me exactly what had happened to Rebecca on that red, laterite road to the east of St Faith's School.

2 Death at the Roadside

They pulled her out by her hair. They seemed to pick on her from the moment they saw her but there was no evidence at the time that they stopped her minibus, rather than any other, because there was a white woman in it. It seemed like fate, bad luck, whatever you want to call it. It turned out it was a carefully organised plan.

The red Hiace in which Rebecca and Annabel were travelling was driven by Cyprian Bogovu, a man of about forty-five with two wives and six children. In the manic conditions of Boromundi's roads he had a reputation as a safe, reliable driver. The women had set out to visit Annabel's mother, a widow who lived about thirty miles from the school, a trip which Annabel took regularly on a Saturday. They had caught the local bus from the school gate into the nearest town, Kaserewe, where they had boarded Cyprian's minibus. The whole journey should have taken a leisurely two hours and they planned to be back at St Faith's before dark.

They were stopped about fifteen miles out of Kaserewe. Minibuses like Cyprian's operate an unscheduled service throughout Africa. As long as they are not full – and 'full' means grossly overloaded – they'll pick up anyone who flags them down. The man who stepped out into the road wasn't known to Cyprian. He described him as tall, probably over six foot, with light brown skin, a thin face and close-cropped, curly hair. He wore jeans, a pale blue shirt which wasn't tucked in and brown leather shoes. The shoes were laced up: it was an important fact which we didn't appreciate until later. Otherwise, the description matches half of Boromundi's adult male population.

Temba saw Cyprian on the Tuesday following the women's deaths, so his memory should have been vivid. Cyprian said that the man surprised him by walking round to his window, which was open, instead of climbing aboard. When he produced a gun which had been tucked into his trousers and hidden by his shirt – it was almost certainly an old service revolver – Cyprian obviously fell apart. From then on his recollections were patchy, the sequence of events confused, and the descriptions of his other attackers even more superficial.

The man ordered Cyprian to switch off the engine. At the same time two other men, both armed with automatic rifles, opened the doors on the passenger side of the vehicle. An older woman, a large lady with a clutter of baggage, sat in the seat next to Cyprian. She had to be persuaded by one of the riflemen, very roughly, to get out. The man became irritated by her slowness. She stood at the side of the road and commenced a keening wail which continued until her attacker turned very suddenly and hit her in the face with the butt of his rifle. She went over backwards, sitting abruptly in the mud, her hands pressing a mouth that oozed blood.

The third man entered the back of the minibus. He seized Rebecca by her hair. He was a big man, well over six foot, very dark skinned, very strong. He dragged her out, moving backwards, tugging as he stepped down from the vehicle with the result that Rebecca tripped and fell forward, plunging out of the door to sprawl full length on the road. It had just started to rain, a vertical deluge which hammered on the roof of the vehicle. The road, like almost all the roads in Boromundi, was a dirt road, strongly cambered. The rain washes the loose surface of sand and dust into the runoffs scraped along the side so, unless the road has been graded recently, it's always full of red, sticky mud. Rebecca fell into this. Cyprian said she was screaming until she hit it.

Annabel followed her. She came out shouting, almost shrieking at the man, begging him to let Rebecca go. Then something happened – from his position in the driving seat Cyprian couldn't see exactly what it was – which turned her tone to anger. He thinks that either the man who had attacked Rebecca or the man who had pulled out the old woman hit Rebecca. As I said, both of them had rifles, probably Kalashnikovs, with wooden butts.

The other occupants in the back of the vehicle, a boy of about seventeen, an old man and two women in their late twenties or early thirties followed the women out. They were made to lie face down on the road with their hands on the backs of their heads.

At this point Cyprian saw two other men emerge from the bush, hurrying out of it. One of these he recognised immediately as Smallboy Mushewa. They were angry, shouting at the other men – as if they had not waited for them, as arranged, before stopping the minibus.

The man with the revolver made Cyprian lean forward

so that his face was pressed against the steering wheel. He could at this point only hear what was happening and was unable to see anything. At least two men entered the minibus and pillaged the passenger's luggage of anything that had any value. There were shouts and laughter. Cyprian was almost certain that they were high, on alcohol, or *bhang*, or pills, or a cocktail of all of them – except the man with the pistol who seemed tense and ill-at-ease.

What appeared, to me, so surprising about the account was that none of the attackers made the slightest attempt to disguise themselves. Temba later discovered – though Cyprian certainly did not divulge this – that Smallboy was related to Cyprian through Cyprian's mother's family. The men must have believed they were inviolable. At the time I didn't appreciate how chaotic things were in Boromundi, that, once they had completed the robbery, it would be easy for them to disappear into the bush until things quietened down.

Nor was there any indication, at this point, that anything was intended other than robbery. As soon as the men had finished in the minibus, they began searching the passengers. One of the women – it may have been Rebecca – began crying. She was told to shut up and, when she didn't, one of the men began cursing her, his voice rising in pitch with his anger. When she still couldn't control herself – she was sobbing, great, gasping sobs – she was hit, very hard. Cyprian said that the impact, probably, again, of a rifle butt, was soft but crunchy. And she stopped crying.

The events that followed were very confused. There were two shots, single shots, closely spaced, probably from the same gun. Then Cyprian was aware of people scrambling back into the bus. The big woman almost threw herself into the front seat in a flurry of mud, and she had begun screaming again. The man with the revolver, who had stood in the road beside Cyprian throughout, hit him with its muzzle. It was no more than a tap on the side of his head, on his temple, though it was enough to cut the skin and draw blood. When Cyprian looked up he was told to drive. '*Nendeya!*' the man shouted – 'Go!' Cyprian didn't wait. He started the engine, revving too hard, crashed the gears into first and let the clutch in so sharply the minibus jerked forward and almost stalled. He was accelerating down the road when the seventeen-year old passenger shouted that the two young women had been left behind.

Cyprian didn't stop. I suppose, by making for the nearest village and raising the alarm, he did the best thing. But he abandoned the two women to their fate.

It looked like they were being raped before the passengers returned to the bus and those in the back continued to watch what was happening as Cyprian sped away. They saw Annabel try to get up. She was already naked but smeared in mud. They saw one of the men lash out with a panga. She raised her arm to ward off the blow. While they didn't see exactly what happened, the blow was vicious enough to have severed the limb. One of the men had started on Rebecca while the passengers were lying on the ground: they could hear his rhythmic grunting. As they left, another lay on top of her. The last thing they saw was a man hitting her with a panga, perhaps using the flat of the blade. This was almost certainly Smallboy Mushewa.

These were fleeting images, described to Cyprian in the chaos after they reached the village. The phone in the shop wasn't working. A passing driver promised to call the Kaserewe police. They took an hour to arrive. By that time the other passengers had disappeared: they knew full well that the questioning by the police would take hours, that it would probably be, at the least, insensitive and, at worst, brutal. Temba doesn't blame them. I don't blame them. After all, people do the same in England for much worse reasons.

We did not know exactly what had happened on the roadside. We did not know why those two shots were fired. They certainly didn't kill Annabel. At the time Temba told me all this, sitting in the darkness, in the rain, whispering it to me against the boisterous racket emanating from the party in St Faith's school hall, I shut my eyes and prayed that those two shots were aimed at Rebecca, that she was dead long before they began to do the terrible things they did to her.

When Temba and I returned to the party I set about drinking myself into oblivion, but it wouldn't come.

Eventually dawn crept up on us and Temba dragged me back outside. We stood, propping each other up. The sky was overcast, a low, featureless murk that was sooty black to the west but held a thin grey that outlined the jagged ridge to the east. The land fell away from the school campus into the same deep valley as was visible from the church. It was filled with mist, its surface like the grey waters of a rising lake – pierced by black, half-sunken objects: trees, a telegraph pole, the roof of a house. The air chilled the sweat on our skin. The atmosphere seemed silent with expectancy.

I felt sick. It was nothing to do with Rebecca. It was the food and the beer and I needed to lie down. I needed to sleep.

'I will kill them,' Temba hissed. He was staring out across the view and, for all the drink, his eyes were as hard as nails. 'I will hunt for them, Armstrong. I will catch them, I will cut them up very slowly. When they are hurting very, very much they will tell me what happened. They will explain to me why they felt it was necessary to kill my wife. Then I will explain to them why I am so angry with what they did. I will explain that, if they felt free to kill my wife in any way they chose, then I must feel free to kill them similarly. Except that it will take me longer, for I will dissect them.' He turned to me. 'You know that my subject is Biology? No? I am a very good biologist. I enjoy dissection. Though I have never done it before, I know how to do it so that a human body will scream and scream even as it is taken apart.' He stopped, glancing at his watch. 'In half an hour I have to teach.'

'Christ,' I muttered.

I'd taught with hangovers, but this wasn't a hangover, not yet. I could hardly stand. When this hangover arrived it would be Armageddon.

'You must sleep,' Temba said.

I said, 'No,' but I remember his arm coming round me to support me. I remember launching myself away from

the hall doors, across the slippery earth towards the main
school buildings. Then I don't remember anything.

I woke about five in the afternoon. I came back very
slowly, swimming upwards through grey glue towards a
painfully bright light, struggling to remember where I was
and what I'd done. And, as each memory came, I screwed
up my eyes and groaned.

Very gingerly, I opened my eyes fully, and that was
when it hit me.

The room I was in was about fifteen foot by fifteen
foot, white walled and very bare. There was a window
opposite the bed. The flimsy cotton curtains had been
drawn back to admit that painful light, and a breeze
licked at their edges. In front of the window stood a desk
on which I could just see a pen tidy and a laptop. I
recognised the laptop and, in the same moment, one of
the books neatly lined up on the windowsill. I'd given
Rebecca *Out of Africa* just before she'd left. Somehow it
had seemed an appropriate title.

I was in Rebecca's room. I had slept in Rebecca's bed.
I'd managed – and I must admit this sick thought – I'd
managed to achieve something I'd worked at for almost
a year: I was naked in Rebecca's bed. It brought me back
to the shocking reality. Rebecca was dead. The body I
had so wanted to lie beside lay a quarter of a mile away
in a wooden coffin. I fought away from the thought and
focused on my need for water.

I retrieved my trousers, neatly hung with my other

clothes over the back of her chair. I had great difficulty walking. The room banked and dived and climbed like an aeroplane doing a stunt routine. The doorway kept falling sideways. When I finally reached it I clung grimly to the upright while I fumbled at the handle. The door opened into a passageway. I found a bathroom and fell across it to clutch at the edge of a row of basins. I worried about drinking directly from the tap but did it anyway – I was desperate. Temba later told me I was right to worry.

There was no shower and I didn't want to take a bath so I stuck my face into a basinful of water and held it under until I almost drowned. Then I tottered back to my room.

Temba sat on Rebecca's bed nursing his head. I think he'd been making the same groaning noises as me, though he had far more justification: he'd taught a full day and taken football practice.

He'd just seen the Head. The Head was in a similar condition but he'd sent a message. I was to go back to Mateka and fly to England the next day with the Wises. The Head did not intend to hold me to my offer to take Rebecca's place. We'd all been a bit drunk, we'd all said some things we probably didn't mean. It had been a splendid evening. And Temba advised me to go. In fact, he did more than that, he *urged* me to go.

It would have been so easy to have shaken hands with Temba, to have thanked him for all he had done, both for me and for Rebecca. I was tempted. I so very nearly nodded and said, yes, that was probably the best thing. I was very low, not only with the hangover but with facing the silent accusation of her possessions and, through them, the stark reality of Rebecca's death. So nearly . . . but I didn't.

I don't know what drove me at that very, very low point. It wasn't any desire for justice or revenge or anything like that, not at that moment. I wasn't angry, murderous, as I later became. I was hung-over and feeling sorry for myself. Perhaps it was partly that I'd worked out that, unless someone did something, the murdering bastards who had killed Rebecca would get away scot free. And I didn't like that idea. Then again, it may have been *Kisasi*. That bird was beginning to haunt me: the idea that I'd go back to England and he'd come down to the little graveyard where Rebecca lay and sing over her grave because nobody had the guts to do anything about the fact that she'd been murdered.

Temba had been sent to drive me back to Mateka. Instead, unwillingly, he led me to the Head's office. Bartolemew Nchanga was a layman, a heavy man in his early sixties with ginger biscuit-coloured skin and a spectacularly large nose the shape of a currant bun, stuck on the front of his face. He was dressed in a dark suit and rose from behind a cluttered desk to greet me. He thought I'd come to say goodbye. Instead, I asked for Rebecca's timetable.

I was still holding his hand when I said it. For a moment, hard, searching eyes held mine, then, very slowly, he nodded his head and smiled. He'd been great fun the previous evening but in that moment was sown the seed of the huge respect I was to develop for this man.

Temba did drive me into Mateka because Bartolemew insisted I saw the Wises and said my farewells to them.

I think he realised that they would find something very special in what I was planning to do.

He was right. They thought a lot of the fact that I was taking over where Rebecca had left off. However, they did try to persuade me to change my mind. Their heart wasn't in it and they gave up very quickly. It made them happy: their Rebecca's work was to be continued by the man who had loved her. It made them bubble with joy.

George and Emily Wise were by now changed people. Their experiences at St Faith's had given them a new purpose. The fact that those good people would care for the grave of their only daughter inspired them. On their return to England they were to set about organising funding on a scale that the school could never have dreamed of.

I slept the night at the hotel. After an early breakfast, with George and Emily due to catch the afternoon flight to Nairobi, a police car collected us. An inspector with Gucci glasses welded to his face, whose silence was so oppressive it suffocated any conversation, drove us at stupid speed, blue lights flashing and siren braying, until we reached the edge of the city. Then he slowed down, turning the lights and siren off, and crept to the point on the road outside Kaserewe where Rebecca had died. It was not a journey that either George or I had wanted. Emily had insisted. She'd said she couldn't leave without seeing the place, without being able to picture where her Rebecca had died.

I'm glad I went. The countryside wasn't anything like I'd imagined. The parts of Boromundi we'd seen, between Mateka and St Faith's, had been densely forested high land. A few miles to the east of Kaserewe the ground fell gently away and the forest drew back to allow clearings of grassland, speckled with smaller, acacia-type trees. In some ways the landscape reminded me of England, of the great forests that had covered the countryside in mediaeval times with their clearings and rides. There was something else: the place seemed depopulated. It looked perfect mixed farming country, but the people simply weren't there.

Rebecca had died beside a very straight road. It came out of forest and ran across grassland. A small stand of trees stood near the point where the minibus had stopped. I suppose the men had hidden in them, had, perhaps, rested or even been asleep under them. There was nothing to show of the incident. I think Emily and George had expected to find skid marks, perhaps bits of wreckage from the bus. There wasn't anything. Knowing the truth, I hadn't expected to see anything – except, perhaps, the two cartridge cases from the shots that were fired, and I searched for them and didn't find them. What's more, it had rained almost incessantly since the event almost two weeks before, so any marks on the ground had long been washed away.

George and Emily knelt in the mud and prayed. They said the Lord's Prayer together, kneeling close enough to touch, while I stood behind them, my head bowed but watching them. I envied them, their closeness, their unspoken communication, their mutual support. And it was while I was warming to this thought that it occurred to me that this might not be the spot.

I stood and turned the concept over and over. We wouldn't know any different. Looking around, it seemed an unlikely site for an ambush. Any escape, if something had gone wrong, would have been across open ground, yet forested cover was available only a hundred yards back down the road. And, if the five men had waited in those trees, why did two of them get left behind? Temba had definitely said two arrived late, that they'd been angry about it.

It wasn't the place, and I knew why. The policeman was afraid. I watched him, the way he fidgeted, the way he kept glancing around. As I discovered later, the police didn't control much outside the main towns. This was bandit country and he wanted to be well away from cover when he stopped.

I noticed something else. In the short time we were there four vehicles passed: a lorry, two cars and a mini-bus. I checked my watch. It was just past ten, perhaps an hour after Cyprian Bogovu's minibus had been stopped. Okay, so that had been a Saturday and this was a Thursday, but I would have expected more cars on the roads on a Saturday. It seemed to me that, wherever it had happened, the chances that no vehicles had passed while events were unfolding were remote.

So there had been more witnesses, people who might recognise the attackers. Despite this, according to Cyprian Bogovu, the five men had made no attempt to disguise themselves.

It reflected the dismissive arrogance of their power over other people. Violent power. And for the first time I felt afraid.

I woke suddenly, lying rigid on my back, all my senses sharp, listening. I was in Rebecca's room but it was so utterly, so tar-thick dark that I couldn't even find the outline of the window. I knew I'd left it wide open and the curtains drawn back because, outside, the sound of torrential rain spattering into the leaves and gurgling in the gutters and storm drains seemed strangely close. I had no idea of the time but it must have been the early hours. I lay, my skin hot and sweaty against the sheets while a cold tingle started at the top of my spine and worked its way downwards, as I wondered what had jolted me awake.

The sound was almost indistinguishable under the racket of the rain: a scratching, no louder than a cockroach might have made scurrying along the skirting, that came from the direction of the door. The sound kept starting, and stopping, and the patter of the rain would wash in behind it; and then it would start again. It might have been a small dog worrying at the door, wanting to come in. It might have been someone working at the lock.

At that thought, terror, like some cold-footed devil, started tying and tightening knots in my guts, squeezing them so I fought to stop myself voiding them into the clean, starched sheets of Rebecca's bed. I couldn't move. I couldn't think – certainly not logically. Someone was trying to get in, someone who planned to kill me, one of Rebecca's murderers sent to complete the job.

I couldn't turn on the light. There was only one switch, right beside the door, and to do so would illuminate the whole room, blind me, and make me an easy target. I could scream, but the rain might drown the sound and I didn't want to then find that my problem had been an overexcited cockroach. I could escape out of the window. If I did I'd get soaked, I didn't know where to go for help, and, again, when someone came back with me they'd probably find nothing, and a right idiot I'd look. It took me an age to work up the courage to crawl out of bed and, standing well to one side of the door, very carefully turn the key and ease it open.

In the faint light that spilled down the passage I saw Temba. He lay spread-eagled on the floor. His hand moved up and down, indicating that I should come down and join him. For a moment, for only a moment, it seemed a faintly ridiculous thing to do. Once I lay prostrate beside him, he manoeuvred so he could whisper in my ear. 'Dress,' he said, 'Then follow.' He spoke so quietly it took two attempts to get the message over, and it sent me scrabbling back into my room to find my clothes while he kept a lookout, moving from door to window and back again, always keeping as low as possible. And it was while he was doing this that I noticed he carried a rifle.

I followed him out into the passageway. We crawled on our bellies to the communal sitting room, through it and into a small kitchen beyond. Temba had come in through the window. We went out the same way, dropping down through a shrub, tumbling into a flowerbed which contained enough plants to shield us as we crawled along it. The rain was, if anything, heavier, a torrent which blanketed sound and vision. By the end of the block we were filthy, wet and muddy, but able to stand before merging into the thick forest that surrounded the school buildings.

Temba led me along dark, narrow paths for about half a mile, slipping and tripping as we worked our way up hill. We finally stopped at some rocks, a heap of rounded boulders of what was probably heavily weathered basalt, clothed in undergrowth. We sat close together against a rock face, peering out through the darkened forest towards the pale light of a clearing in the middle of which stood a small house, Temba and Annabel's house. We looked at the back of the house. The back door stood open and a light burned dimly in what might have been the kitchen.

We sat in the rain, watching the house, for almost half an hour until it eased. It wasn't cold – it was more like sitting in a tepid shower. And then something very strange happened. I heard a noise, like the scrape of a finger along the teeth of a comb, but louder, like one of those rattles they used to take to football matches in the good old days when people stood squashed together on terraces. A harsh sound, long drawn out; then gone. I'm almost certain it came from the forest beyond the house.

Temba heard it and he was up and moving before I could ask him what it was. He worked his way from cover to cover towards the house, using every tree, standing behind each, peering forward until he was quite satisfied, then flitting to the next. I followed, noisily, my chest tight and my guts writhing like a bucket of worms.

The worst bit was the last. In one movement we tumbled through a gate, sprinted along a narrow path between sodden vegetables, and through the back door. Temba went in first, moving like a cat, dousing the lamp as I followed. God knows what use I would have been if there had been men waiting for us: I had nothing in my hands.

I stood in a tiny kitchen, my heart thumping in my chest and my legs shaking, listening to the metallic snaps of contracting metal in the hurricane lamp, while Temba searched the house. When he'd finished, when he was absolutely certain that no-one was there, he came and collected me, leading me through a neat sitting room and out onto a veranda, stopping immediately. The rain had eased and a few stars showed through holes torn in the cloud. There was enough light to see that the clearing fell steeply away in front of the house, wide enough for us to be able to see out across the tops of the trees on the far side and into the dark gash of a valley. I recognized it as the same valley, the school hidden by the trees below us and, although I could not see it, I knew that the church where Rebecca lay stood away to our right.

I moved my lips so they almost touched Temba's ear. 'What's . . . what's happening?'

He did not reply but slowly pointed. He seemed to be pointing out across the valley and it took me some time to realise that the object he indicated was only a few feet away, above the steps down from the veranda into the garden. I moved closer, seeing that it was something about the size of my fist, something suspended from the guttering on the end of a piece of string, something hanging at head height.

'I walked into it,' Temba said without moving. His voice was thick, as if he was fighting back nausea. 'Earlier, when I came out here, I walked into it. My face . . . it slapped my face.'

It looked like a lump of meat. I reached out for it, drawing back at Temba's urgent, 'No!'

'What is it?'

'It is a tongue. A man's tongue, torn out at its roots. I think it is the tongue of Cyprian Bogovu.'

3 Alice

I threw up my first supper at St Faith's, doubling forward as I spewed, and almost headed Cyprian's tongue. I think I'd have pitched down the veranda steps and ended up flat on my face in the mud if Temba hadn't caught me, dragged me back and lowered me to the couch that ran along the back wall of the veranda.

'Jesus,' I mumbled through lumps of carrot and the vile taste in my mouth, immediately leaning forward and throwing up some more across the floor. 'Oh shit!' I spluttered as I fumbled for my handkerchief.

Temba found me a glass of water. I took it and used it to wash my mouth out, stumbling to the veranda rail to spit it out – and saw the tongue again, rotating slowly, with the rain dripping off it, and felt my stomach jump and contract.

But I held it. I held it because an explosive fear grabbed me. Out in that blackness beyond the veranda men were watching, perhaps lining up the sights of their rifles. Men were moving to surround the house ready to rush us, seize us, and start beating and hacking at us with those machete-like *panga*s, screaming with crazy pleasure as they did it. For the first time in my life I was afraid, no . . . terrified, not of something unknown, something in my imagination that might happen to me, but of something horribly real. I was shit-scared that someone would, at any moment, set about killing me, and doing it in the most brutal and agonising way possible.

It was Temba – again – who saved me. I was able to control myself, to finish washing out my mouth, to wipe the dribbles of puke from my chin and the front of my shirt, because Temba appeared with a mop and bucket and made himself busy cleaning up the veranda floor like some proud housewife, mopping, splashing the mop into the bucket, squeezing it out, mopping . . . and all the while, he hummed, a tuneless sort of hum; but he hummed.

And while I collected myself he reached up, untied that dreadful piece of string and disappeared indoors, the mop and bucket in one hand and the tongue dangling from the other. I never asked him what he did with it.

Cyprian was dead. Some time later Temba heard that two men had come to his house, after dark. The poor man had been at supper with his first wife and his youngest daughter. They had dragged him out into his yard. His struggles, his screams, had provoked cackling laughter from his assailants, then violence. They beat him, first with the flat of the axe blade he used for chopping wood, then with a *panga*. In agony, exhausted, he fell silent. Then they began asking him questions. When he'd answered them, when he'd begged them to let him go, for his children's sake, for his wives, they spent a further hour with him. No-one made the slightest attempt to intervene. They finished him by chopping his head off and slicing out his tongue.

They: Smallboy Mushewa for certain and, not as certain, the man who had held the pistol.

But we heard that later. On the veranda, after Temba had emerged from the house clutching a couple of bottles of beer, we sat on the couch listening as the rain built up again, a heavy, unremitting downpour that hammered the tin roof and gurgled along the gutters, that hissed across the ground and smacked the leaves of the trees. At first we sat in silence, I think nursing the same thought: Cyprian Bogovu was dead. The only man we knew who had actually witnessed the incident, who might have been able to identify Annabel and Rebecca's killers, was dead. They'd left it a remarkably long time – it was almost a fortnight since the ambush. It reflected their cockiness, their confidence that they would never be caught. And Cyprian's tongue arriving here meant they knew who he had talked to.

Temba brought me back. He lifted his beer and drained half the bottle in a gulp. Then he sighed. 'Ah, Armstrong, so now you have heard *Kisasi*.'

'*Kisasi?*' I frowned at him

'Yes. That noise, from beyond the house, when we were waiting.'

'What, the scraping sound?' The noise of a fingernail being run along the teeth of a comb; or a slow circular saw, slicing into wood.

'Yes. That is *Kisasi* the Justice Bird. Perhaps this time he was calling for Cyprian Bogovu. But he told me one thing: that there was no-one near, no-one waiting for us.'

So that was why Temba had leapt up so suddenly and charged at the house.

'There is something else, Armstrong,' he went on,

'they did not kill me. They could have done it, very easily. They did not kill you – and that would have been even easier.' He paused while I thought about the open window of Rebecca's room and the rain cascading outside. 'Instead, they have warned us.' He sat, shaking his head. 'It worries me.'

'Worries you?' For Christ's sake! We were alive, weren't we?

'Yes. It worries me very much because it means that there is one of them, at least, who thinks.'

'Oh yes?'

'Yes. One of them thinks, and it is much more difficult to wage war upon the evil that thinks.' He paused. 'This one, he says to himself, "If we kill those boys, then the police will have to do something. A second death, of a white visitor . . . they will have to do something." That is what he thinks.'

I nodded. Temba was right. Their natural reaction after Cyprian had spilled the beans would have been to kill us, and to have enjoyed a bit more fun. But someone had stopped them. They'd decided to frighten us instead.

'So one of them thinks.' I repeated.

'Yes. That is a big worry. People like Smallboy Mushewa, he does not think. So it is the one that thinks whom we will have to fight.' Temba paused, then sank the rest of the bottle. 'But it is worse, Armstrong. Worse.'

I frowned at him in the darkness.

'It is not only that he thinks. It is very likely that he has refrained from the killing of you and me for a reason. He does not want a big fuss because he is planning other, more important things that he does not wish to draw attention to.'

When Temba made that statement my mind went into overdrive.

Perhaps the two girls hadn't died for nothing perhaps it hadn't just been an opportunity killing. Something was happening behind that brutality. In a small, strange way it made me feel a little better about Rebecca's death.

We sat for some time. Temba broke the silence.

'Now we can do nothing. We must not be seen to be seeking information. We must go nowhere near Cyprian's home. We must . . . we must teach.'

I turned that thought over and over for a few moments. It seemed pretty indigestible.

'Okay,' I said slowly, 'But, if we can't do anything, Temba, how do we find them? It's information we need. Information. We have to find who they are, where they are, why they're doing this.'

Temba cut in. 'We can do nothing. We, you and I, Armstrong, we can do nothing. So we have to find others who will listen for us.' He stood and went into the house, returning with two more bottles. 'Today is Friday. Today we will teach.' He laughed quickly, humourlessly. 'Today Mr McKay will teach Geography and Mr Mbanga will teach Biology. And tomorrow, in the evening, Mr McKay and Mr Mbanga, who have been without women for many, many days, will go to a prostitute.'

When it comes to recreational activities, I have principles. I'm quite happy to buy a drink. The one time I went bungee jumping, I fully expected to pay for the thrill. If I go on holiday, I pay the airline and the airport taxes and the hotel. The one recreation I do not pay for is sex. Sex is like catching fish. Your up-front expenditure is low – a few worms. After that, you work for it.

There are disadvantages in having such a principled approach. As part of my pathetic attempts to lay Rebecca, I gave up sex with other girls. For nine months I was celibate because Rebecca kept me that way. When she left for Africa I had several tries at getting back to normal but they didn't work. The girls seemed willing enough but the satisfaction seemed to have gone.

I don't know what Temba was thinking as we drove the school truck down to Kaserewe that Saturday evening. His situation was quite different. He'd been making love to his wife – and by this time I'd seen a photograph of Annabel and had the first inkling of how much the man had lost – only a fortnight ago. But then, as I discovered, it was often very difficult to know what really went on in Temba's mind. He had this small, very round head with the features rather crowded on the front of it, leaving little room for expression. You knew when he was happy because he laughed, or he whistled, or – and this was his favourite – he hummed. You knew when he was very angry because he went horribly silent. In between times, it was damn difficult to tell what was going on.

By the time we set off for Alice's, about nine at night, we'd both fuelled up. We didn't go to a fancy hotel. Temba made straight for the shanty town round the back of Kaserewe, to a rusty corrugated iron shed called The Hollywood Bowl. This magnificent one-room establishment squatted on the edge of an unmade road filled with rubbish and puddles of water, but the atmosphere inside was amazing, good music, cheap beer, low lighting and filled with so many people that there was no danger of falling down. Everyone was shouting. And I joined in. Because one thing I had determined to do early on was to learn ChiMundi. At St Faith's I didn't need it – all the kids spoke English and weren't allowed to speak anything else while they were on campus – but I felt I'd be far more use to Temba if I understood the local language.

I learnt a whole load of useful words at The Hollywood Bowl. *Sex. More. That was great, do it again.* And, *How much?* By the time Temba and I fell out of the place I was ready for anything – except Alice.

Alice was huge. Take a seated Buddha, change it to female by adding even bigger, more pendulous breasts and yet more folds of flesh, paint it pitch black, give it a moustache and you've got something resembling Alice. She sat cross-legged in the middle of a maroon, velvet-covered couch dressed in a peach coloured silk shirt and voluminous cerise trousers smoking 555 filter tips and sipping neat gin from an American shot glass. The house stood in one of the more expensive parts of town, a two-storey building set back from the road behind a high lantana hedge, with plenty of parking out the front for the clients. But to gain entrance you had to get past Alice.

A girl showed us into the room and hovered by the door. Alice sat immobile, her eyes fixed on Temba, while we perched uncomfortably on the edge of armchairs facing her. It reminded me of an interview for a job in a comprehensive, in the headmaster's office, the atmosphere rather tense.

'You wan' a drink, Temba?'

Her voice was sore-throat hoarse, forced up from somewhere deep in that blubbery body.

'Beer.' He waved his hand at me. 'This is Armstrong.'

Alice didn't even glance at me. I was aware that the girl had disappeared.

'You never come here . . .' She had to pause to catch her breath. '. . . for a fuck, Temba, while . . . that good girl of yours . . . not warm in her grave.' It was painful, listening to her, the way she fought for breath. 'You don' come here . . .' she went on, her voice rising, and I suddenly realised she was angry.

'Listen.' I glanced at Temba. He, too, was angry and his voice rose to meet hers. 'Listen, Alice, Armstrong and me . . . we are here for a girl. A girl each. A good, clean girl.'

Alice was still watching Temba. She had bulgy eyes which seemed to water a lot as she kept dragging out a small handkerchief and dabbing at them. The door opened behind us and the girl returned. She carried a small tray on which she balanced two tall and very full lager glasses. She offered one to me first, bending neatly at the knees to lower herself to my level, passing me the beer and avoiding my eyes. She was pretty, dressed in a minute miniskirt and a vest-like top through which her nipples showed; middle teens perhaps, very much the same sort of age as some of the girls in the fourth year class whose legs I had admired last lesson the previous afternoon.

Alice waited until the girl had closed the door behind her before turning back to Temba. 'Okay,' she said. 'Okay, two girls. But . . .' and her voice began to rise again, 'you don' ask me . . . because you don' have to. I know what you come here for . . . you, Temba Mbanga . . . and it insults me . . . you not able to ask direct. You get what you want . . .' and, at this point, she folded into a paroxysm of coughing, the sort of deep smoker's cough that terrifies people like me who are relatively young in the game, finishing with an explosive, 'I swear!'

The length of the sentence seemed to have exhausted Alice, but Temba nodded.

When we climbed back into the truck I hurt. Alice must have seen me watching the girl who brought the beers because, when I was shown to a room, she was waiting for me. She was sixteen – that's what she told me – and her name was Mumbai and she had a repertoire of energetic activities that didn't stop for half an hour and left me physically and mentally limp. She had a great body, slim with just enough flesh on it to be fun, breasts the size and firmness of honeydew melons and a wonderfully tight, pert bum. Except for her nipples, which were a deep damson, her skin was the colour of a Mars bar and so soft and smooth I spent time just running my hands over it: I think she had oiled it in some way. She smelt of lavender. Her hair, black and tightly curly, was cut short against her scalp and there wasn't another hair between her eyelashes and her maroon-painted toenails.

Mumbai should have been a gymnast. She should have been the Olga Corbutt of Boromundi. To her, sex was acrobatics and the bed her mat, while the bloke acted as parallel bars, horse and bar. There was nothing touchy-touchy-feely about it, not at first – it was all good, hard exercise. And, if you couldn't take it any more, when you lay limp as a landed fish, she massaged you – and she was good at that too. The whole thing could have been intimidating but the girl's character saved it: she was simple, unpretentious, warmly cheerful and desperately anxious to please.

I didn't fully understand what had gone on between Temba and Alice but he didn't want to talk, not until we were back at his house and sitting on the veranda with a beer. I was still at the stage where I didn't like the veranda, because I kept looking up to where Cyprian's tongue had hung and out into the darkness wondering who was watching us. It took a couple of drinks before Temba unwound.

'So now we wait,' he said.

I didn't say anything.

Suddenly he turned to me. 'Annabel was a nurse. Okay? She worked in Kaserewe hospital. Her ward was mainly Aids patients. *Slim* patients. You understand? Many of these were prostitutes and she . . . she was sad that these girls were dying, unnecessarily.' He stopped, and I could see how his hands gripped the material of his trousers. 'She became interested in these girls. Condoms. Many were not using them because the men did not want them. I am not talking about Alice's place, because there is no choice, the man must use them. But there are so many other brothels in Kaserewe, and women working out of their own homes because they have children and their man has left them . . .'

I sat in silence under this uncharacteristic deluge. I still didn't understand.

'Annabel knew the women. She understood the pressure they were under. They knew her.'

There are times when I'm very slow.

'Did you talk to Mumbai?'

I frowned at him. 'Yes.'

He nodded. 'Men talk when they fuck. They talk more
if they have a few beers. Not while they do it because
their brains are concentrated in their balls, but before
and after. And, if the girl is good, she can persuade them
to say things . . . did you talk about Rebecca?'

I didn't answer. I sat, rigidly, remembering how, as
time had run out, I had held Mumbai, held her tightly
against me with my face pressed into her neck, and
told her how beautiful Rebecca had been. And Mumbai
had lain very still, listening, not commenting; just listening.

'Jesus!' I whispered.

So that's how we tapped into the most efficient information network in Boromundi. The girls, and particularly people like Alice who ran girls, exchanged
information. They're not fools. Information is more
powerful than an AK47 – I've heard that somewhere and
I'm damn sure it's true. For these women, at the basic
level, the information is about men and their habits. It
helps if you know that a man with a small scar on the
right side of his nose likes a bit of violence with his sex.
At least, then, you've got some choice of whether to take
him on or not and, if you do, of having something ready

to deal with him if he gets overexcited: like a large, leaded club. But the real information is the pillow talk. The drunk, babbling. The man nursing his sadness, wanting someone to listen rather than someone to fuck. Or the man puffing himself up in front of the girl he's about to screw because he's not sure he can do it. Or the man making excuses because his performance was so embarrassing the girl's silently pissing herself with laughter. Talk. Men do it. I did it. When Temba pointed out what I'd done, I was ashamed. And, when I realised the implications, elated.

I saw the whole point of the exercise. We'd covered our tracks. If we'd just gone down to see Alice, it would have been out and around in no time and someone would have wondered why we were talking to Alice and that same network would have told them. As it was, both Temba and I had had a good time – though he was loath to admit it. And we had our first ally, someone who would prove to be absolutely invaluable.

We visited Alice's place at irregular intervals, mostly depending on the availability of the school truck. Each time, we were shown into her room. However established her customers, they always started with Alice. We would go in and a girl – often Mumbai – would disappear for beer, and we'd move over to Alice and shake hands. Sometimes the scrap of paper was slipped into Temba's hand. Sometimes it came into mine. Each time it was accompanied by a quick look, a flick of her bulbous eyes, the glance of a conspirator.

Somewhere in amongst the small talk the question of girls came up. Temba moved around. I tried other girls but Alice said I was wasting my time so I went back to

Mumbai. But we found ourselves spending more time with Alice herself. She was a remarkable woman, fiercely protective of her girls and armed with a barbaric sense of humour. With most of the stories she told I ended up crying with laughter, but with the uneasy feeling that men were by far the weaker, and certainly the vainer sex. They did such dumb things. Like the drunk in a brothel in Kilongalewa who boasted to a girl that he knew a man who had recently taken a white girl's sex organs, and dried them.

Alice wasn't laughing when she told us that. We knew, from the moment we came into the room, that something bad had happened. She tried to skirt around it for a while but, for the first time, she was flustered, unable to find the fun, unable to face us. And, when she did finally come out with it, I collapsed.

I'm still not sure whether Temba already knew. When he'd described Rebecca's body as diced up into little pieces I'd believed him – but I'd imagined a frenzied attack, a man with a *panga*, a man rotten with hatred slashing and slashing at her. I now knew it wasn't like that. She had been very deliberately cut up. Carefully butchered. And bits from that process, parts of her body, had been kept.

Despite the sickness I felt, despite the weight of grey, overwhelming despair, I was determined to know the detail. Alice told me, but, I'm sorry, I can't bring myself to write it down. Suffice it to say that it wasn't a minor piece of surgery like the clitordectomy that many African tribes carry out. Large amounts of skin, flesh and internal organs were removed. No wonder she had seemed so light in her coffin.

And other parts? I asked. What about . . . what about her breasts?

Alice didn't know.

Cyprian's tongue had been bad enough. I hadn't known Cyprian. The idea that . . . no, I can't go on.

I tried to stop thinking about Rebecca after that because, if I allowed it, a stark, vivid picture would jump at me – of a man bending over her muddy, mangled body, slicing at her with a *panga*, like a butcher working a carcass. It was so horrible I blotted it out, and that meant blotting her out. Even now, it's difficult to remember the girl. In two senses: partly because, with time, I've actually forgotten what she was like; and partly because, when I do make the effort to remember, that ghastly picture jumps at me, elbowing aside all the sweet memories. For me, a single act of barbarity has destroyed her.

Nothing in my life had prepared me for the bad things that happened in Boromundi. After that moment, when Alice, for the first time, told us something rather than wrote it on a piece of paper, I managed to scrape myself together enough to go to Mumbai. I had to, or risk destroying our cover. That night, sex wasn't what it normally was. Mumbai was a genuinely sensitive girl who could read a mood. That evening, she was completely different, very gentle, very huggy; and, for the first time, she kissed me on the lips.

Once I'd overcome the physical disgust at how they had butchered Rebecca, I tucked it away. It became less a piece of emotional baggage than a fact, a statistic, almost; something to be weighed. It did some good too: it gave me a bit more spine, a bit more determination, it introduced a new element of ruthlessness; and it prepared me for the bloody time that was to come.

A mass of information, often no more than snippets, came in through Alice. Some were gems. Too many were speculation, rubbish, or irrelevant. All of them, every single one, we stored. Appropriately, they went onto Rebecca's laptop. Slowly, painstakingly, the facts began to slot into place. It was like doing a jigsaw, except that there were extra pieces, pieces that didn't belong, and pieces that overlapped existing pieces. The computer enabled us to juggle them around, look at them from different angles, place them in different contexts. It was detective work. There were times when it was almost fun: Temba and I, sitting together on his veranda with a beer or two, the darkness and chorus sounds of the African night surrounding us and the glow of the laptop in our faces, staring at the screen. There were times when we screamed with frustration. As the Christmas holiday loomed we had three names and some useful information on four of the five. Only the last, the big man who had climbed into the back of the bus and pulled Rebecca out by her hair, remained a nameless, shadowy figure.

And we had everything we needed to know about Smallboy Mushewa except one thing: where was he?

4 Smallboy Mushewa

Lake Kenge forms most of the western border of Boro-mundi. It is a long, narrow lake of immense depth, the fourth deepest fresh water lake in the world. It lies in the western arm of East Africa's Great Rift Valley, yet the ground at its northern end rises steeply. It's as if the rift valley suddenly gets lost. It does, and for good reason: it is buried beneath layer upon layer of lava and ash from three volcanoes that are still spewing fire. These form the Mountains of the Morning Mist or, if you want to learn a little Chimundi, *Mlimuku wa Usubuki Ukugu*, mountains so high that, although they straddle the Equator, they have a permanent cap of snow.

Smallboy Mushewa was born on 27th April 1984 at Kwita-Kwita, a small town in the shadow on the highest of these, Mount Simbilani. In this spectacular world of mists and montane forests, of vertical ravines and rushing rivers, where the active caldera of Simbilani bubbles like some gigantic witch's cauldron amid the deep snows and ice-blue glaciers, the birth of a runt went unremarked.

Smallboy was the youngest of Miriam Mushewa's eight children. From his birth he was an object of suspicion. He was quite unlike any of his siblings, all of whom were tall, pale-skinned and well-formed. The village tittle-tattle suggested that Miriam had been caught by an *umsuka*, one of the dark spirits of the forest, that she had acquiesced – worse, had returned to the forest again and again for her pleasure – and that this *sonku*, this black dwarf, was her punishment. Alice's informants were quite certain that Miriam had had an affair: poor woman, if it gave her any happiness she deserved it, for she never deserved the cross that Smallboy would make her bear.

Smallboy wasn't his given name. In the custom of the country he was baptised with a biblical name – Hezikiah – in the local church, in a ceremony carried out very quickly after his birth in the certainty that he was not long for this life. It was a miracle that this weakling child survived. But Miriam loved him and she was fierce in her protection, utterly determined that he should live and thrive. Along with his seven siblings Smallboy had a total of fourteen half-brothers and sisters from three step-mothers. All were older than him for the simple reason that, a few months before his birth, his father disappeared.

Gideon Mushewa was a self-made man. From humble beginnings in this remote corner of Boromundi he created a thriving transport business. As the business expanded he moved south to set up his head office in Mateka where he branched out into timber and coffee. He bought land, built an office block and houses. Miriam Nyakandisi, one of the secretaries in his office, came from the south-east of the country, a tall, good-looking girl of the Bora tribe, a finely-built, copper-skinned people with Hamitic blood in their veins. She had two children by Gideon before she managed to persuade him to marry her. It was a dreadful mistake: as soon as he did, he shipped her off to Kwita-Kwita, to a life of drudgery in his mother's *boma*. Gideon came home at irregular intervals, to inspect his lands, to get drunk on his mother's beer, and to beat his wife and, later, all four of his wives. In his spare moments he procreated thirteen children off Miriam, of whom five died, four in infancy and the fifth, Gideon's eldest and favourite boy, at the age of seven after being bitten by a puff adder.

Gideon's disappearance was occasioned by the collapse of what was by that time a ramshackle business empire. He had lost most of his trucks in the first Boromundi civil war, hijacked by fighters who either forgot to return them or burnt them to prevent them falling into the hands of the opposition. Worse, Gideon backed the wrong side, throwing himself behind the Popular Front for the Liberation of Boromundi (the PFLB, pronounced 'pflab') who derived their support from the western half of the country and their financial backing from Mobutu's Zaire. When the Boromundi Revolutionary Front (BRF), a loose alliance of tribes from Miriam's area in the south-east of the country, took Mateka, Gideon fled. In the street fighting his office was razed to the ground. His business collapsed. When the two sides met in Nairobi to sign the Nairobi Accord that brought the first civil war to an end Gideon crept back to Mateka but not into the position of influence he had once held. He gathered what capital he could and speculated. One of the few areas which brought in money was 'bush meat', dried game meat – anything from monkey to snake – and animal medicines and charms – leopards' teeth, lions' balls and the scrota of gorillas – which were in demand in the city and available on the slopes of Simbilani. His other affairs, particularly a disastrous investment in a copper mine, lost money. Faced with angry creditors who were threatening to cut off his testicles, or worse, he disappeared.

By this time, Miriam Mushewa's life was a misery. She came from the people who had defeated PFLB, who had ruined Gideon. The other three, junior wives, all from the Kwita-Kwita area, joined their mother-in-law in persecuting the woman. When Smallboy was five his mother gathered her children and fled. She returned to her home village in the Bora lands. Things were little better there. Nobody wanted a woman who had married a PFLB activist and brought with her a locust-hoard of eight half-caste bastards, not even her family. Miriam survived as best she could. In her late forties, but still good-looking, she took to prostitution. Her house was on the edge of a village through which the main road to Tanzania passed. She sold fruit to the passengers on buses that stopped in the village and this gave her the opportunity to solicit. She died when Smallboy was nine, probably of Aids.

In those first nine years of his life Smallboy suffered merciless bullying. His elder brothers and sisters bullied him. His half-brothers and half-sisters bullied him. Because of his small stature and short fuse, and because it seemed to be the done thing, the rest of the kids joined in. Smallboy grew up a permanently cornered rat. He learned his lessons in calculated viciousness in those nine years. The Bora kids stopped bullying him only when, with his mother's restraining hand removed, he nearly killed one of them.

The outbreak of the second Boromundi civil war gave Smallboy the career opportunity of his life. In late 1993, a raiding party from the revived PFLB, renamed the Boromundi National Reconciliation Movement (BNRM, or 'Bunrum' as Temba called it), appeared at Smallboy's school, rounded up the teachers and children and paraded them in the playground. In the chaos, mercifully, half the children escaped. Those that didn't were subjected to the spectacle of watching their teachers shot. Since Smallboy had been unrelentingly beaten by many of them, his reaction to the show was very positive. It may have been this, it may have been other reasons, but Smallboy was selected, along with about a dozen other boys and rather more of the older, better-looking girls, to accompany the guerrillas when they made their escape.

The concept of a child soldier is loathsome but, in the chaos of the Boromundi civil war, they undoubtedly had their uses. Children are inconspicuous. Children are very good at running errands to dangerous places that no adult can possibly reach. Children are quick, surprisingly brave and eat half what an ordinary soldier eats. All they need is training, in the art of guerrilla war and in loyalty. The former is fairly straightforward: for example, Smallboy learned how to fire an AK47, how to clear a jammed breech, how to strip the rifle down and clean it, and how to reassemble it before he had been with Bunrum a week. The lessons in loyalty were slightly more traumatic.

The children were debased. They were made to do all the things they had been brought up believing to be wicked; they were made to carry out mind-numbing atrocities; all the values of their old world were systematically destroyed, so utterly that they could never return to them. And these horrific acts were always carried out in front of witnesses, men, women and children who would hold their dreadful secrets – as long as the child remained loyal. It bound them together. Perhaps, somewhere back in our horrid human past, the concept of blood-brothers is based in this.

Smallboy raped. Some of the girls from his school were the object of his early bestiality. A lot of people came to watch this performance as Smallboy's member was out of all proportion to the rest of his body. Smallboy killed and cut and maimed, decapitated and disembowelled. It was all sold to him as training, training for the great battle to liberate Boromundi. It wasn't. It was inhuman degradation and it was calculated and it was wicked. The trouble is that he enjoyed it and quickly became very good at it. Within a month of his recruitment he found himself in the front line of Bunrum fighters, and later he was present at the second sacking of Mateka, an event that probably matched the horrors of the last days of Troy. Bunrum fighters wreaked a savage revenge for their defeat at the hands of the BRF ten years before, and Smallboy was in the thick of it.

We had a good description of Smallboy from about this time. He was five foot one, with a disproportionately large head on a thick neck, a barrel of a chest and bandy legs which made him walk with a pronounced sailor's roll. His skin was the shade of deeply tanned leather. One of his most surprising features were his hands: the fingers were long and delicate, with very pale fingernails which were beautifully shaped: the hands of a woman. As far as I can tell, this must have been the only feature he inherited from his tall, slim, pale-skinned mother.

His eyes, jet black and sunken, were set very close together. Apparently he could not look anyone in the eye. Instead, his eyes were constantly on the move, darting, watching, calculating. He had a flat nose, rather full, weak lips and, despite his tender age, the faintest wisps of a moustache. And he had an explosive temper. Girls who had been with him and not done exactly what he required, instantly and without question, had been severely beaten.

He was very strong, his movements quick and decisive. But the lasting impression people had of him was his humourlessness. It was said that he never smiled.

The second civil war carried on for nearly three years. For much of that time the country slid into barbarity. Statistics, of mortality, mutilation and family break-up; of the number and type of refugees, of the number of orphans and of rural depopulation; of deforestation, slaughter of game and destruction of farm land, all exist. They're hopelessly inaccurate and virtually meaningless. While the carnage was going on all the outside agencies abandoned the country, returning only when the Boromundi Revolutionary Front once more began to regain control. Bunrum forces were pushed back into the mountainous west and northwest of the country. Many crossed into Zaire, joining in the mayhem there. Smallboy was last seen in June 1996, in Kwita-Kwita, one of the few areas remaining under Bunrum control and one which had solidly supported Bunrum, facts which did not prevent the horrific massacre of a dozen people from the town, mostly female relatives of Gideon's wives. Smallboy was said to have denied any involvement: how could he kill his own people?

Then he disappeared.

This account of Smallboy's background was a result of Alice's information-gathering network. We knew less of the other four men, but by this time we had been able to rate them according to their importance.

Target 1 – the term 'target' was one Temba insisted on using – was, in our view, the leader. He was the one who had dragged Rebecca out by her hair. At this point we knew virtually nothing about him except that he was exceptionally strong, tall (perhaps six foot, six) and very dark-skinned. He did not normally operate with the other four. We didn't know his name.

Target 2 was the man who pulled the fat lady out of the front seat and hit her in the face when she made a noise. He was in his early twenties, a dark-skinned, negroid type with a very short temper. His name was Mophas Mandabanga. Once we had one other key piece of information about him, he was easy to follow up. Mophas was badly scarred. When he was a baby his mother had dropped him into the cooking fire. It's a common cause of infant death and disfigurement in rural Africa. Mophas' injuries included the almost total loss of his left eyelid and severe burn scars to the left side of his face. These left him with a lop-sided, leering look. With these two pieces of information – the name and the scarring – we learnt a great deal about him very quickly.

Target 3 was the man who arrived late with Smallboy and almost certainly entered the back of the minibus with Target 1. Once we'd identified Mophas, target three was easy. He was Onias Matanganesa, Mophas' half brother: same mother, different fathers. He was also Smallboy's closest associate – perhaps the nearest Smallboy ever got to a 'friend'. Again, once we had a name, the information started pouring in.

Onias was younger than Mophas, perhaps seventeen or eighteen, a boy who was dangerous in his insecurity. Given to flares of violent temper, he was described to us as a sadistic killer. Unlike Smallboy, who seemed to rape and kill because it was the normal and natural thing to do, Onias enjoyed his violence. He was renowned as a child-beater, a violent rapist of both sexes who, if crossed (and apparently his brother made some effort to restrain him) was quite likely to go berserk. The girls put his extreme savagery down to one stark fact: he only had one testicle.

Target 4 was Smallboy.

Target 5 was the man who had the service revolver, who held it to Cyprian Bogovu's head throughout the attack. I have already described him, the way Cyprian described him to Temba before his death – as tall, probably over six foot, with pale, almost honey-brown skin, a thin face and close-cropped, curly hair. Now we knew his name was M'Simani Kangalewa. The name is important because it proves that he originated in the south-east of the country. We were also certain that he was given the simple responsibility of poking a gun in Cyprian's face because the rest of the gang wanted him to have an easy job. In other words, they didn't trust him. All he had to do was stand there and threaten. Cyprian was obviously terrified of him, yet there was plenty of evidence in his account to Temba that the man was nervous and didn't do a very good job. For example, when he told Cyprian to go, he screamed at him. He didn't need to. Cyprian was already quite frightened enough.

By this time we were also beginning to understand why these five men had been thrown together.

As the second Boromundi civil war abated through the first half of 1996, the aid agencies returned. With them they brought their new white four-by-fours and ludicrous sums of money which they poured into the bottomless pit of African corruption. Even when they brought food, like sacks of maize or nutritious biscuits for young children, or tents and clothing, it was stolen from under their noses, the food adulterated, and sold on at enormous profit. Out of the carnage of war emerged the blowflies of peace. The fattest of these carrion feeders formed the new regime, a regime which, if it were possible, was even more corrupt than the last. The people, the ordinary man and woman and child, would have liked nothing better than to have been left alone to pick up the pieces of their mangled lives. But they were clamped under fear, under suspicion, as the arbitrary and uncontrolled BRF militias and police sought out those they claimed to have supported Bunrum, mostly people of the negroid tribes of the central belt and far northwest. Thousands died. Thousands more were thrown into prison, with the promise of prompt trials which never took place once the fickle interest of the Western media had moved elsewhere. And, as time went on, the police and militias, like ticks, became bloated and slack.

When I arrived in Boromundi, I had no idea of this history. To me the countryside, with its lush vegetation and washed-clean look, seemed incredibly peaceful and fertile. The people laughed. If St Faith's was an example, educational standards were remarkably high: the kids took GCSEs and the vast majority passed at A grade. I assumed that what had happened to Rebecca had been the exception, that the arrogance of the policeman who drove us that day to see where she had died was unusual.

The fact is that St Faith's, and the villages that surrounded it, weren't a good example of rural Boromundi because both civil wars had, to a very large extent, passed them by. Its main effects had been on individual families whose sons and daughters had been working away or had left to join the conflict. A few of them came back, mentally and physically scarred. Most simply disappeared, leaving relatives aching for news that never came.

It's not that St Faith's didn't take sides. It did. If push had come to shove people like Temba would have fought for the BRF. Of the two it had always been the less extreme, had, at the beginning, adopted a democratic socialist doctrine which sentient beings like Temba could live with. He maintained that it was unrecognisable today, run, as it was, by men who had been successful in the two wars simply because they had been brutal. That sort of background did not fit them for government – not democratic government, anyway. Even less were they qualified to run the nation's economy.

During the second civil war our local town of Kaserewe had had one bad fright. A Bunrum rabble – I think that's the only way to describe the motley collection of armed and semi-crazed men, women and children – had appeared along the main road early one evening. They settled on the town like a swarm of locusts, cleaning out the shops, breaking into and looting homes, and spreading murder and rape, particularly through the poorer parts of town. One small group had the temerity to invade Alice's place, but they were so drunk by the time they arrived that Alice and the girls had got rid of them quite easily. Temba told me they were buried under the carport Alice had been building at the time.

The town had been saved by the arrival of BRF troops the next morning. A sporadic, rather inconclusive battle had raged through the streets. By the early afternoon the BRF were back in control and the Bunrum rabble evicted, leaving about thirty dead. Kaserewe sighed a collective sigh of relief and burnt the bodies.

The day the Wises left, I had stood beside the road whilst they knelt in prayer. The place was only about fifteen miles from Kaserewe, yet had suffered much more. I'd noticed how empty the countryside was. I'd been right: it was depopulated. Before the first civil war the region, a great swathe of country to the south-east of Mateka, had supported thousands of small farmsteads. But in the last thirteen years there had been six years of all-out warfare and seven years of violent peace. Most people were either dead or had disappeared. Those that were left, mostly the old and children, were terrorised by casual police brutality and petrified of the gangs which were the splinters that remained after the shattering of the Bunrum army. In many ways the conflict didn't end. It simply broke up into smaller pieces.

When Smallboy emerged after two years, it was as a member of one of these gangs. The authorities could do little about them, there was too much newly-created space into which they could disappear. In any case, their activities were no more than irritating pinpricks which only occasionally, as happened when Rebecca was killed, caused problems. So, while they were hunted, it was with less and less urgency.

At the time I arrived in Boromundi that lackadaisical approach was changing, for good reason. It was beginning to become clear that these were no longer isolated groups but were operating with some common purpose. It was too late. A new movement was being born, one that was growing unseen but with the speed and malevolence of a cancer; one that was far more repulsive than Pflab or Bunrum, that threatened to wreak a new havoc across the country – a holocaust which would make the first two civil wars look like spats in a kindergarten playground.

5 Training

I moved in with Temba shortly before Christmas. I didn't want to. I'd visited his place a fair bit, and very comfortable it was, but that comfort, and its homeliness, had been made by Annabel. She might have been dead but she was everywhere. I found that very difficult. Also, I was quite content with what the staff wing had to offer. We had electricity until the school generator cut out at ten, hot water running out of a tap, we were fed and the food wasn't bad, the sheets were changed once a week – and I argued that Temba and I shouldn't be seen together more than was necessary. The counter-argument Temba deployed that changed my mind was simple: when the opportunity came to pick off one of our 'targets', we needed to be poised to go after them. By that stage we were beginning to build up an understanding of how these gangs functioned: they slept rough, they lived off the land, they were heavily armed, and they moved around a fair bit. We knew they came into town – quite of few of Alice's contacts had encountered them – but the chance of our catching one of them on one of these recreational visits was small and depended on how prepared we were to drop everything to go after him. It would be like hunting a dangerous wild animal, a man-eating leopard or a rogue buffalo, except that it would be far more difficult;

we wouldn't be planning to shoot them cleanly through the head.

So we had to be ready, and we had to train.

What Temba proposed was exactly the challenge I'd been yearning for. I'd already been out into the Boromundi forest. I'd already met its cathedral-like proportions, its darkness, its muffled silence broken by the drip-drip of its near-constant rain. I'd already, briefly, been lost in its monotonous sameness. I knew what it was like. The concept of having to survive in it challenged me.

But, before I moved into Temba's bungalow, there were one or two things I tried to negotiate. One was that we had someone to cook and do the washing. I drew the line at eating, day in, day out, the sort of thing Temba had been subsisting on since Annabel's death, mostly maize-meal cooked to the consistency of wet concrete, over which he would pour a tin of gristly Tanzanian 'stew'. I'd dined with him a few times and suffered the next morning, so I knew. Fanny, the lady we employed (it wasn't her real name but one I gave her; the real one started Fan – and had six syllables in it), came in at midday, had something ready for lunch at one and cooked a proper meal which we ate at six. I also tried to persuade Temba to install a five kilowatt generator. I offered to pay for it. I said we could have lights that illuminated the area around his house, in case we were attacked. We could play music. I could use my electric shaver. I lost on that one – probably quite rightly.

As soon as I had moved in he began to teach me bushcraft. I had no idea where he'd learnt it, but he was good.

By comparison, I was starting from nowhere. I knew how to tie a reef knot and could manage a bowline as long as I thought about it. I could make twist, that Boy Scout staple of flour, salt and water. That was it.

At first, I couldn't get enough of Temba's training, but what I hadn't realised was how tough it would quickly become. I learned how to travel through the forest, silently, covering my spoor. We slept nights out. I learned to stalk. I was made to lie hidden, immovable, for hours. I was taught how to build a fire out of forest materials that were sopping from months of rain. We survived without provisions for two days, eating what we could hunt and pick up. I baulked only when I was told to climb trees, high trees, then very high trees with precious few branches to hang on to.

If, at first, I was willing, as time went on my body proved weak. I couldn't help moaning. I became depressed. I refused to do things. I wanted to give up. One day, standing in the pouring rain in the forested peaks about three miles west of St Faith's, having spent a whole morning doubled up trying to read the tracks of animals in sodden leaf-litter, with me whining about going home, that I'd had enough, that I wanted a hot bath (in the staff wing – at Temba's place, there wasn't even a shower), that I was sick of all this fucking Tarzan stuff – Temba hit me. He hit me with a straight left that Mohammed Ali would have been proud of, a blow which lifted me off my feet and laid me flat on my back in the mud. He caught me high on the cheek and, for the following week, I sported an impressive black eye. I hated him for it, particularly as Mumbai found the black colouration hilariously funny. But I shut up. I didn't want to be hit like that again. And . . . I knew he'd been right to do it.

While Temba trained me, I did my damnedest to improve our conditions. Without telling him, I sent for a few things from England that I firmly believed would make a difference. My father had to post them twice as the Boromundi postal service succeeded in losing the first package. Thick polythene body-bags for staying dry while sleeping. Light, breathable, waterproof tops and leggings. Quality rucksacks. Two small Maglite torches. Theatrical make-up for our faces, in case I wanted to look black.

I stopped smoking. A smoker, in the unlikely event you haven't noticed, stinks; in the forest, so Temba said, he could smell me half a mile away. I stopped using a bed and slept rolled up in a blanket on the wooden floor. Each night Temba set an alarm clock and put it in a brown paper bag by my head. If and when it went off, usually at about half-past three in the morning, I had to get myself kitted up, out of the house and hidden in the surrounding forest, within a hundred metres of the house, in three minutes flat. Then Temba came looking for me. If I'd been slow, or he found me too quickly, he'd set the alarm again. Once I'd got the idea we swapped roles. Lastly, we walked. We walked miles, with our rucksacks full of stones, in pouring rain and humid heat, across rocky, slippery, soaking terrain, up precipitous hillsides and down into dank, torrent-scoured valleys.

The strain of the training had some nasty side effects. One afternoon, Temba stuck his head round the staff-room door.

'Okay?' he grunted. Just about every day we had taken a walk along a narrow path which traversed the steep hillside, to visit the place where Annabel and Rebecca had been buried.

Normally I'd have pushed aside the books I'd been marking – I preferred to do this in school as, if I left it to the evening, it had to be done by the light of Temba's tilley lamp – and joined him. Instead I said, 'Give me a minute.'

He gave me a good three minutes, then he asked, 'You coming?'

'Yeah!'

He gave me another five, then he said, 'Light's going.'

But I still didn't go. I didn't spend ten minutes sitting on the wall by Rebecca's grave – there was no headstone yet, just a mound of slowly-subsiding red earth that I tried to keep clear of weeds – staring out across the valley, thinking. I wasn't with Temba while he stood over Annabel's mound, his head bowed, his lips working – whether in prayer or in anger, I never knew. I stayed stubbornly at the desk in the staffroom. I tried to concentrate, gave up, and hurried along the path after him – to find the graveyard deserted. When I ran up to the house Fanny hadn't seen him.

By the time he came in Fanny had long left and our supper sat cold on the table.

'Temba,' I said. I reckoned I put everything I meant into that one word but he walked straight past where I was sitting towards his bedroom.

'I'm a fucking idiot,' I added, scrambling to my feet. 'Look, I'm sorry.'

He stopped by his bedroom door and shrugged.

'I was . . . I just wanted to get the marking done.'

He nodded. Each time he moved he spattered rain-water across the floor.

Then he turned away and went into the bedroom, closing the door carefully behind him.

I took myself out, across the veranda and into what had once been a lovingly tended front garden.

The moon, high in a sky devoid of stars, and almost full, seemed remarkably small for the amount of light it generated. The clearing, the face of the encircling forest, the narrow gravel pathway that ran down to the wooden gate, all glowed in a ghostly luminescence, and stood out more strongly for the depth of the shadows behind them. Yet the scene lacked colour. Even the bed of African marigolds that Annabel had planted, flowers that dazzled in their yellows and golds in daylight, cowered under a muddy grey. The forest wasn't silent – there was still the characteristic sawing of the crickets and the warble of the millions of frogs that copulated cheerfully in every puddle and the rustle of the six–inch cockroaches in the leaf litter and the high-pitched squeak of bats zig-zagging after moths – yet each sound seemed discrete, almost apologetic. And the plaintive cries of the bush-babies high in the forest canopy, a sound which, when I'd first heard it, had sent me dashing out on the veranda fully expecting to find an abandoned infant mewling in its crib, seemed thin, half-hearted.

The scene was breathtaking in its frozen beauty, but I felt sick, sick enough to want desperately to go back home to England.

It was partly Rebecca's fault. I'd stayed out here for her yet now I could hardly think about her. I wasn't doing all this for Rebecca any more. It was an idea which I found profoundly unsettling. If I was no longer doing this for Rebecca, what was I doing it for? And, if I had no reason to do it, why was I staying in this foreign place, going through all Temba's training shit with the end purpose of sticking my head out and probably getting it blown off – or worse?

It wasn't that I'd fallen out of love with Rebecca. When I thought of her, when I made the effort to remember what she looked like in England, the way she'd smiled at me, when I recalled how thrilled I would have been if she'd said 'yes' that afternoon in her class-room, I knew nothing had changed. For the first time, I began questioning the whole concept of revenge. I could do the other thing: forgive. If I forgave, life would suddenly be simple again. For a start, I wouldn't have to be in Boromundi any more.

I'd come out here with the Wises out of a sense of duty. That was it. And, when the truth had come out about the ambush, I'd stayed less for the revenge than for the excitement. It had less to do with Rebecca and seeing justice done, more to do with the boredom of life in England. And, now that the action hadn't really happened, now that the prospect was a slow, grim slog, now that I was beginning to grapple with the brute realities, I'd upset Temba. It was my own stupid, cretin-ous fault. I was totally dependent on Temba.

But something else did come into it: justice. The fact was, long before I came to Boromundi, I was fed up with justice not being done. Not in Boromundi – because, with the state of the country, one couldn't expect it – but back at home. Kids disrupted classes, wrecking other children's education and terrifying the teachers, and bugger all was done about it. Clever lawyers paid for by the taxpayer ensured that criminals got away with murder. Street gangs ravaged shoppers in city streets and, when arrested, were let off with a warning. I couldn't get my mind round the weakness of authority. It made me sick.

I was still standing in the middle of the clearing when I noticed the light seemed to have dimmed. I looked up. Something had bitten a neat chunk out of the side of the moon's disk, just like you'd take a crescent-shaped mouthful out of a digestive biscuit. And, as I watched, more and more of the moon disappeared.

I know that, in the old days, eclipses were considered portentous. Watching this one gave me the creeps.

It got worse. Just before midnight, as the last of the moon's bright disk flared and died, the outline of the whole moon reappeared in dried-blood red. And suddenly, around me, the forest fell silent. Nothing moved. It was as if everything, the animals, the insects, even the trees, were holding their breath, waiting for something terrible to happen.

Which it did. The next day, Smallboy broke surface.

It was the Wednesday evening before the end of term. School closed for the brief Christmas holidays at midday on the Friday. Temba and I had visited the girls' graves as usual and walked together up to the house. Things between us had eased. Fanny met us, standing on the veranda holding a note. Fanny was a large lady. When I remember her I think of beef dumplings and apples and tortoises – but black, very black, with a very round face and a sudden white grin that split it in half. Except she wasn't grinning.

I was getting used to the ChiMundi language, but most of the tirade that followed went way over my head. Temba took the brunt of it and he looked like someone being cut up by a bren gun. It all had to do with the lady who had brought the note. Fanny knew her. Fanny was a good Christian, an active member of St Faith's church congregation. Fanny had two daughters at the school. And Fanny was not amused if this ... trollop ... was the sort of company Temba was keeping. I stood by and looked innocent. Temba adopted the head-down look of a man battered by a hailstorm, finally muttering something about 'slim' and Annabel's patients which seemed to mollify the lady. Only then did we get the note.

Temba read it, then pocketed it. Only after our evening meal, when the tilley lamps were lit and Fanny had taken a rather straight-backed leave, did I get to see it. It was from Alice. Smallboy had been located at the Children's Rehabilitation Centre near Bumani. Smallboy was very ill. If we wanted to have a chat with him – that's how she put it – we'd better get a move on.

I dropped my guts. Smallboy might be a sitting duck but he had to be collected – fast. All the bravado, all the bragging about how we would cut him up slowly, came flying back to hit me in the face with the force of a wet haddock. Deep down, I was coldly terrified. I sat, gripping the sides of the chair, my breathing shallow and my guts barely under control. I could feel, really feel the blood drain out of my extremities.

Fortunately, Temba wasn't looking at me. He was

already planning, out loud, leaning forward in his chair with his elbows on its arms and his fingertips touching, almost as if he was praying. He'd heard of the place but hadn't been there. The Bumani Rehab Centre had been built shortly after the first civil war when some of the charitable agencies had begun to accumulate hoards of children who had been separated from their families during the troubles. At that time, child soldiering wasn't a major problem. Mostly, these kids had become lost when their villages had been destroyed, and the centre had been designed to look after them while their relatives were located. It wasn't until after the second war that displaced child soldiers reached plague proportions. Then the centre changed its role, specialising in the so-called rehabilitation of these little nasties back into society.

Temba was surprised that Smallboy had turned up there. He was a bit old for them, and probably far too far gone to stand much hope of being rehabilitated. And they were definitely not a hospice. If Smallboy was dying, there were more appropriate places for him to be – like, I suggested, strung up by his balls from a gibbet.

Temba ignored me, rattling on: the great thing was that we knew where he was, we knew he was helpless – it was merely a matter of going and collecting him.

'But we got a serious problem, Armstong.'

I frowned at him. Only one?

'We got a couple of day's teaching left. Right?'

I nodded wisely. 'Yeah. Day and a half.'

'Okay. So we can't just walk out.'

'No . . .' I began.

'But Alice, she say, time is very short. We must grab Smallboy quick, not just for this personal business but because, if we squeeze him, he can tell us where the others are.'

Temba was miles away, thinking out loud, pacing, his eyes glazed, the thoughts tumbling out one after the other. And I sat listening, holding on to myself.

'Bumani's two hours the other side of Kaserewe in the school truck. Right? And we must do this without being identified, at night and, in that paint stuff you got. So, we don't go this evening, but we do it tomorrow night.'

'Thursday,' I croaked.

'Thursday. But the serious problem is that Bartolemew Nchanga man. We need time off, we need transport . . .'

Transport. The only available transport was the school's ancient Bedford TK truck. It had originally been fitted to carry cattle but the school used it for all sorts of things, including taking the kids to school football matches, so the truck was quite a feature round Kaserewe.

'We have to have Bartolemew's permission,' Temba continued. 'So . . . we have choices. We tell him a story, which is difficult with Bartolemew, or we tell him the truth. That man, he may not be a priest but he's a good Christian, a man of the church, a man who won't take kindly to the concept of revenge, particularly in this present climate of national reconciliation. If he ever knew what we planned . . .'

Temba suddenly turned to me, a frown scrunching up his face so it looked even smaller.

'Lie,' I croaked.

Temba nodded and stood. For the next ten minutes he strode up and down the room. As far as I could see, my only use was to listen. I didn't have to comment.

We weren't ready. This had happened sooner than he'd expected. While he had a gun – I'd only seen it that night Cyprian was killed, and then briefly again – I didn't. So I couldn't be directly involved in hauling Smallboy out of the Centre. Okay: so I would drive the truck. He'd go in and collect the bastard. We'd bundle him into the truck and drive him out of the village, find a quiet spot and settle down to business. We'd need knives, sharp ones; a scalpel, rubber gloves, face masks; oh yes – I could have a *panga* in the truck, keep it on the floor by the handbrake, for the more brutal bits. The more brutal bits . . . Shit!

I sat and listened to all this in a stew of mounting terror and excitement. It was like an avalanche, belting down a hillside straight at me. I was so frightened, so elated I couldn't move. At any moment Temba would be off to see Bartolemew, to pinch a scalpel from Biology, to sharpen the *panga*, to clean his gun . . .

He stopped, standing over me, catching and holding my eye.

'Okay?' he said. 'We do it?'

I nodded. I couldn't speak.

'Right!' And he rattled off a list of things for me to do. Some way of covering the truck's number plate. A quick check of the gear: the neat little serrated-edged sheath knives, the lead coshes we'd made, the lengths of piano wire we'd borrowed from the school piano, the theatrical make-up. A notebook and those fancy new torches (a small glow of pleasure here). Rope to tie the bastard up. Some wide, sticky tape to go across his mouth. Food. Drink. He was marching up and down again, spitting out instructions. Then he suddenly stopped. 'Bartolemew,' he said, and disappeared out of the door.

The story Temba told the Head concerned a young relative of his who had suddenly appeared at the Bumani Rehab Centre. Temba had been asked by his family, who lived in the far north-east of the country, to go and check him out. It sounds thin, a story like that, written here in black and white, but in Boromundi it was horribly common. Temba came back brimming with relief. Bartolemew had taken it. He'd been a bit puzzled as to why I was going. But we had the transport.

I know now what inexperienced troops feel when they're told they're going into action. It's a sickening mixture of breathless excitement and fear. More fear than excitement. My guts surprised me by staying tight and my thinking cleared, but my hands shook when I tried to do things, and I got confused doing simple tasks. I kept wanting to go for a piss, then finding that, as I stood over Temba's open pit, nothing came out. Things were bad – but got a whole world worse when Temba appeared from the bedroom clutching a parcel swathed in oily rags. He sat in the chair opposite me and unwrapped it. It was his gun.

I had only seen it in the darkness, that first Thursday night, a vague outline, something that clattered metallically. Somehow I'd imagined a .22, or a shotgun, or an ancient rifle, an heirloom held together with bits of copper wire, something from the First World War when the Germans had owned Boromundi. It was nothing of the sort. What Temba cradled in his hands was an M16 carbine, an American assault rifle.

I want to stop here and take a break, go away and

pour myself a large whisky. My hands shake with the memory of that black device. I'd never seen one of these things up close, not for real. This was a killing machine designed specifically for the slaughter of humans, producing a hail of over seven hundred rounds per minute with a muzzle velocity of a thousand metres per second, a storm of flying metal designed to smash, tear and explode flesh. Yet, to me, looking at it, it had a slim, graceful, functional yet brutal beauty. So I watched with my mouth open as Temba set about cleaning the thing, deftly stripping it down, oiling it, wiping it, cleaning the barrel with a wad of cotton and a length of string, and, finally, reassembling it. He took all the cartridges out of the magazine, carefully inspected each, then, very methodically, put them back. When he'd finished he leaned the rifle against the side of his chair and looked up. He caught my stare. And gave me one of his rare all-teeth smiles.

The man knew exactly what he was doing. He was just making sure his real friend was ready for use.

When we'd done everything we could, which took us until about one on the Thursday morning, I rolled up in my blanket on the floor of my bedroom. I couldn't sleep. I lay on my back, staring at the darkness, saying, 'Oh, shit!' over and over again. I wanted Mumbai. I wanted her to hold me tight and tell me the world wasn't going mad on me. I wanted her to protect me from what was about to happen. I wanted to be ill, to be nursed by her.

I wanted to bury my face between her firm black melons and forget.

I taught the next day through a haze of anxiety and tiredness. Getting away, stumbling up to the house to find Temba standing by the truck all ready to leave, was a relief. We took turns driving. As we travelled, we underwent a transformation. We turned black, with artistically arranged white splodges, using the theatrical makeup my father had sent. Our clothes became dirty, mudstained rags. If, during the raid, anyone saw us, we wanted them to assume we were Bunrum guerrillas with a bone to pick with Smallboy.

The further we progressed, the more agitated I felt. I worried that we'd be stopped at a roadblock: God knows what they'd have made of the face-paint. I worried that the police would pull us up as we passed though Kaserewe: I suppose we could have pretended we were going to a fancy-dress party. I was worried someone would recognise the truck, and would report it stolen. I was worried, but Temba just whistled through his teeth.

The other side of Kaserewe, Temba suddenly said, 'Soon, you drive.'

I nodded.

'When we reach the Centre, I go in alone.'

As far as words were concerned, I'd reverted to infancy: all I could do was nod.

'I take the M16.'

I nodded vigorously. I wouldn't have had a clue what to do with it.

'If I have any difficulties, I will use it. I must find Smallboy quickly.'

I managed a grunt.

'If that rat cause trouble, I will shoot him, perhaps kneecap him, to incapacitate him. Okay?'

'Yeah.'

'If necessary, I will carry him. Depending on his state, I will either throw him in the back or, if there is any fight in him, I will stick him into the footwell, here, and hold the gun against his head. Okay?'

I nodded.

'Then you will drive like hell.'

Damn right I will!

As you already know, the plan fell apart, like plans are apt to do. It wasn't our fault. It might have worked rather well.

It was late afternoon when we arrived. The rehab centre was set back from the road down a dirt drive. When we pulled up in front of a muddle of single-storey breezeblock buildings painted white, with corrugated iron roofs, we found ourselves surrounded by children. They were anything from about six through to thirteen, perhaps fifty of them, girls and boys, all very scrubbed and shaven-headed and dressed in clean, cheerful tee shirts – one little girl wore a Fat Willie tee in slate grey, just like my niece's, and another wore Buffy the Vampire Slayer – and knee-length shorts and American baseball caps. They stood around us, they looked up at our bizarrely painted faces, they didn't react, they didn't move. Their faces lacked expression, curiosity, life. They were automatons in human form, their personalities stripped out of them.

No one else seemed to be around. Temba climbed out. The zombies watched this huge, dirty man, with his black and white face and vicious gun, and they didn't bat an eyelid.

'Hey!' Temba said.

They put their fingers in their mouths and stared up at him.

'You seen Smallboy?'

They sucked and stared at him, their eyes the size of billiard balls.

'Smallboy Mushewa,' Temba suggested.

Yellow snot, like two naked caterpillars, oozed down the from the nose of a round-faced kid who wore nothing but a pair of shorts and a belly button the size of a door knob.

Temba shifted the M16 and suddenly a lad of about ten pointed back up the road and said something which I didn't catch, something in a high-pitched voice which propelled Temba back into the truck, screaming at me to, 'Drive!' That's how we came to the cemetery.

When we saw what was happening and knew we were too late, we sat for a few minutes in the truck. I won't describe our feelings because you've got an imagination. We could have left it, driven home. It shows how much I had recovered that it was me who suggested we join the group around his grave. We stood back from the other mourners, watching. As the ceremony finished Chloris came straight over to us. She didn't ask our names and she didn't bat an eyelid at our disguise. She was very sweet, explained that she had nursed him and thanked us for coming. I think she thought we were friends of Smallboy's. She even invited us back to the centre for a cup of tea. When we declined she said, 'He was very brave.'

I grunted. I didn't dare say anything and Temba wasn't going to.

'We'd run out of painkillers – again – so it was pretty grim for him. You know, at that stage they've nothing left in them. They're a shell, a weak, helpless shell filled with pain, with . . . unbelievable agony. Most of them have given up but Smallboy, God bless him, kept smiling right up to the end. Poor, poor thing.'

I could have suggested to Chloris twenty reasons why the little bastard was smiling at her, and I could have been pretty graphic about what was going on in his sewage mind, but I didn't, not because I didn't want to speak but because that was the moment when her peace, her serenity, her uncomplicated goodness began to worm their way deep into my soul. I simply could not conceive that anyone could be so loving towards anything as revolting as Smallboy.

She did answer one question, though. The reason Smallboy had come to the Centre was that his father, Gideon, owned the Bumani village shop. So Gideon had reappeared, just like Smallboy reappeared. The man was a natural born survivor. With his mother dead, I could only assume that, when Smallboy became ill, he fell back on his one remaining relative. Gideon was all Smallboy had left. He came home, if you like, to die.

That's why, later that night, after we'd dug up the grave, we decorated the front of the shop with Smallboy's testicles. And, just before we left, we dumped his head on the Centre steps. It was bucketing with rain again. By that time we were pretty worked up. We hadn't discussed it, but I suppose we wanted to make a point: not everyone was prepared to forgive, not everyone was Christian enough to love little bastards like Smallboy; not everyone could be as sweet as Chloris Humphries.

All the way home, battling our way through pouring rain along roads that were muddy ice-rinks, I was elated. Temba could hardly string two words together. By the time we got back it was too late to go to bed. We cleaned our faces and ate a cold, silent breakfast. We went down to the school and taught a morning's lessons. For me, the reaction lay in wait until I was safely back in Temba's house. Then it hit me.

I sat on the couch on the veranda and shook. It was as if something had torn my nerves out by their roots. The paroxysms were so extreme they seemed to crush my chest. My heart hurt. I was afraid I was having a seizure or a heart attack. Slowly, slowly, the shaking died away.

It wasn't what we'd done to Smallboy on that tarpaulin. That was horrible work but I could cope with it. It wasn't being driven by Temba down the darkened village street while I dropped bloody chunks out of the back of the truck. It wasn't what we did at the shop nor the leaving of his head on the Centre steps. No, the shock came from the very fact of my having controlled and overcome my fear. I had been so wound up, so tight – yet I'd controlled it and, I hope, proved myself to Temba.

In fact, there had been times, like at the cemetery, when I'd been cooler, more calculating than he. My nerves might be shot, but, overall, I was pretty pleased with myself.

Temba suddenly emerged onto the veranda, handed me a beer, padded across to lean on the rail and said, 'Nothing!'

'No,' I agreed.

'Gideon is in Bumani. That is all.'

'Yes,' I agreed, struggling to control a new paroxysm of shaking but beginning to understand.

'The other four.' He shook his head.

'They'll come,' I said helpfully.

He pushed himself away from the rail and turned to me. 'Tomorrow we go. Tomorrow, if they look for us, we are not here. Tomorrow . . .' He waved his beer in the direction of the distant tree line. 'Far away, eh?'

'Good idea,' I said.

He turned back to the view. 'But, next time, Armstrong, you have a gun. Okay?'

'Okay,' I whispered.

'A big gun.'

I nodded, but when I took a swig of beer my throat was so tight I had difficulty swallowing, and I had to clutch both hands firmly round the bottle to stop them jumping around like a pair of overexcited squirrels.

Later, as we sat silently on the dark veranda seeing if we could empty a whole crate of beer, *Kisasi* sang for us. I'd never heard him go on for so long. The little bird positively trilled. Temba didn't agree, but it sounded to me like a hymn of triumph.

The next morning, the Saturday, we caught a bus to Temba's family home in the north-east.

6 The Galil

I am unable to reveal exactly where Temba's family home was for reasons which will become very apparent. In any case, it's difficult to describe since it's a long way from the nearest town. The countryside was quite new to me, much more like the Africa I'd seen in films and on those wildlife programmes on telly: dry and dusty, moulded by the sun and the wind and the unreliable but sudden rainfall. Red-brown, flat-bedded sandstones and shales had been dissected by the sheer-sided canyons of innumerable seasonal streams to form a blocky, sharp-edged terrain, the sort of thing you see in cowboy films set in the Arizona or Mexico deserts. Clinging to the thin, sandy soil were low thorn trees, at most twice the height of a man, which formed a grey, monotonous tangle that stretched for thousands of square miles. In the clearings between the bushes knots of scrub grass clung to a precarious existence. Humans were an afterthought in that fierce landscape.

Temba's village consisted of a collection of half a dozen *boma*s, enclosures formed of branches lopped from the thorn trees, within which were clusters of round, beehive-shaped huts, built of mud and wattle. Each *boma* was home to a family – husband, wives, grandparents, children – and each member had their own hut. These were entered by a small, circular door which had a high sill – presumably to keep scorpions, snakes and the occasional floods out – and was windowless. They varied in size from a large dog-kennel inhabited by Temba's youngest half-brother to something the size of a suburban sitting room which was used for living and eating when it rained – which wasn't often. The area inside the thorn fence was baked earth, assiduously swept each morning by the women. The cooking was done on an open fire in a small, lean-to kitchen.

I was given my own hut. I had to crouch, almost crawl, to get in and out. At its centre it was just high enough for me to stand. It contained a small chest of drawers and a crude, wood-framed bed which had springs – if you can call them that – made of what appeared to be plaited grass. On this was laid a blanket, and I slept rolled up in another. A third, very old blanket had been fixed so it could be pulled across the door to give some privacy.

Temba pointed to the floor.

'Nice floor,' he said.

'Yeah,' I frowned. It was a very nice floor, brown and polished, with a neat, hand-woven carpet on it.

As I've said before, there were times when it was impossible to tell what Temba was thinking. This was one of them. He had seemed in a good mood so I thought that, maybe, something was amusing him.

'So?' I said, 'Nice floor. Nice carpet. Nice bed. Nice . . .'

'Dung.'

'Dung?'

'Cow dung, mud, and plenty polish.'

'Blimey!'

Lots of things were like that. Each morning I was brought water in a gourd. The gourd resembled the dried outer skin of a pumpkin, about the size of a basketball, with a hole in the top. Temba's youngest sister, Nzizi, who disappeared into her own smiles each time I spoke to her, had been detailed off to carry out this little task. I felt ashamed to accept it: she'd had to collect the water from a pool a good three miles away, leaving before light and returning with the gourd balanced on her head. I was expected to drink, then wash carefully, in such a way that a minimum of the water would be lost. When I'd finished, Nzizi collected the waste water and sprinkled it onto the family vegetable gardens.

Temba's father was exactly as I would have imagined Temba thirty years older. A huge man running to fat, his hair and thin beard grizzled, he wore the traditional *nchanga*, a six-foot length of brightly coloured and patterned cotton cloth, wrapped round his waist like a skirt, and a very ordinary collared, short-sleeved shirt with two biros in its breast pocket. Temba emerged the first morning dressed in an even brighter *nchanga* and a white cotton vest, his great chest and arms exposed.

The family seemed very much at peace. Their days were unchanging, responding only to the movement of sun and weather, and to the visits of their relatives, particularly of the grown-up daughters who had moved away. Sizwi was one of these occasional visitors. She took after her mother, tall, with wide-set, almond-shaped eyes and skin the colour of Lyle's Golden Syrup. I don't have too many rules when it comes to women but one of them is to stay away from the daughters of the house in which I'm a guest. What's more, Sizwi was married.

I tried very hard to be polite but a little distant despite her smile and the liquid brown eyes that watched me.

The women did most of the work: they milked the goats, worked the gardens, cooked, washed, collected water, made their own clothes and shoes, cleaned the houses and compound, and, occasionally, walked into town to do the shopping. The men sat around and talked, this talk being justified as decision-making – which caused the women to shriek with mirth. The younger men, those below the age of eighteen, took the cattle out, sometimes great distances, in search of grazing, often not returning for a week or more at a time.

For the first couple of days, Temba and I did very little except squat with the other men under the shade tree in the centre of the village; tall, lean men with long faces and dusty skins. Many of them, particularly the younger ones, were armed, usually with old, poorly maintained AK47s. They carried their weapons with the ease with which you and I carry our mobile phones: they were a part of them. We passed our time talking. I was, once again, at a disadvantage: although my ChiMundi was coming on, these people spoke a different language, though they did their best to draw me in. The conversation was very slow, punctuated by long 'Eehs' and 'Nnnns' and the effortless flicking of cow-tail whisks at the swarms of flies. There seemed no emotion in their discussion. All were expected to contribute. One subject seemed to drift into the next. It was quite difficult to pinpoint the moment when a decision was made.

On the third day Temba came to my hut just after Nzizi had delivered my water. He caught me on the hop: I'd just let the child touch my skin – she couldn't believe its colour – and I felt guilty. Guilty, because little Nzizi looked just like her sister and I'd been imagining what it would be like to have Sizwi touch me. Temba eased his bulk though the tiny doorway and squatted beside my bed, lowering the butt of his rifle to the floor, so the top of the barrel stroked his cheek, and grinned.

'We go,' he said.

I had slept extremely well. I felt warm and comfortable. I didn't like the look of the grin or the gun or the idea of going anywhere.

''Nother day,' I suggested.

'We have a meeting.'

'We're on holiday. Cancel it.'

'People wait for us.'

'Apologise. Tell them I'm ill.'

He lifted the M16 and poked me with the butt. 'Now,' he said.

'Jesus!' I pushed myself up onto my elbow. 'It's not far, is it?'

'Half a mile? Maybe a mile.'

The half mile took four hours. Four hours, at an almost ceaseless, loping pace, threading our way through a dry but beautiful wilderness.

There were no paths, no sign of other humans. The sun burned my skin and probed the back of my eyeballs. The heat bleached the colours out of the sand and rocks and trees, and the baked earth cooked the soles of my trainers. We stopped twice. Both times Temba, who was travelling about five yards in front, held out his hand, waving me down. The first time I crouched, listening, watching him. Nothing seemed to happen. Finally he rose, very slowly, and beckoned me forward. Fifty yards on from where we had halted he stood and pointed at the ground. The great, round outline of an elephant's footprint was stamped into the sand. 'A herd,' he whispered, 'here, a few moments ago,' and he showed me how the sand at the edges still fell into the imprint. A big herd. I hadn't seen them.

The thought of being surrounded with wild animals filled me with a heady mixture of excitement and terror. The bush around me suddenly became infinitely threatening: a termite mound transformed into a rhino; a twisted tree a buffalo; a low bank of sand a crouching lion. And yet we had to work our way through it.

The second time Temba stopped, I again saw nothing but this time I heard the rumble of many hooves, away to our right front, and, rising above the thorn trees, the dust kicked up by a large herd. And I noticed that, this time, Temba slipped the M16 from his shoulder and held it at the ready, and waited much longer before he led me on. 'Buffalo,' he said. Bad tempered beasts. *Great*, I said to myself. *Nice to know.*

We arrived at the village in the heat of the day, to be welcomed very formally, each of the village men, who were obviously expecting us, shaking our hands and muttering their greetings. We joined them under their shade tree, squatting, African-fashion, in a rough circle. At first I was uneasy. Without exception, all the men held rifles, caressing them with the ease of long familiarity. Then beer, the same millet beer as I had drunk at Rebecca's wake, was brought in gourds. The gourds were passed round, rather like the port at a gentleman's table, except that we drank it noisily and straight from the container. The talk and laughter rose in volume. The women brought more beer, the little girls clinging to their skirts and staring at me with round black eyes until they were dragged away. Food was served, a goat so lightly roasted that the blood dribbled down our chins as we ate. As the heat began to wane and the colours ran back into the landscape the talk fell away. It was not that the men were sleepy – the beer continued to move between us. There was an expectation in the air.

A small boy approached. He carried something wrapped in cloth and I knew immediately what it was. Temba, who was sitting on the opposite side of the circle from me, caught my eye and grinned. I felt like a child at a party who knows the present is for him but cannot say anything.

The boy shuffled into the centre of our circle, very conscious that he was the object of attention, and, very gently, lowered his burden to the earth. The squatting men studied the bundle until a thickset man in his middle years eased himself to his feet and advanced upon it, slowly and carefully unwrapping it.

The purchase of my rifle took over an hour. Temba commenced proceedings by walking across to the weapon, squatting and stripping it, inspecting every part with ostentatious care, before reassembling it. Even though the language meant little to me, it was obvious that the bargaining that followed was cut-throat. Twice Temba called to me, his voice keen with frustration, saying we would leave. Each time he was persuaded to return, to sit down. As the sun sank and the shadows thickened in the surrounding bush Temba stood, rubbing his aching legs, before advancing on the thickset man and carefully counting out notes from a roll he carried tucked into his *nchanga*. The deal was done. Temba bent to take the rifle, lifted it, turned, and handed it to me.

'Eeh,' the men chorused. 'Eeeh.' It was like the long sigh of a dusty wind.

I would give a lot to know the history of that rifle. It was a Galil, an Israeli automatic rifle firing the 5.56 x 45mm NATO cartridge, the same as Temba's M16. Apparently the design is based on the Finnish Rk 62, itself a variant of the Kalashnikov AK47. It had a neatly-folding stock and a 35-round magazine the same banana shape as the AK47. It was a very well-made, efficient killing machine, capable of firing 550 rounds per minute. What was more important, it was in good condition. I loved it, and it never let me down. But how did an Israeli rifle find its way so deep into the heart of Africa?

I had to stand and watch Temba pay for the rifle and, from the number of notes that he had unrolled, it must have cost a small fortune. As soon as I dared I sidled up to him.

'Temba,' I whispered. There were a lot of people milling around and I was hot and sweaty and none too steady on my feet.

'No,' he said.

'You've got to let me . . .'

'No!' he repeated.

'Temba . . .'

'Armstrong!'

'Shit!'

So the Galil was a present from him and nothing, but nothing I tried over the next few days would persuade him to allow me to pay, nor make a contribution. It was a very precious gift and the gesture bound us closer together.

It was also a dream come true. From a small boy, I'd longed to own something like this. When I was twelve my father had bought me a .177 air rifle. My mother disapproved and made me promise never to shoot anything living, particularly the swarm of small birds she fed so excessively in our back garden that many were virtually flightless. I was quite incapable of keeping my promise.

Before leaving, Temba insisted on loading my rifle, though I wouldn't have known one end from the other if we had run into trouble. We walked into the entrails of a truly bloody sunset, the bush already dark and silent around us. I couldn't see anything, the shadows so thick they obscured the ground, and I was already so tired I tripped over every protuberance and stumbled into every hole. The branches of the thorn trees caught at my face. The day's consumption of beer didn't help. Temba seemed to do much better than me, at times moving ahead, leaving me behind. Had not an almost-full moon risen shortly after seven, the journey might have taken all night.

It was not without incident. The African bush comes alive with the dark. We had no torch and, with me stumbling around, Temba must have missed many of the warning sounds, but he stopped us frequently, waiting as something moved away. I think, mostly, it was harmless, but once we halted to listen to a hoarse, deep-throated cough from a watercourse away to our left. I didn't know it was a lion until Temba told me later, but it made no difference: the sound was primaeval, terrifying. I stood, listening, feeling the cold fingers of an ancient fear dance up and down my spine.

We finally fell into bed just after two the next morning. The Galil slept at my side.

I spent most of the next two days with my rifle. The Galil is a beautifully simple weapon to shoot. My overwhelming recollection of the first time I used it was of the sheer, atavistic joy I found in its power. I wanted to scream as I pulled the trigger, as the gun bucked in my hands and the bullets shredded a small thorn tree. I'd have cheerfully played with it all day but Temba had warned me that its cartridges were more difficult to come by than the standard Kalashnikov's 7.62, so I spent far more time squatting beside a blanket, held down against the hot wind by a large stone at each corner, stripping the Galil, cleaning it and reassembling it, again and again and again, until I could do it blindfolded, and quickly. Every now and again Temba wandered over from the shade tree and stood behind me, using his rifle to point to the different parts and making comments.

By that stage, I was used to the idea that Temba couldn't sit around doing nothing for long, and I was also used to the idea that the one person who would be in complete ignorance of what he planned was me. So I fully expected it when, late in the afternoon of the sixth day of our holiday, he announced we were setting off on an exercise early the next morning. There's nothing significant in this, but the day happened to be Christmas Day. The family didn't plan to celebrate in any way and there was no giving of presents – which is just as well, as I hadn't brought any along.

In some ways I am ashamed of what follows. In other ways I view it as a necessary evil. There were times when it was funny. It was dangerous all the time.

Temba and I were up before dawn, and we travelled fast. We stopped for a first rest in the shade of one of those lovely, flat-topped acacia trees, on a slight knoll, with a view, the sort of spot lions favour so they can watch the passing game and select their next meal. It was midday and, had the flies not been so persistent, I might have been dozing.

'You know where we are?'

I woke up. Temba hadn't spoken for hours.

'America?'

Temba swatted a fly.

'Okay. Where?'

'This is the Malakari.'

I looked around with a little more interest. The Malakari Game Reserve is in Tanzania and was, until the early nineties, one of Africa's forgotten reserves, a vast area of savanna and swamp too remote to be on any tourist itinerary. But the construction during 1996 of a longer runway at Mba, at the eastern edge of the reserve, a new network of park roads, and two large hotels, one overlooking a waterhole in the style of Kenya's Treetops, had begun to open it up.

'We missed immigration,' I said.

Temba pointed. 'You see that Tommy?'

We'd passed hundreds of the little gazelle but I gave him the courtesy of a quick glance.

'Yeah?'

'For the start of this exercise, you must shoot it.'

For a moment I didn't believe my ears.

'Shoot it? Jesus! What for? There are hundreds of Tommies around your village. What's the point of sticking our necks out here, in a national park? If we're caught, we could . . .'

'Who will catch us?'

'The Tanzanian police? Rangers? I don't know . . .'

Then the penny dropped, and my guts turned over. The whole point of the exercise was that we needed some opposition, and the Tanzanian Rangers would be armed and would shoot to kill. I knew that the Malakari had had a bad time during the second Boromundi civil war, with Bunrum gangs crossing into it to slaughter game to feed their fighters. It had almost become a commercial-scale operation, with trucks loading up the carcasses shot during the night and transporting them back across the border to centres where the meat was butchered and processed. This had continued for almost a year after the peace while the Tanzanian Rangers had fought pitched battles with the poachers. The place was peaceful now. That's why the tourists had come back. But the Rangers were still there.

'We won't shoot any of the Rangers?'

Temba shook his head. 'No, no. We must not be seen by them. If we are seen, we have failed the exercise.'

'And . . . we won't shoot many animals. I mean, not the . . .'

'We will shoot very few. The plan is to use them for stalking practice. We will get very, very close, close enough to pull tails.'

I was beginning to understand.

'But,' Temba continued, 'it is essential you shoot something big: a wildebeest; or something difficult like a waterbuck. To understand your rifle, Armstrong, you must feel it kill. You understand?'

I nodded.

'And,' he added, 'we will do some very silly things. Okay?'

Temba is a man of his word: we did do some very silly things.

It was midday on our second day in the park, the heat suffocating, the crickets tearing the air with their screaming. I lay out on a shelf of rock that overlooked the bed of a river. No more than a sluggish trickle of water flowed between green, stagnant pools left from the last flood. Thirty yards below me and on this side of the water, under the shade of a dom palm, a minibus was parked. It was painted in black and white zebra stripes. All the doors and the roof were open against the heat. Scattered around a flat area between the rounded rocks that fringed the water were its eight passengers. Some lay on their backs, their arms thrown across their faces. One or two sat up, gripping their knees, talking to the driver, an African dressed in a khaki bush shirt and long trousers. In one of the high fever trees above them, a colony of bright yellow weaver birds quarrelled around their nests of woven grass.

Below me, Temba lay flat on his face within five yards of one of the women, hidden from her by a low boulder. Slowly, so slowly, he eased himself forward. The woman was in her early thirties. She had short, blonde hair and she wore soiled white shorts that squeezed the fleshy tops of her legs, and a tee-shirt whose lime green material stretched so tightly across her ample bosom that, even from my distance, I could see the bumps of her nipples. She was talking to a man who lay beside her, sitting with her back towards Temba and her arms extended behind her to support her weight; and by her right hand stood a bottle of Coca Cola.

She had taken two sips from it since Temba had begun to stalk it. His first movements had been fairly quick, skimming from one hiding place to the next. Only in the last few yards had he begun to crawl. Yet he was under pressure. As I watched the woman sat forward, turned to reach for the drink, sipped and put it down again. A third of the bottle had gone. And Temba and I were thirsty.

He moved again. I've seen wildlife programmes in which a lioness stalks her pray, her body quivering with the intense effort of slow motion. Temba was like that. A sudden movement, and he would be seen. There were at least three people who were facing towards the woman. He had to rely on her body to shield him from them, her body, the soporific heat, and their sense of security.

He left the boulder. The ground he was moving into wasn't completely bare, there were some tufts of grass and a small thorn bush, but it was thin concealment. If the woman turned, or if her male companion sat up, Temba would be clearly visible.

I have no idea what he would have done had he been seen. Got up and run? Stood and laughed, told some story about his being a member of the Tanzanian Special Forces who were on exercise? Whatever he did, the driver was unlikely to believe him. Did he have a radio in the bus? Would he call up base, or the Rangers, and ask questions? Would the Rangers come after us? Did they have spotter planes? Or . . . is it possible that, if Temba had lain still, if he had not moved, if he had not met her eye, the woman would have said nothing?

Temba was very close. The dust of a day's trekking camouflaged his clothes and his hair and his skin. If I screwed up my eyes he blended into the land, so perfectly he might have been another rock. Using his toes and his elbows, he lifted himself forward. He was almost close enough to reach his prey.

There is a strange human state somewhere between laughter and fear. I was in it. I trembled with fear. My stomach seemed to flutter with it. Yet I wanted to giggle. I wanted to laugh at this huge man, flat on his face in the dirt, his arm reaching out for that precious bottle of Coke. It's a state I remember from childhood, from childish wickedness like a summer raid on a neighbour's raspberry patch, running from it in terror and laughter.

Temba stopped. The driver had stood up. The man stretched. I could hear his groan of contentment. And he was saying something: from his attitude, from his movements, he was telling his passengers that their lunch break was over, that they needed to be moving.

I remember once, as a boy, standing with my father on a wooden footbridge across a weir. On the far side of the weirpool below us, on a bank of mud, a small group of mallard stood preening themselves. A fox stepped out of the reeds behind them, seized one of the ducks, and stepped back into his cover. Not one of the other ducks moved. They continued to preen themselves. After a few moments of incomprehension I turned to my father and said, 'Did you see that?' He hadn't.

Temba had disappeared. While the driver had had the attention of his passengers, he had taken the bottle and melted back into the rocks.

The woman sat up. She was laughing, shouting something to the driver. Then she turned for her drink. She stopped. I saw her head move as her search widened, and the way her body stiffened. Then she turned to her companion, laughing uncertainly as she asked him to give her drink back. He was still lying out flat and opened an eye at her, shaking his head. She was sitting bolt upright now, casting around again before turning back to him. I could feel his anger at her renewed accusation. He sat, and then stood up. He moved around her, looking behind the rock that had sheltered Temba. The woman also stood, joining him, searching quickly. Then she shouted across to the driver. What she said drew the attention of the other passengers. The driver came over to her, spoke to her. I could hear her voice slightly raised, with the first edge of fear.

At that moment Temba slid down beside me. I caught

his grin as he handed me the bottle. It was still cold from
the icebox.

We killed more than Temba had intended. It was I who
did most of the killing, and I hate to admit I enjoyed it
but I did.

I didn't enjoy it for the blood, for the fly-blown, tick-
infested deadness of the beasts I knocked over. I enjoyed
it for the challenge and because I was proud that, when I
chose to kill, the animal died quickly. I never missed.
With the Galil, after all the practice, I couldn't.

To Temba, what we did – the exercise – was deadly
serious. I thought of it as a game, a very dangerous game.
We would select an animal, a lone animal or one that
was on the edge of a herd, and stalk it. We only stood a
chance with those that were close to some sort of cover
– much of the park was open savanna, the grass dead
with the drought, the ground bare and swept with swirling mini-tornadoes – the dust devils of rising, superheated
air. The game was for the player to get as close as he
dared. Temba's idea of pulling its tail wasn't far from the
truth. To succeed, the player had to use every scrap of
cover; had to watch the wind, so he would not be
scented; had to move slowly, methodically – and know
when to freeze, and for how long to stay still. The other,
the back-up man, followed close on his heels, covering
him with his rifle. Mostly, we never got anywhere near
the animal. On the occasions we did, the game was to
push the risk as far as possible, so far that even a

normally docile animal, like the wildebeest or the little Tommies, might react to the sudden shock by attacking. And that's where the back-up man came in. If things went wrong, his job was to kill it.

It wasn't a fair game, really. Temba had a far better understanding of the animals. He had years of experience at stalking. When he was my back-up, he was much more confident that they were unlikely to attack me, however close I might be, however surprised they might be. I didn't have that confidence. Worse, Temba crept closer than I ever dared. So I killed. Temba, rightly, didn't.

But I learned from the killing. I learned how resilient a body is, how it can take terrible injury and still function. I learnt that a 5.56mm bullet has no stopping power on the larger animals: in other words, if the animal is coming at you and you hit it – it keeps coming. I learnt that bullets go into bodies and make small holes, but that they are designed to smash their way through, oscillating and rotating and tearing a progressively larger and larger hole, so that the exit wound is often horrific. I learned to hit an animal in the right place. A single shot to the brain will do the job of twenty bullets in gut and hindquarters and legs.

I also learned that automatic rifles are noisy machines. We knew, from the moment the sound tore the eerie silence of the bush, that we had instantly become the hunted. We waited only long enough to ensure that the animal was dead, to look quickly at the torn flesh and gaping, blood-filled exit wounds. Sometimes we stayed long enough to remove a cut of meat, the liver, the tongue.

'*Nendeya!*' Temba would say as soon as it was done. '*Nendeya!* Let's go!'

The first time, with the Tommy, I hung back. I'd never shot anything as big and fine as this, and I wanted a few minutes with my trophy. If I'd had a camera I'd have wanted a few pictures too.

Temba watched me as I turned the beast over.

'Rangers here in ten minutes,' he said.

The Tommy had a fine pair of horns, curved, like a lyre. I wondered how long it would take to cut them out.

'Five minutes.'

'Jesus!' I said. But we went.

Our job was to put miles and as many barriers as possible between them and us. From the tricks that Temba pulled and from the way he exploited the terrain I suspected he had been here and done this many times before. And I learned from him: how he used bare, hard rock where our tracks would not show; how to double back, and double back again; how to walk into the middle of herds, weaving through them, so that their movement would destroy our spoor; how to use the wind and the lie of the land; how to vary our pace. Always, he explained, the tracker is trying to understand his quarry. Once he understands him, once he sees his intentions, he can follow quickly because he can afford to make less use of the marks on the ground. Therefore safety lies as much in unpredictability as anything else.

If the Rangers ever hunted us, they never got close. We saw what might have been one of their Land Rovers in the distance, but it was travelling slowly along a dirt road and in the wrong direction. But their menace was

ever-present. We took turns to watch at night. We never
lit a fire. We never stayed long in one place. We covered
great distances, never in a straight line, often at night.

In all, I killed seven animals and Temba two. By comparison to the numbers killed in the Bunrum massacres,
our nine was nothing. Okay – so I'm excusing myself. As
I said, in retrospect I really am ashamed of what I did.
But the lessons I learned in the Malakari were to save our
lives.

7 The Kings of the Malakari

We spent four days in the Malakari, a day longer than Temba had planned. They were days that changed things between Temba and me. Until then, I had felt that he was the leader. Temba led, I followed. I was the rookie European in this raw, dangerous land, he the experienced black man teaching me how to survive. When we headed back to Boromundi, we returned as partners, equal partners, as brothers.

If you had asked me, a year previously, whether I could imagine myself living in the middle of the African jungle with a six-foot six black Boromundian whom I reckoned was the greatest bloke in the world, I'd have laughed. It's not that I've ever had any sort of racial feelings about black people. But the blokes I'd knocked around with had always been white. I understood white men, particularly if they came from Essex. I felt natural with them. And, okay, I thought like them.

But Temba was different. Our trust was absolute. I'd put my life in his hands in that stalking game. Twice he'd killed an animal when it threatened me. If he hadn't, I would have been dead. Inexperienced as I was, he, in his turn, had trusted me. Things like that bind people together. We had an intense understanding of each other. I knew what he was going to do almost before he did it.

It was a bit like football, when you're a member of a

team that's really working. When you've got the ball you don't have to look up to see what John or Fred or Jack is doing, you know. Instinctively, you know.

And when they stop dead, so do you.

Temba stood rigidly, like a spaniel, pointing with his nose. But I couldn't, for the life of me, work out what he was so interested in.

'Two,' he breathed.

I was buggered if I could see even one of anything across that flat, dried-up dustbowl – other than a rather fine, flat-topped acacia and, some distance ahead, a small, river valley which, Temba had said, was the end of the Malakari and the beginning of Boromundi.

'Two what?'

'Under the tree.'

I looked. It took me a couple of minutes. 'Jesus!' I whispered.

What I'd shot up to that point had been relatively tame: zebra, wildebeest, antelope, even a wart hog. This was different. This was *simba*, the king of beasts, relaxed, confident, secure within the confines of his national park; a celebrity, the centre of attention, used to the clickety-clack of thousands of expensive cameras wielded by fat tourists in zebra-striped minibuses. To me he was a big man waiting to be taken down.

'Just one,' I begged. 'Please, Temba.'

He was so easy to shoot. I simply walked towards him. Temba came some of the way, then dropped back. I liked that. It meant he was confident in me: I didn't need a nursemaid. I kept walking. The ground was open, bare earth with the occasional tussock of dry grass. I was within fifty yards when the first lion saw me. He'd been lying on his side, stretched out in the late afternoon sunshine, only moving to twitch at the irritation of the flies. His brother was lying on his back, his neck extended like a pussy-cat waiting to be tickled under his chin and his back legs wide apart, perhaps keeping his balls cool.

The one that had seen me didn't react other than to keep his head up so he could watch me. I kept walking, the Galil held loosely in front of me, the change lever on single round, my finger already on the trigger. I was within thirty yards when he made the next move, coming suddenly to his feet, broadside on. His brother stood up too, more slowly, turning to face me. I had to make a decision. I didn't want them both. It was a matter of which, and, as the second turned, I knew it was him.

He was considerably bigger, heavier in the shoulders, darker, more dangerous. I stopped, lifted the rifle, tucked it into my shoulder, aimed between his eyes and squeezed the trigger. The lion collapsed. His legs jellified and he went down like a sack of potatoes. And his brother came at me.

I never saw him tense. I never saw the flick of his tail that's supposed to precede a charge. I didn't see him turn. He just came at me.

An automatic rifle loads the next round as it fires. All I had to do was aim again and squeeze the trigger. But he came so fast, so unexpectedly, that I never managed it.

I remember him hitting me. The bit that connected

was very solid, and it sent me flying. When the world stopped whirling round and I came to rest, I remember thinking that I'd done something really daft; that this was stupid, stupid, stupid. I remember becoming aware of the terrible weight of the lion on top of me and thinking he had very bad breath. Finally, I remember thinking, perhaps this is a dream. Then I passed out.

I was dead. I was dead and I'd definitely gone to heaven.

When you first wake up in heaven you drift into consciousness. It's all very gradual and very gentle. You become aware that heaven's a very light, bright place. It's also very quiet. You lie on your back, suspended. There's no floor or ceiling, just a haze that seems to surround you: clouds, I suppose. You don't feel hot or sweaty, nor do you feel at all cold. You feel wonderfully content.

You lie there, not moving. Bit by bit you become aware that heaven is populated by angels, real angels who drift in and out of your vision. Angels in black with blonde hair coiled tightly on top of their heads and round, pink-scrubbed faces that peer down at you and smile and mouth things in a heavenly language you don't understand. Then you go back to sleep again.

You keep doing this in heaven until finally you wake up and understand what the angel's saying. Like, 'Oh, you're back with us now, are you?'

And when you nod and try and fail to form words like, 'What the hell am I doing here?', 'Who are you?', 'Where am I?' and 'Why doesn't my left arm work?' the angel reaches out and puts a cool, firm hand on your brow and says, 'Ssssh,' just like your mother used to do when you were small and in bed with 'flu.

So, because she's an angel and obviously very much in charge and, therefore, everything's bound to be fine, you close your eyes and stop worrying about such minor matters and go back to sleep. Except that the next time you wake up in heaven you remember where you last saw that angel.

'You're Chloris.' Your voice is slurred and 'Chloris' is quite difficult to say.

She nods. 'I've met you somewhere before, haven't I?'

I try to shake my head but my left shoulder hurts, so I say, 'Don't think so.'

'Weren't you black with white patches last time I saw you?'

I try to frown but she's smiling. And you can't frown at something that beautiful.

'Don't know what you're talking about,' I mutter.

'You were better looking when you were black,' she says, and walks away.

Temba couldn't believe it when I didn't shoot. He was only about fifteen yards behind me, so he saw the whole thing in close-up. But he did something, purely reactional, which saved my life.

In the last micro-seconds of the lion's charge, he moved. He says he stepped forward. The movement caught the lion's eye and he veered. He veered towards Temba so that, instead of hitting me head on, he caught me a glancing blow. It was quite enough to bowl me over, more than enough to send me flying. But before Temba could do anything else the animal had turned and, in one bound, was on top of me.

Temba said that, from that point in, I did everything right. My actions must have been purely instinctive because I have no memory of them. I balled myself up, pulling my knees up into my stomach. By doing this I protected my abdomen from the dew claws on the lion's back legs. These are the claws part way up his leg: if you dare, inspect the cat that's cuddled up on your couch and you'll find them – they're wickedly sharp. While a lion's chewing your face he will hook them into your belly and tear away the wall of the stomach, so your guts spill out. At the same time I used my arms to pull my head into my chest, protecting my neck, head and face.

The lion had intentions on my throat but, because I'd protected it, he seized my shoulder instead. He got a good grip on it, his teeth went deep, and he worried at it.

Then Temba shot him.

He collapsed on top of me. Temba's strong, but he had a hell of a job rolling the corpse off me.

Stupidly, we carried no first aid kit. Temba tore up my tee-shirt, using balls of the material to stuff into the holes that were bleeding worst, then bound my chewed-up shoulder as tightly as he could. He said he managed to stop most of the bleeding, but that was about all. Then he hid our rucksacks on the other side of the river, the Boromundi side, shouldered the two rifles, and carried me the fifteen miles or so back to his family's *boma*.

I couldn't have done that. It frightened me, thinking

about it afterwards. If things had been the other way round I'd have had to leave Temba and go for help. Even if I'd run all the way and the rescue party had run back, it would have taken six to eight hours. Temba could have bled to death in that time; either that, or something else might have come along and finished the job.

The nearest help lay in Tanzania. Temba could have got me to one of the park roads, flagged down a vehicle, and had me in the small hospital in Mba in half the time it would have taken to get me to the nearest hospital in Boromundi. He made the decision not to. Perhaps he was fairly certain that I wasn't that seriously injured. Perhaps. More likely was that he felt that to have taken me into Tanzania would have risked everything we were doing. Suddenly it meant I was less important than the operation.

I do remember being carried by him. It's a memory that came back some time after I'd been admitted to hospital. I recall the agony I felt as he jolted across the countryside. He carried me in a sort of fireman's lift, so I faced down at the ground. It seemed very close. In a detached, remote way I studied its detail: the random stones, the brittle tussocks of grass, the small, contorted thorn bushes and the sudden swathes of reddish sand. It was very uncomfortable, and my shoulder hurt like hell. I remember telling him to put me down, for Christ's sake to stop; and to please, please leave me. When he wouldn't, when he kept going, I remember trying to bite back the pain, then giving up and letting rip: I screamed and screamed. Fortunately, Temba said, for most of the time I was unconscious.

It was dark by the time we got back to his village. Temba was in a state of collapse. His father took over. It wasn't the first time he'd seen a man mauled by a lion: the lads herding the cattle often came across them, and it was part of their job, part of the process of growing up, that they had to drive them off, and occasionally things went wrong. He stripped away the bloody bits of tee-shirt, unplugged the holes and bathed the wounds with a purple liquid, a disinfectant derived from the roots of a plant.

The wounds in my shoulder looked clean. No bones had been broken when the jaws crushed the shoulder. The flesh was badly lacerated and the muscles torn, and the lion's canines had sunk so deep they had almost met in the middle. They patched me up but they had to get me to hospital. The big fear with lion attacks is infection. The meat they eat lodges in their teeth and rots, and could start a nasty infection.

One of Temba's brothers ran through the darkness to the small village on the road where Temba and I had climbed off the bus. His job was to organise a car, to be there ready for when they brought me in. I was carried David Livingstone-style in an affair that looked like a hammock slung underneath a pole. I remember that part of the journey, if the shoulder hadn't been such agony, it would have been very comfortable.

A taxi took me in to the nearest town, Tilubu, some forty-five miles along a dirt road. The jolting of the car through the potholes brought the agony back. At some point I passed out again. My next memory is of Chloris' face.

I stayed in hospital for nearly three weeks and, for the whole of that time, I could do little more than lie in bed and pray that Chloris would come into the room; and then, when she did, lie in bed and watch her, feeling my insides turn over and over like a basket of eels.

I had a room to myself, courtesy of George Wise. When I had first come into the hospital I was in the men's general ward, but they'd moved me almost as soon as Temba managed to contact George. He wrote to me, the letter arriving when I'd been in hospital for about a fortnight, apologising. I don't know what he felt he had to apologise about: I was very grateful to him for what he'd done, as some of the things I'd seen in the public ward had been pretty unpleasant.

My private room was beautifully cool. The hospital was all on one floor, with whitewashed walls and a red-tiled roof. My room opened onto a small veranda that let out into a central courtyard. There were lawns and flowerbeds, and a fountain in the middle; I could hear the water tinkling away all night. A little man with a bad limp spent a lot of his day in this quadrangle, squatting on his hunkers weeding the lawns and flowerbeds, or standing and swinging a steel blade the shape of a hockey stick to cut the grass. Every evening at about five he hobbled around his garden dragging a hose behind him, and watered everything.

I only had a couple of worries: one was that I was letting St Faith's down. The other was that Chloris had recognised me.

Temba and I had always been rather pleased with the anonymity of the raid we'd carried out on the Rehab Centre at Bumani. There had been no evidence that anyone had recognised us, even though we'd been seen by a number of different people. Our dread had been that someone would identify us through the school truck. It hadn't happened. Now, suddenly, the cat was out of the bag. Chloris had enough sense to know that the two grubby individuals she'd seen at Smallboy's graveside were the same people who'd dug him up. And now she had one of them imprisoned in a hospital bed.

She raised the subject again when I'd been in about a fortnight. She appeared in my room and closed the door carefully so the latch didn't click. She hadn't done that before. For a moment it worried me. Then I suffered a great rush of excitement. She was in love with me. She was going to come across the room and stoop to kiss me. She would slide her arms around me and pull me against her, whispering endearments. All her vows . . .

'Why did you do it?' She stood by the bed, just out of reach, her arms folded under her breasts, looking down at me.

I swallowed hard. ' "Do" what?' I croaked.

'You know: cut up Hezikiah.'

I looked up at her. Those deep blue eyes were set wide apart in her face, on either side of a very straight, perhaps a little too long nose. And there were freckles, just a pale sprinkling of them, that danced from the tops of her plump cheeks across her nose.

'I don't want to talk about it,' I muttered.

She looked at me. She had a wide mouth with generous, pinkly kissable lips. 'He was coming to the Lord,' she said.

My reaction was somewhere between an explosion of anger and a roar of laughter. Whatever it was, it brought me upright in the bed and it hurt. 'Jesus!' I said and, as an afterthought, 'Ow!'

'Yes. Jesus. He was coming to Jesus.' I stared at her. She was quite serious.

'He knew he was dying and he was very afraid,' she continued. 'He told me his mother had brought him up in the church, that he'd been baptised and confirmed. He used to go regularly until he was twelve.'

'Balls.'

She frowned at me.

'Listen,' I said. 'When Smallboy was nine he joined the Bunrum murder squads. He specialised in rape and sadism. His favourite recreation was killing people so slowly they hardly noticed. He only told you these lies because, for the first time in his life, he was afraid. He was terrified of dying. Perhaps he thought that, if you gave him a helping hand past the pearly gates, he might be able to carry on where he left off – in heaven.'

She didn't say anything. She stood, looking down at me.

'What are you doing here?' I asked. I wanted to change the subject.

'I was transferred.'

'Why?'

Once again she took refuge in silence. But her expression had changed, fractionally.

It was early days with Chloris. At that time I had no experience of reading her facial expressions. It's not that she didn't have any – she did – but the overriding impression was of serenity. But, when I got good at it, I could read other expressions going on underneath. Not fear, or loathing; nothing like that because she's incapable of them. But sadness, regret, pain (all of these for other people, never for herself), happiness, laughter; and love – but the wrong sort, the platonic sort. Not the lust sort.

'You're a nurse, are you?'

'Yes. I trained as a nurse.' Chloris was moving round the bed, smoothing the sheets, coming to my end of it and putting her arm around me to ease me forward so she could fluff up the pillows.

I took a deep breath. I wanted to smell her as she came against me. She smelt warm and slightly yeasty, like freshly baked bread. I couldn't take my eyes off her.

'You're all right, are you?'

'Yes,' I whispered.

If I'd reached out, I could have touched the coarse, black material of her habit. I wanted to. I wanted to grab a handful of it, hold it very tight and pull her towards me.

'You didn't tell me why you did it,' she said.

'What?'

'Hezikiah.'

'No.'

'Tell me.'

I shook my head. 'You don't want to know.'

She smiled at me. 'Yes, I do.'

So I told her.

I told her almost everything, leaving out none of the gory bits but omitting mention of one or two details, like Mumbai.

When I'd finished, when I'd described what Temba and I were planning, when I'd explained why I'd been chewed up by a lion, she said, 'You can't.'

'What do you mean, "I can't"?'

'Armstrong, didn't anyone ever teach you the concept of forgiveness?'

'Yes, but they were lousy teachers.'

She almost smiled at that and said, 'I suppose you'd know.'

'We're going to kill them,' I explained. 'If we'd caught Smallboy before he died we'd have taken him apart, little by little. We'd have tried to string his miserable life out for as long as possible, so we could inflict the maximum pain. We'd have liked to do it in public because, somehow, we wanted to impress on them some idea of the pain and misery they caused their victims. I wanted him to know. I want him to feel . . .'

'You don't understand,' Chloris cut in. 'You don't understand that forgiveness is the only way to rise above these people, and the only way to lay to rest the victims they've so wronged. There's so much more power in forgiveness; far, far more power than in what you're planning. And forgiveness must be the way forward for Boromundi. Forgiveness, reconciliation, peace. If we go on hating, if we apply the concept of an eye for an eye, this country will tear itself apart over and over again. At some point people have to say, "Stop!" You, intelligent people like you, must show the way.'

I watched her. I hung on every word. Not because they meant anything to me but because she was stunningly beautiful when she spoke so intensely about something she believed in. When she stopped we were silent for a few moments.

'Have you heard of *Kisasi*?' I asked.

'Yes,' she said, carefully.

'I've heard him sing,' I said.

She looked down at me rather pityingly. 'You believe that sort of thing, do you?'

'Yes,' I replied. 'Do you know, the only times I've heard him sing have been at crucial, significant times. Like when he told Temba the coast was clear when we came back to find Cyprian's tongue. And, and he sang very loudly after we'd chopped up Smallboy.'

'*Sarothrura jacobi*,' she said.

It took me a moment. 'Is that what he's called?' She surprised me, that she could remember a name like that. But then, Chloris was full of surprises.

'There was an article in the Mateka Times,' she explained, 'a couple of months back. It's a species of pygmy rail. Very shy, never comes near humans. Never.'

'You remember all this?'

'I'm interested in birds.'

'So am I.'

She wrinkled her nose at me and, very imperceptibly, shook her head, as if I were a pretty hopeless case.

'Why did they transfer you?' I asked to keep the conversation going.

She smiled and began moving round the bed, tucking it in again. 'You'd better get some rest,' she said. 'I'll come back and see you later.'

She made for the door but I called, 'Chloris.'

She turned, came back and reached out, resting her fingers on my arm.

'Yes?'

'You won't tell anyone else, will you?'

'Of course I will.'

Jesus, I thought to myself. Oh Jesus, Christ Almighty, now I've fucked it. I've told her everything and she's going to go straight out of here and spill the beans. If she does, Temba and I have got a couple of days before the bastards come after us . . .

Her hand slipped down to tighten on my wrist. Her face came closer. 'I'm going to talk to God, Armstrong. I'm going to the chapel and I'm going to say some prayers. You know, He's been here, all the time we've been talking. He's been listening and . . . and He's got the advantage over me that He's been everywhere you've been. He's seen what you've done, Armstrong. He's seen into your heart. He knows what you're really like. He knows what's possible with you.' She paused and a smile lit her face. 'So, I'm going to talk to God and together we're going to decide what to do with you.'

Temba borrowed the school truck to visit me a couple of times. On the first occasion he told me that Mumbai wanted to visit too, that she'd got Alice's permission, next time he came. I begged him to find a way of stopping her. I had this horror that Chloris might come into the room whilst she was here.

In between times, my body got better while my mind got sicker. At first, I tried everything to break down the barriers that separated Chloris and I. I tried to persuade her to sit on my bed: she wouldn't. I complained of pains in awkward places: so she called the doctor. I asked her to massage my back, told her that the muscles were knotted up with so much inaction: she brought along a large black lady who pretended she was a physiotherapist. In fact she was a sadist.

Because she was so untouchable but so close, frustration turned the breathless worship of the early days into antagonism. I began to snap at her. I refused to speak to her. When she came into the room I rolled over on my side and pretended she didn't exist. Once I was up on my feet, I looked out for her and went out of the veranda door as she came in from the passage.

Of course, none of this made the slightest difference to Chloris. Day in, day out, when she caught up with me, she was her own sweet self. Her goodness, my loathsomeness, made me feel sick. I hated myself. I lay on my back in the darkness, listening to the fountain and fantasising that she would come to me naked one night and that we'd creep out and dance in the fountain together, the cool water bathing our pale skins. And I swore that, the next time she came in, I would climb out of bed, fall on my knees and implore her forgiveness.

Except she didn't come back in the morning. Nor the next.

I think someone had been spying on us. And they were sufficiently worried by what they saw to move Chloris to the children's ward.

8 Sizwi

The day after I returned to St Faith's the telephone started working. Temba said the system hadn't worked in the Kaserewe area for almost ten years and outlying parts of Mateka, the capital, had only been reconnected within the last six months.

In England, I'd sooner have gone out of a morning without my trousers than without my mobile, so you'd have thought that the idea of being back in touch with the outside world would have thrilled me. It didn't. It was like living in Temba's village, with no running water (every time I remembered it I thought of poor, giggly Nzizi; and then, of course, her gorgeous sister Sizwi), no WC, no fridge, no shops, food cooked over an open fire, snakes, flies, cow dung all over the place – I'd loved it. So, in a perverse way, my immediate reaction was that I didn't want to be anywhere near a telephone. This was Africa. Modern technology spoiled the place.

It meant that Temba and I no longer had an excuse for going down to Alice's place. Even though there was only one line, which came into the Head's office, Alice had a phone so she could contact us any time she needed to. Which was just as well, as Fanny had talked to the Head and the Head had had a word with Temba in my absence. Bartolemew had been very understanding – two young men without women, their physical needs, the lack of appropriate local women, etc, etc – but, two of his staff openly visiting the local bordello, and in the school truck – he couldn't allow it to continue. Fanny had promised to be very discreet (some hope) and a full-blown scandal would, he felt sure, be averted. I think it was quite a relief for Temba. He'd never really enjoyed the bonking side of our visits to Alice's. Me? I was devastated. In fact, I was fucking furious. Despite Temba's warnings, I caught the bus down into town the following Saturday evening and walked out to Alice's place.

Alice hadn't changed in the slightest. She was in her favourite blouse, a silky, long sleeved number in a shade of peachy-pink shot with gold threads that glittered as her breasts wobbled, and the usual pair of tight pink trousers an elephant would have been comfortable in. The minute I entered, she levered herself out of her couch (she'd never done that before) and came across and helped settle me in a chair. Without so much as a how-do-you-do she unfastened and removed my shirt before spending a couple of minutes inspecting my injuries – at this stage, still covered in dressings and very, very sore. Mumbai was summoned and arrived carrying a beer, which I refused on medical grounds, and she joined Alice in poking and prodding at my wounds while I pretended to be brave.

The women entered into an animated discussion in ChiMundi. It started rather seriously but rapidly deteriorated, becoming more and more ribald, much to my irritation. From what I could pick up, I think they were deciding whether it was safe to let Mumbai loose on me and, when they concluded it probably was, the sort of things that she should and should not do. I suppose it's understandable: the last thing Alice wanted was for me to pop my clogs under Mumbai after escaping from under a lion. Anyway, they ended up shrieking with laughter.

Which changed as soon as Mumbai left us. Alice returned to her couch, took a shot of her gin and, wiping back her tears, gasped, 'So you are well . . . very quick . . . Mr Armstrong? Mumbai . . . is very happy.'

'Yes,' I said, watching her while gingerly pulling my shirt back on.

'It is good, very good. Soon, soon you will be very good again.' Her head nodded several times.

I agreed I would be very good, adding to myself that I would be very good indeed once I had my hands on Mumbai, all the while carefully fastening my shirt buttons.

'Mr Armstrong, Mr Temba . . . did not come . . . to see me at all this weekend. He . . .'

'There's news?'

'No. No news. But there is . . . much talk of matters . . . which are not in newspapers.'

I frowned at her. I suspected that the phrase 'not in newspapers' had some special meaning. 'What?'

Alice shifted in her seat, then took a few moments to pour herself another gin.

'People say that a child has come.' She caught and held my eye, her expression very serious. 'A child who is very important for Boromundi. They call this child, the liberator, the new king, the redeemer.'

'I've heard this somewhere before, haven't I?'

'Yes. But this is a black child, a boy. A boy king . . . who is already a warrior.'

'A boy king?' I leaned forward. 'What does this mean?'

Alice shrugged hugely before subsiding into her cushions, gasping for breath.

'You've no idea?' I went on. 'Do you know where he is?'

'I am not sure,' Alice rasped but I think Mr Armstrong, that he is in the north-west, in the Mountains of the Morning Mist.'

'Simbilani?'

'Near Simbilani. I think, perhaps . . . across the border from Simbilani.' She stopped at that point. She was having much more trouble breathing than when I'd last seen her. 'At present,' she went on, 'it is too dangerous for him to come. So he stays in a safe place.' She paused again. 'These rumours are very strong, Mr Armstrong. But there are men . . . who come before him, who must . . . prepare the way.'

'That also sounds familiar.'

She coughed, dabbing at her eyes. 'Yes, yes. Men come, who must prepare his way, so he may come in his majesty.'

'What's he coming to do?' I cut in before she could ramble on, 'Don't give me the fancy words. Who is he? What's he going to do?'

'I do not know. People are saying, "You have heard? He is coming." And they are nodding together, saying, "Yes, he is coming". But they do not know who he is, or where he is coming from, or what he is coming to do. It is like a game. A whispering game. You understand?'

I nodded. A whispering game, like the whispering of the wind in the trees before a gale.

'But you are worried?' I asked.

Alice didn't respond for a moment. Then she nodded. 'Yes. I am. I am very worried. I think this is the start of very bad things again.'

The week after half term, on a humid Thursday afternoon, Temba barged into my classroom and, with no apology to my class, who were engrossed in my vivid description of subsistence farming in the rice paddies of southeast Asia, dragged me out onto the veranda. I stood, listening to the excited chatter from the classroom behind me, while Temba gripped my arm. M'Simani Kangalewa, he hissed, had been spotted near Tilubu.

Temba had been in the staffroom when the secretary summoned him to the phone. It had been his sister, Sizwi. The conversation at Temba's end had been in code as it was a resentful joke in the staffroom that the school secretary listened to every word, filtering out the interesting bits to pass them selectively to Bartolemew Nchanga or her personal friends.

Kangalewa was our target number five, the one that held the revolver to Cyprian Bogovu throughout the attack. All the evidence was that he had been frightened, that he had got himself involved in something that was way over his head. They'd given him the easy job because they didn't trust him, and he'd bodged it.

Temba was fairly certain from his name that Kangalewa came from the southeast of Boromundi. The vast majority of the people in the eastern half of the country had supported the NLF against Bunrum, so Kangalewa was a renegade. Returning to the Tilubu area would be dangerous for him, despite all the talk of reconciliation. If it really was him, it was too much of a coincidence. Tilubu was where I'd been in hospital. Tilubu was where Chloris worked. Tilubu was close to Temba's home. Of the three, which one had drawn him back? Or was it more than one?

That Sizwi had found Kangalewa wasn't pure luck. Temba's family was well aware of what we were doing. They and his closest friends from neighbouring villages, members of his clan and age group, had been briefed on the men we were searching for. They were actively looking for them. It had been Sizwi herself who had spotted someone who fitted Kangalewa's description and had had the balls to go up to him and asked what he was doing in Tilubu. It had been a very dangerous thing to do, but the bastard had been surprisingly forthcoming. He was visiting an aunt who was ill. He was in town to buy her medicine and some groceries. The girl had sharp eyes. In amongst his groceries she spotted a tin of lubricating oil.

Now there isn't much call for light lubricating oil in the average Boromundi village. It has its uses: on bicycles and Singer sewing machines, on padlocks and hinges. But it's also used on rifles. It's not the best oil for cleaning and lubricating firearms, but it does the job. Further, the girl was quite convinced that the weight of the groceries was far more than would be needed by a sick aunt. It was more likely that Kangalewa was camping out in the bush with a number of other people and, if he was, then they were on some sort of mission.

The evidence was pretty circumstantial. But it was enough.

All along Temba and I had known this might happen: that the opportunity to pick off one of the men would arise in school time and that the bastard would be far enough away for us to need the school transport. We'd been lucky with Smallboy. Now we had no choice. I didn't even have to discuss it with him. I left Temba to extemporise on rice cultivation and went and saw Bartolemew.

I took a gamble knowing it was no good doing it by halves. I told Bartolemew everything. I even explained about Alice and Mumbai. I didn't swear him to secrecy, because doing something like that is unreasonable and suggests a total lack of trust, which is a bad way to start. I just told him, as quickly and succinctly as I could.

I'm a firm believer that it helps immensely to have seen a man very, very drunk. Some people go silent. More become loquacious, or self-important, or whiny. The vicious, angry and resentful streaks comes out in a few. In both Temba and Bartolemew's cases they became beautiful, gentle people. And the way Bartolemew came back to me, the day after Rebecca's wake, and said that he would not hold me to my drunken offer to stay, had really impressed me. I liked the way he ran St Faith's. I, like all the rest of the staff, respected him and feared him in the right measures. But none of this prepared me for his reaction.

He listened in complete silence. He didn't ask a question. His eyes, small, dark, deep sunk on either side of his monstrous nose, never left my face. I hadn't sat down when I'd burst into his office, I had stood with my hands on his desk, leaning forward slightly. When I'd finished I stayed like that, waiting for his reaction.

There was a terrible silence. I knew I hadn't done very well. I'd been too hurried. My posture had been assertive, rude. The way I'd busted into his office . . .

He opened the top drawer of his desk, took out the keys of the truck and pushed them across the desk. His eyes never left mine.

'You have a rifle, Armstrong?'

I nodded.

'Enough ammunition?'

I nodded again.

'Then, you and Temba – take care.'

Even though it was after eight in the evening when we reached Tilubu, we found Sizwi at work. She was a hairdresser and her tiny salon was the front room of a corrugated iron shack in a rubbish-filled alley just off Tilubu's main street. It was lit by a hurricane lamp suspended on a length of galvanised wire from the rafters. A large rectangular mirror, its silver rusted by the damp, was screwed to one of the wooden uprights, and a carver chair had been placed in front of it for the customers.

Sizwi was finishing with a customer. We sat on the low wooden bench that ran along the back of the salon and watched her work. She was plaiting the woman's hair, which wasn't more than three inches long when pulled out straight from its tight spirals, then fixing the plaits against her head with tiny pieces of ribbon. The effect was rather like a ploughed field, the furrows running from front to back, with bright flowers growing in it. It was a fiddly, intricate job and had obviously taken hours. The woman, a girl in her early twenties, sat very upright, watching Sizwi in the mirror and never uttering a word. When the job was finished, she stood close to the mirror, turning her head this way and that to inspect Sizwi's handiwork, then left the room. No money changed hands. No word of thanks was given. She went, and Sizwi turned and smiled at us.

'You have come quickly.'

'Sizwi,' Temba said, getting up. It was the way he said it: something was wrong. There was no smile, no warmth. I had thought this was his favourite sister. When we'd been at the Mbanga's *boma* they had laughed together.

Sizwi hesitated, as if she wanted to say something, then turned to me and extended her hand. 'Armstrong.'

Her hand was warm and very delicate, with long fingers and nails that were surprisingly white. Small, firm breasts pressed against the flimsy cotton of a dress that buttoned down the front and showed off the wonderful slimness of her body. 'You are better, now?'

I nodded. 'I am well.' I wasn't. There were times when I felt weak, despite all the exercise I'd been taking. And this, the prospect of catching up with Kangalewa, made me feel sick. The thing with the lion had knocked my confidence. I wasn't sure how much use I would be to Temba. But I wasn't going to miss it. 'And you?'

She hesitated, then turned away quickly without answering, leading us through a door to the back of the house.

There was only one room, the same size as the salon. In one corner was a single bed, a chest of drawers and a rail from which half a dozen cotton dresses hung. The rest of the space was taken up by a small table with upright chairs, a tattered arm chair, a sink unit which was obviously used for preparing food and a wooden cupboard with holes drilled through the doors – presumably some sort of larder. While Temba and I settled ourselves at the table, Sizwi disappeared through a door that led out to a yard at the back.

'Sizwi's husband doesn't live here?' I said it unthinkingly, looking up when Temba didn't answer immediately, sensing his anger.

'I'm sorry,' I said.

We sat in silence for a few minutes. I hadn't meant to upset Temba.

The conversation floundered through Sizwi's simple meal of rice with a vegetable relish.

From the way that her husband was never mentioned, I guessed that his absence might be the cause of the friction between them. Perhaps Sizwi had angered her family by giving him reason to leave. The other thing that we skirted around was what we were about to do. Given those constraints I started working at the two of them, trying to break through whatever it was that lay between them. In the end I gave up, occupying myself with covert glances at Sizwi, very conscious that she was careful to avoid catching them. But Temba did, and the frown he gave me made the earth shake. After that I avoided looking at her. Only when we'd finished eating, when the plates had been stacked in the sink (it had no waste pipe for water to drain from it, so I've no idea how it was used), did Temba ask Sizwi whether she'd found Kangalewa.

She shook her head. 'No. No-one has seen him since yesterday, but I have spoken with the bus driver who took him out of town. You know the Usuki road?' Temba grunted and she continued. 'Well, about six miles out of town there are baobab trees . . .'

'I know the ones.' His tone was curt.

'I think these men are in the bush to the north of that place. The driver saw Kangalewa take the path that runs between . . .'

'There are villages that way. There is a big village not far from the road.'

Sizwi nodded. 'Yes. But they are not in that village because I know the people there and I have asked them. They have not seen any strangers. So I think they are beyond it. There is a river, from which the people draw their water. It is possible that they are staying near it.' She paused, and her voice dropped. 'I am sorry that I have not been able to find them.'

Temba grunted.

'I have tried.'

She seemed close to tears. I felt sorry for the girl.

We sat in silence as Sizwi cleared the remains of the meal. Then Temba and I rolled ourselves in blankets on the floor. Sizwi drew a curtain which shielded her bed, taking the lamp with her, and I lay listening to her. I pictured her every movement as she undressed. I imagined her hanging her dress with the others on the rail.

I saw her nakedness, her small breasts and the narrowness of her hips, as the golden brown of her body slipped between the coarse blankets. I lay, listening to her restlessness. The metal springs squeaked as she turned in her bed.

I couldn't sleep either. The more I thought about it, the more it seemed a good idea for us to share our insomnia. But I couldn't. As I've said, for all the coolness between them, she was Temba's favourite sister. In his present frame of mind he might not have forgiven me if he'd found us together. And I had no idea what had happened to her husband. He might, at any moment, turn up though I thought that unlikely. All I knew was that she'd kept looking at me across the table. Then avoided looking at me. I recognised the signs.

In a way, it was good to have something to take my mind off Kangalewa, but by the time my watch showed one I'd had enough of thinking. Temba's breathing was slow and regular. He was a heavy sleeper but quick to react when woken. I was prepared to risk Sizwi's husband. As I slipped out of my blanket, as I tiptoed across the bare boards, as I carefully lifted and ducked under the curtain, I said a prayer that Temba's sleep would be deep and untroubled.

Sizwi was awake. In the darkness, I felt her lift aside the blanket. I dropped my pants and felt her hand clasp the inside of my leg, pulling me towards her. As I sat, as I put my weight on the edge of the bed, the metal springs squealed. I froze. It took a moment to hear Temba's regular breathing and five minutes for my heart to recover, five minutes in which Sizwi's hand moved and made her intentions quite clear. I gave Temba another minute before trying again, and the springs grated. I stopped. I swear – I would have made it. It might have taken a bit of time but it would have been okay – but Sizwi began to giggle. I had one leg partly under the blanket and my bottom perched on the edge of the bed, touching a warm shoulder that shook with suppressed laughter. My other leg supported my weight on the floor.

I heard Temba move. He was awake. It would take him a moment to see my empty blanket, another in which to seize his rifle. In two steps he would reach the curtain. I could stand to face the onslaught. Or I could . . .

The springs screamed as I threw myself on top of her. Sizwi exploded with laughter, laughter cut off as I crushed her mouth under my lips, as her arms came around me and gripped me, as her legs came apart.

We lay, locked together, trembling and listening. Slowly the sounds of Temba's snoring came to us. Slowly we relaxed.

We coupled without breathing and so cautiously the springs never murmured. It was wonderful: very gentle, very controlled, very deep and very long, and very, very slow. Even when we climaxed together our gasps were soundless.

Somehow, in that narrow bed, I must have slept, because I woke very suddenly when Sizwi got up. It was just before four. She dressed quickly. As she went out the back I ducked under the curtain and made it to my blanket. She returned a few minutes later carrying a lamp and three steaming mugs of tea. Temba and I sat up in our blankets to drink our tea. When Temba went out front to start the truck Sizwi came against me. She kissed me, mouthed the words, 'God watch you,' against my lips, her breath sweet and warm, and kissed me again. As she drew away she smiled.

To my surprise, Sizwi drove: and very competent she was. The Usuki road was a dirt road in appalling condition, rutted, riddled with deep potholes brim full of muddy water, and cut by frequent gullies. The girl drove carefully, hanging on to the steering wheel and leaning forward to peer into the beam of the headlights. In one place, where a culvert had been washed away, she had to leave the road and follow the tracks of other vehicles that had found a way round the obstruction through the bush.

She slowed as she pointed out the stand of baobabs, set back from the road on our right, their pale bark easily visible, but she kept going, finally allowing the truck to roll to a stop about a mile beyond.

The land was impenetrably dark, somehow blacker for the waning moon, the colour of rotten cream, which lay low on the horizon. Temba and I climbed out and worked quickly to prepare ourselves. Then, without a word to Sizwi, Temba led the way back along the road, setting a cracking pace. I followed close behind him. Every couple of minutes we stopped and listened. Had we heard anyone, we would have side-tracked into the bush until they'd passed. We had no need to until the truck came past us. It didn't slow and we watched as its tail lights disappeared back along the road.

With the moon about to set, we turned off into the stand of baobabs. They are the overweight elephants among trees, with bloated bodies and thin, crooked, leafless branches whose silhouettes clawed at the stars.

The ground between them was open, like the interior of some great, satanic cathedral, so the going proved easy. Beyond them we faced a wall of tangled thorn trees. It took Temba a few moments to find the path that sliced through this barrier.

This sort of bush is eerie at night. It is close, hemming one in, and silent, but filled with watching eyes. I fought to close my mind to it, but danger seemed ever-present. Those whom we hunted might be watching along the trail. Puff adders lie out in the residual warmth of paths, too sluggish to shift even when something as large and inedible as a human approaches. Moving as silently as we could, we could still bump into anything: lion, leopard, elephant. We could have taken it slowly, stopping and listening at every turn, working our way along each straight. We didn't have time. Temba continued to press the pace. We needed to be beyond the village and across the river before first light.

We came into the outskirts of the village very suddenly. The bush fell back to reveal small gardens filled with the fallen, brittle stalks of last year's maize crop, but with the remains of pumpkins and tomatoes, cassava and beans. Only the dark leaves of the banana trees looked alive. Temba stopped. We could not go through the village itself for the pye dogs would have heard us and their yapping brought the village men out. So we struck away to our left, following the edges of the cultivated land, stumbling across the uneven earth, snapping the dried stalks as we pushed through the maize.

I lost all sense of direction. It was easy simply to follow Temba, a good five yards behind him so I could see where he trod.

He found a well-used path on the far side of the village and re-entered the bush. We moved more carefully now, stopping to listen, straining our eyes into the gloom. Nothing moved except in my imagination. Other than the scream of the crickets, each note cutting in and, as suddenly, cutting out, the bush lay silent around us. The land began to fall away. At times the path thrashed its way down steep, rocky slopes, offering us views out across the dark riverine trees immediately below us to much more open land beyond.

We came to the river suddenly. The path flattened out. Leaving the tangled thorn trees we plunged into a canyon cut through head-high reeds. Beyond them the going opened out and we trod across loose sand. Above us, mimosa, whistling thorn and some sort of palm formed a high canopy against the stars.

If anything, Temba pushed the pace even harder. I dropped further back, my rifle at the ready, the lever on automatic fire, covering Temba. He crouched, half running across the sand, disappearing suddenly as he leapt down into the bed of the river. The bank was about six foot high, broken down in places where humans and animals had approached the water. The river no longer ran. Dark pools, tucked under the bank on the outside of meanders, reflected the stars and the silhouettes of the trees. Most of the bed of the river was dry, loose sand, covered with the scattered dung of animals, the sand slippery in our haste.

We climbed the bank on the far side, almost immediately entering another reed bed. An animal broke at our approach, a heavy beast which snorted once before crashing, unseen, away to our right. Beyond the reeds the land became more open, speckled with small trees, rising gently to a low ridge.

Temba turned left along the front of the reed wall, found a gap, entered it, and sat down. Uncertainly, I joined him.

I had no idea why we were waiting. We sat, very close but not moving as, in front of us, above the ridge, the sky began to pale. Sunrise was as slow and breathless as the night's lovemaking, and, as the colours came, the pale yellows and pinks and flame oranges of a perfect dawn, as beautiful. The air held a chill, a freshness, a promise. Nothing moved except the slow play of the light as it chased the darkness out of the landscape. I sat spellbound, watching the dawn, and thought of Sizwe. I imagined her sitting next to me instead of her monosyllabic, ill-tempered brother.

Temba's grunt woke me. Without speaking, he rose and led us out of the reeds.

I felt pretty pessimistic about the chances of finding a small group of men in this vast and sparsely populated bush wilderness. I had learned enough in the Malakari to know how easy it was to disappear, even to be active – provocably active – yet remain hidden. This area to the north of Tilubu dropped away towards the savanna lands of Temba's home, but it seemed better watered and the undergrowth thicker. To make matters worse, I was tired. If I had slept, it had only been for an hour or so.

We turned left again along the reeds. I stumbled after Temba, paying little attention to what he was doing. To my surprise, he set a cracking pace, almost as if he knew where he was headed. As the sun rose I began to feel hot and irritated. We were skirting the edge of the reeds and not, as I would have done, working up to the ridge to our right from where we might gain a view across the land; but I didn't say anything. I kept trying to act professional, scanning the surrounding bush, turning frequently to look back the way we had come, concentrating most on the ridge where I anticipated that M'Simani and any men he had with him would be lying up – and watching us. Temba didn't seem to be bothered about it.

We'd been going for about an hour, and I'd become increasingly worried about what Temba thought he was doing, when, in turning to look behind us, I tripped. I fell awkwardly, and just avoided prodding the muzzle of the Galil into the sand. I struggled to my feet and turned on Temba, ready to suggest we should cut this crap along the low ground by the river and get up high – now!

He was down on one knee with his back towards me. For a moment I thought he had resorted to prayer as the only way of finding M'Simani. Then I saw that he was studying the sand.

As I walked over to him he didn't look up or comment, but even I, in my inexperience, could read the tracks he'd found. Somebody wearing trainers had come down to the river. The local villagers didn't possess trainers; they went barefoot. This was a townie, someone coming down to the river to collect water.

We'd found them. By God, we'd found them!

I caught Temba's eye, saw the gleam in it. He was trying not to, but he couldn't help it: he grinned.

M'Simani. M'Simani or one of his gang. Their carelessness was breathtaking.

9 M'Simani Kangalewa

M'Simani Kangalewa was born in 1974, in the village of Shinyua-Bani, out in the grasslands some thirty miles to the east of Bumani, the location of Chloris' rehab centre. M'Simani came from an unusual family. His father, a minor chief in the area, only took one wife, M'Simani's mother, and M'Simani was their only son. He had two sisters, both older than him, one of whom, Daisy, became a senior nurse at the big African hospital in the capital, Mateka.

Most Boromundi men of any wealth or substance, particularly from the cattle-based tribes of the savanna plains, want more than one wife, and certainly want more than one son. Fat wives, like fat cattle, are a sign of success, of affluence. Having only one wife is like, if you were very rich in England, owning a beaten up Ford Fiesta. You don't do it – you buy a Porsche. And sons, sons are what you talk about with the other men, under the shade tree.

M'Simani was a cuddly baby, plump, with pale skin and big, soulful eyes. His sisters fought over who would carry him and both his mother and father doted on him. To put it simply, from the start M'Simani was spoilt rotten. But he was a bright boy, and he did well at primary school, sufficiently well to join the 4 per cent of Boromundi's population who manage to reach secondary school. He was sent to Gororungozi College near Bumani, a boys' boarding school located four miles out of town, beyond the rehab centre. He did well and, by the end of third year, promised to gain 'O' level grades that would progress him to the dizzy heights of 'A' level. He even had an ambition: to be a doctor. I've chosen my words carefully: it wasn't his ambition, it was his father's and mother's and sisters', and it was slung round his neck like a dead vulture. Personally, from what our sources told us of his early life and from what I learned of his character, I don't think M'Simani would have recognised ambition if he'd tripped over it. He was too weak, too much a drifter, a boy who did well while his teachers stood behind him with their sticks, but who would drift as soon as he was cut loose.

And the cutting loose happened suddenly. M'Simani became involved with a group of boys led by an unusual leader. This boy was a troublemaker, one of those rare pupils who has absolutely no respect for authority and is so fearless in showing it that authority quails before him.

Feelings ran high amongst the boys at Gororungozi because the meat they were served in their evening meals was bad. M'Simani was drawn into a plot to stage a boycott of the dining hall. The way it was set up, M'Simani was seen to be the leader of an uprising which, one evening, turned into quite a nasty riot. The boys refused to eat their supper. After an ineffective effort to pacify them, they broke out of the dining hall and ran around in the darkness brandishing sticks and threatening to beat the staff. Some damage was done, particularly to the school kitchens. In the end, and very reluctantly, the head called the police who restored order and carted the ringleaders off for a night in the Bumani Police cells. M'Simani never went back to school and never returned to Shinyua-Bani.

He fled to Mateka. His oldest sister, Daisy, put up with him for a while but, when she caught him dipping into the biscuit tin which contained her savings, she threw him out. I don't think it particularly matters what he did in the following years, but none of it was any good. He became part of the low life that writhed and squirmed in the shit of Mateka's shanty towns. When the second civil war broke out, he joined Bunrum. As with Gideon Mushewa, he had the misfortune to choose the wrong side to join, particularly for a boy from the south-east, but he probably did it to spite his father, who was a local worthy of the BRF. M'Simani saw very little fighting. His main occupation seems to have been in logistics – or, to put it another way, in the quartermaster's stores. It was a cushy, safe and lucrative number which suited him perfectly. When the war ended he slid back into Mateka.

By this time he had a reputation as a procurer. If you wanted something, M'Simani was your man. He was intelligent in a weasily way, and had learned that people will pay a lot for a little of something they're partial to, particularly if it's illegal, like drugs, or risky, like little boys or six-year old virgins. He did well. He bought a bungalow in one of the better suburbs. He dressed nattily – hence the carefully tied shoelaces on that day he stopped Cyprian's minibus. But he never let a woman near him. I believe M'Simani was a homosexual – this in a society where homosexuality is dangerous business.

M'Simani was last seen in his bungalow towards the

end of July 1997. Then he, like Smallboy, disappeared. The next time M'Simani broke surface he was standing at the roadside beyond Kaserewe, flagging down Cyprian Bogovu's minibus.

We followed the trainer tracks up the slope into the rocky outcrops along the crest of the ridge, where we dropped into the dirt and lay squinting into the sunrise. The land fell steeply away, then flattened into a plain broken by kopjes. Kopjes are formed of gigantic, rounded granite boulders anything up to the size of a suburban house, piled on top of each other, some balancing on those below – rather like great grey heaps of elephant dung. Between the boulders, the gaps are thick with small bushes and grass. The flat land that separated these kopjes varied from open pans of bare, pinky-brown soil to dense thorn bush.

Temba moved his face against my ear. As he whispered, I realised it was the first time he'd spoken since we'd left Sizwi.

'From the spoor, I have counted four.'

He caught my eye and I nodded. I wasn't being honest: I hadn't noticed there was more than one.

Then he gestured towards the land that fell away in front of us. 'Armstrong, they are in a kopje. Yes?'

'They're in a kopje,' I repeated. It's where I'd have been.

'Then they are watching. If we wait here, perhaps we will see them move. If one comes for water, we will see where they lie. Then we can take them, tonight. But they may leave, they may go in the other direction, away from us. Then we will lose them.'

I rolled onto my side and looked at Temba. His face was powdered with a pale layer of dust through which droplets of sweat had cut dark runnels. His eyes caught mine and they were black and hard.

'We risk it,' I said.

He didn't wait. He pushed himself to his feet and I followed as, using every scrap of cover, he worked his way down the slope. The trail was easy to follow in the loose sand and scree and seemed to be bearing away to the left, towards the north-east, following the more open ground.

Once Temba had its general direction he stopped following it. We used the thicker cover, moving fast through it, then working our way back to the trail, relying on Temba's skill as a tracker to find it when we crossed it.

It worked well, mainly because these men had, again, been incredibly careless. Their footprints – and by that time I could identify the four – were plain to see. They had made no attempt to conceal themselves, to zig-zag, to use rock outcrops – nothing. It worried me. It was as if they felt either innocent or secure. Was this really M'Simani Kangalewa? And, if it was, then what was he doing here?

An hour later, with the sun well above the horizon, the shadows shortening and the beginnings of the day's heat bleaching the colours out of the landscape, we knew which kopje they were in, mainly because the trail ran straight towards it, and also because it offered an ideal vantage point, an unusually high kopje thickly clothed in vegetation with deep, shadowed clefts cut between the boulders. Working through the bush, we closed on it quickly, circling slightly so we came in from the east, with the sun behind us, dropping into the shade of a thorn tree when we saw that the last few yards lay across open ground. We lay close, concealed behind a stand of dead couch grass, and looked at that gap. It was open hard-pan without so much as a leaf or a stone for cover. I knew then how the men must have felt on the Somme, staring across the emptiness of no-man's land at the waiting Germans.

Temba didn't say anything because he didn't need to: there wasn't a choice. When he got up and moved out into the bright sunlight, I had my rifle trained on the slopes of the kopje but I knew perfectly well that if they saw him, there was bugger all I could do about it. I lay, watching him, anticipating the shot, waiting to see him fall, wondering what I'd do if he did, whether I'd have the guts to go out and collect him or whether I'd just run. He walked very steadily. He seemed, almost, to saunter, yet he crossed the gap remarkably quickly.

After he'd disappeared I lay still for a while, knowing it was my turn. I wanted to stay where I was. I particularly didn't want to get up because my bowels seemed to have liquefied and I was quite certain that, the moment I came vertical, they'd void themselves down my trouser leg. Worse, it seemed pretty obvious that the men on the other side must have seen Temba but had let him come so as they could see how many others would follow him. He was already dead. The moment I walked out into that space, they'd start shooting. And it would be easier than shooting hamsters in a cage.

I pushed myself to my feet and stepped out into the sun, my breath coming in shallow gasps because my chest had locked solid, as if bracing itself for the impact of the first bullet, while some maniac in my head kept running round and round in circles screaming about turning back, for Christ's sake turn back, turn back! 'Walk!' I whispered to myself in time with my tread. 'Walk, walk, walk, you cunt! Walk! Walk slow! Walk, fuck you!'

It was miles wide, that piece of open ground, my legs feeling heavier than tree trunks and the air so oppressively hot it was like pushing through treacle. To make matters worse, as I approached the blessed shade on the other side I saw what looked like a fat Buddha squatting under a bush, watching me come. It was Temba, and the bastard was laughing.

Working our way up the kopje proved painfully slow and dangerous work. At times the only way forward was to climb up and over the boulders. We scrabbled to gain a purchase on the steeper faces where, often, flat sheets of rock weathered off the granite surface threatened to slip away and crash down into the bush below; then we flattened ourselves and crawled on our bellies as we crossed their horribly exposed tops. Worse, our every move was watched by rock hyraxes, beasts the size of an overfed domestic cat which, if we moved too suddenly, sat up on their hunkers and threatened to sound their alarm call and expose us.

We'd made it three quarters of the way up when I smelt wood smoke. I caught Temba's trouser leg and pointed two fingers, like a V-sign, up into my nostrils. He hesitated, his flat nose moving like a rabbit's, before nodding. The early morning breeze was light, fitful, but generally from the north-west, almost straight into our faces. Using hand signals, I suggested that their camp was already below us and on the side that faced the direction from which we'd come. He nodded, turned away, and made to work his way across the face of the next boulder. But I caught at his leg again, and pointed upwards. I was afraid that someone might be near the top, above us, the lookout who'd failed to spot us as we sauntered across that open land. Temba hesitated, then nodded, indicating that he would wait while I went on up.

Usually, the last leg to the summit is the worst but this wasn't. I followed a steep but crumbly slope up a gash between two rocks, scrabbled up a weathered face to my right, squirmed my way across its more gently sloping top, and peered over the edge. This wasn't the highest rock – that rose above me to my right, a great, flat-faced slab that resembled one of those statues on Easter Island – but I was higher than their lookout. He was squatting on a flat surface slightly below me, facing away to my left, towards the river. Dressed in dirty combat trousers, his top bare, he had his eyes closed as he dozed in the warmth of the morning sun, and he was smoking a cigarette. A battered AK47 with two yellow-taped magazines lay on the rock at his right hand.

He wasn't far away from me, no more than ten yards. I lay, watching as he slowly raised his cigarette and drew deeply, the dry tobacco of his roll-up flaring, unable to believe that he hadn't heard me, that he had no inkling I was there. Better still, I could reach him by dropping back from the edge and moving to my right, then down the corner formed where my rock met the big, Easter Island slab. From there, I would be right behind him.

If I'd had the time, I could have made those few yards easily, without making a sound, but I was conscious that Temba was waiting for me, probably wondering what the hell I was up to. Worse, he might get fed up and launch his attack on the others. If he did, this bloke would be directly above him and Temba would be a sitting duck. I had to sort out the smoker-man before the main show began.

I'd hardly moved before I dislodged a small stone which rolled down the slope and dropped away behind me. The rolling made enough noise but it chose to land in a bush, swishing down through its leaves. I flattened myself on the rock and listened, expecting the man to react, but it wasn't until I plucked up courage to peep over the edge that I was sure he hadn't. He must have heard it but perhaps he was used to the hyraxes dislodging rocks; either that, or he was deaf or stoned. As I watched, he calmly flicked his cigarette butt away into space.

Moving cautiously, I wormed my way across the rock into the corner. When I looked again the man still hadn't moved but he was now so close I saw he had skin the colour of used sump oil, very smooth and clean, and that the hair on the back of his head was short and tightly curled. I began to work my way down onto his rock, unable to watch where I placed my feet, the rifle held away in front of me, my bum sliding against the smooth surface. I was expecting that, at any moment, he would hear me, that I would have to shoot him, that what

happened afterwards would depend on whether Temba
had got into position to deal with the others. I kept my
eye on his head, noticing the first glisten of sweat along
the darker creases of his neck, coming with the heat of
the day; seeing how his hair glittered in the sunlight like
steel wool; noticing a fly that had landed on his shoulder,
the way it rubbed its front legs together. As I came
upright at the bottom of the slope, as I took the first,
slow, controlled steps towards him, I felt in my pocket
with my right hand, found what I needed, and began to
draw it out.

He moved incredibly quickly. I don't know what he
heard or sensed, but he knew I was there and began to
twist upwards and away from me. As he rose, his hand
reached for his rifle. If he'd left it he'd have been too
quick and I'd have missed.

The blow caught him on the side of his head, just
above his ear. The sudden, dreadful weight of the swinging lead cosh crunched into his skull. He staggered. His
legs folded and he sank to his knees. I knocked him
sideways, stepped over him, lifted the weight high, and
swung again, down at him, accelerating the weapon with
all my might. That second blow caught his forehead, full
on, and the front of his face exploded like a rotten
pawpaw.

He lay, jerking like a clockwork toy that's running
out of spring. He gave me plenty of time to arrange him
on the top of the rock so that, despite his quivering, he
wouldn't fall off. He was still breathing, shallow and
bubbly, and his eyes were wide open behind a mess of
blood, but he wasn't with me. And he wasn't Kangalewa.

He lay on his side, slightly bunched up. I knelt over

him, my weight pinning him, and put my hand on his chin, pulling his jaw up and back like I'd been taught when I learned to give mouth-to-mouth resuscitation. The knife came easily from its sheath. I got it as far as his neck, so the blade pressed into but didn't quite puncture the skin where it was stretched out, smooth and unblemished. A vein throbbed just under the point of the knife. I hesitated.

I mightn't have done it but a shout and a shot and the 'pfeew' of a bullet passing my head like some supersonic, malevolent bumblebee, gave me no choice. The knife slid in easily enough, then encountering resistance. When I leaned on it, when I had sawn it back and forth a couple of times, it slid easily again. Then, as blood squirted across my hand, I began to work the knife sideways to cut his throat open. The man writhed but he didn't have any strength and my weight overwhelmed him. He might have been semi-conscious but the more I sawed, the more he fought. The sounds he made were horrible, gurgly, choking on the blood that gouted, as from some primaeval sacrifice, and oozed in deep, smeared scarlet across the granite slab. And then there came the tearing sound of automatic fire, and a man screamed.

I rolled off him, tried to stand, slipped in the blood, and dropped off the rock. Spread-eagled to slow my fall, I slithered down its angled face into a gully, landing in a thorn bush. I fought through it, lacerating my hands, trying at the same time to sheathe the knife and pull the Galil round in front of me. I came out, fell flat on my face onto another ledge of rock, and wriggled forward to look over the edge.

The men's camp lay immediately below me. It occupied

a flat bowl of land surrounded on three sides by the rocks of the kopje. A fire had been made in the centre and blankets were scattered about where the gang had slept. One man lay sprawled face down to the right of the fire. He was naked except for a pair of very white Y-fronts and he had a hole the size of my fist in the middle of his back from which blood slowly pumped. Another man stood at the edge of the clearing, almost facing me, his back against a rock, and he held his hands in the air; not high, but at the level of his ears. He was a short, thick-set man with pale brown skin and he had his trousers on, though they were not fastened and had slipped down so his genitals were exposed. He wasn't Kangalewa.

The third man lay on his side, bunched up. It was he that was screaming. I saw Temba to my left, fighting his way down the kopje, trying to keep his eyes on the two men while struggling through the underbrush and sliding or jumping down the faces of the rocks. And it was while he was doing this that the standing man made his move. A rifle lay on the ground a few feet away from him and he lunged for it, the sort of dive you'd do into a swimming pool. It was so very easy to squint down the Galil and, as he hit the earth, shoot him.

By this time Temba had reached the clearing. He lifted his rifle and shot the man again, a short burst that knocked his body back, so it ended up in a heap against the bottom of the rock. But I know he was very dead long before Temba loosed off at him.

I was shaking when I joined Temba, shaking so badly that, had I attempted to aim my rifle, I would have been useless. The reaction, albeit at an early stage, once again threatened to tear me apart. Temba had no such trouble. He was jubilant. He turned and threw his arms round me. I found myself enfolded, crushed against him, whirled round and round, conscious only of the heat and sweat of his body and his bear-like strength and his screams of joy. But he let me go quickly and pushed past me to the man who lay on his side, moaning. He used his foot to turn him over. He was very dirty, his clothes smeared with dust and a mixture of mud and blood, his face contorted with pain, his lips peeled back in agony to expose a row of perfect, white teeth. But I knew who he was.

Then my attention was caught by something up and beyond Temba's head, something that moved down the face of a rock, half way up the kopje, snake-like, its polished skin glistening in the rays of the morning sun. For a moment I didn't know what it was and reacted by raising my rifle. Then I understood. It wasn't an animal. It was rivulet of blood, the life blood of the man I had slaughtered.

I suppose of all the five men who had stopped Cyprian Bogovu's minibus, Kangalewa had seemed to have the least responsibility for the murder of our two women, so I was less interested in punishing him than in using him as a source of information.

So, when we had recovered our breath and I'd narrowly avoided being sick, after Temba had kicked Kangalewa hard in the ribs, hard enough to obtain an assurance from him that there had only been four men in the gang, we settled down to business.

Temba rolled him onto his back. The cause of his screams had been a bullet from Temba which had taken two fingers off his right hand. Kangalewa was no fighter: anyone fired up to do battle would have fought on despite this injury. For him, that nick had been the end of his war.

Once we'd checked that his injury wouldn't deprive us of his company, Temba knelt beside him and, using strips torn from Kangalewa's shirt, spent five minutes binding up the wound and reassuring the man. By the time he'd finished, Kangalewa had quietened down and was capable of listening to and understanding what Temba said, and volubly anxious to be of as much assistance as possible.

Then Temba told a terrible lie. He said that, if Kangalewa told us everything, the truth, the whole truth, voluntarily and willingly and without omitting a single scrap of relevant information, we would spare him. The alternative, he explained, would be a long, agonisingly painful death, so drawn out that, at a very early point, he would be screaming at us to end it. To illustrate the possibilities, Temba dug in his rucksack and unearthed his scalpel, and he treated a shaking Kangalewa to a discourse on his skills in dissection, and how, as a biologist, he knew exactly how much of which living tissue could be removed from an organism without it actually dying. It was a wicked thing to do but it had a magical effect. Kangalewa sang like a choirboy.

Kangalewa sang and we listened in mounting horror. What he told us was beyond belief.

Many of you, who read this account, will have to expand your minds to take in what I am about to describe. You will not want to believe it, not in this twenty-first century. And, when you do begin to come to terms with it, you will dismiss it as, 'Oh, Africa! Of course! Conrad's *Heart of Africa*. Pure fiction.' But I have to remind you that what Conrad wrote was true. He had travelled through Good King Leopold's Congo. He had seen the heads impaled upon the stockades. He had seen the punishment amputations, the razed villages, the brutalized population. It wasn't his imagination. I also have to remind you of the horrors that stir behind the chintz curtains of suburban England, a country that fancies itself as ranking high amongst nations in culture, law, tolerance and learning. A doctor quietly puts down four hundred patients with as little compunction as you or I would step on as many cockroaches. Serial killers, husband and wife together, entrap, rape and then murder their innocent victims. A small girl undergoes years of torture and abuse by her closest relatives, her distress patently evident to teachers, social workers and neighbours, yet nothing is done until the child is discovered dead in a bathtub, starved, naked and covered in her own excrement. We live in a civilised land, yet the forces of evil swirl close beneath its elegant surface.

An eight-year old boy has become a deity. Quite how

he got to this elevated position, Kangalewa is not sure. But his power is now so awesome that to look upon him is certain death. Those few who are permitted into his presence approach upon their bellies, naked, their faces pressed to the floor. They are not there to speak. They come to listen and, when they have left, slithering backwards across the cold marble floor, they hasten away to carry out the minutiae of his every instruction.

What is the basis of his power? When the fit takes him he speaks in tongues. He writhes upon the floor, froth blowing around his mouth, his eyes rolled up into his head to expose their whites. As he recovers, he speaks. It is part prophecy; part instruction; part dogma; part incomprehensible gibberish. The men that are close to him listen carefully, whisper together, interpret, commit his words to paper, issue instructions. To kill. Maim. Torture. Massacre.

He sits on a royal throne of ivory tusks; not any old ivory but the teeth of the rare pygmy elephants of the deepest forests of Boromundi and Congo, a race quite separate from the common African elephant. Across the seat are thrown skins of albino and black leopard. The arms and legs of his throne are crusted with diamonds from the Williamson mine in Tanzania, emeralds from the fabulous Sandwana deposits of Zimbabwe and rubies from Kenya's Tsavo. Two black-maned lions are chained on either side, beasts that dispose of the flesh of those who displease him.

But he is a mere boy. He has toys. His favourite is a Kalashnikov, an AKS74, its metalwork leaved in gold, its bullets tipped with industrial diamonds. He fires these bullets at living targets, and he is very skilled with his toy. Yes, he has all the sadism of small boys, except that his every whim is gratified, encouraged even.

Where is he? Kangalewa is not sure. But, yes, he has been to his palace. He was sent in July, last year, to receive instructions. It is a good three day's drive to the west of Mateka and, from the chill he felt, in the highlands. The Mountains of the Morning Mist? Perhaps. He could not tell. And he saw the king? Of course not. He saw nothing. He was blindfold at all times. Had he looked, even upon the way, his eyes would have been burnt out and his tongue sliced from his mouth.

What are this new king's plans? Ah, that is easy. When he is ready, he will save Boromundi. Boromundi first, then the other countries surrounding it: Tanzania, Zaire . . . The arms, the men, the strategy – all are ready. A conquest, rather than a 'saving'? Of course. He will create an empire that Africa has not seen since the days of the pharaohs, created by an army stronger than Shaka's Zulu *impi*s, a power that even the United States will respect. Why? Because Africa is richer in resources even than the United States. Gold, diamonds, uranium, copper, oil, coal, iron . . .

Who were the other four with Kangalewa that day in October when he stopped a minibus on the road to the east of Kaserewe? Temba waits. Kangalewa has closed his eyes, screwing them shut, and his head drops forward. His face is grey beneath its dust. Ah, says Temba, so you know who we are? He nods.

Temba hits him with the muzzle of his rifle. The protruding sight catches Kangalewa's cheek and thin rivulet of blood flows down it, like a dark tear. For a moment he whimpers. I think he knows that it is hopeless, that his fate is sealed. Kangalewa! Temba's voice is a whisper. Those men: who were they? Mophas Mandabanga? Yes. Onias Matanganesa? Yes.

These ones, Mophas and Onias, where are they? I do not know. I swear, I do not know. They are nothing to me, so, if I knew, I would tell you. I swear. Temba kicks him. His boot jerks forward and connects with Kangalewa's testicles, and the man screams. Where are they? He shakes his head. He kneels before us, his head slumped forward, facing the ground, so we cannot see his expression. But it is the attitude of a man whose despair, whose hopelessness is total.

There were others. Who were they? Smallboy Mushewa? Yes. And? He does not know him. He begins to whimper. I do not know, he screams. I swear. We called him Bullet. That was his only name. I never saw him before, never again since. I swear. But Temba hits him with the butt of his rifle and he falls sideways, his hands covering his head, and it is my turn to kick him. I kick him while he is down, aiming for his head and connecting behind his ear. He screams. I kneel beside him and whisper in his ear: Tell us. Tell us, M'Simani. We need to know. He nods. The man is Bullet. He was the leader. He is someone important. He came for that mission only. That is all I know. I swear! I stand beside Temba, looking down at him. I believe him.

A 'mission'. Like this one? Temba glances at me, catches my nod, and drags Kangalewa upright, shoving the muzzle of his rifle into his mouth so hard it clatters against his teeth and so deep he chokes. You are on a mission now? Yes. I am sent to obtain things. What? I am sent for things which the king needs. That is my job. What things?

Many: guns, other weapons, diamonds, special foods, bulk provisions for his troops, and clothing, fighting kit . . .

'And? Come on . . . And . . . ?'

Mooti. Medicine.

'*Mooti*? What sort of *mooti*?'

It hurts. I can see it hurts Kangalewa to tell us. He keeps his head bowed and he sees our rifles, pointing at the ground, but he knows that the catches are off safety, that it takes a fraction of a second to squeeze the trigger. *Mooti*, he whispers, *mooti* which the king will, when he is ready, give to all his fighters. It will protect them against bullets, against RPGs, against land mines. It will make them invincible. It will make them as powerful, as unstoppable as the army ants, the *zhunghu* that swarm across the landscape eating every living thing that does not run to escape.

'You are looking for this *mooti*?' 'No, no – for some ingredients.' 'What ingredients?' 'Ah, so many.' 'What . . . ?' 'Herbs. Medicines from the shops. Roots. The parts of animals' – he lists the traditional medicines used by the *nyanga*s, the witch doctors: 'the liver of baboons, the . . .' Temba hits him again, a glancing blow across the side of his head. 'Cocaine and pills, many different sorts of pills. Mescaline, psilocybin . . . from Europe. Kangalewa explains: he has the contacts. Obtaining these things is easy, it is only a question of money, of dollars . . .

'So, what are you looking for here, near Tilubu?'

Kangalewa shakes his head. Drops of blood and sweat flick away to mix with the dry dust of the ground. Temba asks the question again, pressing his rifle into Kangalewa's eyeball, forcing his head back. What?

It comes out suddenly, with the speed of vomit. 'A girl. A white girl. A white virgin. That is what the king seeks. He has one but . . .' The man falls sideways. He lies on the ground at my feet, shaking.

I cannot breathe. My chest has a band, like steel, around it, that squeezes me. I cannot breathe. I cannot breathe.

A girl. A white virgin. Now I know why Rebecca died. Oh God, I know why she died. Poor, poor Rebecca. They weren't interested in Annabel. She was a sideshow, a momentary pleasure – thrown like a child's sweet to the likes of Smallboy Mushewa. They wanted Rebecca. For his *mooti*, the king needed Rebecca. So they took a *panga* and they sliced her. I choked suddenly. What they took from Rebecca's body wasn't enough for their needs.

I can hardly hear. There is a great sound in my head, like the buzzing of a million bees – no, harsher, like a saw, a band-saw, a grating, tearing sound. Zzzzzeeeee. Oh God! Zzzzzeeee. It is the sound of *Kisasi* the Justice Bird. Zzzzzeeee.

Temba is speaking again. 'So who are you looking for now, Kangalewa?'

Oh shit. I know. A white woman. A virgin. I know. And my rifle kicks as I squeeze the trigger.

I stripped off bush boots and sweaty socks and walked very slowly, barefoot, across the sand, savouring its softness and warmth against the soles of my feet and the sudden chill as I waded out into water as clear as vodka. The sands were smooth and coral pink and stretched emptily away on either hand, backed by regiments of high palm trees whose fronds whispered in the damp trade wind. Before me a shallow sea of turquoise and jade, tinted sepia where the sea grass swam, ended a mile out in a white line of seething foam where a great ocean broke against a reef, the boom of its destruction rolling in like distant drums across the lagoon. 'Bloody hell,' I whispered. In such an idyll, I wondered, what does a nun wear when she swims? A bikini?

I closed my eyes and breathed deeply, drawing the heavy salt air into my lungs, and allowed my mind to drift. At this moment, M'Simani Kangalewa would still be stretched out on his own patch of sand. He'd been alive when we left him. He probably hadn't known he was alive, and even the best A & E department in Britain couldn't have put him back together: but he was still alive. We could have left the bodies out in the open for the vultures to pick over, but a spiral of vultures wheeling and descending through the early morning thermals might have drawn someone's attention to the gristly scene. So we'd chucked the bodies of the other three men into the bush-filled gullies between the great, rounded stones of the kopje. We'd thrown the pathetic remnants of their goods after them, their cooking pots, their clothes, their blankets, their food, everything except their guns. We'd kicked the ashes from the fire until they blended into the sand, after which we'd broken branches off the trees and obliterated the tracks which traced recent events in that small amphitheatre in the rocks. When we'd finished there was nothing left except the buzzing of the flies from the bushes as they settled upon their feast. Then Temba and I had dragged Kangalewa into the shade of a small acacia growing against one of the kopje's granite boulders and pegged him out. We'd used stakes made from acacia wood to nail him to the ground, and then we'd left him to the ants. They'd be all over him now. They'd probably tickled at first. Now, now they'd be seething over him, covering him like some living suit, exploring his eyes and his mouth and the other holes in his body, natural and man-made, and they'd be so excited they'd be biting. Temba had reckoned it might take them weeks to pick him clean.

'Bwana, sah!'

I turned to find a tall man in a very clean white nightdress which reached down to his ankles. He wore a maroon Egyptian fez, complete with dangling tassel, on his head, a matching cummerbund, and a grin white with teeth.

'Hello,' I replied.

'You have asked at reception for Sister Humphries.'

'Yes,' I said.

'*Njo!*' he commanded, beckoning. I stopped long enough to pull my boots back on, then followed him past the main hotel building through the palms along the back of the beach to the furthest of a scattering of white-walled, thatched bungalows that faced the sea. There I found the answer the question I'd been asking myself: a nun on a seaside holiday wears what she always wears. And, no, she doesn't go swimming, she doesn't sunbathe, she doesn't go snorkelling, and she doesn't prop up the hotel bar. Instead, she sits on a little veranda, sipping Earl Grey tea and staring out at the view and talking with a tiny, black, sparrow of a companion about the sorts of things nuns always talk about. That is, until I arrived.

Chloris didn't say anything when she saw me and I have no idea what she thought because she turned away so her headgear hid her face. The other nun couldn't have known who I was, as she dismissed the man in the nightdress, invited me up onto the veranda, offered me a chair, and began to pour me a cup of tea. Only then did Chloris express the opinion that what was about to happen wasn't a good idea.

'I searched everywhere in Tilubu hospital and couldn't find you,' I explained to the side of Chloris' head. 'First I did battle with a large lady who sat, like some great, quivering chocolate blancmange, behind the desk in reception. "No, Mr McKay," ' I mimicked, ' "Sister Chloris is not available. No, none of the sisters are available. No, the doctor in charge of the hospital is not available. No, no-one is available who wishes to see you. Please, you leave now, okay?" '

'It was easy enough to make a detour round her. I

didn't know exactly where your room was, but I had some idea. I was hurrying down a corridor when I met one of your hospital porters. He was a little smaller than my friend Temba, but not much, and he carried a neat length of lead piping and, from the way he hefted it, he knew how to use it.'

At this point I had the satisfaction of seeing Chloris' hand go to her mouth.

'It didn't prevent me trying to hit him first. I was past reason. All I wanted to do was see you, explain the situation, and persuade you to get out.'

'What situation?' Chloris asked. At least she now faced me.

'What is it?' I asked, ignoring her question. 'Has someone decided I'm a bad influence on you? Is that why you suddenly disappeared from my ward? Is that why half the hospital staff give up ministering to the sick in order to assault me when I come looking for you?'

Chloris was hiding her face again so I rambled on.

'He didn't hit me very hard, but it was enough to floor me. When I next knew where I was, someone was sitting on my head and someone else – and I have a nasty feeling it was the fat lady from reception – was crushing my chest and stomach and preventing me from breathing, while Temba was trying to dissuade the porter from emptying my brains across the concrete floor.'

A sharp intake of breath indicated that Chloris was still listening.

'I spent two days in bed, recovering.' I stopped suddenly. Temba had had to hurry back to St Faith's so I'd been left at Sizwi's and she, bless her, had found lots of time to satisfy my needs. In between, she'd found out

that Chloris had been sent on leave. She'd flown to
Tanzania for a week on the coast. Sizwi even discovered
which hotel she was staying at, the Two Turtles, ten
miles south of Dar-es-Salaam.

Chloris swallowed. Her adam's apple bobbed up and
down in her wonderfully smooth, pale neck, but nothing
came out.

'I never touched you,' I pleaded.

'No.'

'So why were they so horrible??'

'It's not what you did. It's what you thought.' The
words came out strangled.

'What I "thought"? Who the hell's got the right to
decide that they're going to hit me because of something
I'm thinking?'

By this time the little nun had cottoned on to what
was happening, as she withdrew the cup of tea she had
been holding out to me and asked me to leave. I refused.
I said I had to talk to Chloris, that I didn't mind her
chaperoning us as long as she swore that everything she
heard would be kept in confidence. She began saying that
she couldn't do that, that anything she heard . . .

I'd had enough. I grabbed Chloris' arm and hauled
her down the veranda steps. She didn't resist. She came
easily, hanging back only long enough to beg Maria to
come with us. Which she did, walking a few paces behind
us, just out of earshot.

I stopped pulling Chloris when we came out onto the
beach, because the beach was as beautiful as the girl
whose hand I was holding. The sun was beginning to
drop behind the palms and it threw a golden light that
stretched the barred shadows of their trunks across the

sand to the sea. The tide was low, the small, transparent waves lifting suddenly, tinkling as they tumbled onto the sand. In the last few minutes the wind had dropped and the air had become heavy with the scent of frangipani. Chloris began walking down the beach ahead of me and, before we'd gone a dozen yards, she'd stooped and picked up a small shell, inspecting it in the palm of her hand for a moment before handing it to me.

'Look at it,' she said, and she was smiling.

Smiling. This was a girl who I'd just manhandled, just dragged away from her bungalow. Smiling! It took me a moment, but I did as I was told. It was a very small shell. The top was a bluey-grey but the lips around the entrance where the snail had lived were a rich, daffodil orange.

'It's very pretty,' I remarked.

We'd reached the bottom of the beach. She stopped, kneeling for a moment to remove a pair of very sensible black lace-up shoes and grey woollen socks. She stuffed the socks into the shoes and carried them in her left hand. Then she turned to walk along the bottom of the beach so she trod into the swash of the waves, walking slowly.

'Yes, it's God's handiwork. Even a dead seashell is God's handiwork. You – you're God's handiwork, too, Armstrong. I don't understand you, but I suppose that's part of the mystery God creates for us.'

I grunted. I didn't see myself as much of a mystery.

'You're not supposed to be here. You're supposed to be in school today, teaching, yet you've come all this way to find me. So you've come to tell me something horrid again. Every time I see you, it's something horrid. Am I right?'

She was looking at me but I nodded without catching her eye. A wave broke, a larger wave that hissed up the sand, exploding round her feet and coming on to soak my bush boots.

'Shit,' I said, trying to hop out of the way.

'Why don't you take them off?' she suggested.

While I knelt and worked at the laces she addressed the top of my head. It must have been quite a tableau: Chloris, in black, standing holding her shoes while I knelt at her feet. God knows what the little nun thought.

'When I went to confession,' Chloris said, 'while you were still in the hospital, the priest asked me about you. He wanted to know what my feelings were. I told him.'

I looked up at her. One of my laces was knotted and I was struggling with it. 'Why did you . . . ?'

'I told him you disturbed me. Which you do. And I said I didn't understand it because everything you'd done had always been so loathsome.'

'You didn't . . . ?'

'No. I didn't tell him what you confided. You asked me not to, remember? But he said I hadn't to see you again.'

I hauled my boots off and we continued along the beach. I made a point of walking in the water as my feet stank. 'Loathsome'. I repeated the word to myself because it hurt. 'Do you know,' I said, 'six months ago, I'd never heard of Boromundi. I was a teacher in a small town English comprehensive and I lived a very dreary existence. I'd never done anything . . . loathsome, not in all my life. Then five men went and killed the girl I'd asked to marry me.' I paused. 'Smallboy was one. On Friday I caught up with the second.'

Chloris stopped and turned to me. Her lips were tight and her face pale.

'Temba and I found his gang camped in the shelter of a kopje. I think they'd only planned to be there for a couple of days but they couldn't locate the person they were looking for, so they'd stayed on. They'd overused the track from the kopje to the nearest water: it was easy to follow their footprints.'

'How many?'

'There were four of them.'

'No. I meant, how many did you kill?'

'Four. The one that had been present when Rebecca was murdered lasted longest – it took him a bit of time to explain why she was killed. It wasn't a random death, like I'd thought, like I told you. She was carefully selected, and the reasons they'd selected her were the same reasons they had for camping out near Tilubu.'

'Tilubu?' I saw the shock in her face.

'Yes. They'd come to Tilubu looking for you. As the crow flies, their camp was only five miles from the hospital. If you'd been there, if you hadn't been on holiday, they'd have kidnapped you and you'd be dead. I'm not going to tell you what they'd have done before they killed you because I don't think you can take it. It's so evil that even I . . . even I, loathsome, loathsome me, even I am disgusted.'

Her right hand, the one that wasn't holding her shoes, had come up to her face and she was pressing her fingers against her lips. She had beautifully long fingers with neatly clipped, oval nails. She'd moved slightly so the setting sun shone straight into her face, its colour warming her skin, and, if I hadn't already fallen in love with the girl, I'd have tumbled then.

'You can't go back to Boromundi,' I whispered. It was my turn to sound as if I was half strangled. 'Chloris, what's happening is part of a huge conspiracy. It's so big, so evil and so powerful that, if you do go back, they're bound to get you.' I paused because the way I'd put it sounded rather weak. 'They'll rape you and they'll kill you and they'll cut you up and . . . I'll tell you how bad it is. If you say you're going back, I'll push you into the water, there, and I'll drown you. I'll hold your head under 'til you stop breathing. I'd rather do that, Chloris, than risk what will happen if you go back to Boromundi.'

Her hand hadn't moved. It was still pressing her mouth, except that she was shaking her head, very slowly, her eyes wide, and she was saying, 'No, no, no,' over and over.

In those moments as we stood on the beach together, things changed forever. Yes, I felt sorry for her. Yes, I felt a great surge of protectiveness. Yes, if the beautifully shaped fingers pressed against a face that glowed in the failing sun were anything to go by, there was a lovely body underneath waiting to be unwrapped. And, yes, I felt warm about the fact that she had admitted, quite openly, that she had had to confess her feelings for me to her priest. What changed was that indefinable thing, that emotional switch that clicks over, that takes love beyond the chase, beyond the fleshy desires of sex, beyond friendship, companionship, affection – and onto a different plane, something that, when it happened, made me realise that this girl, wrapped in raven black, holding her sensible shoes in her hand while she stood on that beautiful tropical beach, was my woman. I felt as much for her as I did for Rebecca and knew that what I was doing for Rebecca I would do all over again for Chloris.

'Chloris,' I whispered.

She still looked at me.

'I'll come with you. I'll take you anywhere you want to go. Back to England. Australia. Hawaii. The North Pole. Anywhere except Boromundi.'

She nodded very slightly. Then she turned back along the beach and began walking, and I hurried to catch up with her.

I stayed two nights at the Two Turtles. I took a room in the main hotel block, well away from their bungalow, but I spent every moment she allowed with Chloris. We passed our time on the veranda talking, or taking long walks along the beach, finding places in the shade of the palm trees to sit and talk some more. At low tide we paddled out across the rock pools, watching small fish dart amongst the submerged forests of seaweed and coral, and marvelled at their colours.

Poor Sister Maria. She was very sweet, very understanding. At Chloris' request, she came everywhere with us. For much of the time she was no more than a shadow following us. It wasn't that either of us set out to be cruel to her: we simply forgot her. When we remembered her we apologised, laughed, called to her to come close; and, for a few minutes, we'd draw her into our conversation. But it didn't last.

It must have been terrible for her. She was watching one of her order going astray; she was watching a friend break all the rules; she was a conspirator in what could be the end for Chloris. When I mentioned this to Chloris she hotly denied it. She wasn't doing anything wrong. There were no rule that said she mustn't talk to men; there was no reason why she shouldn't enjoy my company; she wasn't . . . But she was. The more we talked, the more we understood of each other, the more we found in common, the closer we drew together, the more dangerous her position became. She said, that first afternoon as we walked down the beach together, that she didn't want to talk about what I'd told her, not yet. So we didn't, and she didn't allow that ugly black cloud to spoil the time we had together. Her strength showed in her determination not to allow me to do anything that might compromise her and in the way she set about converting me to Christianity. I begged her not to, but that was simply a challenge. So I let her try, listening to her as she explained about how Jesus had come to save us, how he always knew what we were thinking and doing, and how we could always talk to Him by praying. I lay back, watching her belief soften her face, and enjoyed it: not what she was saying, but watching her.

Just before lunch on the Tuesday, when Chloris went off to the ladies, Maria reached out and gripped my arm, catching and holding my eyes.

'You must not do it,' she said. She had very dark eyes with rather beautiful eyelashes that curled against her cheek, and she didn't blink. I knew exactly what she was talking about.

'I know,' I replied. 'But I can't help it. And she can't help it either.'

'You can do something, Armstrong. You can go away and leave her alone.'

I nodded. Yes, I could. And, if Chloris was prepared to swear that she wouldn't go back to Boromundi, and if the price was that I would never see her again, I'd pay it. I caught at that thought: that I'd pay the price. It was a thought I'd had in a similar context once before, and I remembered the outcome of that terrible failure.

After lunch I tried to persuade Chloris to come in for a swim. She laughed a lot, but refused. It didn't prevent me going in. We were back at their bungalow. I didn't have swimming trunks so, unthinkingly, I stripped to my boxer shorts. I was about to turn to run down to the water when I looked at Chloris. She'd covered her eyes. And Maria – she'd turned away.

I swam. But I felt sick at the thought of how much Chloris – and, probably, little Maria – would have enjoyed the water. I lay on my back and imagined their laughter, and the fun, and – oh, stupid things like how lovely it would have been for them to have their limbs free from that awful material – then looked towards the shore, seeing them sitting on the veranda like two pied crows, watching me.

My return flight was booked for midday on the Wednesday. I had ordered a taxi for nine. I had an early breakfast with the two girls and then I dragged Chloris back to the beach for a last few minutes with her. As we walked, I lectured her. I laid her position on the line. When I'd finished, when I'd told her that I would do anything, anything to dissuade her from going back, I asked her what she was doing.

Her answer came in a typically roundabout way. She started by saying how good Maria had been, how understanding; and how they'd prayed together, so many times – last night, long into the night. And how they'd talked about the circumstances she found herself in. And how . . .

'Chloris,' I interrupted, 'what are you doing?' I was holding her arm, gripping it through the coarse cloth, squeezing it.

She stopped and turned to me, holding me with those startling blue eyes. 'I'm going back, Armstrong. I'm going back because . . .'

I caught her unawares, so violently that she almost fell, but I lifted her and bundled her down to the sea, dragging her out into the water, even though she was struggling and kicking and screaming, wading out through the waves until I dropped her. Then I pushed her head under and held her down, feeling her hands grasp at me, fight me. And all the time I was screaming, 'No, no, no,' because it had never occurred to me that she would decide to go back. I was so stupid and arrogant and ignorant that I'd never bothered to plan what I would do if she did. And now, for want of that thought, I could think of nothing except what I'd originally threatened: that I'd rather drown her myself than risk her.

Perhaps it was because I was thinking. Perhaps it was because my heart wasn't in what I was doing. Perhaps it was simply that, once she'd recovered from the shock, Chloris had begun to fight back. Anyway, I suddenly found my legs kicked away from under me and I fell, disappearing under water, blinded by the sand we'd thrown up in our exertions, tangling myself in Chloris' clothing, struggling to find something through it, an arm, a leg, something to grab hold of. And then she kissed me.

Her face came against mine. I saw it, through the soupy water. And felt her lips, hard against mine. A kiss, and she pushed away from me.

I'm not a great swimmer, and I was in a state of shock. When I came up, coughing, when I'd found my legs, Chloris was wading, like some half-drowned bat, towards the shore. Maria was coming to her, splashing through the water and screaming, throwing her arms round her and throwing me the dirtiest look I've ever seen. And a couple of men, the mini-briefed, muscular, more-brains-in-my-balls-than-between-my-ears tourist sort, were waddling down the beach looking for a fight.

I gave it to them. It was a good fight, slippery in the sand and heavy work because of my sopping clothes, but it lasted a solid three minutes and in that time one of them got a bloody nose and I got knocked down twice.'

The taxi driver didn't want to take me because of my wet and sandy state, but the hotel manager insisted. And there was a little puddle of salt water under my seat in the plane but I'm not sure whether that was sea water or tears.

'She kissed me. I swear she kissed me.'

Temba, sitting on the opposite side of the dining room table, his face as shiny as an under-ripe plum in the harsh light of the tilley lamp, adopted his incredulous look. It's the sort of sour face ordinary human beings make when they're sucking a bitter lime: all wrinkled up. Except that, with Temba already having all his facial features crowded together in one place, it made his face look like the bottom end of those coconuts you knock off a coconut shy.

'She did. I swear . . .'

'What did she do it for, eh, Armstrong? Why would a nun want to kiss you? To get herself into more trouble?'

When I tried to butt in, he waved me down. 'Listen, my friend. Everything she does, she tells her confessor. Everything. And this man gives her a hard time. Okay? Now, that girl is no fool, eh? So . . . She never kissed you. It was an accident, something that happened as she struggled.'

'She kissed me,' I repeated weakly.

'And now she loves you?'

I didn't look up for fear of catching another withering look, which is a tight mouth stretched out and turned down, and the head oscillating very slowly from side to side. Bugger him. She did kiss me. And she does love me.

And, yes, perhaps if she tells her confessor he'll have her
– pray God – sent far, far away.

'Ooooh!' I moaned, folding my arms on the table and
laying my head on them.

'What's wrong with you now?'

I was crying again. Every time I thought of the events
of that morning, the tears of frustration and misery
squeezed out. 'Temba, she can't come back. If she comes
back, if they catch her, I'll die. I'll put the end of that
nice rifle you gave me into my mouth and I'll pull the
fucking trigger. I swear.'

'Okay, okay,' he said, and leaned forward across the
table. 'We do something.'

I looked up at him. 'Promise?'

'Swear. Now, you listen to me. While you're chasing
nuns around the beach, I've been working. I have told
Bartolemew what that hyena M'Simani told us.'

I didn't say anything. I wasn't sure it was the right
thing to do.

'Bartolemew has many friends.' Temba read my
doubts. 'He knows this place. He is not a politician, but
he understands how they work. He has sympathy for us.'
He hesitated. 'Perhaps he will know who we may see.
Perhaps he may advise us.'

'Mm,' I grunted. Bartolemew might be a good starting
point. But surely someone else already knew about this.
These rumours, the whisperings that Alice had described,
surely someone had heard them and investigated.

'Is this Bunrum, returning in disguise?'

Temba shook his head. It was a stupid question. He
wouldn't know the answer any more than I. All we knew
was that some of the people who had been associated

with Bunrum were involved. But this was so much bigger, so much more menacing, because it unleashed forces which, in Africa, were close beneath the surface and easily stirred: dark forces, primaeval forces of ignorance and fear and violence.

'I've been down to Miss Alice's and done my bit there,' he continued.

'You went back?'

'Sure. I took half an hour with Mumbai, but . . .'

I stopped listening. I didn't like the idea of Temba being with Mumbai. I thought we had an unspoken agreement that the girl was mine. Well, not exactly mine, because she probably serviced ten other blokes in any one day but, as far as Temba was concerned, Mumbai was mine and not his. And then I began wondering whether he'd twigged what had been going on with Sizwi, and whether this was his way of getting back at me.

'And Miss Alice says,' Temba continued, 'that there is trouble around Simbilani. She has heard rumours of fighting between government forces and guerrillas, and of the guerrillas winning. The roads up into Northwest district are closed, the government says, because there is foot and mouth problem, traffic restrictions are necessary. But we have foot and mouth everywhere, so why do they treat it differently in Northwest?'

'It's connected?'

Temba shrugged.

'And it isn't being reported in the papers?'

'No, no. There is nothing in the papers. Tomorrow our President, Mr Bugarimani, flies to the USA for talks about aid. This President Clinton, he is promising big money for rebuilding Boromundi. If there is news of trouble, if . . .'

'Did Alice say anything about the scale of the clashes? I mean, is this a major push or are they feeling their way?'

'Miss Alice thinks it is small, this trouble, but it is the beginning. It is like the first drops of rain before the thunderstorm. Around us, the sun still shines, but the sky is darkening over the horizon.'

'No news of the other three targets?'

Temba shook his head. 'No. And this name, Bullet, it means nothing to her.'

'Shit!'

'Now, Bartolemew . . .'

'Bartolemew . . . ?' I repeated.

'Bartolemew is very angry with you. He thinks this Armstrong McKay is some joker, on holiday here in Boromundi, in Tanzania, where next? Even during term time. He is very, very angry . . .'

'Was this before or after you told him . . . ?'

'Before. When I told him about that M'Simani rat and your concerns about a nun, he shut up. After a little thought he decided we did well. And then I described this trouble, this trouble that M'Simani says will come from the Northwest . . .'

'And what did he say?'

'Nothing. You know Bartolemew: he sat and listened until I was quite finished. You know him – these eyes, how they eat you? He watched me all that time.'

I nodded. 'And?'

'Bartolemew is a good man, Armstrong. He is a Christian. When I had finished, when I was silent for a whole minute, he closed his eyes and said, "May God help us".'

'So he believes what M'Simani said was true?'

'Oh yes. He is quite sure it is true.'

I heaved a great sigh of relief. 'So, what do we do?'

'Nothing. We leave it with him. He will talk to certain people he knows. He will not tell them where his information is sourced. He will not mention M'Simani, Tilubu, nothing. He will ask, he will listen, then he will talk to us.'

I went back to teaching the next day, the Thursday. I gave it a day for the dust to settle, then, on the Friday, I plucked up the courage to go and see Bartolemew. I wanted to apologise. But Bartolemew was out of school. There was a meeting of the St Faith's School Board and, since most of the august members of that body lived in Mateka, it was customary for the Head and the School Secretary to travel to them rather than for them to trouble themselves coming out to St Faith's. Bartolemew was driving. On the way back, late on the Friday evening, Bartolemew's Peugeot went off the road. It careered down a steep embankment into the bed of a small river in spate, and was washed half a mile downstream, rolling and banging its way over the rocks. Both the bodies were still in the car when it was found, shortly before midday on the Saturday.

I'm an ant. I'm standing on a shore, on a sandy beach, looking out to sea. The beach is just like the one where I fell in love with Chloris for the second time, with palm trees and a lagoon with patchwork colours of green and blue, and a little hotel where men in white night-shirts serve ice-cold lager and roasted cashews on the beach, but the far-out, constant white line of the reef has disappeared because there's a wave coming, a great, solid, black, concave wall of water running right along the horizon from one end to the other, a tidal wave that's rising, rising. It's coming at us with a gigantic inevitability and it's already so big it'll go straight over the tops of the palm trees behind me. Along its crest the spray whips back, like the teeth of some primaeval carnivore, more and more as the wave lifts and darkens and curls over. There's millions and millions of tons of water in it along with all sorts of rubbish, chairs, bits of house, corrugated iron, and bodies, and its coming at me like an express bulldozer. I'm dead. I have moments to live, then I'm dead.

We buried them, Bartolemew and the secretary who listened to our telephone calls, like we buried beautiful Rebecca. As usual, it rained. After we'd finished, after the hundreds of mourners had paddled off through the mud towards 'tea' in the school hall, I hung back. I went and knelt by Rebecca's grave, not giving a damn that my best trousers got muddy knees, and I squeezed my hands together and twined my fingers tightly and, with the rain running down my nose, I asked Rebecca to listen. I explained that Temba and I had done everything we could but that the forces lining up against us were too much. Any minute, a wave was going to break, and then I'd be seeing her.

I told her about Chloris. I told her I loved Chloris, and I was honest enough to admit that I loved Chloris

even more than I'd loved her. And I'd loved her a lot.
So much that I'd come out to this Godforsaken fucking
dump, and been here four long months, during which
time things had got so serious that I was now killing
people. Three, so far. Shooting them or hitting them with
coshes and cutting their throats or pegging them out for
the ants to nibble. That's how serious it was.

Then I asked for her help. I said that I was quite sure
that she was with God because she'd been such a wonderful girl here on earth that God would want to make
sure he got to know her. And, since He probably made a
point of talking to her, could she please have a word in
His ear about Temba and me. How we were down here,
doing our best, and struggling a bit.

It was getting dark and the rain was even heavier by
the time I'd finished. I stumbled away through the murk,
out of the little churchyard, splashing and slipping my
way along the path towards the school. And then I
stopped. I realised that what I'd just been doing was
praying. I'd done one of the things that Chloris had said
I should do, one of the things she said would help; one
of the ideas I'd mocked.

I stood for quite some time, alone in the darkness and
the deluge, thinking about that. Then I went on to the
Hall. Temba was there, already flying high on millet
beer.

During period three the following day, the new secretary
summoned me from my classroom, taking my arm and
leading me to the school office where she placed the

phone carefully in my hand; with the difference that she then left, closing the door firmly behind her.

'Hello?' I croaked. The phone shook and because of the alcohol and a severe lack of sleep, saying anything hurt.

'It's me.'

I frowned at the phone. 'Who?'

'Chloris!'

'Jesus!'

'No, Chloris. Chloris Humphries.'

'Chloris! Where . . . ?' So many questions tumbled all over the place, banging around in the pain of my brain, unable to find their way out.

'I'm in Mateka. They're not letting me go anywhere.' A pause. I still couldn't get my brain together. 'Listen, I told them. They believed me.' Told them what? Believed what? God! – not that she'd kissed me! 'There's someone . . . he wants to meet you to talk about . . . you know, what you told me. He'll be in Kaserewe, tomorrow, nine o'clock, first thing. He can't come up to the school because they'll recognise him. So . . . Armstrong? Are you there?'

I grunted. The typhoon in my head was concentrating on blowing around fragments of corrugated iron which banged and clattered.

'Is there anywhere you could meet him? Somewhere discreet, you know, where they won't recognise him?'

Chloris. My beautiful Chloris. In Mateka.

'Armstrong?'

'Chloris! I love you!'

'Armstrong!' A pause. 'Somewhere safe.'

So I gave her the address of the only discreet person I

knew in Kaserewe and, before I could say anything else, she hung up. I tried 1471 but it didn't work on the Boromundi system.

Which left me with several conflicting emotions. Relief, joy that Chloris was, at least, relatively safe. And a certainty, from the way she'd reacted when I told her I loved her, that she loved me too. I wanted to shout with joy, with sheer elation – which I didn't, for obvious reasons. The other emotion was panic. I had no idea who 'he', this man who was coming to see me, was. And I didn't know whether Alice would play ball – after all he might be the chief of police. So I rang her. She wasn't happy, going on and on about 'this wasn't a conference centre' but I began thanking her profusely and, at the same time, hung up. Then I made for Bartolemew's door to beg the school truck – and stopped.

I stood in front of the door staring at the 'Headmaster' plaque, shocked at the way I'd forgotten he was dead. Bartolomew, solid, reliable Bartolemew, the Bartolomew we all took for granted, dead. Bartolomew, the man I respected, dead. He hadn't just been part of the scenery, he'd been part of the alliance, one of the few people who knew, a brick we could rely on to understand and help. And he'd gone. He was over in the cemetery lying with Rebecca, sharing worms.

I'd have been standing there for an hour if the secretary hadn't come back in.

I took a taxi down to Kaserewe the next morning and arrived half an hour early. I was early, but he was earlier.

If you can imagine Churchill in his mid-fifties, but charcoal-skinned and about half the great man's size, you've just about got him. He was dressed exceedingly neatly in a very dark, pin-striped suit, white shirt with plain, dark blue silk tie, and black patent leather shoes. Not a hair was out of place. Not a speck of dust showed on his clothing. He'd settled into the chair Temba usually used and Alice had fixed him up with a glass of orange squash. Even so, he looked ill at ease and the two of them seemed to be making heavy weather of their conversation.

Alice, for a change, was in pink. Pink blouse, pink tights, pink mules and pink toenails. The tights were too tight and her belly threatened at any minute to escape over the elastic and much the same could be said about the relationship between her blouse and her bosom. She managed a cough and an, 'Armstrong', before she pressed the buzzer. She didn't look at me. Mumbai came in wearing virtually nothing except a grin and collected the gentleman and me and led us upstairs to a private room. I wanted to ask her how it had been with Temba but refrained, following my visitor into the room. It was a big, square room largely occupied by a king-size double bed which they'd pushed as discreetly as possible to one side and covered with a counterpane. In the centre of the room they'd set up a folding table with two chairs, a decanter of water and two glasses. The windows overlooked the front of the house and had been thrown open to allow a sultry breeze to stir the curtains, but it meant we had to listen to the cars coming and going and occasional snippets of ripe conversation from some of the customers.

My visitor stood for a moment, looking around. Then he turned back to me and extended his hand. It was like holding a bunch of hot cocktail sausages.

'I'm Father Hutumwe.'

'Yes,' I said, because he wasn't. 'I'm Armstrong McKay.' He wasn't Father Hutumwe because I recognised him. One of the things about teaching in a church school is that they leave all sorts of diocesan magazines and other propaganda lying around in the staffroom in the off chance that someone will read them. And I'm a teacher, so I remember faces. The man lowering himself into the chair opposite me, the man who had just been talking to Alice, was called Muteresa, and he was the Archbishop of Boromundi.

I didn't like archbishops. It's not that I had actually met any of them, but I'd seen senior English versions on the telly spouting off about things which they patently knew bugger all about, and I'd seen the Roman Catholic versions clustered round the Pope in Rome, some of them propping the poor old boy up, and I'd been to a confirmation service in which a truly dreadful cousin had one of them lay his hands on her head, which didn't seem to make the slightest difference to her behaviour afterwards. So the poor man started on a bad wicket. It didn't last. By the time we'd finished, I rather respected him.

He started off by explaining the background. Sister Chloris had come back from holiday with a bizarre story, he said, so bizarre that someone had questioned whether she shouldn't be sent home for a bit of rest and recuperation, and that recommendation had arrived on his desk. He'd met Chloris before, several times, and had liked her, so he asked to see her. What she'd told him about this force up in the Northwest had meant nothing to him. He had sent her away, pending a decision. Then, last Friday, his friend Bartolemew Nchanga had drawn him aside during the School Board's lunch break, and told him the same story.

'I did not believe him,' he said. 'He was my friend, and I did not believe . . . This *mooti*, this killing of white women for . . . no, no,' he shook his head. 'In Zaire, perhaps. Uganda – even in Uganda, no. But here – no! Definitely. Then, less than two hours later, my friend is dead.'

At that point he leaned forward across the table, so suddenly he almost upset the decanter. 'Mr McKay, I have contacts in the police. The authorities will say it was a terrible accident, that his car skidded in the rain. But it is not so. His car was stopped by three, perhaps four men. Bartolemew was murdered.'

'He spoke to others at the Board meeting?'

'I do not know.' He paused, then nodded. 'Yes. I think he did.'

'So they may have arranged . . . ?'

He sat back, extracted a large white handkerchief from his pocket and dabbed at the emotion that twitched his face. 'Bartolemew would not tell me the source of his information, so I went to Chloris and asked her.' He paused. 'You must tell me everything, Mr McKay, everything, however long it takes.'

But I was still chasing my thoughts. 'Who killed Bartolemew? You must have some idea.'

'No.' It was said so very definitely I didn't believe him. It would have been difficult for Bartolemew to have drawn someone aside for long enough to describe what we'd told him without others noticing. Which meant that the other person probably knew that the Archbishop knew.

'And Chloris: Chloris is safe?'

He nodded. I waited for him to continue but he didn't. It was as if that particular subject was closed.

There didn't seem to be anything else I could ask so, while he sat in silence, watching my face and doing little else but nod, I told him . . . well, I told him not quite everything, but everything I thought he needed to know.

When I'd finished he asked some questions. I was afraid he'd say something about my being at the Two Turtles, ask about my relationship with Chloris, but he didn't. Then I asked him what he was going to do, and he gave me the sort of reply Chloris would have given: pray.

'Then what?'

'Information. We need to know what is happening.'

I nodded. I hadn't told him that we already had an incredibly efficient listening network in operation.

He began to get up. 'I will talk with you again, I promise.'

I stopped him. 'I need help.'

He didn't say anything, just stood and watched me.

'Those three men . . .'

'Mophas Mandabanga, Onias Matenganesa and one called Bullet.' I was surprised that he had remembered their names, but perhaps he'd done some teaching too.

'I need to find them.'

He held my eyes for a few moments. I couldn't see that he would help us, being as he knew what we'd do if we found them. I mean, Christians have a bit of a thing about betrayal, don't they?

'I will see,' he said. He busied himself putting the chairs straight and arranging the glasses neatly on the

table. He didn't look at me. I concluded that my useful-
ness had ended, that, for all his promises, I probably
wouldn't hear from him again.

I went across to the bed and pressed the bell and,
while we were standing around waiting for Mumbai to
collect us, I added one other thought. I described how,
only the day before yesterday, after we'd buried Bartolemew, I'd stayed behind and knelt by Rebecca's grave,
knelt in the mud and the pouring rain, and asked for
help. And now . . .

Yes, he nodded. Yes, sometimes we ask and help
comes. But then, sometimes it doesn't.

I liked his honesty.

After that, nothing happened for weeks. Absolute silence.
Silence from Chloris, though I made desperate enquiries
to find out where she was. Silence down at Alice's, except
for Mumbai's little trills of pleasure and her gurgling
assurances that I was much, much better than Temba.
Silence from the Archbishop. Silence between Temba and
I as we flogged ourselves to death training in the forest.
Silence from the Northwest – they even raised the foot
and mouth restrictions. Silence, settling like fog across a
landscape. Silence, except from *Kisasi*, I heard him sing
twice, very insistently, in the forest by Temba's house.

As the term dragged to an end I asked Temba what
plans he had for the two-week Easter holiday. He was
uncharacteristically vague. He might go to his village for
a few days. There was a chance he would have to go

away – there was a friend he needed to see. Mostly he would stay here.

The reasons for his evasiveness became apparent two days before the end of term. Teachers go along to the school office for all sorts of reasons: to pick up the register; to arrange an interview with the Head; to use the phone; to collect a form; to borrow a pencil; and to chat with the secretary. A lot of us began going along for the last reason.

At this point I have the pleasure of describing the new school secretary in some detail. She was a remarkably tall girl, just on six foot, with a body like a figure in a Lowry painting, skin the colour of Californian sun-dried sultanas, a dark-lipped, mobile mouth that ran right across a rectangular face, and a mouth that broke into the most brilliant, toothpaste smile I've ever seen, but the greatest joy was in watching Josephine walk. She walked like a model. Models are usually quite pretty, if horribly skinny, but I don't like the way they walk because it always seems so artificial, so stilted – but Josephine was utterly natural: hips slightly forward, body very erect so her small breasts poked at whatever she was wearing, and a bum that waggled with pure allure – she seemed to flow with a leopard-like languor. Whenever I went in to see her, which was as often as possible, I asked for something I knew was on the other side of the room, or in the head's office, then stood back and watched the show. She was lovely. And she had the personality to go with it: generosity, warmth, humour. Nice girl, I used to think as I left the office.

That next to last day of term I barged into her office

without knocking. It's polite to knock. Usually I do knock. This time I was in a hurry and simply forgot. Temba was there. They weren't doing anything. Josephine was sitting at her computer, very upright, her long fingers parked on the keyboard, while Temba stood to her right, his bulk leaning forward slightly, his hands resting on the edge of her desk. There was nothing unusual, nothing remarkable in the scene, except her face. She was looking up at him and there was something in the wide, open-ness of her eyes and the slight parting of her lips that told me everything.

Temba turned to me. His face was, as usual, quite expressionless. As I asked for some of the school's headed notepaper he left the office. That evening, as we sat working at either end of the dining room table, Temba marking books and me finishing reports, I said, for an opener, 'Nice girl.'

He was writing a comment in an exercise book, using a red biro. The biro stopped in the middle of a word.

'Josephine,' I said, to help him.

He nodded, and the biro began moving again.

'She likes you,' I prompted.

The biro stopped again and, very carefully, he put it down, closed the book, smoothed the cover, and added it to the 'out' pile. Then he carefully selected the next book.

'If you're not interested . . .' I began.

His fist hit the table with explosive force. I shot about six inches into the air and Temba's neat pile of exercise books collapsed, sliding across the table and falling in an untidy flutter to the floor.

'Jesus!' I said.

Temba shoved his chair back so hard it shot across the room, caught on the rug and fell over. He stood for a moment, his whole frame quivering, then turned on his heel and disappeared in the direction of the kitchen. I waited, expecting, perhaps hoping to hear the back door slam. Instead he came back, carrying two bottles of beer one of which he slammed onto the table in front of me, the froth rising suddenly, pouring down its neck to drench the reports remaining on the table. Then he leaned over and poked his face at me, his broad nose stopping an inch from mine.

'Listen, flatulent one,' he hissed. 'For two minutes you shut your anus and open your ears. Okay?'

I nodded, dumbly. I'd never seen anything like this.

He hesitated. Then he turned, collected his chair, and brought it back to the table, sitting on it the wrong way round, so his arms resting on its back. He settled himself, fixing me with those black, impenetrable eyes.

'My father has said that I must marry again. Okay? He said that time is short, that there is too much uncertainty. I need children. He needs grandchildren. When we were at my home, at Christmas time, he told me he had asked the matchmaker to find me a new wife.'

'The matchmaker?'

For a moment I thought he was going to hit me. He regained control, but the next words were strangled. 'Yes. The matchmaker. She is a woman of our clan. It is her task to know the people so, when one of them is ready, she may arrange a marriage.' He paused, as if daring me to butt in again, then continued. 'I respect my father. It would be easy to follow my father's wishes and take a wife from the tribe. She would be a bush girl. She would be happy to stay in my village as long as I gave her many children and even more goats. What I do while I am away working is not her concern.' He paused. 'But I would not love her.'

Not like you loved Annabel, I thought to myself. But I kept the comment buttoned up.

'The matchmaker has already found her. It is not customary for a man to see his future wife. His mother will see her, many of his relatives may see her. If the family approves, the marriage will take place. Even though my father had made this arrangement, I refused. He was angry. He shouted. He threatened. Finally he said to me, "Okay – so you find yourself a wife. But you do it quick!"'

'And you have?'

Again, he controlled himself. 'Perhaps.' He hesitated, then took a pull at his beer. 'But this is the question. I could go to Father Chitembe and ask him to marry us. I could do it as you do it in England. But, because both my parents and her parents are still living in the country, because they are not city people, it will hurt them.' He paused. 'You must understand, Armstrong, that here we have no Social Security. When a man is old, the system must still support him. So girl children are valuable, for they are sold into marriage. A man, such as myself, must earn enough to buy his wife. My family may help me. In the old days the payment was in cows, in grain, in honey and beer, in weapons and copper, in cloth and beads. These days it is mostly cash. In the bush, it is a good system. It also ensures that the husbands have made their way in life before they have children.'

It sounded the sort of system I should introduce in England, but I said, 'So you bought Annabel?'

I tensed myself expectantly, but he nodded. 'Yes.'

'How much did she cost?'

He shook his head and sighed. 'You are rude as well as flatulent, Armstrong. That is a question that only an ignorant, uncivilised foreigner would ask. But I will tell you. Almost half a year's salary.'

'Blimey!'

'Returnable.'

I stared at him.

'If she is no good, if she makes no children, if she is a witch, I may return her and receive my money back. Further, it is customary for the arrangement to be . . .' and he frowned, 'hire purchase?'

'Buy now, pay later?'

'Yes. A deposit is placed. I live with the woman. If she is satisfactory, more money is paid. When she has children, the final payment is made.'

'And if she isn't satisfactory, the money has to be returned?' I'm not thick: as I asked the question I was thinking about Sizwi.

He was silent for a few moments. 'If I ask him, my father will carry out the negotiations for Josephine. Because her home is far from mine, it will take many weeks. And, while my father drinks beer with her father, while they talk of crops and cattle, while my father complains that she is too thin, too tall, too dark and too expensive, while my village gossips, while my sisters laugh, I will wait. Out of respect for my father, I will wait. But,' and he leaned forward suddenly at me, 'should I do it? Is it right that I should draw this girl into my problems?' Before I could ask the question that jumped into my head he lifted a hand. 'No, I have told her nothing. I have not mentioned my feelings for her. She does not know that you and I go out with guns to hunt men. All that has happened is that her eyes tell me everything. Now, what would you do, oh man with his mouth in his pants? Would you marry her according to tradition? Would you marry her the English way? Would you spare her the pain of what we go through and marry the bush girl? Or would you hurt my father and take neither? Eh?'

'Jesus,' I said.

'Ah, Armstrong, for you, it is so easy. You have Chloris. You cling to Chloris as a dream. She is unattainable, so she is safe. You have sex with her in your head while Mumbai satisfies your body. Your total commitment is zero. When this is finished, when five men are dead, you will forget Chloris and you will leave Mumbai without even saying farewell and you will go back to England to find a nice, white girl to bear you 2.1 children. But I, I will stay here. I will make my life here. And life does not wait.'

I sat and stared at him.

'So . . . Armstrong?'

'You must marry Josephine.'

The trouble is that the answer didn't come from me. It came from a tall lady who stood framed in the doorway, a lady who advanced on us like a leopard, who stood over us with her hands pressed against her hips. For a moment I thought she was going to clip us over our earholes, like two naughty schoolboys, but she didn't.

Instead, very quietly, she told us that there had been an urgent telephone call from a woman who had tried to disguise her identity but who had failed, someone she knew ran a business down in Kaserewe. We were needed, both of us, urgently, at a place called Chirwe on the shores of Lake Kenge, where we had to meet two businessmen, two half-brothers. They were there, now, but might move on at any time. To contact them we needed to go to the Lake Hotel in the town centre and ask for a lady called Florentine.

Then she paused. By that time I'd swivelled round enough to be able to look up into Josephine's face. I have never seen such pain in a girl's eyes. Mostly, I suppose, it was because she'd caught us talking about her, making decisions like you'd decide which cut of beef you wanted from a butcher. But she must also have overheard Temba's reference to killing five men. I had no idea what she might have made of that.

Temba recovered first. He was about to say something when the girl stopped him by raising her hand.

'Do not say it,' she said, and her eyes pinned him to his chair. 'Later, Temba, you and I, we talk. Okay?'

The man nodded.

'Alice says you have little time. I told her that the school truck is in Mateka for a service. She has a car, one which you may take. If you wish, I will call for a taxi to carry you to Kaserewe.'

'Yes,' Temba croaked, and cleared his throat. 'Yes, if you will, please.'

12   To Chirwe & Lake Kenge

I suppose I should have guessed the colour of Alice's car. This was the car for which a carport was being built round the back when some of the rag-tag Bunrum army made the mistake of visiting her establishment towards the end of the second civil war. It was a twenty-year old Ford Mustang in A1 condition – bar the paint job, which was messy. When we saw it, in the late afternoon of the Thursday, it was the last car that Temba and I wanted to borrow. For a start, it was so unique that anyone seeing it would immediately know where it had come from. And, since it was obviously Alice's pride and joy, we were terrified of bending it. So – we would hire a car. No, no, Alice insisted. No! There is no time. Take it, take it! In any case – it is all arranged! I'm glad we did. It went like a shit out of a cheetah's arse and it seemed to have a quite magical effect on the police roadblocks, which let us through with broad smiles and knowing winks.

We reached Chirwe on the shores of Lake Kenge shortly after eight in the evening. It had grown as a resort town, a place in which, in colonial times, the whites – civil servants, better-off merchants and armed service personnel – holidayed with their families on 'local leave'. Like all African towns, it was now almost strangled by a noose of shanties, but the old resort centre remained remarkably unchanged. It was strung out along the lake shore and in many ways resembled a decayed and shrunken version of an English seaside town: Eastbourne, Weston-super-Mare, Scarborough. Behind a muddy, litter-strewn beach the concrete promenade boasted bandstand and wrought-iron lamp-posts, public benches and metal bollards. But, if the iron rusted gently in the equatorial rain, the scene was enlivened by brilliant colours from flame trees, jacarandas and beds of bright yellow marigolds. On the shore side of a wide, lazy, lakeside road, we found the Lake Hotel, part of a line of hotels, boarding houses and restaurants that faced Lake Kenge. Parking was easy, and Temba left Alice's Pink Peril in a prominent position where it could be admired by the locals and was least likely to be vandalised or broken into.

For all its peeling paint and faded curtains, the Lake Hotel exuded class. We booked in to a large twin room on the first floor, with wooden, shuttered doors which opened out onto a veranda with a magnificent view across the lake. I was immediately dispatched downstairs to ask about Florentine while Temba made himself comfortable in the bath. Temba in a bath is quite a sight. His body occupies most of its volume, leaving little space for water, which therefore gets cold quickly and needs frequent changing. But it's the magnificent contrast between his skin and the smooth white enamel that is most remarkable. Anyway, downstairs I approached a thin faced, severely dressed lady in reception.

'Hello,' I said brightly.

She concentrated on shuffling papers on her desk but managed a clipped, 'Good evening.'

'Er,' I began, 'I'm looking for . . .'

'She is coming.'

I stared at her.

'Florentine. She is coming.'

'Oh.'

She glanced at her watch. 'She will join you in half an hour, for dinner. In the meanwhile . . .' Her wave towards the cocktail lounge indicated quite clearly that she was dismissing me.

Florentine was late. At first Temba and I managed to be relaxed about it, enjoying our gins in the low-light, mahogany-panelled cosiness of the bar. When she was half an hour overdue, I began going through to reception to ask when and whether she would come. 'Soon come, soon come,' I was told, with a frown that suggested I was asking a daft question. When we'd waited over an hour we gave up and went through to the dining room. We had just settled, were about to place our orders, when she arrived. She and Mirianna.

For some reason, I had expected Chirwe's equivalent of Alice. Perhaps, having seen Chirwe, she would be old, white and heavily made up, a faded flower left over from the town's glory days. Temba, so he told me later, had expected a 'fat, black woman'. What threaded its way through the tables, what silenced a full dining room, what minced towards us were Boromundi's answers to Marilyn Munro and Eartha Kitt.

Florentine and Mirianna were both in their late twenties and both about five foot six with near perfect figures, but there the resemblance ended. While the powder-puff white of Florentine's skin contrasted gloriously with skin-tight black pedal-pushers and a dinky halter-neck top

knotted under the bust for quick release, Mirianna's skin
was blacker even than Temba's, so black it was as if
her body were some sort of astronomical black hole in
which light and even matter itself ceased to exist. She
had done her hair in a spectacular Afro, she wore a gold
micro skirt with sequins, and the matching vest in silver
struggled to contain the wobbly magnificence of her
breasts.

Florentine came first, teetering on high heels, extend-
ing a limp hand as she reached our table. 'Armstrong,'
she laughed, 'Cherie! It is so, so good to see you again.'
She had an oval face, eyes that were somewhere between
lilac and blue, and corn-coloured hair that fell in twisted
ringlets all the way down her back to her waist; and she
closed her eyes and puckered her lips into a kiss, folding
them out to display nicotine-stained teeth.

What do you do in such circumstances? Me – I'd had
enough gins to join in the fun. I threw my arms round
the girl, crushed her to me with enough energy to crack
her ribs, and stuck my tongue down her throat. She
hadn't been expecting it.

Give Florentine her due: when she came up for breath
she was still laughing. I glanced at Temba. He was
holding Mirianna off her feet, making a great show of
being pleased to see her, but keeping a good Bible's
thickness between them. A rigid smile was pasted across
his face and the whites of his eyes showed like some
terrified horse.

Florentine turned and surveyed the gawping faces.
With a flick of her hand she dismissed the people and
the place. 'We do not eat here,' she announced in what
I took to be a French accent, turned on her heel and led

us back through the tables. I walked immediately behind her, grinning and watching the way the low-slung cheeks of her bum swung as she strutted towards the entrance. But, once through the foyer, once out into the darkened street, she changed. She grabbed my hand and led us quickly towards the Pink Peril.

'You did ver' well,' she said.

'It was a bit unexpected.'

'But it is normal. Alice, she send us the customers. Many come often.' She was organising us into the Pink Peril, sitting next to Temba in the front and putting Mirianna in the back with me. 'They come for some days – you understand? – to relax, to have a good time.' We were moving out of the hotel entrance and, on Florentine's instruction, turning right, northwards, along the front, when she twisted round in her seat so she could see me.

'So,' she said, and her tone was businesslike. 'Now you have your alibi. Mirianna and I, we will cook supper. Everyone thinks you will spend your night with us. Then, at two, three in the morning, we will return to the hotel, very drunk, very noisy. *Bien?*'

I nodded. 'Good. So, where are they?' It was difficult to be as businesslike as Florentine: in the darkness Mirianna's right hand was like a small mouse, gently exploring exciting places.

'I will explain.' Florentine turned to Temba and indicated that he should fork left into a tree-lined avenue, leaving the main road which had suddenly veered inland from the lake. 'They have been here for two days.' She paused. 'I do not know your business with these men, but . . .' and she laughed quickly, 'these are not men I wish to spend time with.' She twisted back to me. 'There is already one girl here in the town who is hurt.'

'Who did it? The younger one?'

'Yes. That is how we know of them. He was with her and her hand found that he is only, how do you say, half hung? Perhaps she holds his precious jewel for a moment too long. Perhaps she squeeze it.' I felt, rather than saw, her shrug.

'What are they doing here?'

'I do not know. Ver' little. They are spending time in the bars. When they are drunk they are talking ver' loudly. They are angry at the government, they say the taxes are too high, the prices are too high, the wages are too low, and the country it is ruined.' She paused, then dropped her voice. 'You are police? CID?'

'What gave you that idea?'

'Alice. She says that you are ver' important.'

I laughed. 'No.' For a moment I was tempted to tell the girl why we were here. 'No. It's a personal matter. Money.'

She nodded and turned away from me. To our left, through gaps between the trees, I could see that we were still travelling parallel to the lake shore. Florentine hissed, and, on her direction, Temba slowed and swung left into the entrance to a drive. We stopped facing wrought-iron gates, leaving the engine running until a small man appeared who, after a great deal of clattering with a heavy chain and padlock, managed to open them. We finally drew up in front of a large bungalow with a low-pitched, corrugated iron roof, set well back from the road. Temba parked the car in the dense shadow of a mango tree, switched off the engine and eased himself back into his seat.

The night was moonless and, beyond the dark foliage above us, the stars pointedly bright.

'You wish to come in?' Florentine asked.

'No.' It was Temba who answered, his voice a growl. Mirianna's hand suddenly stopped moving. 'Where are they?'

A lighter clicked and Florentine's face was caught in the flame's glow as she lit a cigarette. She sat back, drew deeply, and exhaled slowly. Temba wound his window down and turned away from her.

'They are at Upure-Maje. This is a village, not three kilometres from here, along the lake shore, that way,' and she waved to the north. 'The main road, if it is followed, will take you to it. The road moves from this lake, then it crosses a hill, then it falls to a river. There is a bridge. Then you reach Upure-Maje.'

'Can we get to it by foot from here?'

'If you wish. You may pass through this garden to the lake shore, turn right and walk. There is only one difficulty. Before you will attain Upure-Maje there is the river. It may only be crossed by the road bridge.' She stopped and dragged at her cigarette, lighting Temba's face in a ruddy glow.

'How wide?'

She shrugged. 'Fifty metres? But, with the rains, it runs strong.'

'So we must go by car,' Temba said.

'No.' Florentine shook her head. 'No. I also have a

boat, a rowing boat, on the shore. You may reach the place easily using this boat.'

I thought about that. It sounded a good idea, with the night moonless and the lake very still.

'The house, where they're staying, it's by the shore?' I asked.

'No. There is a petrol station which backs to the shore. You will see it easily because it has a light, high – a floodlight. Yes? Their house is on the other side of the road, facing the petrol station, a house with yellow paint.'

'What sort of house is it?' I asked.

'It is small, a bungalow. It is run by a woman called Umbempa. It is like a small hotel.'

'How many rooms?'

'For guests, three. With Umbempa and her daughter, there will be seven or eight people. The room for your men is at the back, to the right. There is a back door, but the men pass in and out through the front.'

'They won't be there now,' Temba said.

'No. They will be in the bars. But tonight, Thursday, it is quieter, so they will return early, perhaps midnight.' She paused. 'You know what they look like?'

'The older is the taller,' Temba said, 'a black man with a scarred face. The other is short, poorly fed, eighteen, nineteen?'

'Yes. He has a limp.'

I watched Temba as he nodded. Then he turned back to me. 'Armstrong?'

'I like the idea of the boat.'

'It is on the shore,' Florentine said. 'There are oars. You have rowed?'

'Yes.' I waited for Temba to say something, but he didn't, so I said, 'It's okay by me.' I had a fair idea now of how we could do it. I pushed my hand forward and found Florentine's bare shoulder, and squeezed it quickly. Mirianna was already climbing out of the car but I reached out and caught her hand, pulling her back. 'We won't be long,' I said.

Mirianna's face came into the car and, after a couple of tries, her lips found mine.

Shortly after we left the shore a film of low, mucky cloud, lit on the underside by the town's lights, drifted across the sky, obscuring the stars. The wind dropped and the night grew warm and heavy. Sheet-lightning weather, I thought. And it'll rain again soon.

The boat, a twelve foot, clinker-built rowing boat, slipped through the still, Coca-Cola dark waters of the lake. If I turned and looked across the bow, I could see the lights of Upure-Maje drawn out in long, zig-zagging reflections towards us. It was very quiet as we worked our way along the shore, keeping about a quarter of a mile out, the only sound the distant bump of music from the lake-side clubs, the ripple and suck of wavelets along the side of the boat and the swirl of the oars as I dug them into the water and laid my weight into them. Temba sat in the sternthwarts, silent, leaning slightly forward, his hands gripping the sides of the boat – from which I guessed he didn't like boats.

After half an hour we turned to approach the shore. Over my left shoulder I could see the petrol station with its single, high yellow floodlight. Each time I looked I tried to find people, dark shapes moving through the patterns of light and darkness. I had a dread that, as we approached the shore, we would be hailed by some cheery man who would offer to catch our painter. But there was no sign of anyone, no movement except the occasional headlights travelling soundlessly along the road, the cars' progress lost behind the bump-bump of music.

The beach came at us suddenly. I had time to whisper, 'Temba,' before the keel ground onto shingle. As I shipped the oars he was past me, wading quickly ashore and disappearing into the shadows at the back of the petrol station. I vaulted over the side and, having pulled the boat up onto the beach, found my rifle and rucksack and followed him, stopping when I reached a low bush.

Two petrol pumps stood like lonely sentries in the centre of a largely empty lot. It had been separated from the beach by a steel mesh fence on a frame of angle iron but several of the uprights had collapsed and now leaned at drunken angles, and, in places, the rusting fence had been peeled back. To the left of the pumps stood a corrugated iron shed – presumably the office – on my side of which were parked two car wrecks and a Bedford tow truck. The floodlight was perched at the top of a steel pole which projected up from the hut, a single bulb with a shade like an upturned, white enamel soup-dish. Pools of standing water reflected the lights from the line of low buildings on the opposite side of the road.

There was no sign of Temba. He would have gone either to the left or right of the petrol station, crossed the road, then made his way round behind the targets' house.

His first job was to see if they were home. We didn't expect them to be. If they were, he would signal for me to join him.

But I needed to be closer so I stood, arranged the Galil across my shoulder so that it hung from its strap and pointed down my back, forced my way through the wire and walked across the lighted area of the lot. I didn't hurry. If anyone saw me they would think I was returning from relieving myself.

I went round to the front of the office and checked the door. An impressively large padlock secured it. The front of the building lay in a wedge of shadow so I squatted against the corrugated iron wall, looking out across the road. The yellow house was exactly as Florentine had described it, its door forty yards away, behind the low concrete wall that separated its front yard from the road. The street, the petrol station lot, the yards of the houses – all were deserted.

In the next half hour nothing happened. Three cars passed and one man walked down the street. He was drunk and concentrating too hard on avoiding the water-filled potholes to notice me. My only worry concerned a dog, an emaciated, dung brown animal the size of a small collie with a tail which curled almost over to touch his back. He appeared round the end of the petrol station office, walked briskly to the pumps, lifted his leg and peed onto the hose of the unleaded pump, sniffed around the diesel, then walked straight across to me. It was as if he'd known I was there all the time and wanted to show off what he could do. I didn't move. He stood and inspected me, his head on one side. His curiosity satisfied, he continued his journey towards the road, stopping on the concrete screed in front of the pumps, sitting suddenly, lifting his back legs so his bum came in contact with the concrete and pulling himself forward with his front legs so it scraped across the ground. I've seen dogs do it on grass: the poor bastard must have had terrible worms.

Nothing else happened, not even inside me: approaching M'Simani's kopje I'd had to fight to stop shitting myself. This time, nothing. I was terribly exposed, squatting in full view in front of the shed with a rifle in my lap, but it didn't seem to bother me. Okay, I felt tight inside, like you do just before a needle football match. But that was all.

The traffic increased around midnight, more pedestrians and more cars and one bloke on a very unsteady bicycle. None of them came into the lot; none of them worried me; and none of them approached the yellow house. I was beginning to think we were in for a very long night when a couple appeared, walking from my right, along the far side of the road.

The man was about six foot, dressed in a pale, short-sleeved cotton shirt and jeans. He was drunk, not badly drunk, but unsteady enough to feel he needed to drape himself across the girl's shoulders. She was tubby, and the short skirt of her dress had ridden up to reveal fleshy thighs. A strong girl, but she had the greatest difficulty steering him. They stopped outside the yellow house. The girl tried to struggle free of him but he held her. I could hear his voice, the tone alternating between slurred anger and pleading, but I couldn't distinguish the words. He was obviously urging her to come in with him. The girl hesitated, then answered him sharply, still struggling to free herself.

He certainly wasn't Onias Matanganesa. He might be Mophas Mandabanga. He was far too far away, in a street of half-light and heavy shadows, for me to be able to see his face, to see if it was damaged. I could do nothing except watch, my heart bumping in my chest, and wait for Temba to move. When he wanted me, he would signal. I sat, motionless, as the couple argued.

The man won. Suddenly he took the girl's arm and led her into the house. I tensed, gripping the Galil. If this was Mophas, Temba would call me now.

The crickets in the bushes at the back of the lot screamed as tightly as my nerves. I waited.

It couldn't have been Mophas. He was the right height for Mophas but too heavily built. Temba and I had already agreed that, if the two came separately, we wouldn't be greedy: we'd take the bird in the hand. We'd take one, worry about him first, and pick up the second if we could. So it couldn't be Mophas. Not unless something had happened to Temba.

Not knowing is bad. I don't mind trouble so much if I know what's going on, even if it's serious trouble. Not knowing, being in the dark – that's what I can't take.

Temba: was he all right? Why hadn't he called me across? Had they caught him? Were they, at this moment, pulling his toenails out, one by one? I became more and more wound up.

More people and cars passed. I kept saying to myself, 'Give it another five, Armstrong, then you'd better go across, see what Temba's up to.' But, by the time the five was up, I'd convinced myself I had to stick to our plan, that moving might give the game away. So I said it again: 'I'll give it another five . . .'

A group of men came along the road, again from the right. There were five of them walking in the centre of the road, none of them talking. When I saw that one of them was much shorter than the other four I was absolutely certain, from the way he favoured his right leg, that this was Onias Matanganesa. And there was a good chance that one of the other four was Mophas.

They walked diagonally across to, and through, the gate in front of the yellow house. One of the taller men hung back at the front door, allowed the others to enter, then leaned against the house wall and lit a cigarette.

I couldn't move. Although I was in shadow, as his eyes became used to the dark he might see me. And, from the position he was in, he might prevent Temba from signalling.

The street fell silent. Nothing moved. After an age the man walked to the corner of the garden nearest me, facing me. For a moment I thought he had seen me, and I clutched the Galil tightly until I heard the sound of water hissing against the wall.

'Come on Temba,' I whispered to myself, 'Come on, come on. Take him. Take him now.' I couldn't stand much more of this.

The door opened and the girl emerged. She saw the man and hesitated. He zipped himself up and walked across to her. They spoke together for a moment and she began shaking her head. But, the more she shook her head, the louder she giggled. Suddenly she moved, leading the man into the darkness round the far side of the house.

The muscles along the backs of my legs hurt. I'd been squatting, African fashion, for almost two hours. Carefully, I extricated each leg in turn from under me and stretched it out. The muscles screamed as I eased them. All the time, I watched the corner of the house.

The girl reappeared, pulling her skirt down. She stopped for a moment by the front gate to brush at the back of her blouse. Then she looked up and down the street before setting off to my right, back the way she had come.

The man did not reappear. The stillness, the silence, the eerie light and the way it created dense shadows in which a hundred men could conceal themselves – all were beginning to drive me crackers. I again began to think I'd have to go and find Temba, that he must have got lost. For the hundredth time I checked that the lever on the Galil was selected for automatic. I moved and felt for the knife in its sheath at my right hip. I checked the bulge of the lead cosh in my pocket. Where the fuck was Temba?

I don't know how long he'd been standing at the corner of the house. I hadn't been looking for him there because that's where the man had taken the girl. He was beckoning me.

I sprinted across the garage forecourt, zigzagging between the puddles. I didn't wait to see if anyone was coming down the road but, half way across, when I looked, it was deserted. As I dodged through the gate into the yard, Temba turned and dived in through the front door and I followed, almost tripping on his heels. A single bare, low-watt bulb lit a passageway which ran straight from the front of the house to the back. It was empty. Just inside, doors led off either side; then there were two more doors near the far end; and a back door, facing us.

Temba darted down to the end of the passageway, moving fast but silently and, without waiting, lifted his foot and smashed it against the door on the right. The door sprang back in a splintering of wood, hit the wall with a terrible whack and rebounded. I was right behind him as he went through but he stopped and I couldn't see anything except that the room's ceiling light was on. There were two shots. They were very close together and the sound, in the confines of the room, was ear-splitting.

Temba's bulk still blocked the doorway. But it was enough: he was standing, so the shots had been his. I could leave him to it. I turned, my back towards him, my rifle up, glanced back along the passage and, when I was sure it was still clear, stepped to the back door, seized the handle and threw it open. It let out onto a small garden full of shadows, very dark, with odd corners lit by patches of light from the street. Nothing moved. Behind me I heard Temba's voice, his words sharp, controlled, like razors.

I stood for what felt like an age in that back door, watching, waiting, until behind me, there came a heavy bump, as if Temba was moving a sack of potatoes. Then another.

I wanted to look. I wanted to turn and follow Temba into the room to see what had happened. But I didn't. I ducked out through the back door to stand at the edge of an unkempt garden, looking right and left, again seeing nothing; then I swivelled round to check the passage. There were other people in this house and they would have been woken by the explosion of those gunshots. But they didn't show. The other three doors remained firmly closed. Then he called me.

He stood in the entrance to the room holding what looked like the body of a child. It was very limp, floppy, more like a doll, with the legs and arms tied and the head lolling from side to side. I turned my back and Temba draped him across my shoulders. As soon as I'd settled his weight and secured a firm grip on his legs and arms, so that I held him in what approximated to a fireman's lift, I made for the front door.

It was still open. I stopped for a minute to check the road. Everybody in the street must have heard those shots, yet it appeared empty. The only change was that it was coming on to rain, Boromundi-style, a growing, steady, vertical downpour, as if a thousand giant taps were being turned on, the bullet-sized drops hammering the ground. And then I was out, fighting my way down the path to the gate, accelerating through the gap and across the road.

Onias wasn't heavy. He was more awkward, a deadweight, and I was trying to carry him on top of my rucksack while holding the rifle in a position where I could use it if I needed to. I staggered across the road. In trying to look around me, I missed the potholes and kept tripping in them, splashing and losing my balance and plunging forward under his weight. I was conscious all the time that, if others of his group were in neighbouring houses, they would be watching me, might be lining the sights of their AK47s on me; that, at any moment, I might feel the tearing impact of a bullet.

I headed for the fence running down the left of the petrol station lot, out of the main light. Onias became heavier and heavier with each step, his weight shifting, like dead meat. My breath came in increasingly short, painful gasps and my vision seemed to contract into a tight grey tunnel. Twice I had to stop to heave him higher on my shoulders. The second time, the Galil slipped out of my fingers, falling into a puddle. Cursing, retrieving it, I felt the first cramp of fear – fear and a mixture of anger and frustration.

Then Temba overtook me. He had Mophas on his back and he was going like a steam locomotive. My weakness, his strength, sparked a rage in me that sent me charging after him, swearing and spitting curses through the rainwater that ran down my face and into my mouth. I fell through the fence and cut diagonally across the beach, slipping over the wet pebbles until I reached the boat. Mophas lay in the bilges, a dark, formless shape. I dropped Onias, none too gently, on top of him.

I stood away from the boat, my chest banded with pain. Temba leaned forward, his hands on his knees, catching his breath. Then he stood and punched the air with his fist.

'*Bwishu*!' he shouted, his fist slamming upwards into the downpour. '*Bwishu*, Armstrong! *Bwishu*! *Bwishu*!'

Victory! Perhaps. But I wasn't celebrating. I was at the bow, leaning against it to push the boat out, running as it slid away. As I jumped in I heard, behind us, back in the street, the first shouts of pursuit.

13 Mophas Mandabanga & Onias Matanganesa

Mophas and Onias were cousins, not half-brothers, the confusion arising because Mophas' mother, Jumaya, brought Onias up. Their mothers were sisters, Jumaya being almost ten years older than Kika.

At the age of seventeen, after a village upbringing, Jumaya was married off to a much older man, Sindisweyo Sosonye Mandabanga, a rich man who lived in a neighbouring village. She was his fourth wife and her wide hips and generous breasts, so much favoured by local men, made him very happy. Jumaya was happy too because, almost immediately, she fell pregnant, the old man having been unable, in the previous eight years, to attain such a feat with any of his other three wives. Sister wives very often get on well together – after all, they have a common object for their humour – but Jumaya's successful pregnancy and the increasing infatuation shown by the husband brewed jealousy and whispering. The baby, so one murmur went, wasn't the old man's: she'd brought it with her.

Things began to fall apart for the young mother when, while cooking the old man's meal, she dropped three-month old Mophas into the fire. It sounds such a crass thing to do, but it is a common occurrence when babies are carried everywhere by their mothers and the cooking is done over an open fire. The swatch of cotton cloth that held him to her breast suddenly came undone. The child fell. He was snatched from the coals, but the damage to the boy's face was severe. In their remote location no modern medical aid was available, so he was treated by the senior wife with a traditional salve. Mophas screamed through weeks of agony. That he survived was testament to Jumaya's love and care for her sadly disfigured baby.

A month later the old man died in Jumaya's bed. He shouldn't have been there – the rites of their tribe gave a new mother six moons' respite before the husband could return to her. The poor old goat probably had a heart attack. With what had happened to Mophas and his father, and with the series of events that followed – the failure of the rains, a sickness in the cattle and, worse, a severe mauling of the senior wife's youngest son by a hyena – the village turned against the girl. In the normal way, the dead husband's brother would have taken responsibility for his widows. Understandably, he refused to take on Jumaya. Worse, the whispering began to coalesce into an accusation: Jumaya was a witch.

A *nyanga*, a doctor, was summoned to the village to see if she could smell out the witch that brought them such misfortune. The old woman was dressed in a stained cow-hide skirt with monkey tails hanging from her belt, a leopard-tooth necklace, and cowries tied to her ankles. A small leather pouch filled with her grotesque medicines hung round her neck and bounced between her wizened, pendulous dugs. To prepare herself for the ceremony, amongst other things, by smearing herself with a mixture of ash and fat, she retired to a hut – where, of course, it was easy for someone to tip the old crone off. Predictably, therefore, after hours of dancing, screaming, frothing and seizures, she struck poor Jumaya in the face with a cow-tail fly whisk dunked in a mixture of urine and cockerel's blood. The crowd cornered the wretched woman in her hut. After a short, vicious fight she was dragged out and severely beaten before having medicines, prescribed by the *nyanga*, forced down her throat. Jumaya was a big, sturdy peasant girl, used to hardship, but there was a limit to what she could take. In desperation, and in the face of antagonism from her family who feared they would have to repay the bride price, she fled to Mateka.

A country girl, ignorant even of electricity, she stood little chance of worthwhile employment, but an accident, involving a dog, a bicycle and a young Mrs Standish, won her a position as a menial domestic in a European household. She proved to be a good worker, she was quick to learn, the wages were fair, and she was well treated. After a few months in the household she was unrecognisable: clean, smartly turned out and confident. When Mrs Standish had her first baby, Jumaya was promoted to the position of *ayah*, or nanny. She was given a uniform, a starched white dress and white plimsolls, and she was expected to work from seven in the morning until eight at night, six days a week, with an afternoon off on Wednesday. The girl couldn't believe this was happening to her: the money was generous by Boromundi standards and she loved the baby, a gurgling child called Mary. Her employers trusted her enough for Mrs Standish to return to her work as a secretary, leaving

Jumaya alone to care for her daughter for five mornings a week.

Mary's death wasn't Jumaya's fault. European children in Boromundi always had a rest after lunch. That day, a Tuesday, Jumaya laid the nine-month old Mary down in her cot shortly after half past one. Mr and Mrs Standish were still at table and Mr Standish, as was his custom, stuck his head into Mary's room at quarter past two, just before he returned to work. When questioned by the police, he was quite sure that Mary was breathing. But when Jumaya, concerned that the child had not woken, went to her room shortly after three, she was dead. The doctor performed an autopsy but no cause of death was established.

Jumaya was sacked. It was not an unreasonable thing for the Standishes to do. They did not blame Jumaya for what had happened but they could not face daily contact with her. Being people of conscience, they gave her a good reference and a generous parting gift – but she never found re-employment. Nobody, knowing what had happened, would risk having her in their house.

If Mophas' physical injury was not burden enough, his treatment in the years while Jumaya worked so happily for the Standishes was worse. In the absence of family or friends in the Mateka slum in which she took a room, Jumaya had no choice but to drop the little boy each day with a child-minder. This woman 'minded' anything from five to eight children ranging in age from a few months to seven years, confining them in a shack the size of an English bathroom. She was paid little for the service, and gave the children even less. Mophas' hideous physical aspect made him the target of cruelty, both from the other children and from the men who came to enjoy the old lady's other source of income: cheap, illegally brewed millet beer. Poor Jumaya. She knew the terrible price Mophas was paying for the job she needed – and so enjoyed. He grew up hating his mother, hating her even more when the job upon which she had pinned her hopes for their future came to an abrupt end and, in desperation, she turned to prostitution. Mophas now had to face a new pressure: the succession of drunken and drug-crazed punters who physically abused both his mother and, when she could not prevent it, him.

Jumaya managed to keep a roof over their heads. Matters improved when her sister, Kika, the baby of the family, ran away from home to join her. At least, then, one could care for the boy while the other worked. Unfortunately, shortly after she arrived, Kika fell in love. The object of her affection was a short, irascible man who ran the protection racket that covered the slum area in which the two women operated. I don't think he gave a damn for Kika, an ignorant bush girl, but she was a fool for him, enough of a fool to allow herself to fall pregnant. Her pregnancy infuriated him. One night, accompanied by his men, he came to their house and, while Jumaya and Mophas were forced to look on, beat Kika to a pulp with a lead-filled truncheon, after which he inserted the instrument viciously, several times, into Kika's vagina. As a result, Onias was born prematurely. The story of the rat and his testicle wasn't true: he only ever had one to start with and, to make matters worse, the member that went with it was shrunken and the foreskin split along its length – the penis equivalent of a hair lip. His tackle therefore became an object of some wonder when he joined the droves of naked piccaninnies that swarmed like blowflies in the streets around his home.

Two years later Kika was stabbed in a bar-room brawl. She was rushed to the city hospital where she survived for twenty-four hours. When his mother died the responsibility for Onias' upbringing fell upon Jumaya. By that time Mophas was thirteen and earning an income running errands for the men who peddled drugs in the mean streets of Mateka. He did well. He had inherited a fine physique and a dogged persistence from his mother, and had learned brutality and low cunning from his slum upbringing. That there was ten years' age difference between the two boys made no difference: where Mophas went, Onias followed, leaving Jumaya free to ply her miserable trade.

Jumaya died in 1994. This was during the second civil war. Her departure left Mophas and Onias free to join Bunrum when it was at the height of its success. They left Mateka and attached themselves to a 'flying column' led by the brutal John Dobo. This rabble can best be described by likening it to a swarm of locusts. It moved through BRF areas, settling on villages and small towns and gobbling them up. When the means of sustenance was finished or, as happened more frequently, the alcohol ran out, John summoned his swarm with a bugle call and led them on. Rape and murder, vicious beatings and torture were normal, day-to-day occurrences. Onias was thirteen by the time the war ended. He had discovered an almost orgasmic enjoyment in inflicting pain on his victims. Further, after all the laughter at his sexual organ, he discovered that it responded very well to certain stimuli. Mophas, who rapidly became a drunkard, had little truck with the bestiality which switched Onias on so, when they entered a village, Onias would disappear. Heavily armed, he would select his victims with care – usually a house remote from others – and would remain there until the summons to move on. He made no attempt to conceal the horrors he had perpetrated so, when the Bunrum mob departed, what had happened was plain to see.

When the war ended the two returned, openly and unashamedly, to Mateka. The BRF militias and, later, the new government's police had others to worry about: the political and military leaders and middle cadres of Bunrum. Filth like Onias were of little concern to them so long as they confined themselves to where filth belonged – the slums – and kept a low profile.

To use the business buzzword, Mophas and his cousin were head-hunted for the operation to capture Rebecca. The man who recruited them was Bullet Shibane.

You'd have thought we would have learnt from our encounter with M'Simani Kangalewa, but we hadn't. After all the months of training, after the detailed planning and clockwork execution of the operation that netted our two targets, we had no clear plan for what we would do with them once they were in our hands. Obviously, revenge was important. A slow death would satisfy that. But we were well beyond having it as an end in itself. Now we needed information.

While I rowed us out into the lake, quickly losing sight of the shore in the torrential downpour, Temba secured our unconscious prisoners. He was more worried about Onias than Mophas. The lad was a compact knot of muscles, as lethal as a hand grenade with the pin pulled out so, with his legs bound together, he was dropped overboard and towed behind the boat by a painter secured to his wrists, the rope short enough to keep his mouth above water level. In the water he rapidly regained consciousness yet he remained utterly silent throughout the hour we spent with Mophas.

Once Mophas was tied so he was spread-eagled naked in the bottom of the boat, a bailing tin of water brought him round. For a time he was silly from the blow that Temba had administered to his head. I was afraid that he was so severely concussed that he would prove useless to us but it rapidly became apparent that he was acting. Unlike M'Simani, we didn't think he would have any illusions as to what would happen once we had finished with him, so we didn't start off by trying to win his co-operation. What he told us was obtained in the same way you would juice a lemon.

I won't describe what Temba did to him except that it was done by the light of a torch and mostly with the point of a scalpel and, by the time he was finished, the bilges of the boat ran with a mixture of blood, faeces and urine. Don't get me wrong, I'd have been just as brutal, without a shred of compunction. It was simply that Temba, as a biologist, was better at it than me. There were times when I hit Mophas, but only when I lost control and struck out in rage or agony, or when Temba told me to.

As I said, we had no plan for this crude interrogation but we kicked off reasonably well. The facts came out in short, strangled sentences. They came out in a random order as Mophas' mind became increasingly deranged. Frequently, a question was asked and asked again, particularly when we didn't believe the first answer. We kept plugging away at the most important until we were sure we had the truth. What follows is a tidied up version of the early part of the interrogation.

I started it. I wanted to know, however much it hurt, exactly what happened on the side of the road when Cyprian Bogovu's minibus was stopped. I wanted the detail.

Mophas had been the one who had pulled the fat lady out of the front passenger seat. He was then in a position to see everything that happened. What he told us differed little from the patchwork story from Cyprian and the bus passengers and from the few observations we had obtained from M'Simani. Yes, Annabel had been raped. Only one person raped her on the side of the road while the minibus was still there and that was Smallboy Mushewa, and he was dragged off her by Bullet, who was furious with him. Their instructions had been quite clear: they were after the white girl. The operation was intended to be low-key. Keeping the black girl was a spur of the moment decision and only for a bit of fun after the business was finished – and this only because the black girl had turned out to be such a vicious vixen whose strength, fuelled by an insane anger, had threatened the whole operation. When Bullet had thrown Rebecca to the ground when he first got her out of the bus, Annabel had been right behind her, and had gone berserk. That's why she'd been hit, very hard. With Annabel temporarily quelled, Bullet had concentrated on a vital question: he needed to be sure Rebecca was a virgin. So he had torn away her clothes and carried out a rapid and brutal examination. Smallboy, arriving late and crazy with the pills he'd been popping most of the night, had mistaken what Bullet was doing and had jumped on Annabel.

Rebecca's resistance to the assault of his fingers had been more desperate than Bullet had expected so, to subdue her, he had fired two shots almost against her ear. He could have killed her, but he didn't because, if she hadn't been a virgin, they'd have let her go. We might not believe him, Mophas screamed, but Bullet had said that. The shots had had the desired effect and Rebecca was a virgin. It was when Bullet had finished his examination that he'd noticed what Smallboy was doing to Annabel and dragged him off. The men had then pillaged the bus – again, to muddy their motives – before allowing the passengers to get back on board. And, yes, as the bus drew away there was a free-for-all on Annabel. All, even Bullet, had participated.

I kicked him then. Half standing, holding on to the bulwark, with the boat wobbling from side to side, I kicked him again and again, stopping only to ask a question, waiting moments for an answer and, if it didn't come, kicking him again.

'Was she dead?'

'No.' I'd bust his face so badly every word came out in a spattering of blood and teeth.

'So who killed her?'

'Onias,' he screamed.

Temba was doing things low down his back and it was as if he'd pulled the plug on a dam, because Mophas began babbling. 'Onias, Onias do it. Onias . . . Jesus! . . . that fucker out of control. He get his *panga*, he hit her, again and again, he slash at her. Ahhhhh! He hit her breast, her face, her arm. Ayiiiii! He hit her arm so bad it come away.'

'Was she conscious?'

He nodded.

'All the time?'

'Onias make her conscious.'

I kicked him in the face again.

'And you killed her?'

'No, no,' he spat. 'Onias. But she just die. Too much blood.'

I took a good step back and slammed my boot into his throat.

Mophas' screams had turned to shrieks by this time. I sat back, breathing deeply, struggling to regain control by looking out, beyond the charnel-house of our boat, across the placid waters of the lake. The texture of the rain had changed. The droplets were smaller and seemed to fall more slowly, blowing slightly, like silk curtains in a light breeze, hemming us in. But I couldn't close my ears: as Temba worked, Mophas' hideous cries tore the silence.

Rebecca wasn't raped. It didn't matter what Temba did, nor that I repeatedly told him that the passengers had seen her being raped: Mophas was adamant. To have raped her would have spoiled the whole point of the operation, which was to obtain certain body parts from a white virgin. 'How did you know she was a virgin?' I asked.

'Bullet, he felt . . .'

I had to close my eyes then, and swallow at the cold slug of vomit that poked at the back of my throat.

'No,' I managed. 'The whole operation depended on her being a virgin. So . . . How did you know?'

I saw Temba's hand move. Mophas' body tensed, arching back until it was as taut as a violin string. His eyes bulged, and his mouth, a mass of blood and broken teeth from the damage we had done, opened wider and wider. Suddenly he screamed. 'Bullet. It was Bullet. He was certain.'

We gave him no rest, no relief. As Temba worked on him he swore that Rebecca's end had been painless: they had cut her head off before Bullet operated. Again, Onias had done it with his panga, a single stroke. So she was dead. Certainly, dead. Unlike poor Annabel, she had died quickly.

That he'd got the worst out seemed to calm him. For the next few minutes I asked questions and he answered them.

'So what happened then?'

'They were cut.'

'Cut up?'

He nodded.

'Why?'

'So they would not be recognized.'

I think he felt Temba move because he added, 'Also, because of what we took.'

'What who took?'

'Bullet. He cut the white girl. He has supermarket plastic bag.'

I closed my eyes, trying not to imagine it, not to think about it, holding myself.

'Who cut the black girl?' It was Temba that asked.

'Onias.'

'And cars were passing?'

'All the time. Onias hold up some meat but they do not stop.'

Afterwards, Mophas said, they had split up. He and Onias had returned to Mateka. He didn't know where M'Simani and Smallboy had gone, but they'd gone in different directions. Bullet, with his prize in a polythene bag, had cut across country to where he had parked his Toyota Land Cruiser.

So – Bullet. Who was this Bullet?

We squeezed Mophas but he seemed to know little. Much of what he offered – for example, that Bullet was tall, very solidly built and dark-skinned – we already knew from M'Simani. But he did tell us that his surname was Shibane. He thought he was a general in the new Movement – Rebecca, he explained, had been that important: they'd sent a general to collect her. And he told us one other thing: Bullet came from the north-west, from a town not far from Smallboy's home.

The Northwest. Mophas had just come from the Northwest two days ago, hadn't he? Had he seen Bullet? No. But he'd been there, so he could tell us what was going on there, couldn't he?

In all, we extracted very little from him. After what happened that night I'm quite sure that years of training go into making a good interrogator. It probably didn't help that Mophas knew we would kill him. We tried some of what we thought were the standard interrogational ploys – like Temba acting the cruel man, and me trying to persuade Mophas that, if only he'd spill the beans, I'd make sure he didn't die. It didn't work. If we pushed the pain over a threshold, he slipped into oblivion and time was wasted bringing him back. We sought facts, but we didn't know how to deploy, as part of the interrogation process, those few we already knew. Deliberately, at an early point, Temba revealed that we had talked to M'Simani. I think it was because of this that Mophas started by being quite open about the general thrust of what was happening, though he was light on detail.

There was a boy king who was to be the Saviour of Boromundi and, in due course, the emperor of a new African superstate. He was already rich, very powerful, inspired, god-like, and the dispenser of a potent medicine which would render the fighting men of the Movement immune from death in battle. This medicine, as a result of Bullet's success with Rebecca, was available and had already proved its worth. But when we began digging for specifics – like when the main campaign would start and how many men had been recruited and where the men were – we got nothing. And we quickly realised that, on such few points as he gave us, he was often lying. What M'Simani had told us about the boy king's throne, about the way people approached it – we fished for this information but we didn't get it: the boy lived in an ordinary house, he went to school, etc, etc.

I could see the anger and frustration building in Temba. We began pushing for facts about the Movement. How far had it evolved within the population heartlands of Boromundi? Were the other men who had been with Mophas part of a recruitment cell? How many local people, here in Chirwe, had they recruited, how were they doing it, and how successful was the process? To these and related questions we got no answers. He and his brother had been on a visit to friends – that sort of shit. We knew he was lying but it didn't make the slightest difference what Temba threatened or did. Perhaps the man was, by that time, in such agony that a little more had no additional effect. In the end Temba exploded. Ever since Mophas described what had happened to Annabel he'd been holding himself back, like some great, black steam boiler building and building pressure, and he simply let himself go.

He took him apart section by section. He had swapped the scalpel for his *panga*, a big instrument in my hands but like a toy in his. While I sat on Mophas' body, and struggled to hold him still, Temba knelt, pinning his head between his knees. He started with the man's hands. As he removed the first finger he whispered, 'This is for Annabel's wedding finger, okay? She wore my ring here. You understand, Mophas? My wedding ring!' The finger came away and, as Mophas screamed and writhed, Temba silenced him by pushing it into the man's mouth. 'Eat it,' he growled, as he clamped the bloody, broken jaw with his great hand, 'eat it so you understand,' and he stuffed it deep into the back of his mouth before holding Mophas' nose until he felt him swallow.

Finger after finger, he stuffed the man's mouth until he choked. Then he sliced away the stump of the hand in a single stroke and rubbed it into Mophas' face, while he whispered, 'Annabel. My Annabel!' When he had finished he threw it overboard, after which he tied a tourniquet to stop the bastard bleeding to death.

Then he gestured with the *panga*. 'Pull his trousers, Armstrong.'

When he'd wreaked his revenge, when the man had ceased to react, he cut Mophas free, attached him to a line and, trussed up like a Christmas turkey, threw him – or rather, most of him – overboard.

He couldn't swim in the state he was in. I imagine he drowned fairly quickly, but I'd like to believe the story about drowning people: that their life passes before their eyes as they go. I have this vision that all those wretched souls whom Mophas had wronged during his evil, vicious life came along to haunt him in those few minutes. And that he then went straight to the sort of hell described by Dante.

Temba looked at me. 'How you doing, Armstrong?'

'I'm fine,' I said. I was. There had been moments, and I felt filthy from the blood and the rest of the shit that was splattered all over me, but most of it had been good.

'This one,' Temba said as he began hauling in on Onias' rope, 'we need to squeeze harder. Okay?'

'Yeah,' I said. 'My pleasure.'

Onias came over the side like some gigantic carp. His skin was grey and pulpy from the hour he'd spent in the frigid waters of the lake and he shivered uncontrollably. For a short period, and to my surprise, it looked as if we would get much more out of Onias than we'd expected. But he was the same as Mophas: the minute we got on to detail about the Movement, he clammed up. By that time he'd revived a bit, and his refusal to give any more information was sudden and arrogant. In effect, he said that we could do what we liked to him, but that was it. He defied us.

When I remember what Temba did to him in the next few minutes, I also have to remember what Onias did to Annabel. And I didn't see everything because, after a while, I had to turn away. For a time Onias took it in silence, his teeth grinding together as he bore the pain. Then he began to scream. And it was while he was screaming that the boat took off.

It was as if some giant hand had seized it from underneath, flinging it backwards through the water. The initial movement was so sudden that I was thrown off my seat. I dropped my torch and landed on my back in the blood and filth and entrails that swilled around in the bilges. Temba had been leaning over Onias and he was pitched forward on top of him. For a moment Onias managed to hook his bound legs round Temba, pinning him to the side of the boat. As I fought to recover, to find my torch, to go to Temba's aid, I was aware of a brief, vicious fight. Although the boat was still moving in short, sudden bursts, I managed to struggle upright, seeing immediately that Temba didn't need me. But I saw the cause of the boat's movement: the painter that was attached to Mophas' body was jerking, as if a great fish had taken the bait. I shouted, pointing at it, and Temba turned quickly and cut it away. As the boat steadied, I shone my torch down at Onias. He was dead, his throat cut from ear to ear.

'Christ!' I said, collapsing against the side of the boat. Temba ignored me. He picked up Onias' body to throw it over the side but the boy's guts spilled out, a sloppy, writhing mess of pink and purple, slipping down into the bottom of the boat. Temba pitched the body overboard and collected the intestines, throwing them after it. Then he set about washing himself in the lake.

'What was it?' I whispered. I was shaking almost uncontrollably, my reaction to the horror of the events in the last two hours and the shock of what had just happened to the boat.

Temba didn't need to answer. The water, a few yards behind the boat, swirled and, in the light of my torch, I saw the body of a reptile, a great, long, scaly beast that rotated, the pale flesh of his belly clearly visible as he rolled and rolled and rolled again.

'Crocodile,' I whispered.

'Lake crocodile,' Temba said, following my gaze. 'Big one.' And then he began to cry.

The better women who ply Florentine's trade are sensitive to the needs of men. When we returned, soaked, filthy, stinking, shaking with cold, we needed tenderness and care, and that's what we got. A bath. A change of clothes. A gin and tonic, strong, with plenty of lemon and rattling with ice cubes. A hot meal. By that time the shock was affecting me so badly I could hardly hold the cutlery. Mirianna helped, sitting close against me with one hand in my lap and the other spooning rice and meat into my mouth. When we'd finished, relaxing in Florentine's ornate sitting room, we began to drink seriously. We'd planned to return to the hotel pretending to be drunk. By the time Florentine swung Alice's car into the car park in front of the Lake Hotel, no pretence was needed.

I have no recollection of how the evening ended. Honestly. I know that, when I woke, shortly after ten the next morning, Temba's bed had not been slept in and mine looked as if the battle of Agincourt has been fought across it. Mirianna, emerging from the shower, stopped to look down at me. The towel she held was big and white and fluffy, a wonderful contrast to the oiled jet of her wet skin, but all I could do about it was lie back limply and watch as she dried herself and dressed. I must have slipped back into oblivion because, when I next woke, I was alone and it was after one. I managed to crawl downstairs for lunch. The dining room was strangely deserted. I was sitting at a table, struggling with a bowl of oxtail soup, when I saw a police inspector threading his way between the tables, followed by two armed constables. Even though there was no-one else in the room, it wasn't until they stopped at my table that I realised they'd come for me.

The police inspector was a small, sinewy man smartly dressed in a khaki uniform with a slightly paler khaki shirt and faded black tie which matched his skin. He had a thin face that had fallen in on itself, as if the flesh had been sucked out from under the skin, leaving his eyes bulging, the quick, darting eyes of a rat. He led me out into the foyer, turning to throw a question at me. Did I have a car? Yes, I replied. What sort of car? I had hardly started to describe it when he stopped me. A pink Mustang, driven by a very large black man? Yes. And I was here for tourism? Yes. Not business? No. He nodded, turning quickly away.

It's difficult to write this sort of conversation because, in such circumstances, while you're talking your brain is working overtime. On the one hand it's trying to guess what the man's after, because, once you know where he's going, you can modify your answers accordingly. On the other, it's trying to make sure that everything you say and do is innocent-looking, which is very difficult if – as on that occasion – you know you're guilty as hell. You're asking yourself questions like, 'If I were innocent, how would I behave when three policemen come and dragged me away from my lunch, particularly when I need that meal badly because I've got a rhinoceros of a hangover?' Would I be angry? Would I be understanding, co-operative? Would I be asking what the hell's this all about? And at what point would I start muttering darkly about lawyers and the British High Commission? Thinking was a bit of a struggle but I was more worried about dropping my guts because I'd heard enough about the Boromundi police and what went on in their warm little cells to know I didn't want to play with them.

I was quite certain this interest in me was something to do with the previous evening. They'd done pretty well to catch up with us so quickly. I couldn't see where we'd gone wrong. Our alibis, thanks to Florentina and Mirianna, should have been watertight – unless one of the girls had decided, for reasons we wouldn't understand, to grass on us. And, as far as I could tell, nobody had seen us during the attack on Upure-Maji. The rain and the mist had hidden the boat from our pursuers – though, when I'd thought about it afterwards, I'd realised that much of our conversation with Onias and Mophas might have been heard on the shore – the sort of noises they made would have travelled incredibly well over water. It didn't bear thinking about if the whole of the waterside population of Upure-Maji had been listening.

The inspector began shouting at the two constables. By that time I'd decided to go on the offensive, so I tried to catch his attention to ask him what was so important that he'd had to disturb my meal. It came out a bit sharper than I intended, but it didn't make any difference. He ignored me.

Just then I spotted our overnight bags. We hadn't packed them so someone else must have done. They were beside the front door and a hotel porter was standing over them, shifting his weight from one foot to the other with a hunted look on his face. Almost immediately the inspector turned to me and indicated that I should accompany one of his constables. I hesitated, but I couldn't see any choice, so I followed him through the door, seeing, out of the corner of my eye, the porter pick up our luggage and follow me. Two police cars, both white Peugeot 404s with blue strobes on top, were standing at the bottom of the hotel steps.

I stopped, and the porter nearly ran into the back of me. I stopped because, in the distance, along the lake shore away to my right in the direction of Upure-Maji, I could hear the unmistakable sounds of fighting: the chatter of automatic rifles and the occasional bump of an explosion.

The constable brought me back. He had said something and he was holding the back door open, frowning heavily as if he was keen for me to get in; and the porter skirted round me and scampered quickly down the steps to drop our luggage into the boot.

The drive to the police station took all of two minutes. It was done at breakneck speed, with the sirens howling and lights flashing even though the streets of Chirwe were ominously silent and empty. As we swept through the gates of the police compound I caught sight of the Pink Peril parked to one side with a number of other saloon cars, and next to them stood an armoured car, a beaten-up old Saracen in camouflage colours with the Boromundi flag painted on its side and men in army fatigues lounging around it.

The police car skidded to a halt. By the time my head

had caught up with me I'd climbed out and Temba had
sauntered over, joining me as I retrieved our bags from
the boot.

'What's going on?' I whispered.

'Fighting.' He hesitated. 'We talk as soon as we leave.'

'Leave?'

He nodded. 'We are being evacuated.'

Unwittingly, Temba and I had precipitated the third
Boromundi civil war. The five men we'd killed were the
cell that was organising the Movement's infrastructure
in Chirwe. In the previous war, most of the local population had been firm supporters of Bunrum so the Movement confidently expected to build a good following
there before hostilities commenced. Unfortunately for
them, because we'd been in and out so quickly, what
had happened at Upure-Maji had been blown out of all
proportion by the few, rather distant witnesses. A com-
mando had come ashore in a rigid inflatable. Four, six,
eight heavily armed men had stormed the yellow house.
They had looked like government special forces. And so
on.

Boromundi was awash with arms from the previous
conflicts. Those recruited by the Movement in Chirwe
concluded that the game was up, that the government
was on to them. Effectively, by taking out Mophas' cell
we'd chopped their head off and they didn't have anything to think with, so they panicked. When police and
army units were rushed to Upure-Maji, they were shot
at. Within an hour a major fire-fight had developed.

Government reinforcements were rushed in from the big barracks at Iweni, near Mateka. The evacuation of Chirwe started with foreign visitors being taken out in armed convoys, though, by the time ours went out, the roads were crowded with local refugees.

As we crawled along I raised an important question. What had Mirianna and I done last night? Temba kept his eyes on the road. 'Go on,' I croaked through a sandpaper throat, 'Tell me.' He didn't want to discuss it. When I pressed him his irritation surfaced. We'd made fools of ourselves in the hotel, demanding drinks at the bar and then creating trouble when the night porter wouldn't serve us. Florentina and he had had the devil of a job getting us up to the room. What had followed was so disgusting that they'd left us and gone for a long walk.

'A long walk?' I sniggered.

Yes. A long walk. And – before I got any ideas – they'd done nothing except talk.

I told him I didn't believe him.

I suppose he proved it by telling me Florentina's life history. It would make a book in itself, but suffice it to say that she'd been born in Mauritius, English father, local mother, and had been brought up in Madagascar (hence her rather odd but attractive French accent) and worked the early part of her life in South Africa. She'd followed a man to Boromundi, a Dutchman who'd promised her love and riches – neither of which, of course, had materialised by the time the Dutchman disappeared a month later. And Mirianna? Mirianna, said Temba with disgust, Mirianna was local.

Temba lapsed into silence and I was left wondering about the detail of what I'd done the previous night. I always feel bad after I've got very drunk and done stupid things, particularly if they've upset my friends, and more particularly if I can't remember what they were. It seems a waste, having wicked fun and not remembering it.

It was a dreadful journey. The convoy crawled along crowded roads, stopping frequently. I offered to drive but Temba wouldn't let me, so I slept most of the way. We stopped off at Alice's and she, after a meticulous inspection of her beloved car, drove us on to St Faith's. On the way up we gave her Bullet's surname. It didn't mean anything to her, but she said she'd ask around. We finally arrived back to school at half past nine at night and, as we passed the staff quarters, we could hear the end of term staff party in full swing in the communal sitting room.

After Alice dropped us at Temba's house Temba made a bolt for his bedroom but I got in the way.

'Armstrong,' he pleaded.

'Listen,' I said. 'No excuses. You did nothing with that Florentina girl all night. Remember? You "talked". So there's plenty of juice in you. Okay?'

The big man shook his head.

'The trouble with you, Temba, is that, considering how black you are, you're hopelessly transparent.'

'Transparent?'

'Yes. You're afraid of Josephine, aren't you?'

He shook his head.

'You're afraid, or you're not afraid?'

He kept shaking his head, but his eyes were closed and his face had that hurt, wrinkled-prune look.

'Okay then, you're not afraid. So you've got ten minutes to make yourself beautiful.'

She was there. If I'd left Temba to it, he would probably have got pissed first and then he might, and I stress the word, might, have gone over to talk to her. So I cut a corner for him, catching his arm as we walked into the warmth and the din and not giving him any choice. I almost dragged him and, when we'd come up to Josephine, I said, very loudly so half the room could hear me, 'He promised he'd talk to you.'

I don't think Temba got as far as a drink. I saw them a few minutes later dancing together. They were dancing very slowly and very close, and the phrase 'they only had eyes for each other' fitted them perfectly. After that I didn't see them again that evening and, when I finally fell into bed, Temba wasn't at home.

He still hadn't returned the next morning so, after I'd cleaned the rifles and tidied up the rest of our gear, I wandered down to the school office. Josephine normally worked Saturday mornings and I was interested to see if she was there, which she wasn't. Instead I ran into a very irate Father Chitembe.

August Chitembe, you'll remember, was the priest who had done such a good job at Rebecca's funeral. He had also been deputy head so, when poor Bartolemew Nchanga was murdered, he was promoted to acting head. It was not a job he enjoyed, particularly as the School Board expected him to continue with all his existing responsibilities as well as taking on the head's, and particularly when his new secretary seemed to have disappeared without even ringing in with an excuse.

Worse, he'd been unexpectedly short-staffed on the last day of term so the first thing he wanted to know from me was why.

There are people I trust and there are people I don't. Father Chitembe may have been a priest. He may have been a very good man indeed. But I didn't trust him, not like I'd trusted old Bartolemew. So I didn't tell him the truth. I gave him a variation on the 'lost relative' story we'd used when we went to visit Smallboy, but it didn't hold water and he didn't believe me. Matters were made worse when he asked me whether, by any chance, I knew where Josephine was. I told another lie and, again, I think he saw straight through it.

I hung around the office for a few minutes, hoping he'd go away so I could use the phone. It was fairly obvious, in the desultory conversation which followed, that events at Chirwe hadn't been reported in the local media. When the silences became strained, August removed himself to his office. I gave him a couple of minutes to settle back to his paperwork before I rang the Archbishop's office. He wasn't there, but I left a message giving him Bullet's surname and asking him to call me back. Then I saw the chance to earn a few Brownie points and, at the same time, stay in the office, so I stuck my head round August's door and asked him if there was anything I could do to help. I spent the rest of the morning filling envelopes and licking stamps.

It was the sort of task that allows your mind to wander. Mine didn't wander far. It went back to Chloris and, particularly, to the kiss she'd given me as we floundered in the surf at the Two Turtles. I spent some time trying to evaluate that kiss, comparing it, say, to an athletic night with Mumbai or six hours of debauchery with Mirianna. They didn't compare. I'd have cheerfully swapped both for a peck on the cheek from Chloris.

I wondered where she was. I realised I should have asked if someone else in the Archbishop's office could tell me instead of just leaving a message for the Archbishop. I'd have to find out, when he got back to me. And perhaps, during the school holiday, I could visit her, see her, talk to her. I could pretend I was ready for conversion, but only by her.

After that, I spent a fair amount of time daydreaming. They were nice warm, comforting little dreams, with Chloris dressed in a minuscule bikini lying out on some tropical beach and me fighting swarms of sharks and alligators that seemed to be hell-bent on crawling up the beach to eat her. And then, when I'd won, she was so grateful she said she'd love me forever and began taking her bikini top off.

These gentle dreams were rudely interrupted when Jenny Muzikwa crashed into the office.

'Armstrong!'

Jenny was one of the teaching staff, a lady large in every dimension who had the same beautiful brown eyes as a gorilla. Attached to her, as always, came the chemistry teacher, a silent, grey little man called Silas Zindhe.

'Armstrong – you have heard? There has been a coup! The radio station in Mateka has been taken by revolutionaries.' She was very out of breath. 'They are broadcasting military music.'

'A coup . . .?' I began.

'There has been an announcement. The Boromundi Salvation Movement has overthrown the government.'

'The who?'

'Bosmo.' It was Silas. I think that was the first time I'd ever heard him speak. God knows how he conducted his classes.

'Bosmo,' Jenny cut in, in case Silas overdid it. 'Yes, they have called on all military units to return immediately to their barracks, and for all civilians to go home and stay indoors. A state of national emergency has been declared!'

August Chitembe emerged from what had been Bartolomew's office. He'd obviously been listening to the radio too because he asked whether anyone knew what had happened to President Bugarimani.

'Bugarimani?' Jenny sneered. 'That one? He is still in the US. He is always in the US!'

I remembered then that the newspaper had said he was been visiting President Clinton and the World Bank, the IMF and anyone else who would listen, in an attempt to drum up aid for the bankrupt Boromundi economy – though there was also a strong rumour that, while he was over there, he and his family had snatched a week's holiday at a celebrity hotel in the British Virgin Islands.

One of the school's gardeners and the school nurse joined us, and the six of us stood around in the office making coffee and listening to the radio. There were no further announcements so August rang a friend in Mateka who was a senior civil servant in the Ministry of Agriculture. It surprised me that the phones were still working. His news was that there had been some fighting in the streets. It had started about ten. By eleven the radio station had been taken and, shortly after, the central police station had been overwhelmed in a vicious frontal assault. From his office now he could see the presidential palace and it was on fire. He'd heard that the fighting had moved out in the direction of the big military base at Iweni but his understanding was that the few reliable units there had been deployed to Chirwe the previous day, so he didn't expect the base to hold out for long. The airport, most of the main ministry buildings, the telephone exchange and the Bank of Boromundi were still in government hands. The man sounded very laid-back, very civil-servant.

I began worrying. Chloris was supposed to be in Mateka. If this Bosmo lot were who I thought they were – another word for the Movement – then she would be in serious danger. There had been horror stories of nuns being raped and murdered in the last civil war. Bosmo would definitely be far worse than Bunrum as it probably consisted largely of Bunrum who had had lots of practice at this sort of thing. I began hoping that the British government would do something about her, like evacuating her, quickly, before things got too bad, knowing that it was Saturday and most British civil servants would be at home eating their crumpets and not available 'til Monday. I began pacing about the office, wondering what the hell I could do. Ring the Archbishop again? Contact the High Commission? I couldn't think of anything direct I could do until I knew where she was

While I was going through this, the Boromundians played with the radio dial, picking up what they could from the BBC World Service and Kenyan and Tanzanian stations. As the opinion that emerged suggested that Bosmo was another name for Bunrum, they became increasingly nervous and despondent. They knew, far better than I, what was coming. They'd had more than enough of it in two wars and didn't want a third. After a lot of discussion, there didn't seem to be anything anyone could do so people began drifting away. I was about to do the same – I certainly wasn't going to go back to licking stamps in the circumstances – when Temba bowled in.

'August! Jenny!' He frowned. 'You here, Silas?'

'You have heard the news?' Jenny asked.

Temba nodded then turned to me. 'Septic tank needs emptying.'

Septic tank . . .? It took me a moment to remember what that meant. I headed for the door.

As we hurried towards his house Temba said, 'We have to put this project on hold.'

I slowed. 'Oh?'

'I was at a friend's last night.' He frowned a warning at me. 'People are saying that what will come now will be ten times worse than we have already seen. So we are preparing.' He paused.

'Preparing?'

'There is a defence force being assembled in Kaserewe.'

'Which you're joining?'

He shrugged. 'What is important is that your High Commission is organizing evacuation . . .'

At that point I stopped. I stood in the middle of the muddy path through the trees that led up to his house and thought about what he'd just said. He was insinuating that this cook was getting out before the kitchen heated up and I wasn't quite sure that's how I saw things. When I'd been in the office with that sad little group of worried Boromundians, I hadn't been thinking about how I would escape. I was worrying, same as any of them. As I stood there, vaguely aware that Temba had stopped and was coming back down the path towards me, a second thought impinged: I wasn't quite sure that, if Temba was going off to fight a bunch whose supporters included the heirs of Smallboy Mushewa, M'Simani Kangalewa, Onias Matanganesa and Mophas Mandabanga, I might not want to join in.

Temba was talking at me but I wasn't listening. There was something else. Temba and I had travelled a long way together. Yes, he was right to have no expectations of me in a war that involved his country tearing itself apart, but that didn't preclude me from joining in, did it?

It felt remarkably like that time outside the school hall when Temba sat with me in the rain and described how Rebecca had died. Then, I hadn't planned on revenge but once I knew what had happened and realised that no-one else was going to do anything about it, I had no choice but to commit myself. This was the same except, this time, it wasn't five men I would be out to murder but the whole of Bosmo.

'Armstrong, you all right?'

'You're not going without me,' I said flatly.

Temba began to say something, then stopped. 'You sure?'

'Yes. I'm bloody sure.'

Temba borrowed the school truck. I don't think he asked August – the poor man was last seen, head bowed, shuffling along the path towards the church. As we bounced our way down the road towards Kaserewe it occurred to me that, if only I knew Chloris were safe, all this might be rather fun. I even cracked a couple of jokes but Temba was too preoccupied to see the humour and finally shut me up by telling me to shove a slug up the Galil's spout, to keep the change lever on automatic and not to hesitate to blow away anything that looked suspect. I didn't take this instruction very seriously until we came to the outskirts of Kaserewe and I saw the first bodies in the streets. Then I sat up.

Temba drove to Josephine's house first. She lived in one of Kaserewe's nicer suburbs, not far from Alice, and she came down the veranda steps as we pulled up. She was dressed in a dark shirt and trousers, and she carried a small canvas holdall which I rather assumed contained sandwiches for Temba and I. However, she went round to the back of the truck and threw the bag in, and I was still sitting in the front like a lemon when Temba told me to get out and let her sit between us. Only then did I wake up to the fact that she was coming, too.

We drove into the centre of Kaserewe, to the hall attached to Kaserewe church. A motley collection of vehicles littered the road with groups of bored-looking men sitting in or lounging against them, smoking and talking. Temba tried for the car park. Its entrance was guarded by half a dozen raggedly-dressed men carrying rusty rifles, but they let us through. The little man guarding the side door of the hall directed us to a small room.

It contained about twenty men. One or two of them I recognised, like the man who ran food supplies up to the school kitchen in a beaten-up Ford Transit. They'd pulled chairs into a rough circle and were involved in a noisy debate but they shut up when we came in. It wasn't Temba. It was Josephine and me they looked at, and it felt uncomfortable. It felt even more uncomfortable when one or two of them began upbraiding Temba for bringing us along. At that point I felt Josephine's hand on my arm, and we beat a tactical retreat.

We sat ourselves in the warm afternoon sun on the steps leading down to the car park and talked. As you'll appreciate, I didn't mind this in the slightest, not with Josephine. After about ten minutes, an ancient one and a half ton Bedford with a canvas top swung through the gates into the church hall car park. It was driven far too fast, bucking through the potholes until it slithered to a halt in front of us. Two armed men dropped the tailgate and threw the canvas back before jumping out. I could then see their cargo. The driver and two militia men came round the back and, amid a lot of unnecessary shouting and cursing, they began to off-load.

They were in a pitiable state, their clothing torn and many wearing nothing but their underwear. Most were bleeding, some badly, and several had obviously been beaten so savagely they could hardly stand. Once the living were out, two men climbed into the back and began pulling bodies to the rear, throwing them out into the puddles.

'Perhaps some of them are Bosmo supporters, perhaps they are not.'

I turned. Josephine's face was expressionless.

'It is the same again,' she continued wearily. 'For some of our people, this is a chance to settle old disputes. They will say a neighbour supported Bunrum, or supports Bosmo, or they are people from the Northwest. It does not matter what the truth is. He will be taken away, questioned, beaten, perhaps killed.' She paused. She had her arms folded round her knees, hugging them, and her face was very set, her chin jutting out slightly, as if she had her teeth clenched. 'It will be that sort of war, Armstrong.'

We watched in silence as the prisoners were hustled away round the front of the hall. When the militiamen returned, they began dragging the bodies into the far corner of the car park, piling them up. They were all freshly killed, their muscles loose, arms, legs, heads flopping.

'For this, black is better than white,' Josephine said.

I frowned at her. 'What do you mean?'

'The blood, the lacerations, the bruises – they do not show as starkly against black skin.'

'Jesus!' I whispered.

'You must become used to it, Armstrong. You must become as we are; detached.'

I shook my head.

Then Josephine said, 'I know you do not want me to come.'

I gestured at the growing pile of corpses. 'I just don't like the idea of seeing you like that.'

After a moment's silence she said, 'Our people do not want you to come, either.'

'I know.'

'Then let us understand each other. We have a particular purpose. We are together to watch after Temba. Okay?'

I nodded.

'And you will also watch for me, and I will watch for you.'

I nodded again. I felt empty at that point, because I knew exactly what Josephine was talking about.

A spectacularly bloody sun was setting over the mango trees at the back of the church when Temba finally emerged. There followed a fair amount of hanging around, with people shouting at each other, before we finally set off in a convoy of half a dozen vehicles, driving out of town in the direction of Mateka. It wasn't until then that Temba explained to us that, far from joining some sort of Home Guard which might, might have to defend Kaserewe, we were going on the offensive.

15 War

War's like so many things you embark on in life: you
start off excited, nervous, heady, and, like any new boy,
doing things self-consciously, enthusiastically, and not
very well; and you end up worn out and pissed off and
wishing you were anywhere but where you are. The only
difference is that, with war, you pray you do get to the
end so you can feel pissed off, worn out and wishing you
were anywhere but where you are.

I'm proud of one thing. I fought a real, close-up,
footsoldier's war. We lost the school truck early on, not
from enemy action but from old age. On the fourth day,
on the road to Mateka, the big end went and we simply
abandoned it. By that time, several other Kaserewe vehicles were parked on their sides in ditches. Temba and
I were lucky. Because we'd planned to fight our own
private war, we had reasonable footwear that survived
the slog. Most of the others, including Josephine, didn't,
and they ended up either walking barefoot or falling
back on those splendid all-terrain African sandals made
from the tread of a tyre scavenged from one of the
vehicles that no longer needed them.

I don't suppose that my experiences of war, such as
they were, were much different from any other footsoldier – except that they were in Africa. Like, firstly, it's
confusing. You've no idea what's going on – and that

includes people like Temba who, by a process of popular acceptance, seemed to end up in charge of our little militia. Things were probably worse with us because we didn't have radios, and the telephones stopped working the evening we left Kaserewe. If news came, it came by word of mouth, from people moving along the road, from scraps of paper that were thrust into Temba's hand; and if orders found us it was a miracle, and by the time they arrived they were often dangerously out-of-date.

Secondly, you can be hit by awful, numbing boredom. For most of the time you're either sitting around waiting for something to happen, or walking towards somewhere where something is supposed to be happening which, when you get there, isn't happening or has already happened, so you have to walk back again. And, in Boromundi, whatever you're doing, it's hot and sweaty and if the flies aren't having a ball it's because it's raining.

Thirdly, the food's lousy. Nobody provided us with any so we lived off the country. Which, to put it simply, means you steal it off people after you've shoved a rifle in their face. If you're like me and have anything resembling a conscience, you therefore eat badly – except, every now and then, you stumble upon a legitimate feast and make a pig of yourself, after which your shit runs yellow and liquid for a week. When it comes to drinking, you try to stick to water, however stagnant and full of mosquito larvae it is, or the nectar of bottled or canned soft drinks if you can find them, because getting involved with alcohol at a time when a clear head and quick reflexes are essential is stupid. But when you find the booze you drink it. Quite a few of the blokes with us used drugs of different sorts as well, anything from the local *bhang*, which was fairly harmless, through to a cocktail of pills which made them alternately high and low. When they were high they were even more dangerous, and when they were low they were ugly.

War is an emotional thing. Mixed in with the emotions I've already described, there's the feelings about home. In many ways I was lucky. I didn't have to worry about Chloris because she was almost certainly with the rest of the Brits, safely back in England. Most of the others had family in the Kaserewe district and they fretted about them. They'd seen what a Bunrum flying column could do to a town and, from everything we were hearing, Bosmo was ten times worse. They missed their kids. They missed their wives and girlfriends and struggled with the thought that they were fornicating madly in their absence. Like all men, they had a sex drive which, with them living on their nerves, they needed to relieve. So we had problems with men pestering local girls in the towns and villages we passed through. Mostly, the girls either coped or were pleased to oblige. Occasionally it went well beyond pestering and Temba had to be seen to do something about it. When one of the Kaserewe men raped a girl, Temba shot him. At first I thought he'd gone too far. Then I learned that the girl had been eight and that, if Temba hadn't done it, quite a few of the others would.

With all this, you're permanently tired. You never seem to get enough sleep and, when you do sleep, it's somewhere that's uncomfortable, wet, noisy, infested with vermin, fleas and cockroaches, and insecure. I react badly to lack of sleep. I get irritable. I get overtalkative. I move through a world that seems slightly unreal, dream-like, detached, with the consequence that my reactions slow. Which is the most dangerous thing of all because, in amongst the interminable stretches of boredom, things do happen. And, when they happen, they happen suddenly and you come up hard against that essential element of war: fear.

The BRF's general plan was to advance along the main roads from the east and south-east towards Mateka, the capital. During the first five days, we met up with a number of other groups like ourselves, and this little peasant band had been taken under the wing of some army officers and soldiers who'd become lost in the confusion but had stuck with the government side. With the Kaserewe men deployed to cover the right of the general line of advance along the main road, we were working our way along paths and dirt tracks, roughly parallel to it. On the sixth day, at about eight in the morning, after a night without shelter in pouring rain, we came out of some trees and the track dipped into an open, grassy valley before rising the other side towards a ridge of low but fairly thick woodland. The sun had scorched away the night's clouds so it was already hot, it was humid from the rain, and the flies were warming to their work. I was going through my first bad go of diarrhoea and, the last time I'd squatted, I hadn't got my pants down fast enough so I'd soiled myself. I stank, and Josephine was walking beside me and pretending not to notice that I stank. In my depressed, introverted state I wasn't too aware of what was going on around me.

As we walked out into the open an infuriated hornet passed close overhead, followed by a scatter of small, sharp explosions from the general direction of the hill opposite. I hit the ground so hard it jarred my elbows, my heart banging in my chest and my guts writhing like a bucket of maggots. My rifle had been carelessly slung along my back and it was while I was struggling to untangle it and pull it round into a firing position that I saw Josephine. She was down on one knee and squinting along the sights of her rifle, and, as I watched, she squeezed off a single shot.

'Get down!' I hissed. 'For Jesus Christ's sake . . .'

I scrambled towards her and almost knocked her over, throwing my arm across her body and leaning on her so she couldn't do anything damn stupid like getting up again. By that time the air around our ears was being shredded by the 'Pfew', 'Pfew' of passing bullets followed by a slapping, tearing sound as they ripped into the trees behind us, so we lay with our faces pressed against the gritty earth. I prayed then, the words spat into the dirt in tight, sobbing gasps, feeling the tenseness of Josephine's body under my arm and hearing the whimper of her breathing.

As the blizzard of bullets eased, and we could hear the background, staccato hammering of short bursts fired at us from the opposite ridge, I gingerly poked my head above the tuft of grass that was my only cover. There was no sign of the enemy so, in my anxiety to be seen to be doing something constructive, I shoved my rifle in front of me and squirted half a magazine blindly at the trees along the ridge. I felt, rather than saw, Josephine poke her rifle in front of her, but when she opened fire it was with single, carefully placed shots. We carried on like this, aware that less and less were coming back at us, until Temba began to bawl at us in an attempt to restore some order.

After that, I think we did pretty well. A dozen of us stayed where we were and continued sniping in a desultory fashion into the trees while Temba sent the rest to work their way around to the right. Bosmo read what was happening, knew that there were more of us in the direction of the main road, realised they might be caught in a pincer movement and opted for a tactical retreat. So, after about half an hour, Temba began to move us forward in short rushes down the open ground into the valley bottom. It was bad going for a few minutes, with bullets whacking into the ground and whining over our heads, but, as we charged up the last slope towards the trees, screaming and yelling and firing as we went, the last of the opposition melted away – all except one, and he was dead.

We called him Jaws because he'd taken a bullet in the face and this had dislocated his jaw, so he lay on his back with his mouth wide open and askew, and his lips peeled back from his teeth, almost in a snarl. The bullet had entered very cleanly just below his nose and travelled slightly upwards, exiting the back of his head, blowing a hole the size of your fist and spraying chips of skull and globules of gore and brain all over the place. He must have been hit early on because, by the time we arrived, he was stiff and the ants and flies were well into their feast. He was a young man, not more than twenty, with a stocky, muscular body. At that stage I still had some emotion left, enough to feel that he'd been unlucky to be dead.

Which is the final side of war: people get wounded and people die. There's no dignity in violent death. We saw a lot of dead people, men, women, children and babies, who'd died in an unimaginable variety of ways. You quickly build an immunity to the corpses. You've got to. They become no more than an unpleasant part of the landscape. They stink. In the broiling heat the soft bits melt off them and the maggots writhe in the Marmite-coloured juices that were once flesh and muscle. The local dogs get to them. The wild animals scatter their bits across the landscape. We made no attempt to bury them, they weren't worth the time and the emotional price. Early on, we saw things we found so repulsive we couldn't control our emotions. Most of those involved children. After a while we stopped bothering about them, the anger they generated wore us out.

The dead were one thing, the wounded quite another. Other than Bosmo's people whom we dealt with quickly, there wasn't much we could do for them, whether they were our own men or the local population. Josephine's carefully hoarded supply of first aid materials was quickly exhausted. In the humidity, in the unhygienic circumstances in which we lived, the smallest wound, even something as minor as a blister, became infected. The flies helped no end. A cut became an ulcer. A wound suppurated, oozing pus, the flesh around it rotting in a strange, sweet stench. Gangrene became common. For many, a minor lesion became a slow death sentence. And there were not a few who, driven crazy by the pain and disgusted by their body's weakness, walked away and sat under the shade of a tree, placed the muzzle of their rifle in the roof of their mouth and took the fast road to eternity.

How do you survive this? Josephine got it right that first day: you look after yourself and you look after your mates. As far as I was concerned, the rest of the BRF fighters were only of any use in that they helped to achieve my aim: that Temba, Josephine and I should come through this unscathed. We stuck together at all times. We slept side-by-side. There was nothing embarrassing about this as Temba didn't touch Josephine. If one of us went for a shit, one of the others went too. It wasn't ideal, having three of us, it would have been much easier if it had been just Temba and me, but I respected his decision to bring Josephine. For a start, she was a good soldier, a damn sight hardier than I was, and she didn't moan. And, in his position, had Josephine been Chloris, I wouldn't have left her behind and worried about her.

I guess that many people who have fought a footsoldier's war would recognise much of what I've described. But there was, in my war, another dimension: this was an African war. Africa is a place of effervescent colour, of raw savagery, of breathtaking contrast – and that's how its children fight. They wore everyday, high-street clothes, designer sunglasses and baseball caps alongside talismans given to them by their local witch-doctors. They took names like General Jo, Mickey Mouse and Rommel and strutted around the place, or lounged and preened themselves. They were high, not necessarily on drugs, then miserable and whiny because they wanted to go home. Some of them were yellow one moment, so craven that you had to threaten to shoot them before they'd do anything, and crazily brave the next, standing out in the open in the face of a withering fusillade and squirting bullets back at the enemy. And there was something else: war seemed to strip away the façade of civilisation, most of the men were quick-tempered, dangerously and illogically violent, their aggression sudden and unprovoked.

I carry images of my African war like a man carries photos of his family in his wallet. They're colour photos, stills that suddenly flash into my head at the most unlikely times. A girl, slightly built, perhaps eight years old, dressed in a beautifully clean, bright, cotton frock, lying amid the pumpkins in the *shamba* at the back of her house, as if asleep. But you know she's dead. And butterflies flit around her, land on her, feel at the cloth of her dress, urgently, a myriad, shimmering cloud of yellow forest butterflies that beg her to get up, please get up, and fly with us. And a woman, propped with her back against the mud wall of her hut, her head nodded forward as if in sleep and her legs splayed out in front of her, her feet with pale, calloused soles and overlarge toes; the toddler leaning against her has unfastened the buttons down the front of her dress to expose her breast, a large, full breast with an elongate, flattened nipple which the child holds loosely between her lips while following me with the whites of her eyes. All around them the earth is stained red.

We fought our way up the road towards Mateka for almost four weeks. Mostly the opposition were rubbish, hurried recruits who'd joined Bosmo after they'd taken Mateka and looked like the winning side. We pushed them back steadily until we were almost into the suburbs, some ten miles from the city centre. Then a truck appeared and we were ordered aboard. This was in the dark, at about seven in the evening. We drove and stopped, drove and stopped, until midnight. Finally we were off-loaded in a small village. The road running through it was a dirt road, strongly cambered, its ditches full of water with bodies floating around in various states of bloated decay. Even by recent standards the stench was disgusting. The houses, mud-walled with corrugated iron roofs, were badly shot up, burned out and in darkness. A very smart captain in Boromundi Army uniform appeared in an equally smart Land Rover and drew Temba aside. When Temba returned, he was shaking his head.

Mateka International Airport, he explained, was about a mile and a half to the north of us. At six in the morning we would join the assault on it.

At this point we stopped being a local militia making its piddling contribution and became part of the big picture, the main assault to retake Mateka.

What Temba and I achieved at Upure-Maji did the government/BRF (as far as I'm concerned, they were one and the same thing) a huge favour. Basically, we kick-started Bosmo's assault some ten days before it was scheduled. So it was hurried, and more of a mess and a muddle than it otherwise might have been. Their attack had two prongs. From the Northwest Highlands and the Mountains of the Morning Mist the first, smaller assault drove almost due south along the lake shore to Chirwe, picking up strong support as it came. But this one, because of what we did at Upure-Maji, drew the best units of the Boromundi army and was stopped dead at Chirwe. It should have swung east to join up with the larger force which had thrust straight for Mateka, but it didn't.

The coup in Mateka caught the government on the wrong foot but, because the advance from Chirwe didn't arrive on schedule, Bosmo failed to net the whole city. The government, strongly supported by BRF militias and police, was able to counterattack, clearing Bosmo out of several of the key buildings. This success continued until the main Bosmo force arrived from the highlands. Some very messy fighting followed in which government forces were slowly pushed out of the city. The main reason they lost was simple: Bosmo had deployed some of its crack troops, the troops it had been training and arming for months across the Zaire border, including units of the what they called *Wazhunghu*.

An *mzhunghu* in ChiMundi is an ant. Not any old ant, but a soldier ant. Soldier ants are the heavyweights nasties of the ant world, 1.5cm long and shiny black. They march across country in columns of millions. From a distance, the column resembles some sort of furry snake slithering through the grass. They eat anything they come across, picking a carcass clean to the bones. They can even drag down quite large animals. If enough of them manage to climb on board and fix their jaws into its flesh long enough to pump in the vicious poison they carry, the animal will collapse. Usually they do best on immobile, defenceless prey. There are horror stories of columns of *wazhunghu* entering a house and finding the baby in its cot or the pet poodle tied by its leash. It was an apt name for these Bosmo units. They were well armed. They were ruthless. They were drug-crazed. And they'd been doctored with Rebecca's medicine.

They were easy to distinguish as they tied a reddish-brown rag around their heads. It was, so they were told, a white cotton cloth that had been dipped in the boy-king's *mooti*. It made them untouchable. They had other characteristics. Many wore a cheap imitation of Aviator sunglasses. Copying the US special forces, they didn't have a uniform, preferring fashionable gear like Levi jeans and Gucci denim shirts. With their new Kalashnikovs, metal-buckled leather belts and high leather boots, they looked like models posing for a photoshoot. The most irritating thing about them was their cockiness. Even when you had them on their backs with their guts tangled across the road and a rifle barrel stuffed down their throats, they still didn't believe they were going to die.

We hadn't come across them before. But the nice army man in his Land Rover warned us before he left that units of *Wazhunghu* were defending Mateka airport.

Temba did well that night. He had only the vaguest of instructions as to how to reach our jumping off point, a miserable, three mile trudge away through the bush, but he found it. We then snatched a couple of hours' sleep. As usual, it began raining, a thin drizzle, at about three thirty, so we woke up cold and wet.

The main road to Tanzania runs down the western

side of the airport. There are two entrances. The one nearer Mateka leads to the passenger terminals, the second gives access to the freight and service areas. There is a single runway, aligned south-southeast/north-northwest, and from the service area a perimeter road leads round the inside of the south and eastern boundaries of the airfield. At the end of this road, half way along the eastern boundary, stands a low, white building. This building was our objective: we were to take it and hold it.

We had no idea what function it served. Thick bush ran to within twenty metres of the fence so, at about quarter past five, we were able to crawl up to the edge of it and peer out. We couldn't see much: it was still as dark as the inside of an elephant's intestine and the rain was, if anything, heavier. The building was single storey with a low-pitched, box-profile metal roof. It lay a further thirty metres or so within the fence and it had three windows close together at the left hand end of the wall facing us. We couldn't see if the windows were locked or unlocked, or whether they had burglar bars on them. We knew that there was a door on the far side, facing a taxiing area that led to the main runway.

We'd started off from Kaserewe with twenty-one men, including Temba, Josephine and me. By this stage we were down to sixteen, but the intervening weeks had mostly weeded out the weaker brethren. Our main problem in carrying out our assault was less numbers than the limitations of our weaponry. All we had were rifles: no grenades, no rockets, no machine guns. To make matters worse, we were running short of ammunition. Our only hope lay in getting in close. By this time Temba was established as our leader; there hadn't been any other serious contenders. The men respected him because he was cautious and he thought before he did anything. His plan was typically simple. By half past five we would have cut a hole in the fence. We would then rush the building. If the windows round this side were accessible, we'd go in through them. If they weren't, we would charge round towards the front and find a way in.

It doesn't sound much of a plan because it wasn't. And it had one major flaw. If anyone saw us coming, we wouldn't have a chance. The ground on either side of the fence was open and such grass as there was, at six inches high, offered no cover. Once out of the bush there would be no going back.

Temba crawled forward alone to cut the pig-wire fence. He was fairly safe doing this as it would have taken an owl with night vision goggles to spot him. But the job itself promised to be difficult as the only tool we could muster between us was a pair of cheap, snub-nosed pliers. In the event, it proved easy, the base of the wire was so rotten with rust he simply lifted it away and folded it up.

We were supposed to go at 05.55. Shortly after 05.30 Temba gave us the thumbs-up and we crawled over to him through the wet grass. Then we lay, feeling cold and damp and miserable, and waited.

Waiting is murder because all I do is imagine the terrible things that are going to happen to me in the next few minutes. I didn't think we would get away with this one. We were up against professionals, well armed and trained, and ruthless. As soon as we went through the wire we'd be cut down. If we didn't die instantly, shredded into mangled corpses and scattered in pieces across the wet grass, which seemed the better option, we'd be lying in agony until they came out to collect us. I didn't want to think about what they'd do to anyone they found alive.

So I was frantically going through the last minutes of my life. I had missed out on too much for this to be the end.

Temba lifted the fence and began to wave us through. I glanced at my watch. It was 05.50. He had had the good sense to send us through the gap five minutes early. It was self-protection, he didn't want the balloon to go up on the far side, where the main attack was taking place, before we'd reached the building.

I sprinted across that wide stretch of slippery grass, but not so fast that I left Josephine behind. It's the longest thirty metres I've ever done, the blood drumming in my ears and my sight doing the same grey, tunnel-vision trick it did at Upure-Maji. It wasn't until I was up and running that I realized that first light was coming through the low overcast, so we were quite visible. I cursed whoever it was that hadn't started the attack a quarter of an hour earlier, in the dark, spitting the curses as I ran. I was first to the building, throwing myself at its wall, pressing my back against its hard security, reaching out to grab Josephine and pull her against the wall next to me. Temba, who'd waited to see everyone safely through and so had been the last through the wire, was some way behind us, coming fast, his arms pumping and his breath hissing through his teeth as he charged towards us

A quick check showed that all the windows were

closed and were made of toughened glass. I couldn't see any handles. In the blockwork wall below each was set a grey metal box which emitted the cheerful hum of an air-conditioning unit, so the windows probably didn't open.

We didn't wait for Temba but darted round the side. At the same moment the undersides of the cloud in the direction of the airport buildings were lit by a yellowish flash which was followed by the bump of an explosion and the clatter of small-arms fire. I kept running. I passed two similar windows in the end of the building so, stooping as I went, I shot past each, throwing myself round the front of the building.

Two newish-looking Toyota Land Cruisers and a Daihatsu Trooper were drawn up in front of the deep veranda that ran the length of the front. Low chairs and coffee-style tables were neatly arranged along it. The entrance to the building, double wooden doors at the back of the veranda, was nearer my end and, as I hesitated, as I caught my breath, they opened.

The men who emerged were soapy, sopping wet and semi-naked. They clutched towels and trousers and uniform tops with gold braid matted across the shoulder lapels. As they gushed out I shot them. In the face of the hail of bullets from the Galil, they rolled over like rabbits in a cornfield. And, as I fired, others from the Kaserewe squad, Josephine with them, bundled past me, treading and tripping over the bodies and falling through the doorway, and I heard the battering of their rifles.

Then, very suddenly, everything went quiet. Our people began to trickle out of the door, grinning and giving thumbs-up signs. I turned and leaned against the cement block balustrade that ran along the front of the veranda and stared out across the airfield. I was shaking and so emotionally exhausted I wanted to cry. What kept me from tipping over the edge was the pyrotechnics going on across the far side. Silhouetted against the yellow glow of flames and the intermittent flash of grenades stood the tilted tail-fin of a burnt-out jet which had been caught on the ground during earlier fighting. The sound of battle seemed to roll across slowly, heavy and muffled by the dampness. The airfield was utterly empty between us and the jet. If we moved the three vehicles, no-one could approach us from the front unless they came in a tank. And we could cover the back and sides by knocking out the windows.

Temba appeared and flopped against the balustrade next to me. His head was bowed and his shoulders hunched forward, and he was sobbing. I knew instantly, through a haze of weariness, that it was Josephine. I felt the beginning of that awful despair you feel when you know that something terrible's happened, something irrevocably awful that means that life will never be the same again but a continuing, unending misery. I reached out and gripped his arm. 'Temba,' I whispered, but inside me a little voice was saying, 'Oh God, oh no! Please God, please don't let it be . . .'

'You know what this place is, Armstrong?' His voice was so tight he could hardly speak.

I turned and frowned at him. He wasn't crying. He was laughing.

'VIP lounge. This, this is a VIP lounge.' It took him a moment to recover, while I continued to stare at him, wondering if he'd gone mad. 'This place,' he continued, his chest heaving, 'was for president Chunguaye, the one that built the airport in 1983. In there,' and he jerked his thumb behind us, 'in there is a bar and rest-rooms, big, comfy seats and ... Armstrong ... !' He could hardly control himself, leaning against me and shuddering with laughter. 'Armstrong, inside there is a hot bath.'

The bath was the size of a small swimming pool, one of those sunk into the floor jobs. The floor around it was dark blue, mosaic-style tiles and the walls were tiled from floor to ceiling in a rather overwhelming yellow. And the bath was full of water.

The officers from the *Wazhunghu* units guarding the airfield obviously came across each morning to avail themselves of the facilities. It was a risky thing to do. I suppose they had patrols out, perhaps some in vehicles round the inner edge of the perimeter wire, more on foot on the outside – though we'd seen none of them. Perhaps they'd had men guarding the place but had sent them away for half an hour for some privacy while they bathed. I don't know, but I do know that we'd been incredibly lucky.

We counted six bodies, the most senior a colonel. We dragged them out and threw them down the veranda steps. Temba smashed holes in the windows and set lookouts, with more on the front veranda, and then we bathed, quickly, in groups. We all agreed that Josephine should go first, alone, but she was having none of it. So she bathed with me and another of the Kaserewe men, removing everything except her rather frayed knickers. She seemed used to displaying her breasts, because it didn't seem to worry her in the least. But they worried me. They were small and very firm and when she soaped them I had to shut my eyes.

What comes now is a description of what were, for me, some of the worst moments of that whole wretched war. It wasn't my war. It wasn't a fight I had to be in. I'd chosen it and, because I'd chosen freely and voluntarily, I was determined to stick with it. But, by that stage, I was weary, worn out, hurting, dejected. The bath had helped, Josephine's tits had helped, but they offered no more than a momentary lift.

It was the worst part because it went on for a very long time and because, strangely, so little happened. We expected the *Wazhunghu* to counterattack at any time. From just before seven onwards, they showed their intentions with some gentle sniping. I was at the back of the house with Josephine, manning the middle of the three windows, while Temba wandered around keeping everyone on their toes. Every now and then a bullet came through our window with a 'pfeew-smack' as it passed us to flatten itself against the far wall. Some of the early ones took out the rest of the window, showering us with shards of glass. After that they arrived at irregular intervals.

The trouble was that, in order to keep an effective watch, we had to keep poking our heads above the level of the sill. We did it from different sides of the window, at different points, and for varying lengths of time, but

I lived in dread of the moment that the sniper's bullet coincided with one of us taking a look.

I hated it. I tried to think of ways round the problem. A periscope would have been perfect. I tried to prise a mirror off the toilet wall but it wouldn't come – then, when it finally came, it smashed, the shards too small to do an effective job.

The counter-attack started shortly after ten. As we'd expected – because it would have been suicidal to have come from the airport side – it came from the bush, the same direction as ours, and they started by blowing holes in the fence using grenades. They might have a great faith in their *mooti*, but they weren't daft enough to try crawling, one by one and in broad daylight, through the small hole we'd used.

So we knew they were coming and we were as ready for them as we could be, but we weren't prepared for the way they came. They just ran straight at us. There were only seven of them. They came out of the bush, sprinted to the holes in the fence and threw themselves through. They charged straight across the thirty yards of open ground between the fence and the building, and, as they came, in their denim and sunglasses, in their designer tee shirts and trainers, with their Kalashnikovs spitting at us and their dried blood-coloured kerchiefs tight around their foreheads, they screamed.

They were terrifying. I have to hand that to them – they were terrifying, in the blindness of their bravery, in their white-eyed, open-mouthed madness, in their total belief in their invincibility. But as they came at us we knocked them down. And it was so very, very good knocking them down, even the ones who, when we looked at them later, were little more than boys. These had a reputation as the cream of Bosmo's troops, the men who had killed and pillaged and raped their way across Boromundi. These were men who, because of Rebecca's *mooti*, couldn't die. Killing them was the only good part of that long, agonising stay in that shit-hole VIP building.

None of them got as far as the building. If they had, if they'd been able to crouch along the wall under the windows and lob grenades through them, we'd have had a problem. But they didn't make it. Josephine and I stood side by side at the window, with others at the other two windows, and we blew them away.

After that, nothing happened. The sniping stopped. The bodies lay where they'd dropped and attracted the attention of the flies. One boy, the one who'd got furthest, now lay staring at the sky just outside our window. Josephine and I continued the miserable job of poking our heads above the parapet. It went on all day. As the light faded into evening it simply got worse. We had to expose ourselves for longer, squinting into the darkness, imagining movements that weren't there.

The fighting for the main airport buildings continued into the early hours of the following day. From three in the morning onwards, an eerie silence fell across the airport. In the pitch black darkness it began to rain again. We couldn't see anything, and we had no idea who had won. For all we knew, Bosmo had come out on top and was lining up tanks and armoured cars to come over and squash us. The silence, the not-knowing, simply made our agony worse.

Temba stood us down for a rest, one at a time, as often as he dared. But there were so few of us, and we were so afraid of being caught off our guard, that we spent most of the time watching. We may have thought ourselves used to war but I don't think any of us slept that night.

16 Njomba

There are few constancies in this life, things which accompany you, unchanging, each and every day. One is your face. You get used to your face. You don't see it often. In fact, if you think about it, other people see a great deal more of it. When it's your turn it's usually in the mirror first thing in the morning, not the best time to pay it any real attention. You wash it, scrape off the stubble, dry it, perhaps apply a dab of *CK One*. You don't inspect it too closely. You don't worry about it. It's there, familiar, a friend.

I didn't recognise the thing that stared back at me from the Sun Hotel's mirror. At first sight, it appeared black. The lower part, around the jaw and across the upper lip, had sprouted a dark, fungal mat with a faintly green tinge, as if it was acting as a very successful culture for some weird species of airborne algae. Such skin as remained visible was stretched thinly and tightly between the more protuberant bones of the skull and was, on closer inspection, walnut-brown rather than plain black, and wrinkled, with deep crows feet radiating out from the corners of the eyes, while the skin of the forehead resembled a horizontally ploughed field. The furrows of this permanent frown, despite vigorous and soapy scrubbing, remained ingrained with dirt. And the eyes, blood red things surrounded by skin that was truly black, almost as black as Temba's, had sunk into the sockets. But far, far, far worse, was the hair. That face used to have nice hair above it, strong and dark with a cheeky bounce in it. It was washed three times a week with *Head and Shoulders*, so it never had dandruff, and it was cut regularly. What I saw wasn't my hair. It was long and tangled and unkempt. It had none of its usual curl, none of its old body. It lay flat against my skull, as if it were tired, like dead seaweed that has been too long in the sun, and a fair amount seemed to have gone AWOL.

But I was alive. I was alive and billeted for a week's rest and recreation, along with the rest of the Kaserewe unit, in the Sun Hotel, a small private establishment in the eastern outskirts of Mateka. If an AA inspector had seen it he'd have died laughing: it had a single shower, cold water only, we slept four to a room, and we shared the place with a couple of other armies, of cockroaches and bed-bugs. However, the place did have food, basic, simple Boromundi grub in generous helpings, which we made the most of. It had American lager and cans of Coke and Marlboro cigarettes and Hershey bars, all for sale at extortionate prices. And, for the Kaserewe boys, it had women, hoards of them, poking their faces against the windows and offering nirvana for a few cents.

The VIP lounge at Mateka airport was already a dim memory. We knew we'd won when a plane landed. I don't know much about planes but I recognised this one. It was a Hercules C130 transport and it sported American roundels. During the following weeks C130s became as common in the skies above Mateka as vultures and, once the place had been tidied up, their fresh-faced pilots became a noisy feature of the bar in the Palace Hotel.

We noticed the difference the planes made because within a week us footsloggers got presents of as much ammunition as we wanted and some very neat little American fragmentation grenades. Unfortunately the improvements didn't extend to the food: we still had to forage for what we needed. Sadly, a number of much less useful things came in on these planes, including President Bugarimani and his entourage. He hadn't been in the Virgin Islands at all, so he said. When the war broke out he'd been in Washington DC, ideally placed to beg a little support from his friend Bill Clinton, which is what he got.

We might have been knackered, but Temba's dwindling band of Kaserewe militiamen had to fight their way into Mateka. We dwindled not because we were deserting and going home: deserters – we knew from witnessing it – were shot in the back of the head. We dwindled because the fighting continued with, if anything, renewed frenzy. At the end of each day I looked at Josephine and Temba and wondered how much longer we could survive unscathed. It was as if some hand, some force, was protecting us. There were moments when it occurred to me that it was Chloris, tucked away in the security of her convent in Surrey or Berkshire; Chloris, shielding us with her prayers.

Some foul things had happened in Mateka under Bosmo. For example, the stadium in which a remarkably good Boromundi football team had, back in March, swelled national pride by thrashing Nigeria one-nil, became an execution-ground. Each Saturday Bosmo had lined up hundreds of prisoners and suspected BRF supporters and, exercising their imagination, had massacred them, often using the goalposts as gibbets. The locals swore they'd been forced to come and watch the show. I don't think that's the truth at all: I think many went along because they were curious, only to discover that watching people die is even more exciting than watching your favourite football team win. Londoners did it at Tyburn until the last hanging in 1783, and some of us would probably do it today, given the right victim, and I could name a few.

Anyway, as, street by bloody street, we liberated the place, anyone suspected of having supported Bosmo and, particularly, anyone who might have informed on neighbours and who had, therefore, directly contributed to the show at the national stadium, was dragged out into the streets and beaten. Since many of the beatings were carried out with *pangas*, the subjects of this chastisement didn't last long, and their decomposing remains were added to the carnage already cluttering the streets.

I found a pair of blunt scissors and chopped my hair so close against my head that you couldn't see the alarmingly increasing grey, washed what remained several vigorous times using a large bar of *Sunlight* soap, expended an hour and four priceless Gilette razorblades shaving off the beard, and then, feeling a little more attractive, trotted along to see Temba. I told him that the only person who could confirm that Chloris was safely back in England was the archbishop, so I needed to see him, now.

Archbishop Muteresa lived in a smart suburb of Mateka – all wide roads and big gardens and impressive gateways

in high walls with broken glass sprinkled along the top –
but most of the houses showed signs of having been
attacked and looted, with stuff strewn all over the lawns.
Some had been burnt, their walls standing as blackened
shells. The archbishop's abode was a large, colonial-style,
two storey house, whitewashed, with a red tile roof, set
well back from the road in a neatly kept garden surrounded by a steel fence with very sharp points on the
top. There was an ornate gate locked with a substantial
chain and padlock. I stood at the gate for five minutes
and shouted but no-one responded. Temba, who, along
with Josephine and three of the Kaserewe boys, had
insisted on coming along, had less patience, so I followed
them over the fence and, moving quickly from ornamental shrub to ornamental shrub, approached the house.

In contrast to the houses on either side, the archbishop's home looked untouched by war, which made us
suspicious and very alert, so we carried our rifles cocked
with their change levers on automatic. The house had
matching upstairs and downstairs verandas to the right
of its facade, and windows, protected by wooden lou-
vered shutters, to the left. The verandas were deserted,
but half an army could have been watching us from
behind the shutters.

I suppose that, by this stage in the campaign, we'd
grown used to an unprotected approach to houses that
might suddenly spit bullets. The idea that we might, at
any moment, get mown down had become, if not boring,
at least mundane. But I never got away from the little
surge of relief as I reached the protection of a wall, as
I pressed myself against it, feeling through my shirt the
residual warmth of the sun.

We worked our way round to the downstairs veranda and pushed through some expensive-looking cane furniture to the front door. It lay invitingly open, so we went through, coming into the cool, restful shade of a well-proportioned hall. If the shade was pleasant after the broiling sun, the stench wasn't. It was one we recognized too well: roasting flesh. It wasn't very strong, not the stink we met when we came to a burning house in which bodies were sizzling as they roasted. It was damp, slightly musty, as if the smell had been around some time. What also puzzled me was that, despite the invitingly open front door, the interior of the house, like the exterior, seemed in perfect order, with no sign of any damage.

We began to search the place. It had a large and comfortably furnished sitting room that ran from behind the veranda to the back of the house, one of those strange tropical rooms in which the main feature is a York stone fireplace complete with mantelpiece, fire dogs and electrically glowing logs. The dining room was large and airy and boasted a beautiful table in what might have been rosewood, with twelve matching chairs, while the cutlery in the sideboard was silver and the plates Royal Doulton. By this time Temba had checked round the side and discovered that there was a second building, fairly obviously the diocesan offices, and a large garage round the back. He set off with Josephine and two of the Kaserewe men to investigate it.

With the remaining man, I carried out a quick search of the rest of the downstairs before we went upstairs. There were four large bedrooms, all but one unoccupied. The archbishop's bed had been slept in, though I couldn't tell how recently. From the fact that his paisley patterned cotton pyjamas lay neatly folded on the bed, that his hair brush, complete with a selection of tightly curled, black hairs, sat on the chest of drawers, and his toothbrush nestled in its pyrex glass in the adjoining bathroom, we knew he wasn't off travelling. It was quite interesting poking round his room. His underclothes were Marks and Spencer and he favoured bright red braces.

As I came back onto the upstairs landing the light came on. For a moment I was alert, pulling up my gun and flattening myself against the wall. Then I realised what had happened: Mateka's electricity supply had been restored.

We forgathered in the dining room. Temba emerged from the kitchen carrying a handful of beers.

'Kenyan,' he announced, knocking the first top off on the edge of the Archbishop's lovely table. 'Tusker lager.'

They weren't cold, the fridge hadn't had time, but they were good.

After Temba had drained half a bottle he wagged a thumb in the direction of the diocesan offices. 'They are deserted.'

'There is no damage,' Josephine added. 'No thieving, no disturbance. The archbishop, his staff, everybody has . . .' and she shrugged her shoulders eloquently.

It was while we were sitting round the archbishop's table, drinking his beer, that we found him. I was nearest the door into the kitchen and I heard an intermittent, metallic clicking coming from behind it. We also began to notice that the burning smell was getting worse. Temba commented on it. It took a few moments for the penny to drop. I put my beer carefully down on the spotless, polished table and went through to the kitchen.

The archbishop must have enjoyed entertaining, because the cooking was done on an impressively large electric range. The oven was on, and hissing, spitting noises came from within it. It was a large oven, quite large enough to accommodate the archbishop. I didn't open the oven door, not immediately, because it wasn't necessary. His shoes, the same black patent shoes he'd worn at Alice's, were placed neatly beside the machine, but they'd been taken off without unfastening the laces. The archbishop would never have done that. I didn't do anything except turn the cooker off.

I felt utterly dejected. As I went back into the dining room to tell the others what I'd found, I felt as if I carried a great weight on my shoulders. But Temba and Josephine, bless them, were positive. There were other ways of finding Chloris. While the men attacked a crate of beer they'd found in the pantry the three of us walked across to the diocesan office and ransacked the filing cabinets. Josephine found the Humphries file in the archbishop's secretary's office. She came across and handed it to me. I took it away with me afterwards and I'm glad I did as it contains some lovely mementos of Chloris as a nun. For example, little Sister Maria had written a very precise report of what had happened between Chloris and me on the beach at the Two Turtles, and it included a statement that she had clearly seen Chloris grab and kiss me as we thrashed around in the surf.

But when I opened her file that day in the diocesan offices in Mateka, the first piece of paper I found was a letter from Chloris to the archbishop. It was dated 18th March, just a week before Temba and I set off for Chirwe, and it was addressed from the Holy Sisters

Convent in Mateka. It was written in Chloris' round, schoolgirl hand and the ink had run where her tears had splashed onto the vellum. It begged him not to send her to the mission at Njomba. It repeated my plea that she be kept somewhere safe – like in Mateka – until the threat from the Movement was lifted. She even suggested she be transferred to the UK for a period, though she declared her determination to return and continue her work in Boromundi. But it ended, sickeningly, with a promise to obey him, whatever he ordered.

Stapled on top of it was a memo. It simply said, *Phoned Sister Magdalena. CH to go Saturday.*

I managed to hand the letter to Temba.

'Where's Njomba?' I whispered.

He was reading the letter and didn't seem to want to answer me, so I collapsed into the secretary's swivel chair and buried my face in my hands. Temba was too busy reading the letter but Josephine replied. Her voice was thick and low and I could feel the pain in it, and, as she spoke, she came and wrapped her arms round me from behind, holding me so tightly against herself I could feel the way I crushed her breasts.

'It is to the north-west of Mateka,' she whispered, 'about forty, fifty miles.'

'So the Archbishop deliberately sent Chloris into Bunrum territory.' As I said this I saw how Temba's eyes were fixed on my face, small and hard and unflinching. I met them, and held them. Slowly he began to nod.

'Yes,' he said, 'I think the Archbishop was working with Bullet. There is no other explanation.

'The confessional,' I whispered.

Temba frowned at me but Josephine was much quicker on the uptake.

'Temba, you wondered how Bullet knew that Rebecca was a virgin. Armstong is suggesting that the Archbishop instructed a priest to find out.'

I lost it completely then. I have vague recollections of throwing Josephine off, of hurling myself out of the door and pitching across the yard into the kitchen. I know I opened the oven because the stench punched me in the face, and I have a vivid recollection of the arch-bishop, naked, trussed up like a Mohommedan praying, his skin sloughing off to reveal pink flesh as he sizzled in his own juices. But I do remember, very distinctly, throwing his shoes in with him, slamming the stove door, switching the cooker back on, and turning the oven to 'high'.

While a couple of the Kaserewe men sat on my head until I'd calmed down, Temba and Josephine went back to the diocesan offices. They didn't spend long there but when they came back they carried another file. This was one of those suspension files and what was interesting about it was that it was empty. Josephine had found it in the archbishop's private office, in a small, locked filing drawer in a desk the size of an American nuclear aircraft carrier. The drawer had been forced, probably with a screwdriver.

Temba broke the silence. 'The archbishop keeps files on priests who have . . . strayed. There are about twenty of these. Between the names Sandehu and Tananga there is an empty file.'

He turned to look at Josephine, and she grinned. 'I am an expert on filing,' she said. 'Unless this type of suspension file has been fixed properly, things may drop between them.' From behind her back, like a magician hauling a rabbit from a hat, she produced a sheet of paper. 'These are notes on the appointment of a certain Joseph Murunda Shibane to the parish of Gwelea.'

'Joseph Murunda . . .' began one of the Kaserewe men.

'Yes,' Temba cut in. 'Joseph Murunda. We have heard of Joseph Murunda. Joseph Murunda is one of the leaders in Bosmo. Yet Joseph Murunda Shibane is also a priest with a special file. Is it a coincidence that the one we call Bullet is also Shibane? Is it a coincidence that the filing drawer in which this empty file is kept has recently been broken open and that the archbishop is dead? Is it . . . ?' He stopped then and it was obvious he was thinking very hard. 'Am I being very imaginative, or is it a coincidence that the archbishop was at the School Board meeting when Bartolemew was asking selected people whether they knew anything of this Movement? Is it a coincidence that Bartolemew died immediately after asking those questions? Is it a coincidence that the archbishop comes to Kaserewe to talk to Armstrong about the Movement, perhaps to find out how much he knows? Is it a coincidence that the archbishop does the one thing with Chloris Humphries that he is asked not to do? Or, or am I putting too many bricks end to end?'

I didn't say anything. I thought he'd got it right.

We were now pretty sure that Bullet Shibane the murderer, Joseph Murunda the Bosmo leader and Joseph

Murunda Shibane, the priest with a history, were one and the same man.

Josephine and Temba had also found something else in their wanderings: the archbishop's car, sitting in the garage round the back. It was a big black Mercedes diesel with tinted windows, the sort of windows that big-headed filmstars favour, that enable you to see out without people on the outside seeing in. I shook my head in disbelief when I saw it. People in Boromundi are fundamentally very friendly. If they see a car they know, they smile and wave. The idea that the archbishop couldn't be seen by his flock as he travelled around passed all belief. However, it proved useful now. We had no difficulty in liberating several jerrycans of the archbishop's diesel, but considerably more difficulty in finding the key for the padlock on the main gate, but we left the archbishop's house in grand style, all six of us, with Temba driving and Josephine and I in the front, and the Kaserewe men in the back, with room to spare. The Mercedes sported a little purple flag on the right front mudguard with the archbishop's crest on it which flapped in the slipstream; and, as we drove through the streets of Mateka, the few people who had ventured out waved and crossed themselves as we passed.

We took with us the contents of the archbishop's larder. There were two more crates of beer, soft drinks, and a goodly selection of foodstuffs, including things like a case of Abernethy biscuits and three catering size tins of ham. At first Josephine, who was an upright Christian, objected. Temba calmed her down. At a time like this, he suggested, it should be looked upon as an act of Christian charity.

We started with a brief tour of Mateka, searching for news of Chloris. The Holy Sisters convent had been burned to the ground but neighbours told us that none of the nuns had been harmed. They had been taken away in a Bosmo truck – they didn't know where. Except, there was one . . .

Sister Clementine was very old, very small, very frail, very stooped and with a face like a pug. She had escaped the destruction of the convent simply because she had been visiting a sick woman. The local people had hidden her throughout Bosmo's stay. We found her sitting in the sun on the front steps of a house that had been hit by a shell. Rubble, clothing, smashed furniture and a mangled child's doll were strewn across the street.

Josephine did the talking.

'Sister, we are looking for a Sister Chloris.'

The old girl's eyes lit up.

'You knew her?'

She nodded, her jowls waggling.

'Please . . . Did Sister Chloris go with Bosmo?'

The lady's face fell, but, slowly, she shook her head. I could have jumped up and down and screamed.

'So . . . Is she here?

Sister Clementine shook her head.

'So . . . Did she leave before?'

She began speaking, then, very rapidly in a high-pitched whine. I was able to follow enough of it to understand that Chloris had already left – she had been transferred to Njomba Mission some time in March.

'Njomba?' Josphine asked. 'Are you sure?'

'Yes,' Clementine squeaked, nodding vigorously, 'Yes, I am certain.'

'Sister, do you know of a priest called Shibane, Joseph Shibane?'

The old thing smiled. 'Joseph Shibani? Eeeeh! Joseph! That Man! Eeeh! For many years that one was an associate of Archbishop Muteresa, but . . .' She pulled a face. 'Later he was transferred.'

'Transferred? Where?'

Clementine screwed up her face so that her eyes almost totally disappeared. When they emerged she chirruped, 'Kwita-Kwita. I think, yes, near Kwita-Kwita.'

Kwita-Kwita, you'll remember, was where Smallboy was born.

As we moved back to the car I again asked Josephine where Njomba was. Temba answered.

'It is to the west.'

From the way he said, 'to the west', I knew he meant it was well inside Bosmo territory.

'Chloris was sent there in March.' I was thinking aloud. 'So she'd have been there when the war broke out.'

'Unless she was transferred back.'

'I'll have to check,' I said.

'Check?' Temba exploded. 'What you mean, "check"?'

As we drove back to the hotel it turned into quite a row, conducted across Josephine, sitting between us, who stayed strangely silent. Temba still didn't believe that Chloris felt anything for me. I hardly knew the girl. I hadn't even kissed her. I finally scotched that by insisting he pull over onto the shoulder while he read Sister Maria's description of Chloris and I tangling in the surf at the Two Turtles. He grunted when he'd finished.

By the time we reached the hotel Temba was deep in

thought. He muttered something about needing to contact HQ and wandered off with his radio. I spent time with Josephine, who'd borrowed a road atlas of eastern Africa which showed the main roads of Boromundi. We sat on the front veranda of the hotel and found Njomba. There were two ways to reach it. One way was to follow the main road from Mateka to the north-west, branching off about thirty miles out. But there was another road which seemed to lead directly to Njomba. From the uncertain way it was marked on the map it would probably be a horrendous road, but it might avoid the worst of the fighting.

We were still discussing the two routes when Temba returned. He'd changed completely. He seemed fired up. It was just before lunch but he commandeered the hotel's dining room and called the men together. A couple of them had disappeared – according to the others, to have their spines straightened in the local brothel. We were splitting up, Temba announced. Three of the Kaserewe boys, the three that had accompanied us in the morning, were coming with us on a special mission. The remainder would stay on at the hotel until reinforcements arrived from Kaserewe where, now that the BRF was evidently winning, recruitment had been brisk. His speech was interrupted by babble from his radio, another present from the Americans. As he slapped it against his ear he announced we would be leaving at two, immediately after lunch. Then, as he began shouting into his infernal machine, he groped his way out of the room.

For a moment, it warmed my heart that my friends were supporting me in my time of need. Then I began to worry. What we were going to attempt would be virtually suicidal. We would have to break through Bosmo lines and then go foraging round behind them, looking for a girl who might be safe in England but who otherwise was probably dead. If, as a result of this, one of my friends was killed or injured, I would never forgive myself. No, I couldn't let them do it. Impossible. So I went to find Temba and begged him to call it off. But he wouldn't. And when I tried reasoning with Josephine I was given even shorter shrift.

Temba had decided to go by the more direct route but, when we set off from the Sun Hotel in the archbishop's Mercedes, instead of driving towards the city centre he headed for the northern suburbs. I didn't understand what he was doing, even less when we found ourselves back at the archbishop's house.

After parking round the back, Temba led us to a small room adjoining the archbishop's office. The door had been smashed off its hinges but had been propped drunkenly back in its frame. He lifted it away and turned on the light. The room was full of clothes, not ordinary clothes but the gear bishops, priests and choirboys wear. I stood, staring at them. And, slowly, daylight dawned.

It was a mad dash: a bishop, a deacon, three priests and a very pretty choirboy, all in a large, black Mercedes. Temba drove with his hand on the horn. If soldiers didn't shift the road blocks in time, if he was forced to stop, he exploded out of the car, raised a large, silver crucifix high into the air and began cursing them. Temba, as you know, is a pretty imposing figure at any time, but dressed in purple with a matching hat on his head – he was magnificent. I don't know where he'd learnt the language, but if I'd been one of those poor soldiers, I'd have been terrified – and I don't believe in hell.

Inside the car we relaxed in luxury. One of the men had discovered a small, well-stocked bar set into the back of the front seats. The car was air-conditioned. The harsh light of early afternoon was dimmed by the tinted windows. The big engine purred and the springs soaked up the punishment meted out by the ruts and potholes. When he wasn't cursing soldiers, Temba hummed.

There is no such thing as a front line in the sort of war we were fighting. At some point Temba stopped excommunicating BRF and began excommunicating Bosmo. It didn't make any difference – we sailed through. For a short distance we even had a Toyota, with a large machine gun mounted on the back and three Kalashnikov-toting soldiers on board, as an escort.

We reached Njomba shortly after five. In the lengthening shadows of late afternoon, we found the centre of this small market town torn apart, many of the buildings roofless and blackened, the bloated corpses of men, women, children and animals still strewn in the streets. The only sign of life was a group of soldiers dressed in the very latest fashion who were draped around the veranda of what had once been the town's general store. Temba skidded the car to a halt beside them and clambered out. Those of us left in the car wound down the windows and fondled the guns and grenades concealed in the folds of our clothes. I was on the wrong side of the car but if anything had happened to Temba, I'd have been out of the passenger door and blasting the shop apart in a fraction of a second.

Temba had dealt with kids for long enough to feel a situation. To have shouted at or threatened a dozen *Wazhunghu* would have been counterproductive. He was very reasoned with them, almost apologetic, but firm. Could they help him? He was looking for Njomba Mission. An urgent matter relating to a devil that needed exorcism.

They lounged like our English kids lounge around our shopping centres. The arrogance seeped out of them. Their sunglasses hid the glaze in their eyes and the bottles of beer and the rolled-up spliffs alternated in moving back and forth to their lips. For a desperate couple of minutes I thought we would have to kill them and, if we did, we'd have to take on the hordes that would erupt out of the surrounding buildings. It would be like kicking a wasps' nest. And then, suddenly, one of them pointed. He was a lanky lad sporting a 1994 Brazil tee who wore the vertical cuts of tribal markings on his cheeks and a San Francisco Giants baseball cap, but something from his Christian past must have stirred. He spoke a few terse, dismissive words, and pointed up the road with his beer bottle before returning it to his mouth. Temba thanked him gravely. As he climbed back into the car, for the first time since we'd stopped, I breathed.

We found the mission about five miles along the main road to the west of Njomba. A group of girls, dressed in gratifyingly brief gymslips in a colour that matched the wall of forest that defined the mission's extensive, red-earthed clearing, played a lively game of netball in the sloping rays of late afternoon light. The screech of the teacher's whistle cut the still air. From the small, open-walled cluster of classrooms to our left came the chant of the sort of rote learning that African schools seem to enjoy. At the back of a large central quadrangle, shaded by trees, lay the hospital, identifiable by a small queue of women carrying babies, while the church, with white-washed mud walls and shingled roof, stood away to our right. It was as if we were suddenly back at St Faith's, as if the war had never happened. It was like a different world.

As Temba slowed the car in front of what looked like the mission offices, a nun was coming out, a diminutive young woman dressed in exactly the garb Chloris wore. My heart surged. She stopped, poised like some fright-ened antelope, until Temba climbed out. At the sight of his cloth she broke into a round-faced smile.

For all my impatience, for all the suddenly rekindled hope that, somehow, miraculously, Chloris would be okay, I controlled myself. It was like holding down the lid on an exploding dustbin.

It was clearly understood that Josephine and I would stay in the car. Our rifles lay across our knees. Hand grenades weighed down the folds of cloth in our laps. Parked like this, surrounded by buildings, if the *Wazhun-ghu* were watching we'd stand about as much chance as coconuts in a shy where the punters were using Kalash-nikovs. As Temba moved up the steps with the nun, our heads never stopped turning as we scrutinised our surroundings. The scene remained utterly peaceful. A pupil, a small, barefoot boy in overlarge shorts and blindingly white shirt, tripped down the steps and set off in the direction of the classrooms. Yet there was something strange about the place, something unnatural, something discordant.

I kept telling myself that the only thing that was wrong was me. I no longer recognized a peaceful scene when I saw it. My imagination was working overtime, my nerves frayed to breaking point. I was too tired, too wound up, and worried to distraction about Chloris. Relax, I kept saying to myself. For Christ's sake – relax. It's going to be all right. She isn't here, she's in England.

Temba was in the building for what seemed an eternity but was probably no more than twenty minutes. He came out quickly, slid behind the wheel, started the engine and accelerated away, the tyres skidding as we turned sharply across the wet ground. When the buildings had disappeared behind the first bend in the road, he drew the Mercedes to the side of the road. He reached forward and deliberately switched off the engine, remaining leaning forward, gripping the wheel. I knew what was coming.

He swung round. 'They have not heard of her. They do not know who she is.'

The relief hit me like a bucket of icy water. She wasn't here because she'd never been here. She'd stayed in Mateka. She was now in England.

'But they are lying.'

It took a moment for Temba's words to sink in. I stared at him. 'Lying?'

'Yes. I was taken to the sister in charge. There was

something about this woman that I did not understand. She is not what one would expect – the nun who showed me in said that Sister Teresa had left, that this Sister Mary had taken over.' He sat there, slowly shaking his head. 'You know how, in class, you have a child that lies? One that is not very good at it? Well . . .'

We heard them before we saw them, and were out of the car in plenty of time to meet them: one of the Kaserewe boys whom we'd left to watch the road was dragging the little nun who had met us on the steps. His hand was so large it covered her whole face and he'd twisted her arm halfway up her back with such force that her feet barely touched the ground. And, following them, came the other two boys, grinning and wheeling an ancient Raleigh bicycle.

Temba towered over the woman. His hands went to his hips and he smiled. 'Ah,' he said, 'A little bird, a plump little bird.'

We chucked the lovely old Raleigh bike into the undergrowth and bundled the nun into the back of the Mercedes. She didn't need much persuading. As Temba drove, she sang.

17 Bullet Shibane

Joseph Murunda Shibane was born in 1963, the year of Boromundi's independence, with a swelling silver spoon in his mouth. At the time, his father, Dembe Shibane, was already doing well (for an African) as chief clerk in the Mateka branch of the Pan African Trading Company (PATCo), a thriving British import-export business based in Nairobi with branches throughout eastern Africa. The company was going through a revolution at the time. Under political pressure, reluctantly, and rather later than most other European-owned businesses, it was Africanising its senior management. The old tradition of recruiting all executive posts in the colonial mother country had to stop. And Dembe was sitting like a vulture over rotten carrion, waiting.

In the next five years Dembe moved up to become Managing Director (Boromundi). This meteoric rise reflected his ability: he was a shrewd businessman, he was respected by his staff and he had the good sense not to flinch at the sort of bribery that was rapidly becoming endemic in the Boromundi commercial economy. But he needed one other thing: the social graces to entertain the European representatives and directors who came out to tour their investments. He learned them, quickly. His wife couldn't.

It entailed a divorce. Joseph's mother, Kinanewa, a

very black, cheerful lady who weighed in at eighteen stone, was quietly pensioned off to her home town of Njomba. Joseph and his younger sister, Annie, were not permitted to accompany her. They were to become part of the atmosphere that Dembe wished to create in his new house, a beautiful, rambling colonial bungalow three doors along from the Archbishop of Boromundi. It was to have six servants, a swimming pool, two beautifully scrubbed and turned out children and, most importantly, Dembe's new wife.

Peony came from Blackpool but Dembe found her in London. She had a stolid, middle class background, but her father became a violent alcoholic after being made redundant so, at the age of seventeen, Peony left the ravaged family home and moved to London. She worked in restaurants and, over the years, rose to manage a prestigious place in the City catering for business lunches. She was a large lady, not fat like Kinanewa but well-built and imposing. By the time Dembe was introduced to her establishment on one of his increasingly frequent visits to head office in Fenchurch Street, she had been married and divorced twice. The thrusting executive from Boromundi took one look at Peony and knew he'd found what he wanted. Peony took one look at Dembe and felt instant repulsion.

But Dembe was never one to give up. In a good, old-fashioned way, he set about wooing her. She was everything he wanted, a talented cook, a stickler for etiquette, skilled in dealing with business and government people, tastefully dressed and attractive in her heavy way. Her plied her with flowers, perfume, a ticket to the Centre Court on men's Final Day and a weekend in Paris. Dembe delayed his return to Boromundi for a further week to press his suit. When he finally got her into bed, he hardly gave her time to come up for air.

But when it came to it, it was a business arrangement. The sex was good (Dembe once described it as resembling the mating of frantic elephants), but Peony came to Boromundi to do a job and be paid for it. They never married, though, if questioned, they referred vaguely to a civil ceremony in Dallas at the beginning of their honeymoon in the US. There was never any question of children for the two that were already in residence were, to Peony, a dreadful encumbrance. When Dembe was around she was as sweet as African honey with them. As soon as he left the house she was cruel – cruel as only a shrewd, scheming, evil woman can be.

Joseph escaped. He was sent to boarding school in Kenya at the age of seven. He returned to Boromundi only for his holidays. It was Annie, therefore, who suffered the brunt of Peony's spite. Joseph loved his sister but it was impossible to tell his father what was happening. He made sure his mother knew, but the poor woman had no influence and could do nothing but watch from a distance and in increasing despair.

When Annie was twelve she committed suicide. Suicide is unheard of in Boromundi and Dembe succeeded in covering it up. Annie's action in hanging herself by her dressing gown cord from the big Bombay mango tree in the garden was explained away as a childish prank that had gone wrong. The doctor wrote 'accidental death' on the death certificate and left the house with a bundle of crisp US dollars in his pocket. For Peony, the loss of little black Annie was a relief.

What had happened to Annie rocked Joseph. He had known things were bad but not in his wildest nightmares did he believe that it could come to this. There followed a period of intense introspection, after which he made two decisions which were fundamental to the rest of his life. The first was that he would revenge little Annie's death on every white woman he could lay his hands on. And the second was that the best place to succeed in this calculated and violent vendetta was from the safety of the church.

It was a combination of genius – but that should be expected of a young man who was intelligent, devious and ruthless. I have no idea of what horrors he perpetrated while he was being trained abroad. In what little I know from the popular media of rapists and serial murderers in civilised places like the UK and the US, in both of which Joseph lived during his training, it is amazing how much they get away with before they are finally caught. I am not only talking of murder: women who have been horribly abused often prefer to remain silent.

When Joseph returned to Boromundi, he set about working his way up the church ladder. He was appointed to his first parish towards the end of the first Boromundi civil war, in an area that had supported PFLB. There were few white women left in Boromundi by then, but one of them was Peony. In 1990 she was burned to death in an horrific motor accident just outside Mateka. Her body was so badly charred as to be almost unrecognisable, and I am quite sure she suffered the torments of hell before she died. Dembe knew of no reason for her to be driving out in the direction of the airport, though there was tittle-tattle in the chattering community that she was leaving him. Coincidentally, Joseph was at home when it happened, though it was never suspected that he was involved.

Joseph's career stalled shortly after the appointment of Archbishop Muteresa – the gentleman I met at Alice's. In 1991 Joseph was effectively banished to a parish in the far north-west, a parish which included Kwita-Kwita, Smallboy's birthplace, and the foothills of the great volcano, Mount Simbilani. I have no explanation for this sudden move, though it may be that the church had some inkling of his involvement with Peony's death. He remained in exile throughout the second Boromundi civil war. That he was untouched by the aggression of Bunrum was not surprising: his mother came from the region and he was, by then, strongly sympathetic to the Bunrum cause.

If he could not progress in the established church, then Joseph had a choice. He could either leave the church or he could do what, in the end, he chose to do: establish his own. Over the past three decades the churches in Africa, of whatever type, have shed innumerable splinters which have rooted as locally-based, indigenous churches, often weird mixtures of Christian and animistic beliefs. There were already far too many of these, even in his own area, for Joseph to make much headway unless he found some new twist, something that would give his church an edge.

The birth of his illegitimate son, Mganga, gave him the idea. The boy was one of twins, the other of whom died at birth, throttled by Mganga's umbilical cord. Even in modern Boromundi times, twins are seen as the work of a devil and, despite the protestation of Christianity by virtually the whole population, are frequently left out one night for the hyenas. It was this intertwining of primitive superstition and Christian belief amongst his people which led Joseph Murunda to make some suggestions to the boy's mother. The poor woman, no fool herself except in the matter of the local priest, saw the possibilities in what Joseph whispered into her ear during confession. She saw to it that the boy was brought up in such a way as to make him precocious. He was encouraged to do things that were blatantly wrong and to be opinionated beyond his years. Whatever he said or did, he was praised to the skies, whenever possible in front of adults, even to the extent that they were silenced when he wished to express an opinion. His mother doted on him, and Joseph's money helped her to spoil him rotten.

When Mganga was two she began telling her neighbours of the strange things the boy was uttering. The priest was called. At first dismissive, he suddenly found himself able to interpret the boy's statements. There were prophecies, several of which came spectacularly true. There were instructions – for the creation of a new church, for the building of a house for his mother. And there were visions – of a new religion that would bind all Boromundians together, of a Boromundi empire, and of a sort of Pan-Africanism led by his small country. When the time was ready, Joseph, who knew the pressure points in the now-prescribed and largely exiled Bunrum, invited senior figures to come in secret to Mganga's village to see the new prophet and to talk. Some hard bargaining took place, after which the boy, his mother and Joseph disappeared across the Zairian border.

For Bunrum was far from dead. At the end of the

second civil war, tens of thousands of its supporters had fled across the border to live in squalid refugee camps run by Bunrum's foul soldiery. The children were taken from their mothers at an early point to be educated – which meant they were indoctrinated into the new religion. The 'educators' included such teachers as Small-boy Mushewa. The recruits were, as usual, also debased, deflowered and defiled, then trained to utter obedience to their leaders, and trained to fight. They were organised into cadres based loosely on the traditional year group-ings that were used for initiation ceremonies. The elite joined the *Wazhunghu*. The others joined cadres of dif-fering capacities, down to some of the rather dim girls and boys, who became a cadre of prostitutes.

The relationship between Joseph Murunda and the leaders of Bunrum was a difficult one. Ownership of The Boy gave him an influence which became a source of envy. His church was expanding at the speed of a grass fire. One example of his power was the way he won the battle for yet another name for what he saw as the political wing of his church. Having initially called his church *Jamia ma Muendo*, the Movement Church, he felt that the name of the old political movement, Bunrum, was outdated, inappropriate and tainted with failure. The Boromundi Salvation Movement, or Bosmo, he felt, was far better.

Joseph had another brilliant idea: if the Moslems had Mecca and the Romans, Rome, his church must have its place of pilgrimage. With active support from Bosmo he built a small wooden hut, a shrine, in Zaire. In no time, as the fame of The Boy grew, thousands began to make the pilgrimage, from both sides of the border.

With pilgrims came money. With this, and with money poured in by Bosmo and its supporters, Joseph built the temple, complete with the rubies, emeralds, gold, ivory and lions, that M'Simani Kangalewa had described in such detail. He'd thought it was in Zaire. It wasn't. It was at Bo, a small village high on the slopes of Mount Simbilani, deep in the *Mlimuku wa Usubuki Ukugu*, the Mountains of the Morning Mist. And, with the increasing flow of pilgrims from Boromundi, came more recruits for Bosmo.

Many other things followed. As the Bosmo army expanded and trained, Joseph Murunda – or, rather, The Boy – came up with the idea of *mooti*, the medicine that would give Bosmo troops immunity from the bullets of their enemies. The idea was an old one in Africa: the Zulu *Ngangas* dispensed it before the great battles of the Zulu wars. It was always a mixture of witch doctors' medicines and drugs that would make the warriors so crazy they didn't feel their wounds. The only unusual things Joseph Murunda added – his personal touch, if you like – were certain parts of a white woman.

In a way it was a stupid thing to do. It meant he had to obtain them, and it was made more difficult by stipulating that they had to be from a virgin. But it fitted into Joseph Murunda's sick mind as a continuance of his lapsed vendetta against white women. When he announced that Mganga had decided these bits were needed, Bosmo told him that, in this matter, he was on his own. To cover his identity – because he couldn't resist going along himself – he called himself 'Bullet'. M'Simani Kangalewa, the procurer, drew together a small group of men to help him do the job. And it was M'Simani who located the girl. Rebecca.

A lot of information came from little Sister Eunice whom we caught hurrying from Njomba mission to summon the *Wazhunghu* from Njomba town. For Eunice was strong supporter of the Movement. She had even been on a pilgrimage to its shrine at Bo. It was she who detailed one of the subtleties of Joseph Murunda's church, his plan to infiltrate and absorb the established church. He knew its structure intimately. He knew its weak points. He knew the frustration felt by the local priests, monks and nuns at being so far from the centre of decision making and their sense of despair that their church was incapable of making its doctrines and ceremonies more relevant to the needs and tastes of local people. He was lucky in winning one or two key converts early on. In their turn, they drew others with them. This infiltration was done in great secrecy, in the name of The Boy and the Movement, and in the name of God.

At this point I have to ask a question, though I do not know the answer for certain. Was Archbishop Muteresa one of these turncoats? Did he run with the hare and hunt with the hounds? Did he, for his own protection or as a tool for blackmail, keep a file on Shibane? Did Shibane know of this and did he visit the Archbishop, and is that why Muteresa died in his oven? If this were so, it would also explain the death of my friend Bartolemew Nchanga, the Head at St Faith and, possibly, how Bullet ascertained that Rebecca was a virgin.

The Movement's infiltration of the established church explains why some churches and missions, such as the one at Njomba, remained untouched by Bosmo. Only the old Sister-in-charge, Teresa, was killed. Everyone else had either already defected to the Movement or converted with alacrity at the point of an *Mzhunghu* Kalashnikov. Further, the Njomba mission was close to where Kinanewa, Joseph Murunda's mother, lived. She prayed in its church. So it was always going to be safe from the full ravages of Bosmo.

Little Sister Eunice told us all this very willingly. She didn't feel there was any secret in it, not now that Bosmo – so she'd been told – had nearly won the war, not now that the Movement was spreading across the whole of East Africa.

We questioned the girl in the darkened car, pulled well off the road, with Temba, Josephine and I turned round in the front seat while one of the Kaserewe men held her. But when we asked about Chloris she clammed up. Nothing would induce her to say anything. I'm not proud of what followed. She might have been petite and, in other circumstances, a rather likeable girl, but we needed the information quickly. We broke a finger first. It was a rapid way of demonstrating how serious we were, but it didn't work.

I'm glad the car was blacked out. But the windows were closed, so her screams filled the interior. In the end she told us and, when she had told us, we all wept. Because she had liked Chloris, and the reason she hadn't wanted to tell us was that what had happened to Chloris had been one of the few things that had upset her about the Movement.

Chloris had arrived on the 21st March and had started work in the hospital immediately. They had been short of trained nursing staff for months, so her arrival had been welcomed. The war had passed them by until, less than a week before our arrival, a lorryload of *Wazhunghu* had arrived. They had known exactly what they were doing. Sister Teresa was caught, dragged out into the centre of the quadrangle and knocked to the ground. The men found Sister Chloris in the men's surgical ward. She was very brave, insisting that they did not touch her but allowed her to walk to the lorry. The last Eunice had seen of Chloris had been as the lorry drew out of the mission leaving Sister Teresa's body lying, like a heap of waste paper, in the middle of the quadrangle.

She had no idea where they had taken Chloris. She was sure? Yes. No idea? No ... well, yes, perhaps she had. Where? It was possible ... where? Maybe she had been taken to Bo.

That's when I heard *Kisasi* again. But he wasn't safely out in the forest. He had climbed into my head. Zzzzzzeeeeee. Zzzzzzzeeee. It was like a buzz-saw, a klaxon, a scream. Like a high-pitched shriek that never paused for breath – the sort of scream the Japanese soldiers emitted as they flung themselves at the US Marines landing on the bloody beaches of Iwo Jima and Okinawa; it was the scream of the 11th Hussars as they galloped into the mouths of the guns at Balaclava; it was the scream of the Zulu *impi*s as they hurled themselves hopelessly against the British Gatling guns at the massacre they call the battle of Ulundi.

In my case, it was the scream of a man who had given up hope, who did not care except to hunt out and slaughter those he held responsible for the destruction of everything that remained dear to him. It was a scream that held no fear, not of death, not of wounds, not of anything that anyone could inflict on him. On the contrary, it was a scream that invited death, that craved death, that sought release in death – as long as he took certain others with him.

At first it filled my brain. Then it fell back, into a constant background, like tinnitus. So it did not exclude rational thought, as long as that thought was targeted. In some ways it was good in that it suppressed anything that was irrelevant to the accomplishment of that final mission. If Josephine had stripped naked in front of me, I wouldn't have noticed her. It was a scream that rose to drown all sentiment.

When Eunice had finished telling us about Chloris, because we didn't dare let her go, we tied her up. We put a splint on her finger. Then we gagged her and blindfolded her and stuffed cotton wool in her ears so she couldn't hear what we planned and laid her on the floor in front of the back seat. It had begun to rain, fine droplets that whispered across the Mercedes' roof.

'I've got to find him.' I was fairly certain they all knew who I meant, but, just in case, I added, 'I'm going to kill Joseph Murunda 'Bullet' Shibane, I'm going to kill him myself, all by myself for a change, without any help, preferably with my bare hands, and, if possible, slowly and bit by bit. Along the way, I'm going to find out how Chloris died.'

Josephine drew in a breath with a sharp hiss.

'Josephine?' I asked.

'You say she is dead?'

'She's dead. I know she's dead. I intend to make sure she has a decent burial and that the spot where she lies is marked in some way – so she'll be like Rebecca, knowing she's not forgotten. But . . . I can't let you – any of you – come any further. I've lost everything. Temba: you've got Josephine. You two,' and I looked at the other lads, 'You've done far too much already.'

'Bullshit, Armstrong.'

I hadn't realised Temba knew words like that. But I persisted. 'You can get back, same way as you got us here. But I think you need to leave now, quickly, and try and get back through Njomba at night.' I hesitated. 'Please!'

'No,' Temba said. 'No! You and me, Armstrong.'

'And me.' That was Josephine.

'No!' That was Temba again.

That was the start of a quite complicated conversation.

Temba was adamant that what faced us was so suicidal he couldn't do it with Josephine along. Nor, in fairness, did he want the Kaserewe men – they'd done enough in risking themselves that far.

But, when he said this, the others became angry. If I went, if Temba went, they would go. I jumped in, insisting they return, then turning to Temba and pointing out that they stood little chance of making it back without his theatricals. There was one hell of an argument.

We found a way forward in a compromise. We would drive the Mercedes as far as we could get safely, heading west-north-westward towards Bo. When it could go no further, or if things became dangerous, we would hide it, and Josephine and the three Kaserewe men would lie up while Temba and I went on. It broke our cardinal rule – that we should not be separated from Josephine – and both she and the Kaserewe men objected strongly to being left behind but, like all fudges, it enabled us to get back to business.

Josephine had found a more detailed road map of Boromundi in the glove compartment of the Mercedes. It showed Njomba, with Kwita-Kwita about forty miles away, as the crow flew, and Bo some fifteen miles beyond. The area was shown as criss-crossed with roads. The main Mateka-Zaire road, which we wanted to avoid since this would be congested and dangerous with the main retreating Bosmo army, ran to the south of us, about ten to fifteen miles away, crossing the border some five miles north of the northern tip of Lake Kenge. Temba had a compass in his rucksack. We turned the Mercedes back onto the road and began to work our way west-north-westwards.

It was a night of fumbling along dark roads as slippery as the pip of a newly sucked mango; of feeling our way further and further into the foothills along muddy, potholed tracks that narrowed and deteriorated and petered out; of turning the car round and working our way back until we could turn on to yet another track which did the same; of hope and anger and frustration. We became stuck frequently, wasting precious minutes cutting brush to stuff under the wheels of the heavy car, then pushing, heaving, until it suddenly came free. Very occasionally we found a good section of road and made some progress, but too often those roads veered away from our direction: it was as if these better roads were determined to lead us down to the main road and the jaws of the *Wazhunghu*.

The terrain became more and more savage, the valleys deeper, the valley sides rockier and sheerer, the forest that hemmed us in darker and thicker and higher. Sitting in the car as we plunged along the dirt tracks, it was as if we travelled through some sort of endless, rain-filled black canyon, with the sky a pale ribbon high above us. We pounded through streams in spate, Temba gunning the motor and fighting the steering wheel to bring us through. If there was a moon that night, we didn't see it, nor was there any hint of it behind the clouds. Of human habitation we saw little, just the occasional small village or the grouped huts of an isolated *boma*, all dark and saturated in the rain. When we stopped the car and climbed out to ease our cramped legs the darkness, the rain and the forest seemed to blot out all sound except the steady drip, drip of raindrops in the trees.

Shortly after three in the morning we gave up, exhausted. We had no idea where we were, except that we stood at the end of another track that had petered out. We had no certainty that, during seven hours of driving, we had made any progress at all. Josephine, calling on reserves of energy and cheerfulness that I certainly couldn't find, took charge of us, insisting that Temba and I sleep while she and the Kaserewe men took turns keeping watch. She also had the humanity to untie forlorn little Sister Eunice and take her for a short walk.

I know I slept, bunched up in the front seat, waking moments later to find a pale dawn seeping into the eastern sky. I climbed out, feeling wretched, and looked around.

The track had stopped in a small clearing, probably cut for firewood. To our right, the ground fell some five hundred feet to a stream whose white water bit at its rocky bed. To our left, a broken slope rose almost vertically, disappearing into swirling mist. I leaned back into the car to retrieve the road map. Seven hours travel. Even at an average speed of five miles an hour, we should be approaching Kwita-Kwita. I looked around, straining into the mist. If we were where I thought we were, the summit of Mount Simbilani would be less than thirty miles away, its snowy peak easily visible – if only the rain would lift.

I couldn't see any point in continuing in the car. This seemed as good a place as any to leave it. Josephine and the men could climb the slope and hide in the forest that probably continued above the clearing. They had water and an abundance of ham and Abernethy biscuits, as well as a couple of crates of well-shaken Kenyan beer. As Temba and I moved away, we would be able to identify some sort of landmark that would enable us to find our way back.

I was about to fold myself back into the car to find a few more minutes' sleep when a hand gripped my elbow, so sharply I almost yelped with pain. It was Josephine, coming up against me and pointing down into the valley.

Something moved, just the other side of the stream. For a moment, in the uncertain light, I was sure it was antelope, forest antelope. But no, it was people, two of them . . . no, more . . . several people, a scattered group of them, in single file, walking remarkably quickly.

They were half a mile away, walking upstream towards us. Our car was largely hidden from them by the curve of the slope but, if they had looked, they might have seen its roof and our heads silhouetted against the sky. But they didn't look. They were as weary as we were, as bedraggled from the incessant rain, trudging along what must have been a narrow path.

I put them down as refugees, wretches fleeing the fighting. I was about to turn away when Josephine's grip pulled me back. Her face came close against mine. 'Look,' she whispered.

I looked. There was obviously something, but I was too tired, my eyes too gritty . . .

'Look, Armstrong,' she breathed into my ear. 'Look at what they wear.'

I looked. The one thing we did not have was a pair of binoculars. I stared at the distant figures. Josephine's eyesight must have been so much better than mine. But they were coming closer. And then I saw.

The majority were women. Boromundi women wear a head-dress which is rather like a turban. It is usually formed of cotton cloth printed in cheerful colours with a variety of bold pictures and patterns. These all wore yellow, a very plain canary yellow. A little girl, who was being dragged along by her mother, wore a yellow skirt. And the one man I could see had a length of yellow cloth tied around his waist.

I climbed into the back and, rather brutally, shook Eunice awake. I already knew the answer, but I wanted to hear it from her.

Yellow is the colour of the sun. Yellow is the colour of a bright, new morning and the colour of a coming day. Yellow is the colour of hope, of expectation, of birth. Yellow's also the colour of an ageing Pope, but he shared it, for a short time, with a small black boy called Mganga. Yellow, was the colour worn by The Boy's pilgrims.

As Temba was well aware, I'm not very good in trees. When I was a kid I didn't mind apple trees too much, particularly if the apples were worth the effort, but climbing fifty foot up a damp forest giant which offers nothing but pine cones is no fun. But Temba had insisted. It was the ideal place to keep watch, he said, and he was buggered if he was going to do all the work.

Getting up was bad enough, the branches too far apart and horribly slippery, but at least the struggle gave me something active to do to keep my mind off falling. This tree, being on a steep, west-facing slope and, therefore, open to the light, had retained most of its lower branches, so I was able to climb it by hand. The bigger trees, in the deep forest, have vertical, branchless trunks which soar a hundred foot without a handhold. Temba had once shown me how to use a rope to scale these, slinging it round my lower waist and buttocks, then round the trunk, and leaning back against it, moving up in a series of terrifying jerks. I hadn't got ten foot off the ground before I started screaming.

There's an awful lot of space underneath you when you're high up. I have a vertigo thing whereby, if I look down at a long drop, staring into its emptiness, I get this urge to fall into it. It's like a magnetic pull, like being sucked. I've never actually fallen, but the impulse is terrifying. So I didn't look down. I looked out, across the steep, forested side of the valley to a hill on the far side.

We had followed the pilgrims. We had kept off the path, working our way through the forest, so progress had been slow and, the further we went, the slower it became. Partly it was because the terrain became ever more precipitous, broken and wild. It would probably have been beautiful too, if we could have seen the views, but the clouds were so low they clamped us in an eternal, cloying mist. We also realised that we were far closer to Bo and The Boy's shrine than we had expected, and that meant we had to move cautiously, leaving no sign of our passage. Because, so Temba argued, the area would be swarming with *Wazhunghu* patrols. To Bosmo, this little Mganga and his shrine were worth their weight in gold as propaganda weapons and a source of income.

We must have passed Kwita-Kwita in the car, some time during the night. I reckon that we finally stopped the Mercedes not more than eight to ten miles south of Bo. But it was a very heavy few miles, and I wasn't wedged into my tree until almost midday.

Far below me, the ground dropped almost vertically into the seething white torrent of a mountain stream. The hill beyond rose steeply, a conical, lozenge-shaped hill elongated in a northeast-southwest line and stripped clear of forest – altogether a bit like a bald man's head. The forest on a separate slope to my left, separated from the central hill by a tributary valley of the stream, had been thinned for the pilgrims' campsite and, in the thin light, a hundred cooking fires smouldered, their smoke rising vertically in the still air.

It was exactly as Eunice had described it. She had

made the pilgrimage about a year before, when she had first decided to support the Movement. It had been such an uplifting event, she said, such an experience that she had never doubted her decision to change. Along with two other nuns from the mission, she had camped a night in those trees. In the evening, after they had cooked and eaten their meal, they had crossed the small stream and climbed towards the shrine. When the approach had been cleared of forest, they had laid some of the fallen trunks on the ground to act as seats. She had sat on one of these, looking up the slope to the hut at the top.

This hut, a circular affair with a thatched roof, was open towards the camping area. Inside – and, from where I sat, I could not see this – inside, said Eunice, was a simple altar covered with a bright yellow cloth. On it stood a five-foot high statue of The Boy holding a crucifix above his head. It had been carved in a black wood, ebony perhaps, and highly polished so it glistened in the light of the candles. She knew this because, during the service, there had been communion. The blood hadn't been wine but a traditional beer brewed from honey; and the bread hadn't been the tasteless wafers the mission used but some sort of sweet, sugary African cake. It had been very like a Catholic service. In fact, some of the hymns had been borrowed. But there had been new songs, sung to the beat of drums, which had been very exciting. And one of the priests had spoken. He'd been a very big man, almost as big as Temba, dressed in a white robe, a bit like a cassock, with a yellow stole around his neck. On his head he'd worn a head-dress of white feathers, big feathers like ostrich feathers, which waved as he moved. He'd told them how this new church, the

Movement Church, *Jamia wa Muendo*, wasn't trying to take over from the old church. It was growing from it, a natural evolution that fitted itself into the African landscape. It was a church that understood black people – not only their souls but also their everyday needs – like it knew that they wanted to throw off the yoke of the present government, a government that did little but carry out the wishes of the old colonial masters and the World Bank.

Poor little Eunice. She obviously hadn't understood much of what the priest had spoken about. But, she said, after the service, when they went back to the campsite, they hadn't been able to sleep. So they had joined the other pilgrims in singing, each bringing a candle with them so the whole forest was lit with pinpoints of light. They had sung to The Boy. They had sung his praises just like they used to sing the praises of the other boy, Jesus. Except that, as one woman had explained to her, Jesus had been a white man who had died in a place called Palestine, two thousand years ago and as many miles away, whereas this Boy slept close by, in the great temple up beyond the altar, not two hundred yards away, and could probably hear their singing. And this Boy was simple. He was a boy who talked with God, who interpreted for black people what God said. There was none of the complexity of the other Boy being part of a Trinity, part of God himself, something so obscure it required hierarchy of priests and bishops and archbishops to explain it. More – this Boy, their Boy, was the warrior leader the other Boy said he couldn't be. He was leading a war that was wiping bad people from the land. 'Eeeeh,' had said the people who had been standing round listening to the woman. 'Eeeeh!'

The hut that held the altar was set into a fence made of tree trunks which ran round the summit of the hill to form an enclosure perhaps a hundred metres in diameter. In the centre of this was another enclosure, the wooden palisade surrounding this being higher than the outer one. Just visible inside it, and sited on the very top of the hill, stood a rectangular building. Its walls were made of tree trunks, but the bark had been stripped and the wood painted, mainly in yellow and white, with other colours used to show pictures, rather like primitive bushman paintings: mostly of armed black men chasing and killing smaller people, depicted in red. This building, the temple, had a steeply-pitched thatched roof.

Eunice had said that, when their impromptu midnight service had been reaching its climax, some men had arrived, shouting that they must listen. The Boy, they said, had heard their singing and liked it. They must come, now, and see him.

In fact they hadn't seen him, but had been led, clutching their candles and singing, through a gate in the outer fence and round and round the outside of the inner palisade. It had been so exciting, knowing that the Boy King was listening to their singing. They'd been doing this for about an hour when a voice had been heard, a great voice that boomed out from the building, a voice which praised them and thanked them. After which, trembling, they had returned to their campfires and a sleepless night.

They hadn't seen The Boy because he didn't live in

that temple on the top of the hill. He lived in a neat European-style bungalow at the north-eastern end of the conical hill, in a house hidden from their view which he shared with his mother and his two-year old sister. We knew he had his creature comforts because the thump-thump of a generator sounded day and night, and the dish of a satellite TV receiver nestled on the roof. There were other houses there for the priests, one of which was probably used by Joseph Murunda Bullet Shibane. Below them, on the slope that faced towards us, there were some large rectangular buildings rather crudely constructed of breeze-blocks and box-profile metal roofing. Again, from our initial reconnaissance, we knew what these were: barracks, wash-houses and kitchen facilities for the *Wazhunghu* who guarded the site. We estimated that there were about fifty of them in all. We'd seen some, seen how well armed they were and how they set out for regular patrols around the site. So we knew that, with the place so well guarded, any attempt to break in would be suicidal.

But we hadn't seen The Boy. And we hadn't seen Bullet Shibane. So we waited, taking turns up our dripping tree, staring across at the conical hill, watching and praying for them to show. And wondering what had happened to Chloris.

She was probably dead. They'd probably fed her to the lions that M'Simani Kangalewa had told us were chained to The Boy's throne. They'd probably tortured her first. And that's where I stopped thinking. I'd seen so much that was so horrible in the past few weeks that I was able to shut out the thoughts that followed. So, in a way, I didn't 'wonder' what had happened to Chloris.

I remembered her. I felt sad that we hadn't ever got anywhere together. And I prayed that she was in those buildings, still alive, waiting for us.

I was up the tree when it first happened. At about four in the afternoon the tree moved.

I heard it first, like a great sigh, coming towards me from across the conical hill. For a moment I thought it was the wind, perhaps the precursor of a sudden tropical squall, but the air remained still, the mist hanging like the grey curtains of a funeral pall over the upper hillsides. The sound was upon us in a trice, and the tree swayed.

Like I said, I'm no good in trees. I'm awful in forest giants that thrash around, that bend and sway as if they're in a hurricane. I hung on for dear life, cursing and swearing as the tree lashed from side to side. I was dimly aware that, all around me, the other trees were moving, beating their branches. And the noise became a rumbling, mixed in with a dreadful cry, from away to my left, from the direction of the pilgrim's camp; a cry of terror that was cut off by the boom of a mighty voice.

I couldn't hear what it said – except I was pretty sure it was coming from some sort of loudspeaker. And then the motion stopped.

I was down that tree faster than a squirrel. Temba stood at the bottom, grinning. If I'm bad up trees, I'm even worse when I've been terrified shitless by something up one, and then find that, when I reach safety, I've a big black bastard grinning at me.

'A little earthquake,' Temba explained.

'Little? Jesus!'

'Common occurrence here.'

'Jesus!' I repeated, beginning to feel not a little ashamed. I should have known. I'm a geography teacher. We were close to Simbilani, a volcano in what is, tectonically, one of the most active belts of plate movement on the earth's lithosphere. For the Great Rift Valley of eastern Africa is, literally, a line along which the earth's outer skin is being torn apart.

'But,' said Temba, 'You notice how they use it, eh? That voice from the loudspeaker calls on God to desist and, almost immediately, He does. So the pilgrims are very impressed.'

We waited through the evening of the first day, for two full days, and into the early morning of the fourth, and nothing happened – other than a couple more, but rather smaller tremors. Sometimes we were both in the tree, watching the shrine. Mostly we took turns.

Men came from the houses up to the central temple. They were dressed in white and were evidently the priests of the new religion, and they spent time in the temple. The area around the compound was regularly patrolled by *Wazhunghu*, usually in pairs. They were very relaxed about this, their only job appearing to be to turn back pilgrims who strayed round the edges of the outer stockade. But these movements were useful in showing us the gates in the fences. Both had two big entrances, closed with wooden doors, one at each end. In addition, the priests could get from the main compound into the altar hut through a small door.

When it rained, when sounds were drowned by the spatter of droplets through the leaves, we whispered ideas about how we could enter the place. Because we knew that, the moment we had both The Boy and Shibane together, we had to act quickly and decisively. There might only be one chance.

At night one of us stayed in the tree until late. I didn't mind this late shift – at least, in the dark, I was less aware of the drop below me. And every night the pilgrims poured across the stream and worshipped below the altar, then went back and sang together in the trees. It was very beautiful, with the lights of the cooking fires outlining the dark hillside and the flickering candles flowing, like some lighted stream, as the people moved. And, of course, the singing was wonderful.

We snatched sleep on the ground through the early hours, sleeping lightly, conscious that at any moment we might hear the movement of a *Wazhunghu* patrol. We knew they operated, because we saw them leave their camp and plunge into the forest, but none came near. There was, as I later discovered, a reason. The patrols weren't looking for enemies. They went out in search of the girls from the camp site who scoured the forest to the west of the hill for firewood.

On the morning of the fourth day the weather changed. The sun rose behind us and bathed the hills in a watery light. And I was lucky enough to be on the early shift up the tree when the mist, very suddenly, lifted.

I swear I could have reached out and touched it,

Simbilani seemed so close. It rose immediately behind the temple, towering over it, its lower slopes a hazy grey-blue in the early light, its steep, upper, snow-covered summit so blindingly white it was almost impossible to look at it. And, behind it, the sky glowed a glacial blue.

I heard the pilgrims' gasp and, when I turned towards them, saw the way they were streaming out from the trees onto the cleared lower slopes by the stream, standing in groups gazing up at Simbilani. It was that beautiful.

And then it changed. A cloud, like a great cumulus thunder cloud, like some sort of gigantic, slow-motion cauliflower head, starkly white in the early sunshine, boiled up from its summit. Simbilani was erupting. Millions of tonnes of superheated ash and steam were punching their way up into the stratosphere, yet there wasn't a sound. It was eerie, terrifying, watching that great volcano blow.

Shortly afterwards the earth began to shake and, with it, the trees. It continued to do so every few minutes as the cloud rose higher and higher, until it seemed to hang over us. But everyone seemed very calm, and the pilgrims, after watching the spectacle for a few minutes, drifted back to their cooking fires.

About an hour later a Toyota Land Cruiser drove up to the bungalows. Obviously following it, two three-ton lorries bustled round the end of the hill and drew up beside the barracks. I could see clearly what was happening around the barracks, but couldn't see any of the movement near the bungalows. The *Wazhunghu* were being formed up. It was a useful moment because I was able to count them; sixty-three in all, including the officers. Most of the men were ordered into the lorries and, without waiting for the Land Cruiser, these set off back up the road. The remaining troops clustered round an officer, who was obviously briefing them, before proceeding at a run along the hillside facing me. For a moment it occurred to me that we had been seen, that the men in the trucks were being moved to encircle us, but the soldiers ran straight along the hillside, across our front and in full view of us, through the logs of the worship area, down into the stream and up the slope towards the pilgrim encampment.

A thin, smoky haze, glowing in places from the warm rays of the early sun, lay across the campsite. Many of the pilgrims were still rolled up in their sleeping blankets, the rest were up preparing breakfast. It made no difference. The *Wazhunghu* began shouting, beating them, hitting them with the butts of their rifles, picking up sticks to strike at them. There were screams and shrieks, entreaties to allow them to collect their belongings, to find their children. All were ignored. Within minutes the miserable creatures, several hundred men, women and children, were fleeing the campsite, many half naked, their possessions abandoned, streaming up the hill towards the thick forest.

What happened next horrified me. Instead of letting them go, the *Wazhunghu* began shooting at them. They used well-spaced, single shots. It was as if they were using the pilgrims for target practice. The screams became shrieks and moans. Many ran faster, stumbled, dropped what possessions they carried, while others stopped or turned to face and plead with the soldiers, and to pick up those that had fallen. It made no sense, the way the *Wazhunghu* allowed them part of the way up the slope before opening fire. They murdered them in such a languid way, as if there was no hurry, as if it did not matter how many were killed, wounded or escaped. It wasn't as if they enjoyed their sport: I heard no laughter, none of the usual banter, just the sharp punch of gunshots across the valley.

I watched for too long. When I came to my senses, I was down that tree faster than a squirrel on roller-skates. Temba stood at the bottom. He'd been woken by the shooting and was already kitted up.

'Temba,' I gasped, at the same time pulling on my rucksack and checking my rifle. 'The *Wazhungu*!'

It was all I needed to say. We charged down the slope together, running, dodging trees, slipping in the wet leaf-mould, only slowing as we came to the edge of the forest, where it faced across the stream to the cleared area of the conical hill.

We were not a moment too soon. The *Wazhunghu* came sauntering back, a tight group of them, laughing, their rifles slung across their shoulders. They were the usual motley lot in their wrap-around ninja sunglasses and back-to-front baseball caps, in their stone-washed jeans and tattered trainers, and their distinctive, red-stained cotton head bands. I could not be sure that these were all of them, that some hadn't remained to ransack the pilgrim's possessions, but that was a risk we took.

It was very quick, very clinical and, to anyone who might have been listening at the far end of the hill, it probably sounded like a continuation of the massacre of the pilgrims.

Later, I found out what had happened. On April 30th the Boromundi government invited Tanzanian troops to assist them in suppressing the Bosmo uprising. I do not know, and history does not yet relate, what prompted this, but I have a feeling that it was occasioned not out of any desire on the part of President Bugerimani to hasten the end of the war, but because the US demanded it as a condition of its continued support.

The Tanzanian army is good. It was Tanzanians who, finally, in 1978, spoiled Idi Amin's fun in Uganda. Their units were in Mateka within two days, and by the 18th of May they were rolling Bosmo back in the direction of the Zaire border faster than you and I can roll up a carpet. What we saw was the *Wazhunghu* troops at Bo being pulled back westwards. Bosmo would regroup in its old training camps in Zaire and await another day.

We didn't know any of this at the time. All we knew was that Bullet owned a Toyota Land Cruiser, so, with the *Wazhunghu* patrol polluting the local water supply, Temba and I splashed through the stream and ran along the slope in the direction of the main buildings.

The only person we met as we careered past the barracks was the *Wazhunghu* officer. He came round the corner of a building, probably expecting to meet his men. The startled look on his face was almost comic. Temba got to him before he could open his mouth or draw his pistol, hitting him with a thwack that sounded like the chop of a lumberjack's axe. While Temba sat on top of him, giving him the last rites, I ran on towards the bungalows. I ran round them twice before I could accept that the Toyota was no longer there.

Struggling out of my rucksack, I dropped the Galil on top of it, and leaned back against the wall of one of the bungalows. I felt empty, drained, emotionally wrecked, for, if the Toyota was Bullet's car, then Bullet and The Boy had escaped and there wasn't any point in carrying on because I'd lost my last chance of discovering what had happened to Chloris. I began to slide down the wall, my back scraping against the rough blockwork, my hands coming up to cover my face. As I was about to close my eyes in final defeat I saw the gate of the outer stockade. It was open.

I seized the Galil and stormed up the hill, accelerating, bursting through and seeing the inner gate also open and, parked beyond it, the Land Cruiser. The adrenaline rush of relief propelled me on, my lungs bursting, that familiar grey fog obscuring my lateral vision as I stumbled past the car and plunged through the entrance at the back of the main temple building at the summit.

I stopped in a small room lit by a single, bare electric bulb. To my right, a low bench ran along a wooden wall. Various vestments for the priests, including two of the magnificent feathered head-dresses that Eunice had described, hung above it. To my left, a clutter of equipment, including loudspeakers and amplifier, tarpaulins, flags and pots of paint, lay scattered across the floor. And, ahead of me, closed, was a door.

I stood, staring at it. If those behind it had heard me or seen me, they would be waiting for me. Since it was hinged on my right, and opened outwards, towards me, I moved to its left, flattened myself against the wall, the Galil held in my right hand, stretched out my left for the handle – one of those handles you depress downwards – and, very slowly, worked the latch.

The door began to open, swinging slowly and silently away from me. I gave it a moment to open fully, tensed, and was about to throw myself through when the smell hit me, an animal smell, an acid smell, sour and strong, catching me in the back of my throat. For a moment, it was so disgusting it knocked me back. Then I went through.

I found myself in a darkened room which stretched the width of the building to my right and left. It was empty but the stench was far worse. Six feet in front of me, a woven screen, about eight feet high and formed of long but closely woven branches, wattle perhaps, extended almost the length of the room, leaving a narrow gap at each end. Above, the roof rose some thirty feet to a dark apex. From beyond the screen came voices.

Very slowly, very carefully, I tiptoed to the screen and put my eye right against one of the gaps in the weave. I could see through it quite clearly, through into a long room that ran the length of the rest of the building.

The first thing I saw was Chloris.

The sight took my breath away, not because she was right in front of me, almost at my feet, lying on her side with her back towards me and, as far as I could tell, unhurt; not because her hands and feet were bound, tightly, with thick sisal twine; not because her lovely hair had fallen free from its customary coils, the golden cascade of her locks haloing her head; not because I had never in my life, never, ever seen anything quite as beautiful; but because she was almost naked. She reclined, like something off page three of the Sun, her pale, translucent skin wonderfully contrasted against the dark, heavy cloth of the coarse African blanket she lay on, her only clothing a small, bright yellow skirt formed, it seemed, by two household dusters tied together.

Then I saw that she was chained. A silver chain ran from her bound wrists towards my left, to the throne. I could see the carved ivory of the nearer arm and part of the upright below it, and the stones set in it, mostly green ones, that glittered in the glare of two spotlights suspended from the ceiling, immediately above the man who faced me, and faced Chloris.

Bullet Shibane was a big man, very dark-skinned, with a head that resembled a block of concrete except that it was quite unusually black, upon which sprouted a tight tangle of black hair. His nose, momentarily, reminded me of Bartolemew's, a thing the shape of a potato stuck on the front of his face. But his worst feature was his lips, big, thick lips torn back into a grimace of fury and, as he spoke, flecks of saliva spat from them, some projected on to the floor while others collecting to dribble whitely down his chin.

I have never seen an angrier man and never, in all my life, have I so instantly and terribly hated someone. And it was that hatred, that fierce, mad loathing, that prompted me to do something so stupid I shall curse myself for it for the rest of my life.

Because it would have been so easy to have shot him through the screen. The Galil, at that range, would have torn him to shreds, would have propelled the smashed remains of his body the length of the room. I could have done it. I could so easily have consigned him to instant hell. Dear Christ, something in me – vanity, a sense of triumph, a desire for the ultimate in revenge, perhaps just a niggling concern that this might not be the right man – prevented me.

19 Simbilani

I have seen an estimate that the world has built some thirty million Kalashnikovs of the AK series (AK47, AK74, AKM and variants made in other Communist countries). It beggars the imagination as to how many people between the year of the AK47's introduction, 1947, and today those machines have shot. Had I been shot by an ordinary one I might have felt cheated, rather as a man who has been run over by a Ford Fiesta might wish he'd had the privilege of a Rolls. All I can boast is that the Kalashnikov that got me was probably unique in that it was encrusted with gold.

My stupidity was that I had forgotten The Boy. I should have guessed that the bastard was probably with his father but, in my excitement, I forgot. And I made it worse. As I've said, I had this crazy idea that I mustn't shoot Bullet, not yet. It wasn't that I wanted a 'High Noon' type confrontation, a dramatic finale, me against him. It was simply that I wanted to be quite sure he knew why he was dying, and I wanted him to go very, very slowly, with Rebecca on his mind.

He bore the responsibility for all this. It was he who, through the growing strength of the Movement, had enabled Bosmo to carry out its successful invasion of Boromundi. The *mooti* for the soldiers had been his idea, *mooti* that must contain the essential ingredient which had resulted directly in Rebecca and Annabel's deaths. It had been Bullet personally who had organised the attack which had killed Rebecca. Then it had been he who had done the killing, but only after subjecting her to the most appalling, degrading assault. Finally, he had butchered her, removing the most intimate parts of her body to carry away.

It was the death of his little sister, Annie, following the torture inflicted on her by Peony, his English step-mother, that had turned him against white women. Rebecca's death had been part of his twisted concept of revenge. Now, now it was no longer justice I sought. What I wanted was something far more primaeval: revenge.

I recall that, as I watched him, as he frothed and spat at Chloris, in the seconds it took me to move to the end of the screen, I controlled my emotions and the *Kisasi* scream that filled my head – long enough to weigh the odds. He was much heavier, taller and, probably, stronger than me, but his size made him slower. I was fit. Temba had taught me some hand-to-hand combat. Irrelevancies! The essential thing was that I wanted him to know why I was going to kill him. And I wanted him to suffer as he went. So I made my decision, a decision which seems, in retrospect, to have totally ignored Chloris' plight. As I came round the end of the screen, I propped the Galil against the wooden wall.

Such a mistake! Such a vain, dumb, stupid mistake with such dreadful consequences! Moreover as I came out into the throne room, I never looked around. I was intent on Bullet. But he didn't notice me. He was so immersed in the stream of invective he was pouring on poor Chloris that he didn't see me. Perhaps, also, it was the lights. They shone from above and slightly behind him and pointed straight down on her; where I came in, I was in shadow. So I began shouting at him, calling his name – but my control snapped. I began swearing, screaming that I was going to kill him, kill him for what he had done to Rebecca, what he had . . .

Sitting on his throne of ivory, all The Boy had to do was lift his golden toy and squeeze the trigger.

I wasn't aware of being shot, as such. There was the noise, I was struck by an almighty force, and the whole world went spinning. My disorientation was total. By the time my brain caught up with my body, I was on the floor with Bullet standing over me. Nothing hurt. On the contrary, I had a strange feeling of warm wellbeing. I lay, awkwardly, uncomfortably, staring up at him and struggling to put together where I was and what had happened.

Then The Boy entered my vision and I began to understand. He stood over me, holding his glittering, golden toy loosely in his right hand. He bent towards me and, idly, poked my chest with the muzzle. He was dressed like most modern six-year-olds, in denim jeans and a dark FILA tee shirt. His face was rounder than his father's, as dark, but rather mild looking, and he'd had his hair cut very short. I had the impression that he was rather disappointed that my reaction to the poke he'd given me proved I was still alive. Certainly, the muzzle of his rifle drifted up towards my face and he said something to his father.

Through a sharp, mounting pain, centred somewhere to the right of my chest, Bullet's face swam back into my vision. His mouth was open, its corners white with his spit, and he stared down at me, his eyes strangely wide. I think the man was in shock. Certainly his brain wasn't working. Had I been him, my first concern would have been whether there were others like myself seeking to kill him. But I saw the dawn come. I saw the flash of panic across his face. I saw him grab his son's rifle, almost knocking the boy to the floor in his haste, and I saw the rifle shorten as he lifted and pointed it at my head.

I was dead then. The muzzle velocity of the bullet from a Kalashnikov is some three thousand feet per second, and this one had less than two feet to travel. The black hole in the end of the machine seemed to grow larger, as if it were expanding to swallow me. I have no recollection of any sense of fear. Perhaps it was that my disorientation had numbed my brain, perhaps it is that, when faced with the inevitability of death, the human spirit gives up and accepts it. All I knew was that I was dead.

Until the rifle disappeared. It disappeared very suddenly and, at the same time, there was a bump, the sound of the collision of two heavy but soft bodies, followed by a metallic crash and the noise of scuffling and blows.

There was enough stuffing left in me, enough determination from the training Temba had given me, to propel me to my feet. By that time my side was hurting like hell, as if the devil was riding on my back and stabbing at my right kidney with an eleven inch kitchen knife. But what I saw sent me hurtling across the room.

Temba was on top of Bullet. In size, the men were pretty evenly matched but Temba's charge had knocked Bullet off his feet and sent him sprawling across the floor.

The two of them were slugging it out, leaving The Boy to wreak more mischief.

In his fall, Bullet had dropped the golden gun. It had spun away and come to rest a few feet beyond where they struggled. I could see it, glowing, just outside the pool of light thrown by the spotlights. And little Mganga was going for it, was, at the moment I launched myself, bending to pick it up. But I beat him to it. I made no attempt to wrest the gun from his hands: there wasn't time. I simply kicked him, kicked his arse with such force that my injured side screamed as he staggered away from me.

I swear I never saw her. Before Chloris' God I swear I never noticed either her or her mate, not in those first few frantic moments in the throne room. M'Simani had said they were there. I'd smelt them as I came in. But the two thoughts had not connected. Not that it would have made any difference. If I'd known she was there, I might have kicked little Mganga even harder, in the full knowledge of what I was doing. And I might have enjoyed it the more.

My kick sent him sprawling with such force that he cannoned into the lioness. Her reaction, for all the months of chaining, of undernourishment, of taunts and outright cruelty, was instant and devastating. M'Simani had said she was a man-eater, and she obviously knew her business. She swirled round and cuffed the boy. Her paw struck the side of his head with such force she must have broken his neck instantly. I think, though I don't know, that he was already dead when she seized him, when her canines sank into the back of his neck, when she placed her right paw onto the small of his back to pin him while she growled a warning at me.

Chloris says that I could have done something. She was watching, so perhaps she knows best. I don't think I could – no, for God's sake, I could! I could have risked my life by dodging past the lioness to pick up the Kalashnikov. Then, perhaps, I could have shot her. But The Boy was already dead, of that I'm sure. But I didn't make any effort to save him because I didn't care. I was more interested in what was happening between Temba and Bullet Shibane – worried, too, that others might come in and interrupt us. I checked quickly that Temba had the better of his opponent, ran back past Chloris, scooped up the Galil and threw myself round the end of the screen and through the small anteroom. At the entrance I stopped. The Land Cruiser stood in the compound. Sunlight sparkled off its paintwork. The heated air shimmered above its roof. There was silence except for the screech of the crickets. Nothing moved.

Quickly, I turned and hurried back into the throne room. I passed Chloris again, ignoring her screamed entreaties and the frantic way she gestured towards Mganga. No, I walked over to Temba, catching his eye as he turned to look up at me.

Bullet was crushed under him, on his front with his cheek flattened against the floor. They may have been much the same weight but you have to remember that Bullet had been a priest, a man who had enjoyed too many years of fat living. And he had no training in the art of death, not the training and practice that Temba had had. So I knelt next to Bullet, almost as if I were praying like a Moslem, placing my lips against his ear, a strangely small, intricately whorled ear. And I whispered her name to him, over and over again. 'Rebecca,' I said, 'I want you to remember a girl called Rebecca Wise. A pretty girl, a young girl, twenty-three to be exact, a lovely girl with her life in front of her. A girl with beautiful hair and sparkling brown eyes, a girl who laughed, who cried.'

I reminded him, in case he'd forgotten, where he'd met Rebecca and what he'd done to her. Then, when I was quite sure he understood – and it took a couple of firm pokes with the Galil to obtain a response – I explained who I was and who Temba was, and I described to him how we'd killed his friends: Hezikiah 'Smallboy' Mushewa, Mophas Mandabanga, Onias Matanganesa, and M'Simani Kangalewa. I described to him how they'd suffered. I'd have liked to have gone on, to have spun it out, but I couldn't. There wasn't the time. So I told him that we were now going to show him something that would give him a taste of how we had suffered.

I stood, and helped Temba haul the man to his feet. Then we frog-marched him over to where the lioness held his son.

It was a terrible thing to do to a father. It's like so many things I did in those seven months in Boromundi – I have no pride in it. But when I heard his moan, when his breath choked in his throat, I remembered how Rebecca's parents had cried. And I remembered Temba's misery as he grieved for Annabel. And I remembered the heat of my tears for Rebecca. And I felt a great elation, as if my whole body had filled with a golden, liquid joy.

Enough. Oh God, enough! Sufficient now to say that he must have guessed what was coming. He screamed. He fought with suicidal desperation, twisting momentarily out of Temba's grasp. But we were too much for him. Temba caught him in a great bear hug, and we held him, held him so he watched his son. The lioness had already begun to eat him. She had torn open his stomach and, with the same slurping noises you would make over a good minestrone soup, had now begun to consume his intestines.

We made Bullet watch. If he closed his eyes, I hit him. If he turned away, I struck him on the side of his face with the butt of the Galil. Finally, when we'd had enough, when the wretch had gone limp in Temba's arms, we dragged him, screaming and struggling and begging us for mercy, across the room to where the lioness' mate paced at the full length of his chain. For a moment Temba hesitated. I think he'd had the same thought as I – that, if we didn't kill him first, Bullet might escape. But we didn't kill him. We simply threw him at the lion.

I have no idea what horrors had occurred in that so-called temple. M'Simani had said that anyone who displeased the regime was eaten by the lions. Certainly, from the way the lioness had fielded Mganga, she needed no tuition in how to catch and kill her human prey. The lion was as quick. He'd fallen back a little as we approached but, as Temba pushed Bullet towards him, and with a great rattle of his chain, he sprang. The man – a good six feet, six – simply crumpled under his charge. But his scream, his shriek of naked terror, echoes in my skull to this day.

The lion straddled him. With lightning speed he seized Bullet's throat, clamping his fangs into his neck, then subsiding onto him, crushing him like a lover. I stood, my left hand gripping Temba's arm, as we watched him die.

Bullet died slowly. He died of strangulation, of asphyxiation, of choking and, hopefully, of sheer terror. As he died, he twitched. His legs, free of the lion's weight, jerked, at first weakly, then more and more convulsively. Somehow, he breathed, the desperate, bubbling, sucking noises evidence of air dragged in through the bleeding puncture holes made by the lion's fangs.

The twitches slowed. The body relaxed. Effortlessly, the lion rose, glanced back at us, and dragged the corpse away across the floor, trailing a long, dark smear of blood. Only when his prey was in the shadows, as far from us as his chain would allow, did he stop. Then he turned back, his head low, his eyes dark with hatred, and snarled.

I was only just in control of myself. I was shaking, fighting back an insane sobbing, but that sound, that snarl, broke me. My feelings of hate and triumph, primaeval feelings, spilled out, like black waters tumbling through when some great dam is burst. I remember opening my mouth and screaming, hurling obscenities across the room, jabbing my rifle at the ceiling and jumping up and down. I remember the shouts fading, as if someone had pulled the plug on my energy supply. I remember turning to Temba and throwing my arms around him. I remember hugging him against me and burying my face in his shoulder. And I remember the tears coming, great wracking sobs that tore at my body. Then everything stopped.

Chloris brought me back. I became aware, along some long tunnel of darkness, that she was shouting, that she had never stopped shouting. The sound impinged, slowly. It wasn't the begging tone she'd used when she saw what was happening to Mganga. This was firm, angry, commanding.

'Armstrong!

Weakly, I eased myself away from Temba, feeling his hand take my arm and grip it.

'Armstrong!' Chloris' voice, an octave higher.

'You okay?' Temba whispered.

I nodded, wiping at the snot that had collected around my nose.

'Armstrong!'

I turned and, very unsteadily, tottered towards her. She was standing, holding her wrists out towards me. The chain, bolted to the floor beside the ivory throne, had been wrapped tightly round them and fixed with a large padlock. In the brightness of the spotlight I could see how the steel had cut into the pale, almost translucent flesh. I saw the bruising and the blood.

'Get this off me!' The anger in her tone!

'Okay,' I muttered, but I hesitated. What stopped me was not the problem of finding a key or bolt cutters or a hacksaw, it was the way she stood. Remember, she wore nothing except a tiny yellow skirt. This was a nun, standing naked before me, yet she made no attempt to cover herself. It was as if her nakedness had no importance, no relevance. On the contrary, she seemed to stand majestically in front of me, shoulders back boldly, firm breasts squeezed between imprisoned arms, the nipples proud, while I stood in front of her with my mouth open.

It was Temba who dropped a cassock over her head. It was Temba who, following her instructions, used a bamboo pole to break the thin, silver chain from around Bullet's neck and manoeuvre the bunch of keys away from a frenzied lion. It was he who, finally, unfastened the padlock.

'Thank you,' she said, pushing her arms through the sleeves of the cassock and coming towards me. For a moment I thought she was going to kiss me but, instead, she turned me sideways and tore at the tatters of my shirt, exposing my wound. For a moment she inspected it, then she said to Temba, 'Get me another of those cassocks.'

While Temba tore it into strips, she bound me up. That done, she propped her hands on her hips and said, 'Lucky again, eh?' and, before I could comment on how lucky I was that it hurt so much, she turned away. 'Now, that shooting. There are people hurt. Shall we go and see?'

Temba and I spent the rest of the day working under Chloris' supervision. At first, we worried. We worried that some of the *Wazhunghu* guards had escaped and would reappear. They didn't. We worried about the other occupants of the bungalows but, when we searched them, the buildings echoed with their emptiness – presumably the priests and the rest of Bullet's family had fled into the forest. We worried about the road, afraid that the *Wazhunghu* who'd left in the trucks would return. Every few minutes we'd break off and go and check. No-one came. So, after a while, we stopped worrying. There was too much to do.

We collected the wounded pilgrims from the slope above the camping area, carrying them as gently as possible to the soldiers' barracks where Chloris did what she could for them. It was miserable work, for most of them were either women or children and some of the wounds were horrific. Worse, after half a day in the hot sun, all were in a pitiable condition. Chloris' task was almost impossible. She had found some first aid materials in the soldiers' barracks and more in one of the bungalows, but they were hopelessly inadequate. While she worked, we did what we could to clean the barracks. The rooms were disgustingly filthy, the water polluted, the toilets blocked, and the flies, Christ, I've never seen so many flies.

About three, as the dark shadows of the forest crossed the stream and began to climb the hill towards us, Temba drew me aside. He must go back, he said, to find Josephine and the Kaserewe boys, to make sure they were okay. We didn't consult Chloris. He went, on the understanding that, as soon as he could, he would send help.

I don't think Chloris even noticed he'd gone. As soon as the last of the wounded were gathered, she sent me off to bury the dead. I don't know where she thought I would find the energy to dig so many graves. The fact was, with my side once again oozing blood, I couldn't. Instead, using an old wheelbarrow, I transported the torn and shattered remains up to the temple. I wrapped them in blankets from the barracks and laid them in neat rows near the main door, as far as I could from the throne – as if that would, in some way, dissociate them from the chewed remains of the monsters at the other end.

That job done, I took a few moments to look around the temple. The spotlights were still burning, providing enough light to see into the shadows where the two lions had dragged their prey. Hardly anything remained of the boy and rather more of Bullet: his head, upright and with his eyes wide open and staring at me, most of a leg, and part of his torso. A gory mess – but I felt nothing but a tired elation. Then I walked round the rest of the room.

I have to say that the ivory throne was magnificent. M'Simani's description of the stones was accurate. They were uncut, but that didn't detract from their beauty. There were some fine rubies and one or two that might have been diamonds, but the best were the emeralds, their magnificent deep green set off against the old white of the forest ivory. There were a number of other features which M'Simani hadn't mentioned. For example, a rock had been cut as a surround for the dais on which the throne stood. It was a very bright green, the texture rather fibrous, with centimetre diameter red blotches in it. I've asked about it since, and was told that it was an unusual rock called eclogite, probably from Tanzania.

Thousands of hours of work had gone into that building, thousands more into the throne. The value of the ivory, stones and skins must have been considerable. Yet its destruction took minutes.

I was aware of it first through the soles of my shoes, a vibration, as if the earth was trembling. Then I heard the noise again, that same noise I'd heard in the tree, just before the first shock. Except, this time, it came as a roar, the sound of an express train bearing down on me, or a thousand articulated lorries thundering down a cobbled street. Then the earthquake hit the building.

I was thrown to the ground. For the next few seconds the temple behaved like a rowing boat at sea in a hurricane. As the ground pitched and heaved a fearful roaring, grinding sound filled the place. The timbers of the walls seemed to flex as they groaned. Rafters cracked and plunged down from the roof. The spotlights came away, shorting and sparking as they clattered to the ground. I lay in darkness, unable to move, as a writhing hell surrounded and engulfed me.

I think Chloris must have been praying again. She tells me she was, though she takes no credit for what happened. But I'm quite sure her prayers saved my life. For a few moments, the movements stopped, and, in those moments, I struggled to my feet and ran. I ran the length of the temple, throwing myself out of the great doors that faced south-west towards the pilgrims' encampment. As I came out into the bright sunlight, as I drew a great breath of relief, the next and even more violent series of shocks struck the building.

They knocked me down again. I lay on the ground, my fingernails clinging to it as it flexed and leapt and swayed, while behind me, in a shriek of tearing and splitting wood, in a series of sharp explosions as joints and ties gave, the temple collapsed. I didn't see it go – my eyes were tight shut and my faced pressed into the dirt – but I heard the final roar of its destruction. And, when the earthquake waves once again passed, as I levered myself up and turned towards the great ruin of that place, I saw the first twists of smoke rise from it.

It was probably the spotlights. I'd seen them fall, seen the electric flashes as the wires shorted. I know that, when I ran screaming down the hill to search for Chloris, the generator was still working. Whatever it was, the building caught quickly and, once it was going, that evil, evil place burned beautifully.

Chloris and I remained at Bo for three days. For me, they were days of pain and exhaustion punctuated by sudden terror. Simbilani continued to erupt, pumping great columns of ash into the perfect blue skies, and glowing like some monstrous, throbbing coal through the night. On the second day an immense cloud drifted across to blot out the sun, and ash began to fall like grey, smoky snow, blanketing the ground and blowing in drifts against the sides of the buildings. It stuck in our noses and it tickled our throats. It weighed down the roofs of the buildings and it turned the clear waters of the streams into liquid porridge.

I saw little of Chloris. The first time I bumped into her I grabbed her arm and dragged her into the protection of one of the buildings. 'Chloris,' I said as I held her, 'You know what a lahar is? You've heard of pyroclastic flows? Landslides?'

She didn't react.

'Remember, when Mount St Helen's blew, how it took away the whole of the side of the mountain?

Millions of tonnes of it? You know what happened in Pompeii? And St Pierre in Martinique? And . . .'

Even as I spoke, as if supporting my point, an earthquake rumbled beneath us. They'd been increasing in frequency and power, and the red glow of Simbilani's eruption had reached such intensity that it was now visible in daylight.

'Chloris, we've got to get out of here. Please. We can't help these people. I'd love to but . . .'

Very gently, without looking at me, she eased herself away. And I stood, feeling sick at myself, watching as she returned to her charges.

I did what I could to help. As you probably realise by now, I'm not a terribly sympathetic person and I find dealing with illness – mine or other people's – very difficult. To make matters worse, many of the twenty-six people who lay on the bare, metal beds in the wreckage of the soldiers' quarters were in a pretty bad state. Some of the children, in particular, were in a pitiable condition. But I did my best. When I was in the wards – as Chloris called them – I tried to be cheerful, I made pathetic jokes, and was amazed at how the patients responded. At times I insisted on taking over, to give Chloris a break, time to lie down and snatch some sleep. But it always seemed that, as soon as I heard her breathing regularly, as soon as she was safely asleep, some sort of crisis would occur and I'd have to wake her.

After a while she seemed to give up speaking to me, except to issue instructions and to explain what we should do for individuals and to improve the general conditions for the patients. I don't blame her: we were worn out, drained, going about our tasks like zombies. It was getting to the point where I knew I couldn't take much more, that the combination of my wound, which was suppurating, the escalating threat from Simbilani, the lack of sleep, the events of previous weeks, and the misery of our patients were pushing me towards a crisis.

Around five in the afternoon of the third day, I heard an engine. By the time I'd found the Galil and dragged myself to a point where I could overlook the road, a truck was already parked beside the bungalows and two men were climbing out, rather pale-skinned white men in khaki bush suits.

I didn't go down to them. I sat with the Galil laid across my knees and watched as they were met by Chloris and led round to the barracks. She told me later they were doctors from Médecins Sans Frontières.

Simbilani was taking a rest but the atmosphere remained heavy. The scenery reminded me of one of those deep winter days in England: a grey half-light with the snow falling silently, settling to smooth out the contours of the land and bend the trees under a burden of snow. It was very quiet.

I sat and allowed my weariness to possess me. The war was over. What I'd come to Boromundi to do was finished. This whole traumatic phase of my life, seven long months of it, was drawing to an end. And, as far as I could see, any hope of making progress with Chloris was as wrecked as the *Titanic*. I could go home. I could make my way back to Mateka airport and hitch a lift on one of those C130 vultures to Nairobi and catch the British Airways flight to Heathrow. I could drink watery beer again and chase pretty English girls and do something mind-blowingly mundane like teach recalcitrant kids Geography. It would be summer in England. I could . . .

No I couldn't. There were too many things here I liked. I liked Temba. I liked Josephine. I liked a hell of a lot of people, including the villagers I met on the paths near the school who stood aside for me and said, 'Good morning, Teacher,' as if a teacher was a person worth respecting. I liked the way the sun was hot when it came out and I didn't mind the rain, because the rain fed the torrential streams that cut those magnificent, deep valleys, it watered the plants that sprouted in such profusion and it nurtured the trees that grew and grew upwards to disappear against the sky. And I liked the mists in the morning that sat down in the valleys and the way that, at night, when the clouds allowed them out, the stars burned like white fire in the sky and so close you could reach out and touch them.

And there were things I needed to do here. Like I needed to put in a full term at St Faith's, something I hadn't yet managed. And I needed to see that Temba and Josephine got married, that the process was done properly and that their children were brought up in a Godfearing and respectful way. And there were a few people whom I needed to thank for all they'd done to help me. Only I could do it, because I needed to explain how much Rebecca would have wanted to thank them for their support, for their understanding of my foibles, for their kindness. And some of those people weren't the most likely of people, but they'd been fun and they'd been supportive and I realised I had come to love them.

There was something else. I'd done a lot of killing. I'd

seen just about as bloodthirsty a war as has ever happened, and I'd learned how lousy war was and I didn't want it again. I particularly didn't want it again for this place, this little emerald of a country, Boromundi, because it had had quite enough of it. And I was pretty sure in my mind that Temba would have a few ideas, over and above organising an even stronger Kaserewe militia, which might help prevent it happening again – and I wanted to be part of that.

So – no, perhaps I wasn't going home. Perhaps I could stay and do a bit of planting and cherishing instead of killing.

'Armstrong?'

I almost jumped out of my skin. She'd crept up behind me.

I turned and looked up at her. I couldn't see her face properly in the half-light as the ash kept getting in my eyes, so I looked away. For want of anything better I asked, 'Everything all right down there?'

She didn't reply, but came and sat beside me, tucking her feet under her, then struggling to untangle them from the cassock. I glanced sideways at her. The cassock was grey with ash and its front smeared with blood and puke. She'd tried to tie her hair back with a bootlace but it escaped in greasy ringlets, thick with ash, which she kept pushing out of a face that was crusted grey and had collapsed in on itself, the eyes sunk into deep hollows and the mouth like a dark, jagged crack. And she smelt worse than the warthog I had shot in the Malakari.

'How's your side?' she croaked.

'It hurts.'

She didn't react to that. There was no sympathy, no

suggestion that we should go down and get one of the doctors to look at it. Instead, she said, 'Listen.'

Someone else had said this, in the same ambivalent way, outside St Faith's school hall in the pouring rain on the night we had buried Rebecca.

'What do you hear?' she prompted.

I knew, then, exactly what she was getting at. 'Nothing,' I whispered.

'Quite sure, Armstrong? No bird?'

I shook my head. 'No bird.'

'Certain?'

'Certain.'

We sat in silence for a while until she said, 'Mganga saved me, you know.'

I didn't react. I knew what she was going to tell me and I knew I wasn't going to enjoy it, but I didn't think that anything I might say would stop her, nor would it make any difference.

'His father wasn't shouting at me when you came in. He was shouting at his son.' She paused. 'His son liked me. He'd looked after me. They were having a blazing row because Mganga had stopped him shooting me. He wanted to take me with them.'

'Shit,' I said.

Suddenly she leaned forward and, with her index finger, drew a line in the ash in front of me, a firm, very straight line.

'There,' she said.

I looked at the line. It was a very good line but the sides were already falling in and the continued ashfall would obliterate it within minutes.

'Armstrong, I want you to promise me it's the end of

all this. I want you to draw a line under what's happened.' She paused, and I waited.

She turned and caught my eye. The rest of her might be grey, filthy and smelly, but those eyes were as blue and as clear and as beautiful as they'd always been and still are.

'Promise,' she said.

I wasn't sure what I was drawing a line under, nor what I was promising. To be brutally honest, I wasn't too worried. What interested me was that, if I said I would draw a line under whatever it was, if I promised, it sounded as if she was going to make me some sort of offer. So I said, 'Okay.'

What Chloris did then was something I really hadn't expected. She leaned across and kissed me. She kissed me on my cheek. It was a pretty bad kiss, thin and wettish without being firm, but then nuns don't get too much practice at that sort of thing. So I took hold of her shoulders and moved her round so I could kiss her properly, on her lips, very gently, just to show her how it should be done.